Ludocrats

VOL. I: BEING THE FIRST VOLUME IN A ONE-VOLUME SERIES.

THE LUDOCRATS: VOLUME 1. First printing. November 2020. Published by Image Comics, Inc. Office of publication: 2701 NW Vaughn St., Ste. 780, Portland, OR 97210. Copyright © 2020 Lemon Ink Ltd., Big Robot Ltd., and Jeff Stokely. All rights reserved. Contains material originally published in single magazine form as THE LUDOCRATS #1-5. "The Ludocrats," The Ludocrats logos, and the likenesses of all characters herein or hereon are trademarks of Lemon Ink Ltd., Big Robot Ltd., and Jeff Stokely, unless expressly indicated. "Image" and the Image Comics logos are registered trademarks of Image Comics, Inc. No part of this publication may be reproduced or transmitted in any form or by any means (except for short excerpts for journalistic or review purposes), without the express written permission of Lemon Ink Ltd., Big Robot Ltd., Jeff Stokely, or Image Comics, Inc. All names, characters, events, and locales herein are entirely fictional. Any resemblance to actual persons (living or dead), events, or places, without satiric intent, is coincidental. Printed in the USA. For rights inquiries, contact Law Offices of Harris M. Miller II, P.C. (rights.inquiries@gmail.com). Does anyone still read the indicia looking for extra jokes? I'd hope so. You're our kind of people.

ISBN: 978-1-5343-1703-1

 MAGE COMICS
PROUDLY
and only
SEMI-RELUCTANTLY
PRESENTS

WORD
SCIENTIST

KIERON
GILLEN

A FURTHER
WORD SCIENTIST

JIM
ROSSIGNOL

WORD
VISUALISATION

CLAYTON
COWLES

DELINEATOR
OF AREAS

FERNANDO
ARGÜELLO

PENCILS, INKS
& DEMIURGERY

JEFF STOKELY

PALETTE
EMPRESS

TAMRA BONVILLAIN

TAMER OF THE
UNTAMED

CHRISSY WILLIAMS

ARRANGER OF
BEAUTIFUL THINGS

SERGIO SERRANO

and also WITH THE HELP OF THE MOST EXCELLENT
MARCO ROBLIN,
WHOSE ARTISTIC CONTRIBUTION TO A NOTABLE SECTION
OF SEQUENTIAL ART ADDED MUCH TO THE
OVERALL LUDICROUSNESS OF
THE WORK

THE Ludo

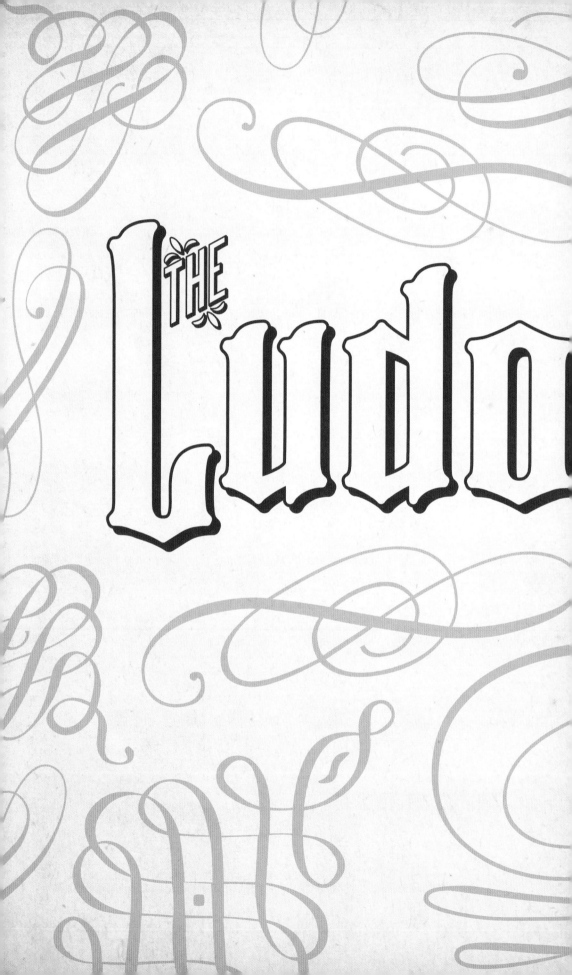

crats™

VOL. I: BEING THE FIRST VOLUME IN A ONE-VOLUME SERIES.

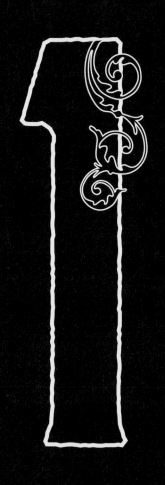

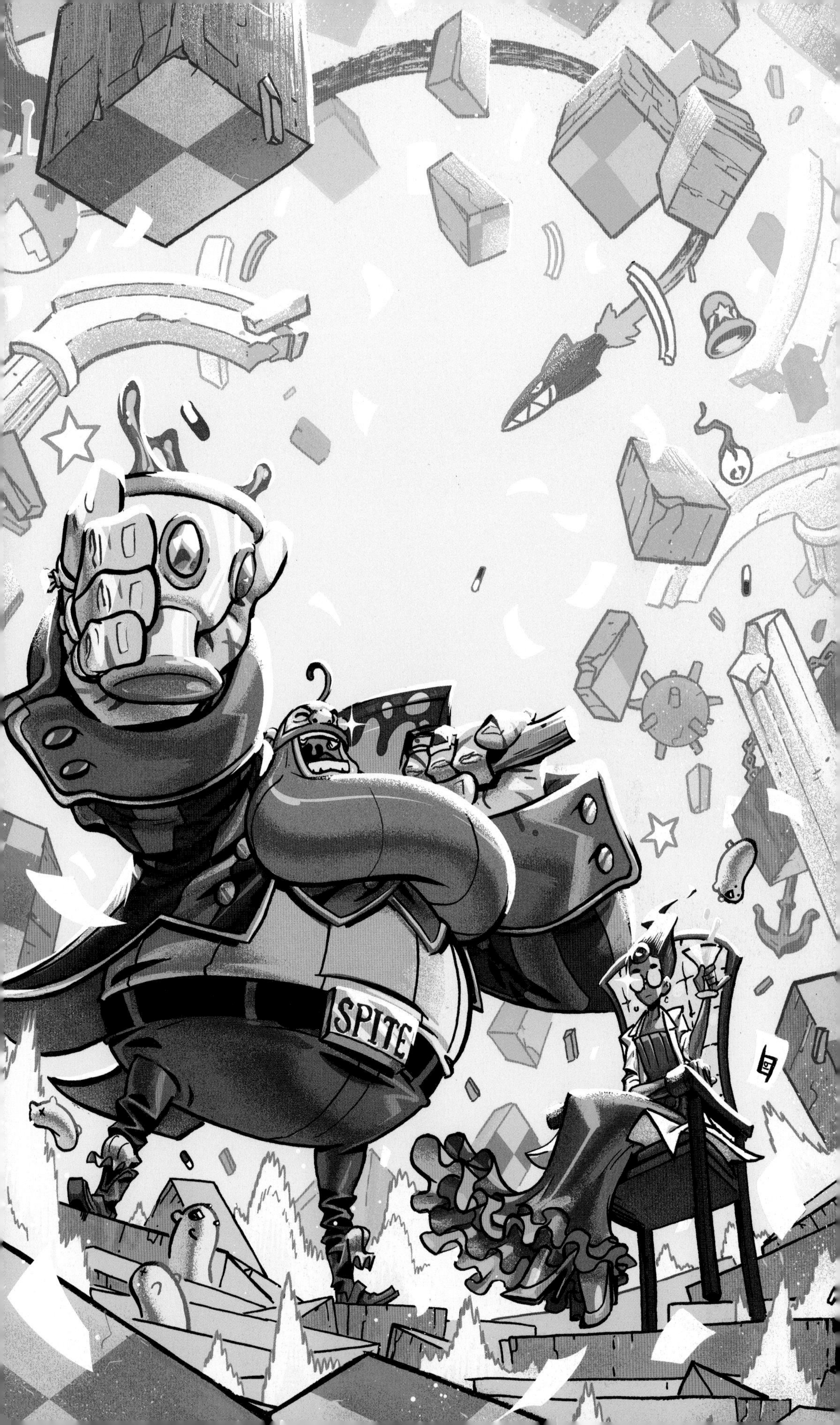
SPITE

E TRIED *to* IMAGINE *a* BETTER WORLD.

WE FAILED.

Instead, WE DID THIS.

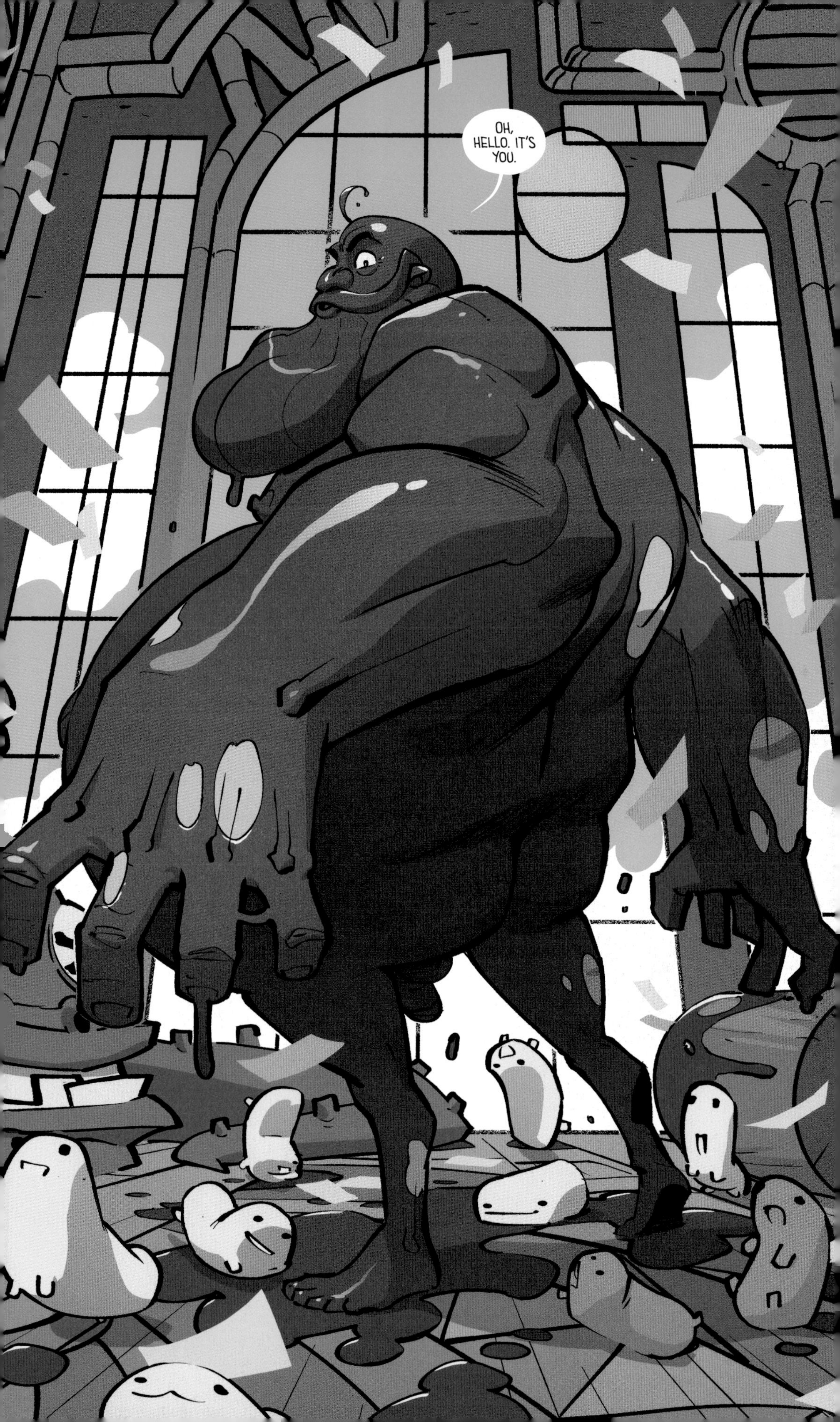
OH, HELLO. IT'S YOU.

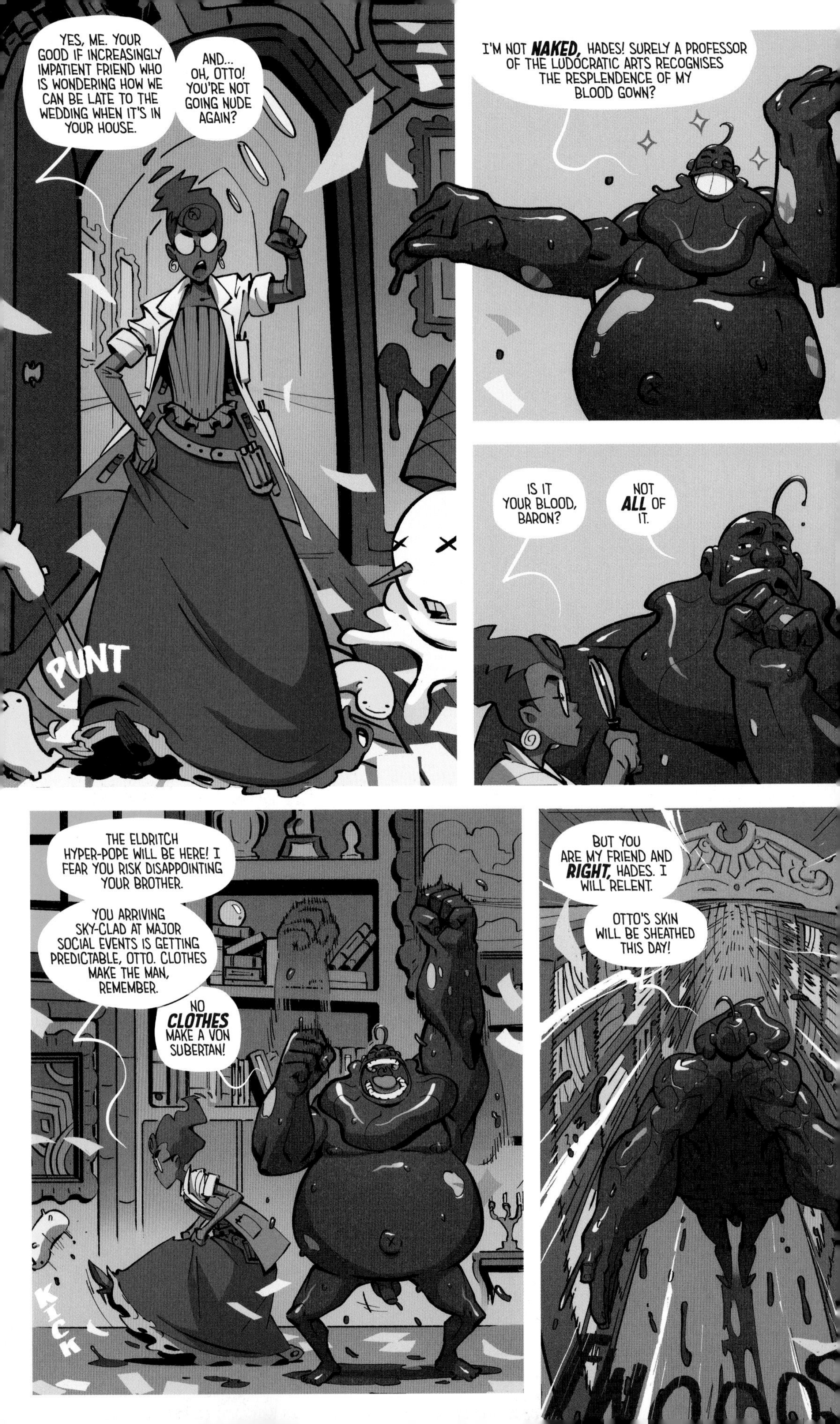
YES, ME. YOUR GOOD IF INCREASINGLY IMPATIENT FRIEND WHO IS WONDERING HOW WE CAN BE LATE TO THE WEDDING WHEN IT'S IN YOUR HOUSE.
AND... OH, OTTO! YOU'RE NOT GOING NUDE AGAIN?
PUNT
I'M NOT **NAKED,** HADES! SURELY A PROFESSOR OF THE LUDOCRATIC ARTS RECOGNISES THE RESPLENDENCE OF MY BLOOD GOWN?
IS IT YOUR BLOOD, BARON?
NOT **ALL** OF IT.
THE ELDRITCH HYPER-POPE WILL BE HERE! I FEAR YOU RISK DISAPPOINTING YOUR BROTHER.
YOU ARRIVING SKY-CLAD AT MAJOR SOCIAL EVENTS IS GETTING PREDICTABLE, OTTO. CLOTHES MAKE THE MAN, REMEMBER.
NO **CLOTHES** MAKE A VON SUBERTAN!
KICK
BUT YOU ARE MY FRIEND AND **RIGHT,** HADES. I WILL RELENT.
OTTO'S SKIN WILL BE SHEATHED THIS DAY!

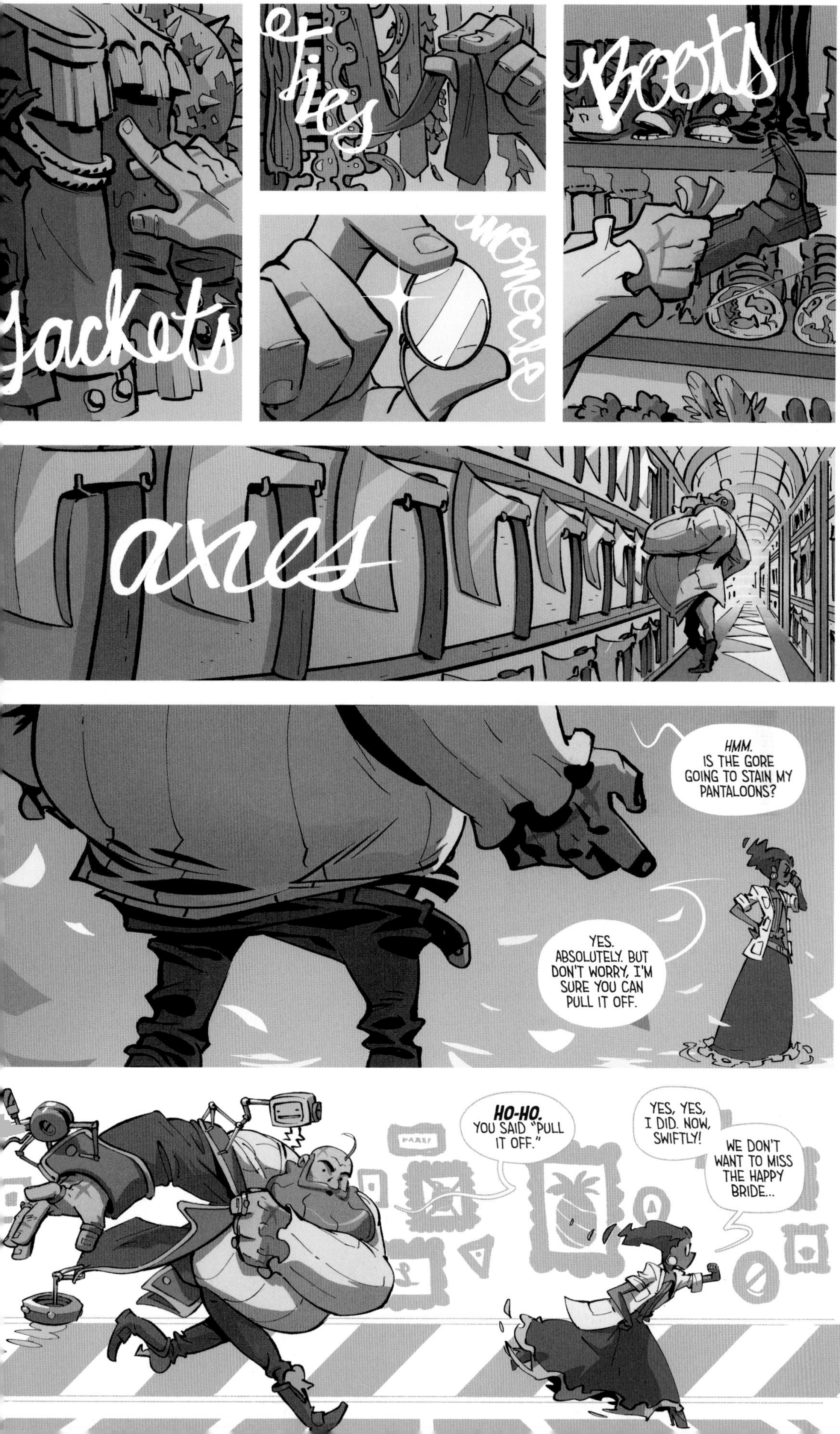
Jackets
Ties
Monocle
Boots
axes
HMM. IS THE GORE GOING TO STAIN MY PANTALOONS?
YES. ABSOLUTELY. BUT DON'T WORRY, I'M SURE YOU CAN PULL IT OFF.
HO-HO. YOU SAID "PULL IT OFF."
YES, YES, I DID. NOW, SWIFTLY!
WE DON'T WANT TO MISS THE HAPPY BRIDE...

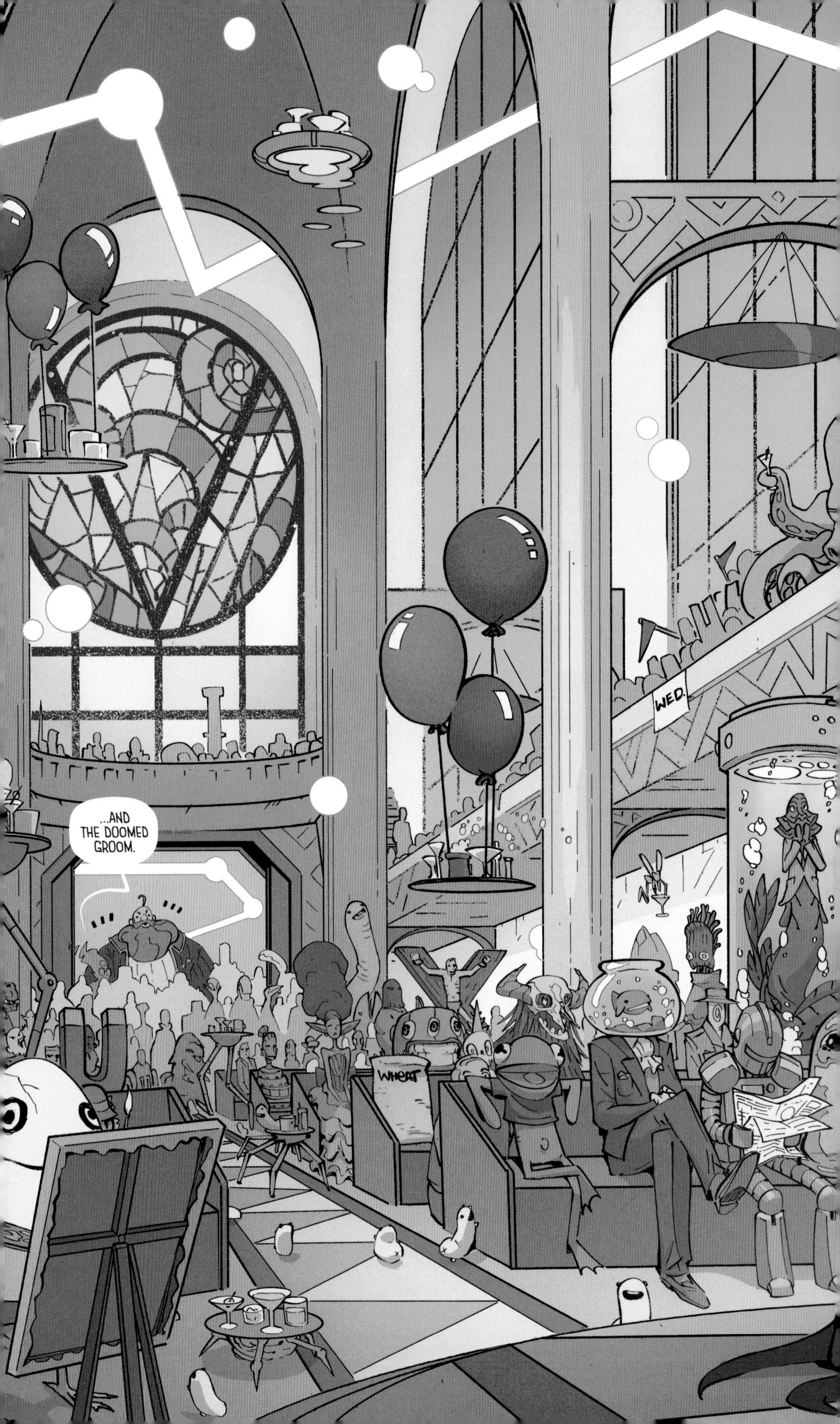
...AND THE DOOMED GROOM.
WED.
WHEAT

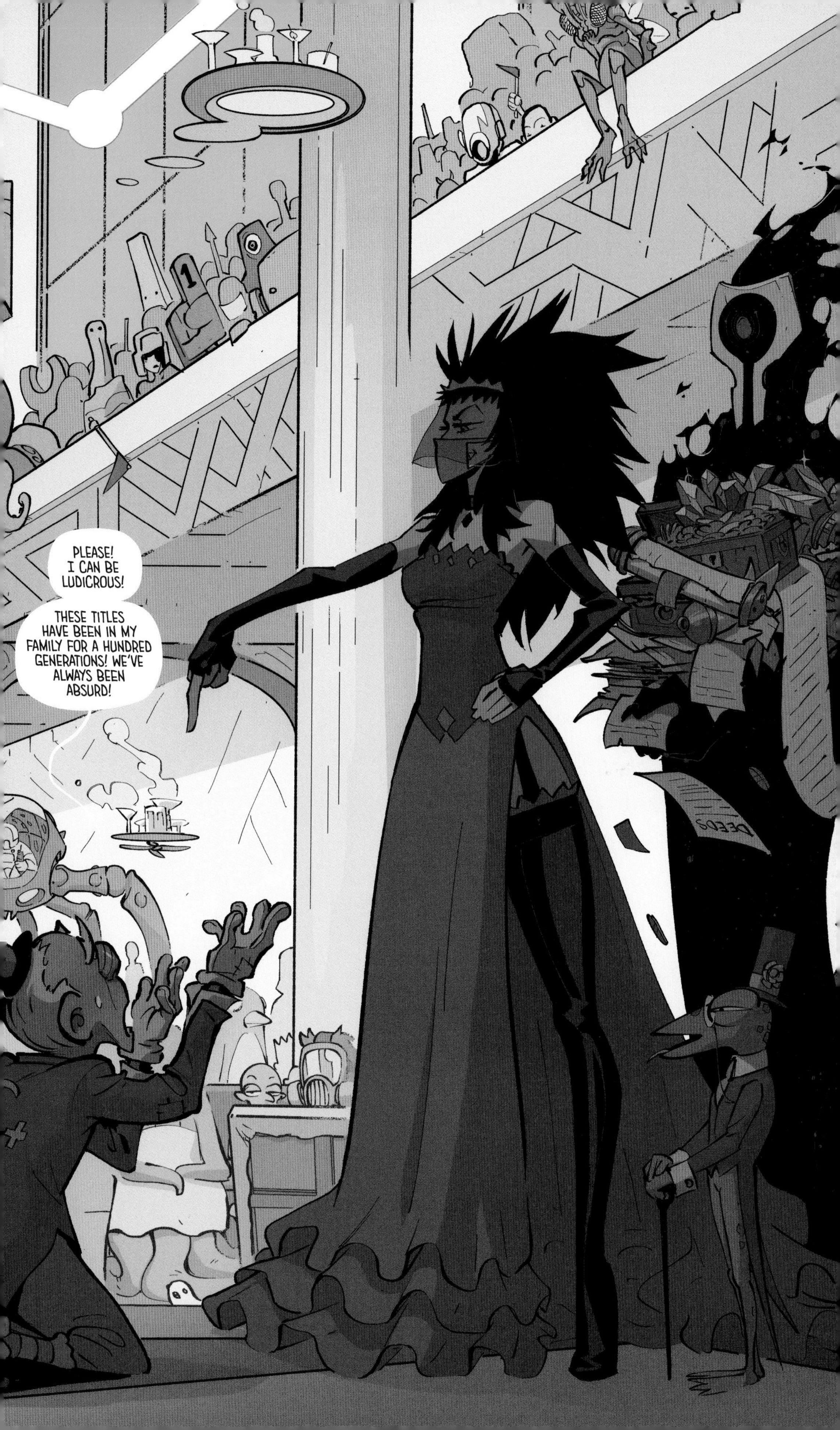
PLEASE! I CAN BE LUDICROUS!
THESE TITLES HAVE BEEN IN MY FAMILY FOR A HUNDRED GENERATIONS! WE'VE ALWAYS BEEN ABSURD!
DEEDS

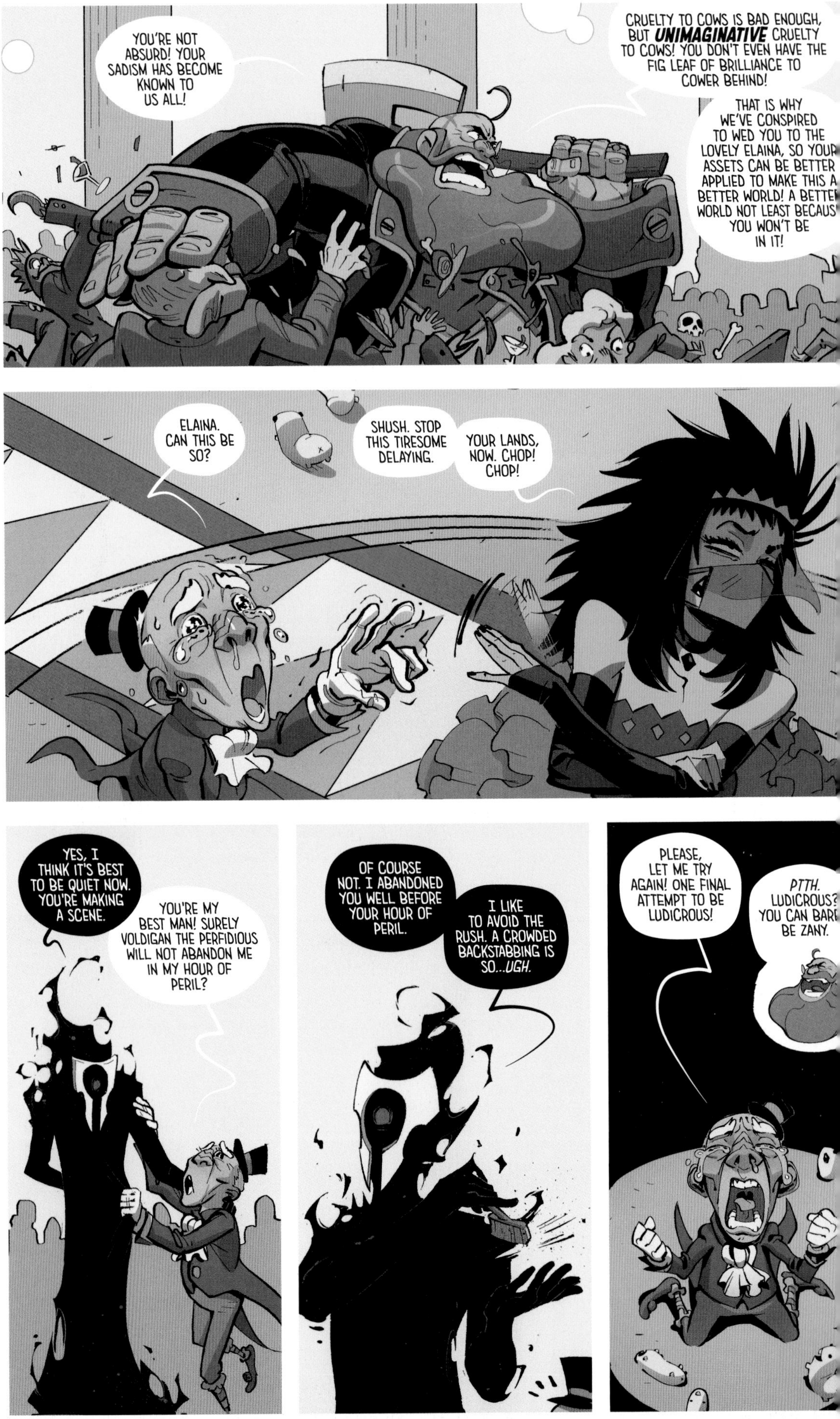
YOU'RE NOT ABSURD! YOUR SADISM HAS BECOME KNOWN TO US ALL!
CRUELTY TO COWS IS BAD ENOUGH, BUT UNIMAGINATIVE CRUELTY TO COWS! YOU DON'T EVEN HAVE THE FIG LEAF OF BRILLIANCE TO COWER BEHIND!
THAT IS WHY WE'VE CONSPIRED TO WED YOU TO THE LOVELY ELAINA, SO YOUR ASSETS CAN BE BETTER APPLIED TO MAKE THIS A BETTER WORLD! A BETTE WORLD NOT LEAST BECAUS YOU WON'T BE IN IT!
ELAINA. CAN THIS BE SO?
SHUSH. STOP THIS TIRESOME DELAYING.
YOUR LANDS, NOW. CHOP! CHOP!
YES, I THINK IT'S BEST TO BE QUIET NOW. YOU'RE MAKING A SCENE.
YOU'RE MY BEST MAN! SURELY VOLDIGAN THE PERFIDIOUS WILL NOT ABANDON ME IN MY HOUR OF PERIL?
OF COURSE NOT. I ABANDONED YOU WELL BEFORE YOUR HOUR OF PERIL.
I LIKE TO AVOID THE RUSH. A CROWDED BACKSTABBING IS SO...UGH.
PLEASE, LET ME TRY AGAIN! ONE FINAL ATTEMPT TO BE LUDICROUS!
PTTH. LUDICROUS? YOU CAN BAR BE ZANY.

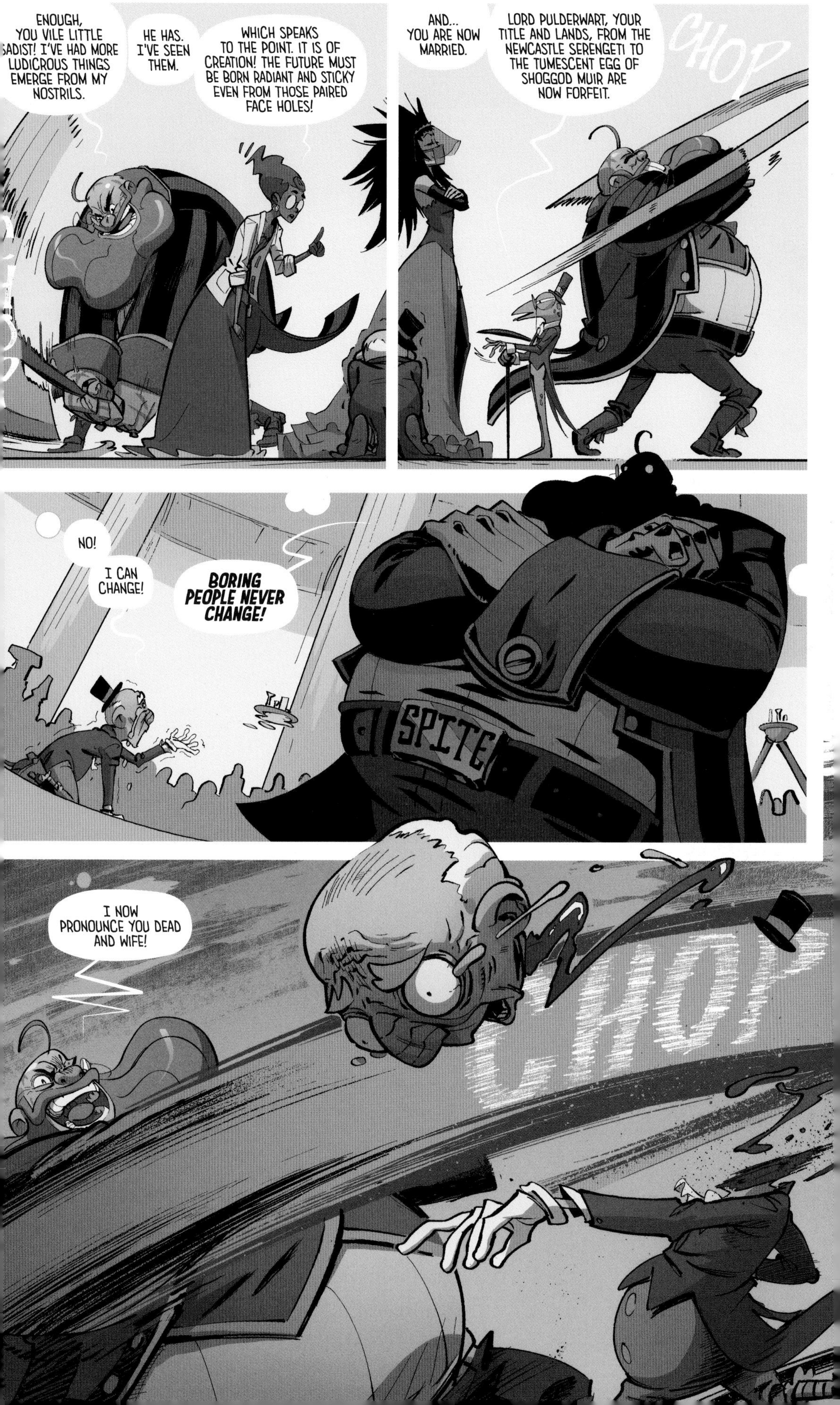
ENOUGH, YOU VILE LITTLE SADIST! I'VE HAD MORE LUDICROUS THINGS EMERGE FROM MY NOSTRILS.
HE HAS. I'VE SEEN THEM.
WHICH SPEAKS TO THE POINT. IT IS OF CREATION! THE FUTURE MUST BE BORN RADIANT AND STICKY EVEN FROM THOSE PAIRED FACE HOLES!
AND... YOU ARE NOW MARRIED.
LORD PULDERWART, YOUR TITLE AND LANDS, FROM THE NEWCASTLE SERENGETI TO THE TUMESCENT EGG OF SHOGGOD MUIR ARE NOW FORFEIT.
CHOP
NO!
I CAN CHANGE!
BORING PEOPLE NEVER CHANGE!
SPITE
I NOW PRONOUNCE YOU DEAD AND WIFE!
CHOP

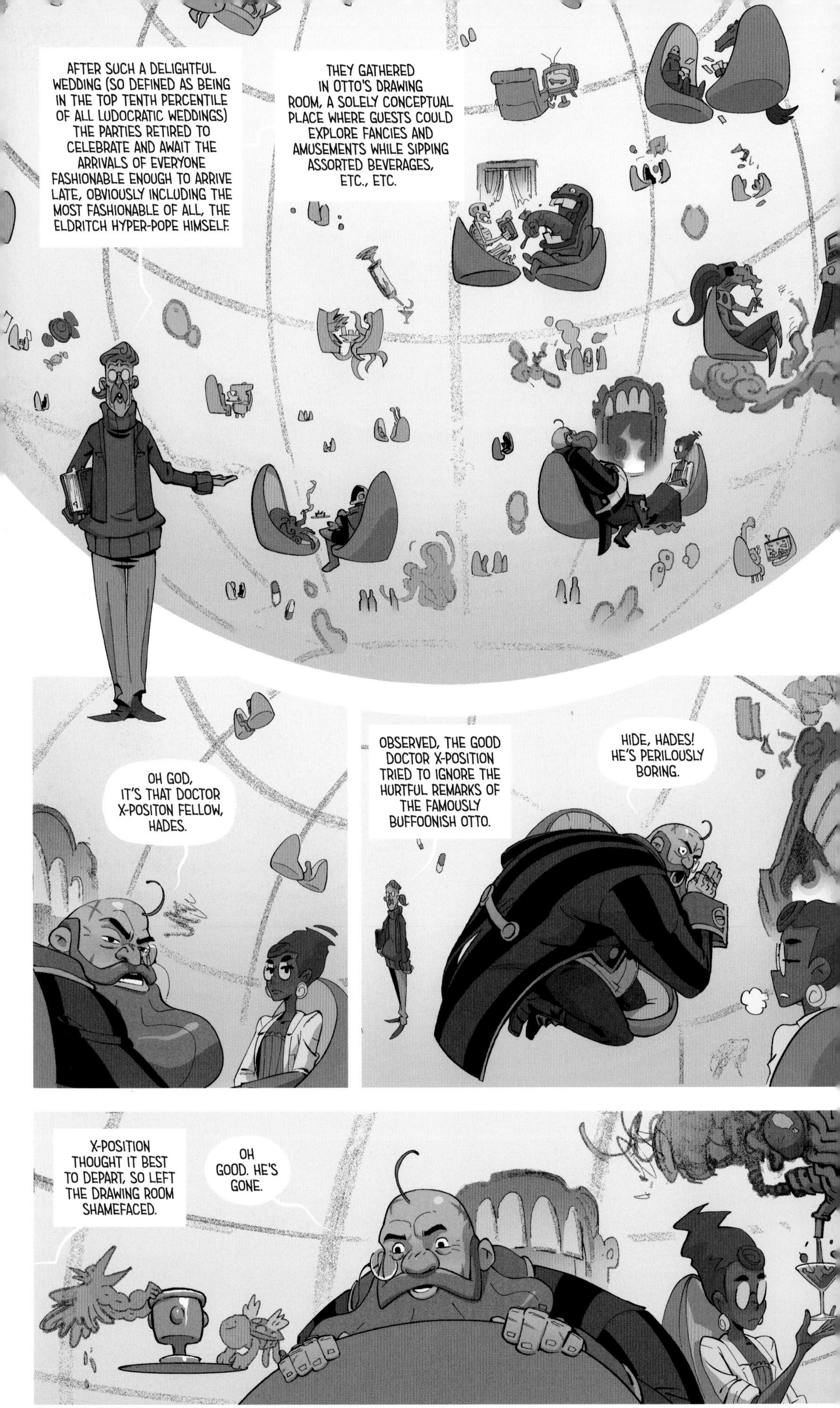
AFTER SUCH A DELIGHTFUL WEDDING (SO DEFINED AS BEING IN THE TOP TENTH PERCENTILE OF ALL LUDOCRATIC WEDDINGS) THE PARTIES RETIRED TO CELEBRATE AND AWAIT THE ARRIVALS OF EVERYONE FASHIONABLE ENOUGH TO ARRIVE LATE, OBVIOUSLY INCLUDING THE MOST FASHIONABLE OF ALL, THE ELDRITCH HYPER-POPE HIMSELF.
THEY GATHERED IN OTTO'S DRAWING ROOM, A SOLELY CONCEPTUAL PLACE WHERE GUESTS COULD EXPLORE FANCIES AND AMUSEMENTS WHILE SIPPING ASSORTED BEVERAGES, ETC., ETC.
OH GOD, IT'S THAT DOCTOR X-POSITON FELLOW, HADES.
OBSERVED, THE GOOD DOCTOR X-POSITION TRIED TO IGNORE THE HURTFUL REMARKS OF THE FAMOUSLY BUFFOONISH OTTO.
HIDE, HADES! HE'S PERILOUSLY BORING.
X-POSITION THOUGHT IT BEST TO DEPART, SO LEFT THE DRAWING ROOM SHAMEFACED.
OH GOOD. HE'S GONE.

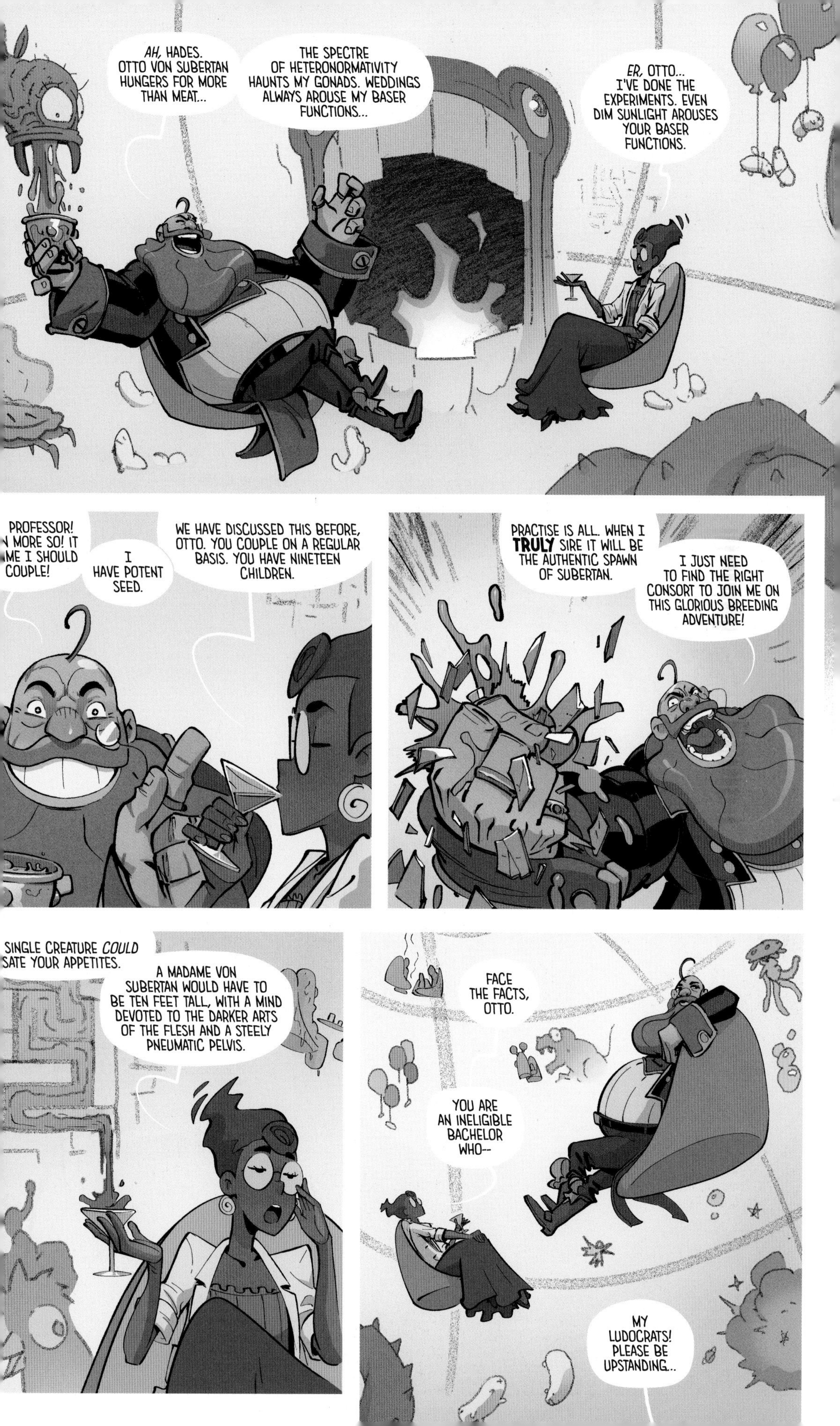

AH, HADES. OTTO VON SUBERTAN HUNGERS FOR MORE THAN MEAT...
THE SPECTRE OF HETERONORMATIVITY HAUNTS MY GONADS. WEDDINGS ALWAYS AROUSE MY BASER FUNCTIONS...
ER, OTTO... I'VE DONE THE EXPERIMENTS. EVEN DIM SUNLIGHT AROUSES YOUR BASER FUNCTIONS.
PROFESSOR! ...N MORE SO! IT ...ME I SHOULD COUPLE!
I HAVE POTENT SEED.
WE HAVE DISCUSSED THIS BEFORE, OTTO. YOU COUPLE ON A REGULAR BASIS. YOU HAVE NINETEEN CHILDREN.
PRACTISE IS ALL. WHEN I **TRULY** SIRE IT WILL BE THE AUTHENTIC SPAWN OF SUBERTAN.
I JUST NEED TO FIND THE RIGHT CONSORT TO JOIN ME ON THIS GLORIOUS BREEDING ADVENTURE!
SINGLE CREATURE *COULD* SATE YOUR APPETITES.
A MADAME VON SUBERTAN WOULD HAVE TO BE TEN FEET TALL, WITH A MIND DEVOTED TO THE DARKER ARTS OF THE FLESH AND A STEELY PNEUMATIC PELVIS.
FACE THE FACTS, OTTO.
YOU ARE AN INELIGIBLE BACHELOR WHO--
MY LUDOCRATS! PLEASE BE UPSTANDING...

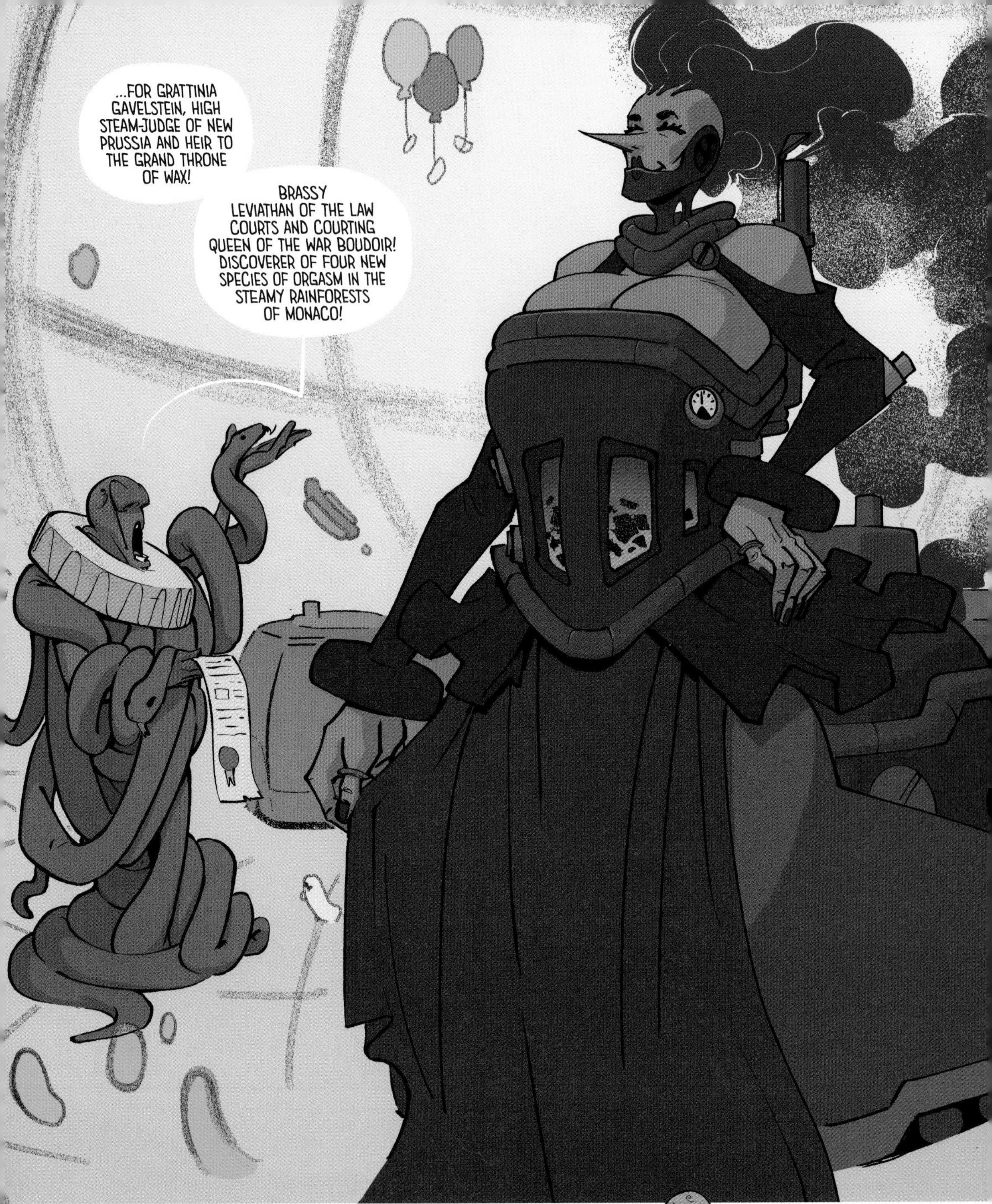
...FOR GRATTINIA GAVELSTEIN, HIGH STEAM-JUDGE OF NEW PRUSSIA AND HEIR TO THE GRAND THRONE OF WAX!
BRASSY LEVIATHAN OF THE LAW COURTS AND COURTING QUEEN OF THE WAR BOUDOIR! DISCOVERER OF FOUR NEW SPECIES OF ORGASM IN THE STEAMY RAINFORESTS OF MONACO!

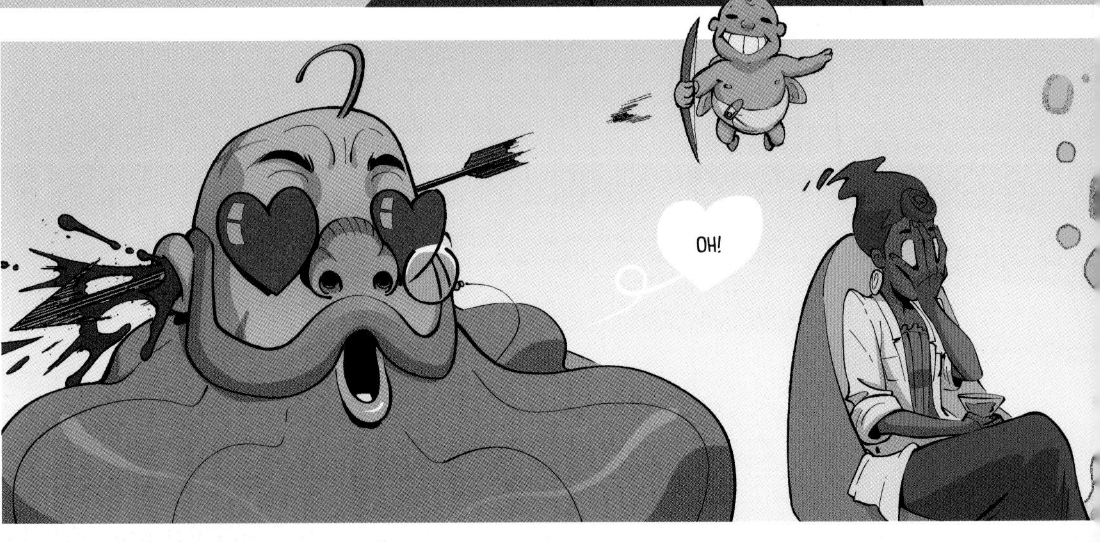
OH!

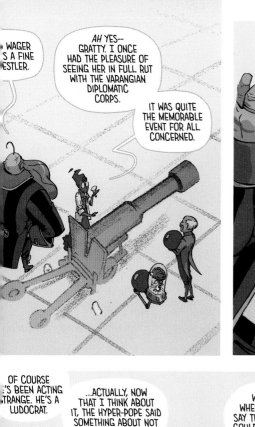

WAGER S A FINE ESTLER.

AH YES-- GRATTY. I ONCE HAD THE PLEASURE OF SEEING HER IN FULL RUT WITH THE VARANGIAN DIPLOMATIC CORPS.

IT WAS QUITE THE MEMORABLE EVENT FOR ALL CONCERNED.

THEN AN INTRODUCTION, HADES! I WOULD MAKE MY ACQUAINTANCE WITH THE STEAM-JUDGE OF NEW PRUSSIA *IMMEDIATELY.*

THIS WEDDING IS ABOUT MORE THAN THE FLOW OF SEED, OTTO.

WE REQUIRE AN AUDIENCE WITH THE HYPER-POPE. THERE ARE MATTERS TO DISCUSS. HE'S BEEN ACTING... STRANGE.

OF COURSE 'S BEEN ACTING TRANGE. HE'S A LUDOCRAT.

...ACTUALLY, NOW THAT I THINK ABOUT IT, THE HYPER-POPE SAID SOMETHING ABOUT NOT TURNING UP.

WHAT? WHEN DID HE SAY THAT? WHAT COULD BE MORE IMPORTANT?

SWRR

I FORGET.

CHNK

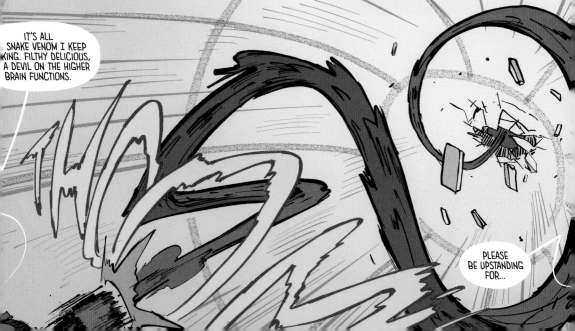

IT'S ALL SNAKE VENOM I KEEP KING. FILTHY DELICIOUS, A DEVIL ON THE HIGHER BRAIN FUNCTIONS.

PLEASE BE UPSTANDING FOR...

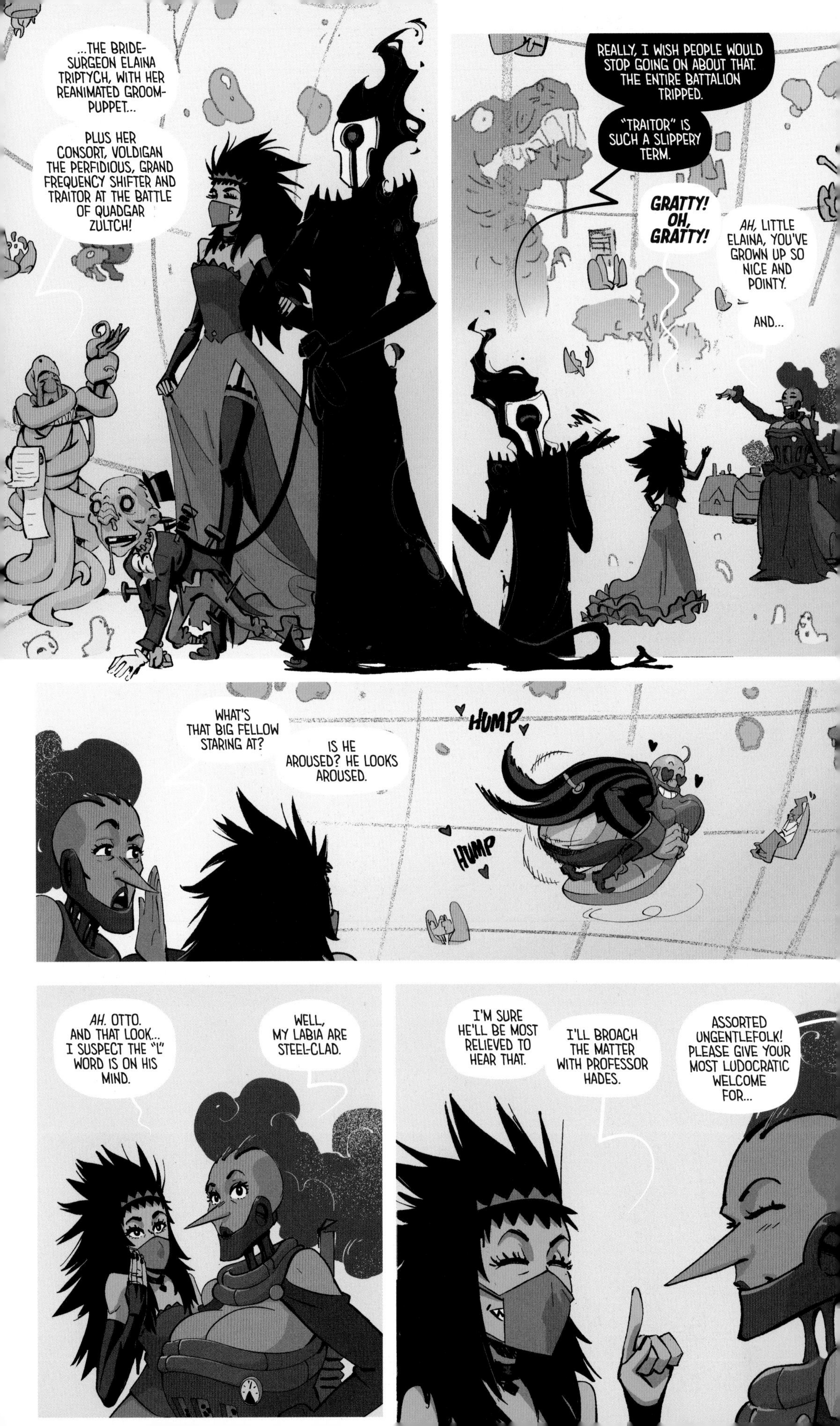
...THE BRIDE-SURGEON ELAINA TRIPTYCH, WITH HER REANIMATED GROOM-PUPPET...
PLUS HER CONSORT, VOLDIGAN THE PERFIDIOUS, GRAND FREQUENCY SHIFTER AND TRAITOR AT THE BATTLE OF QUADGAR ZULTCH!
REALLY, I WISH PEOPLE WOULD STOP GOING ON ABOUT THAT. THE ENTIRE BATTALION TRIPPED.
"TRAITOR" IS SUCH A SLIPPERY TERM.
GRATTY! OH, GRATTY!
AH, LITTLE ELAINA, YOU'VE GROWN UP SO NICE AND POINTY.
AND...
WHAT'S THAT BIG FELLOW STARING AT?
IS HE AROUSED? HE LOOKS AROUSED.
HUMP
HUMP
AH. OTTO. AND THAT LOOK... I SUSPECT THE "L" WORD IS ON HIS MIND.
WELL, MY LABIA ARE STEEL-CLAD.
I'M SURE HE'LL BE MOST RELIEVED TO HEAR THAT.
I'LL BROACH THE MATTER WITH PROFESSOR HADES.
ASSORTED UNGENTLEFOLK! PLEASE GIVE YOUR MOST LUDOCRATIC WELCOME FOR...

...CASANOVA QUINN, DISGUISED AS A SEXY DINOSAUR, TRYING TO STEAL SOMETHING AS HE'S A FAMED INTERDIMENSIONAL THIEF AND THAT IS SIMPLY WHAT HE DOES.

APPEARING HERE COURTESY OF THE *"CASANOVA"* PERIODICAL OF IMAGE COMICS FAME!

SHIT.

OH GOD. IT'S A **CROSSOVER.**

LET ME DEAL WITH IT, HADES.

OH, HADES! HADES!

MY GOOD FRIEND BOGOL THEEN, THE CHAINSAW GASTRONAUT, AND MYSELF WERE TALKING, AND WE ENDED UP HAVING A WAGER WE HOPED YOU COULD SETTLE...

WE WEREN'T.

RIIIIGHT.

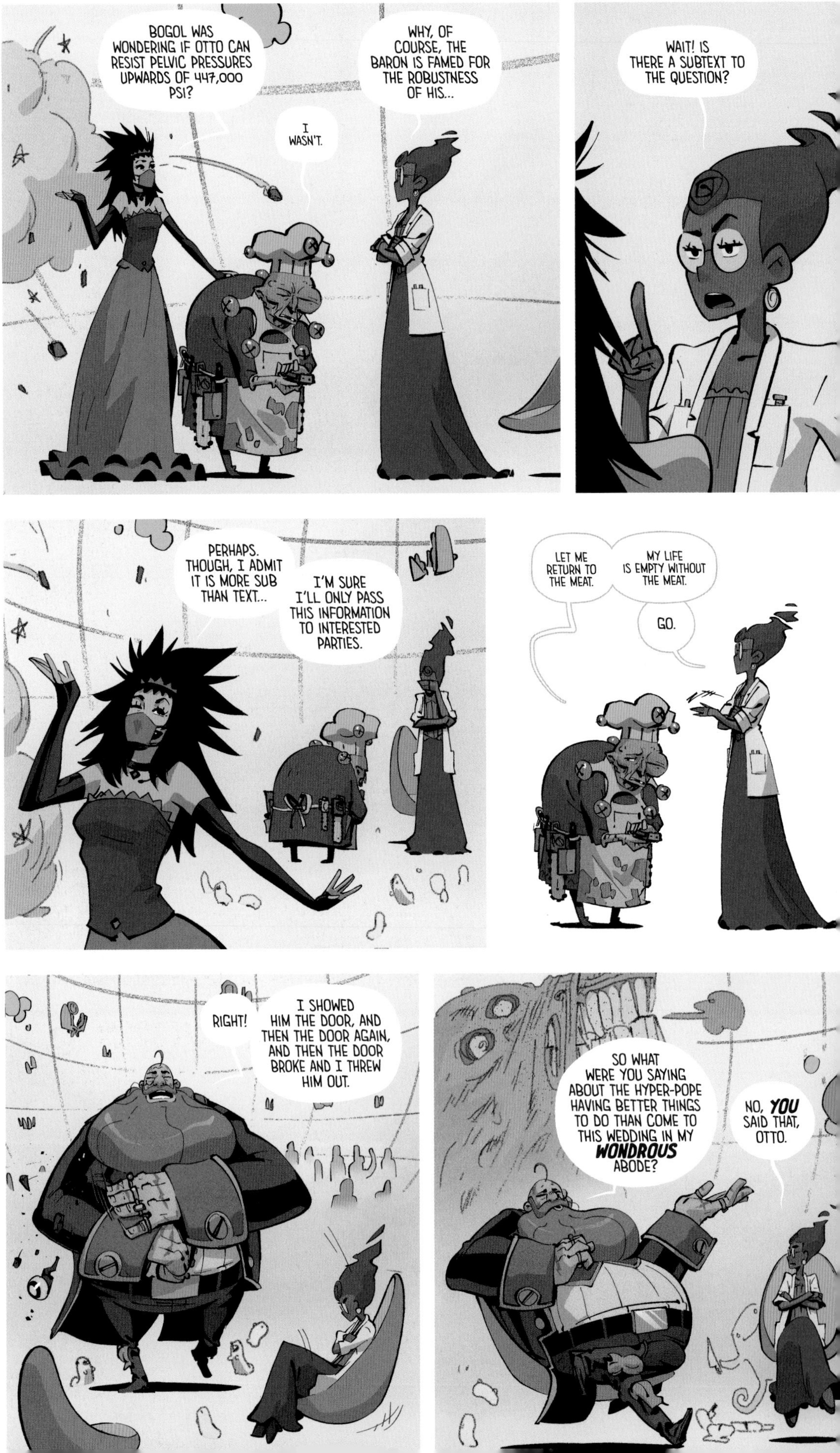

BOGOL WAS WONDERING IF OTTO CAN RESIST PELVIC PRESSURES UPWARDS OF 447,000 PSI?
WHY, OF COURSE, THE BARON IS FAMED FOR THE ROBUSTNESS OF HIS...
I WASN'T.
WAIT! IS THERE A SUBTEXT TO THE QUESTION?
PERHAPS. THOUGH, I ADMIT IT IS MORE SUB THAN TEXT...
I'M SURE I'LL ONLY PASS THIS INFORMATION TO INTERESTED PARTIES.
LET ME RETURN TO THE MEAT.
MY LIFE IS EMPTY WITHOUT THE MEAT.
GO.
RIGHT!
I SHOWED HIM THE DOOR, AND THEN THE DOOR AGAIN, AND THEN THE DOOR BROKE AND I THREW HIM OUT.
SO WHAT WERE YOU SAYING ABOUT THE HYPER-POPE HAVING BETTER THINGS TO DO THAN COME TO THIS WEDDING IN MY **WONDROUS** ABODE?
NO, ***YOU*** SAID THAT, OTTO.

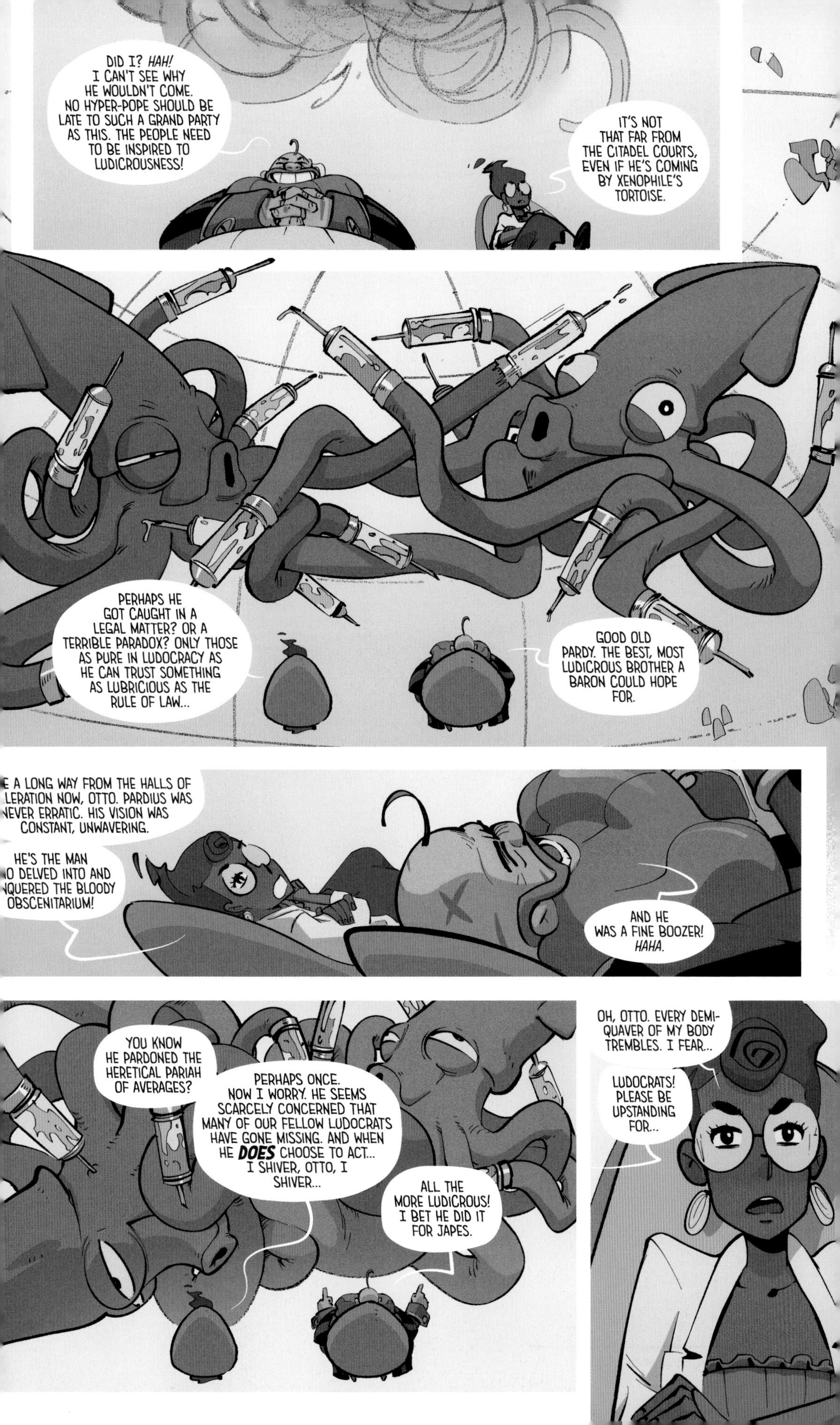
DID I? HAH! I CAN'T SEE WHY HE WOULDN'T COME. NO HYPER-POPE SHOULD BE LATE TO SUCH A GRAND PARTY AS THIS. THE PEOPLE NEED TO BE INSPIRED TO LUDICROUSNESS!
IT'S NOT THAT FAR FROM THE CITADEL COURTS, EVEN IF HE'S COMING BY XENOPHILE'S TORTOISE.
PERHAPS HE GOT CAUGHT IN A LEGAL MATTER? OR A TERRIBLE PARADOX? ONLY THOSE AS PURE IN LUDOCRACY AS HE CAN TRUST SOMETHING AS LUBRICIOUS AS THE RULE OF LAW...
GOOD OLD PARDY. THE BEST, MOST LUDICROUS BROTHER A BARON COULD HOPE FOR.
E A LONG WAY FROM THE HALLS OF LERATION NOW, OTTO. PARDIUS WAS NEVER ERRATIC. HIS VISION WAS CONSTANT, UNWAVERING.
HE'S THE MAN O DELVED INTO AND NQUERED THE BLOODY OBSCENITARIUM!
AND HE WAS A FINE BOOZER! HAHA.
YOU KNOW HE PARDONED THE HERETICAL PARIAH OF AVERAGES?
PERHAPS ONCE. NOW I WORRY. HE SEEMS SCARCELY CONCERNED THAT MANY OF OUR FELLOW LUDOCRATS HAVE GONE MISSING. AND WHEN HE DOES CHOOSE TO ACT... I SHIVER, OTTO, I SHIVER...
ALL THE MORE LUDICROUS! I BET HE DID IT FOR JAPES.
OH, OTTO. EVERY DEMI-QUAVER OF MY BODY TREMBLES. I FEAR...
LUDOCRATS! PLEASE BE UPSTANDING FOR...

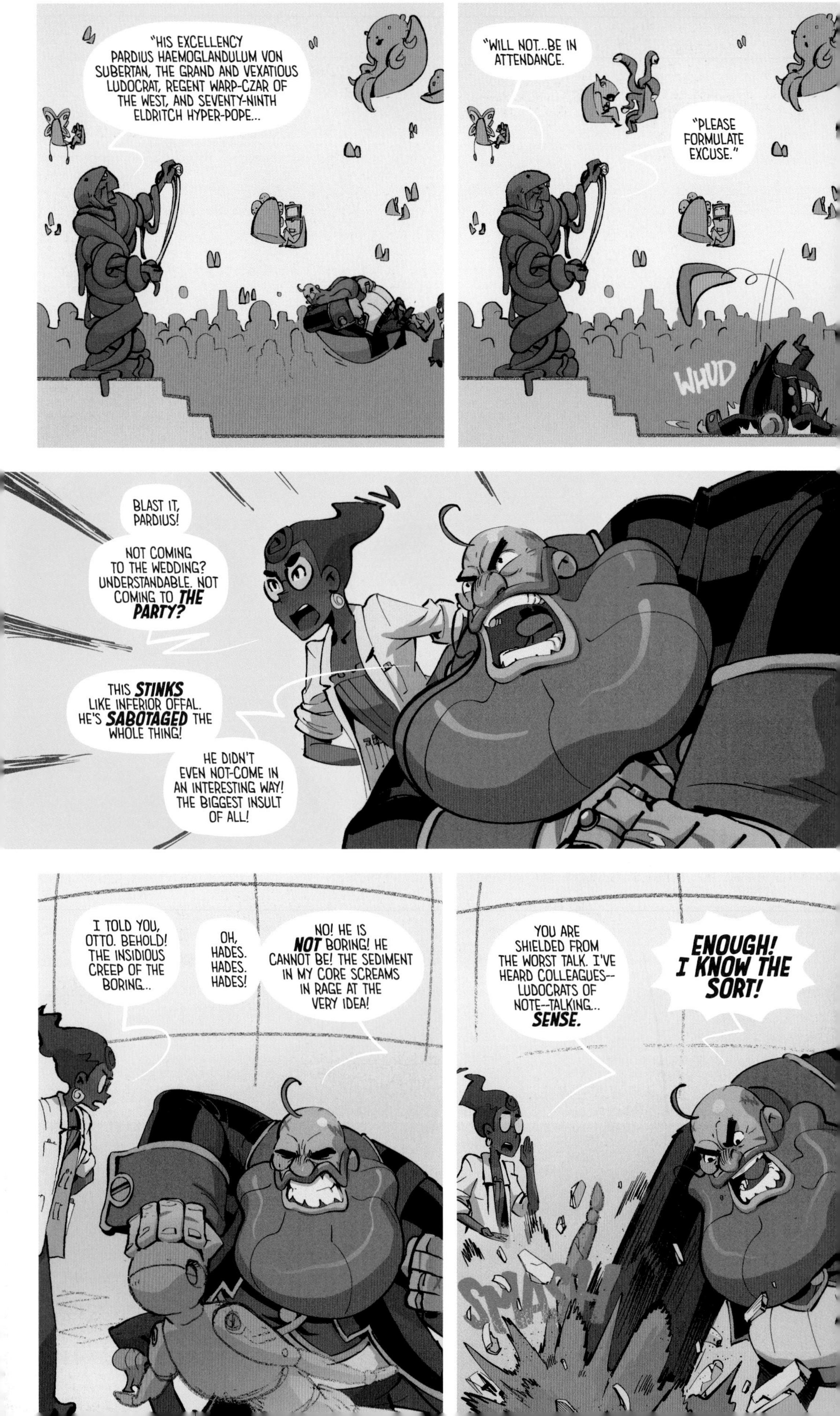
"HIS EXCELLENCY PARDIUS HAEMOGLANDULUM VON SUBERTAN, THE GRAND AND VEXATIOUS LUDOCRAT, REGENT WARP-CZAR OF THE WEST, AND SEVENTY-NINTH ELDRITCH HYPER-POPE...
"WILL NOT...BE IN ATTENDANCE.
"PLEASE FORMULATE EXCUSE."
WHUD
BLAST IT, PARDIUS!
NOT COMING TO THE WEDDING? UNDERSTANDABLE. NOT COMING TO **THE PARTY?**
THIS **STINKS** LIKE INFERIOR OFFAL. HE'S **SABOTAGED** THE WHOLE THING!
HE DIDN'T EVEN NOT-COME IN AN INTERESTING WAY! THE BIGGEST INSULT OF ALL!
I TOLD YOU, OTTO. BEHOLD! THE INSIDIOUS CREEP OF THE BORING...
OH, HADES. HADES. HADES!
NO! HE IS **NOT** BORING! HE CANNOT BE! THE SEDIMENT IN MY CORE SCREAMS IN RAGE AT THE VERY IDEA!
YOU ARE SHIELDED FROM THE WORST TALK. I'VE HEARD COLLEAGUES--LUDOCRATS OF NOTE--TALKING... **SENSE.**
ENOUGH! I KNOW THE SORT!

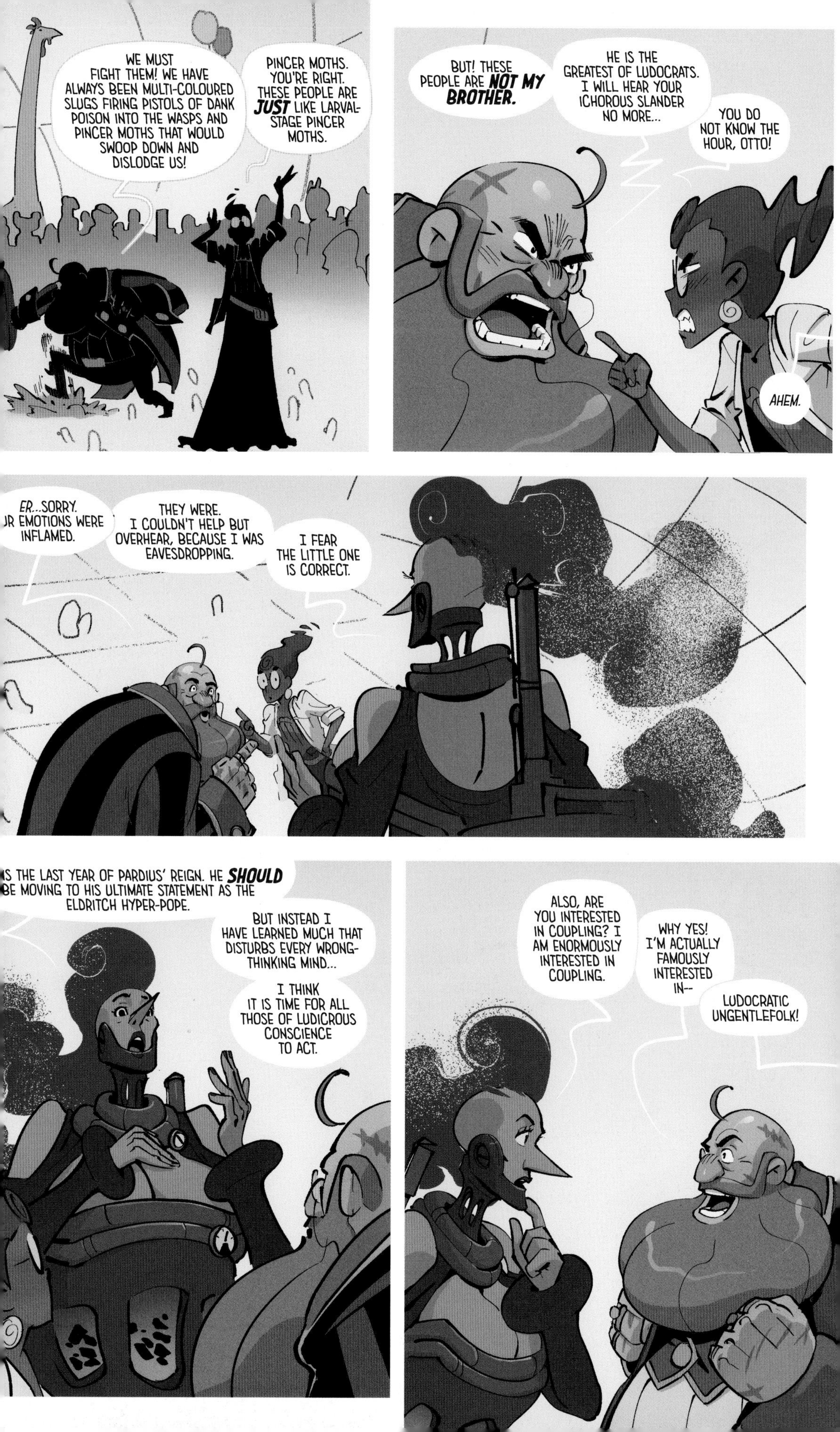

WE MUST FIGHT THEM! WE HAVE ALWAYS BEEN MULTI-COLOURED SLUGS FIRING PISTOLS OF DANK POISON INTO THE WASPS AND PINCER MOTHS THAT WOULD SWOOP DOWN AND DISLODGE US!
PINCER MOTHS. YOU'RE RIGHT. THESE PEOPLE ARE **JUST** LIKE LARVAL-STAGE PINCER MOTHS.
BUT! THESE PEOPLE ARE ***NOT MY BROTHER.***
HE IS THE GREATEST OF LUDOCRATS. I WILL HEAR YOUR ICHOROUS SLANDER NO MORE...
YOU DO NOT KNOW THE HOUR, OTTO!
AHEM.
ER...SORRY. R EMOTIONS WERE INFLAMED.
THEY WERE. I COULDN'T HELP BUT OVERHEAR, BECAUSE I WAS EAVESDROPPING.
I FEAR THE LITTLE ONE IS CORRECT.
S THE LAST YEAR OF PARDIUS' REIGN. HE **SHOULD** BE MOVING TO HIS ULTIMATE STATEMENT AS THE ELDRITCH HYPER-POPE.
BUT INSTEAD I HAVE LEARNED MUCH THAT DISTURBS EVERY WRONG-THINKING MIND...
I THINK IT IS TIME FOR ALL THOSE OF LUDICROUS CONSCIENCE TO ACT.
ALSO, ARE YOU INTERESTED IN COUPLING? I AM ENORMOUSLY INTERESTED IN COUPLING.
WHY YES! I'M ACTUALLY FAMOUSLY INTERESTED IN--
LUDOCRATIC UNGENTLEFOLK!

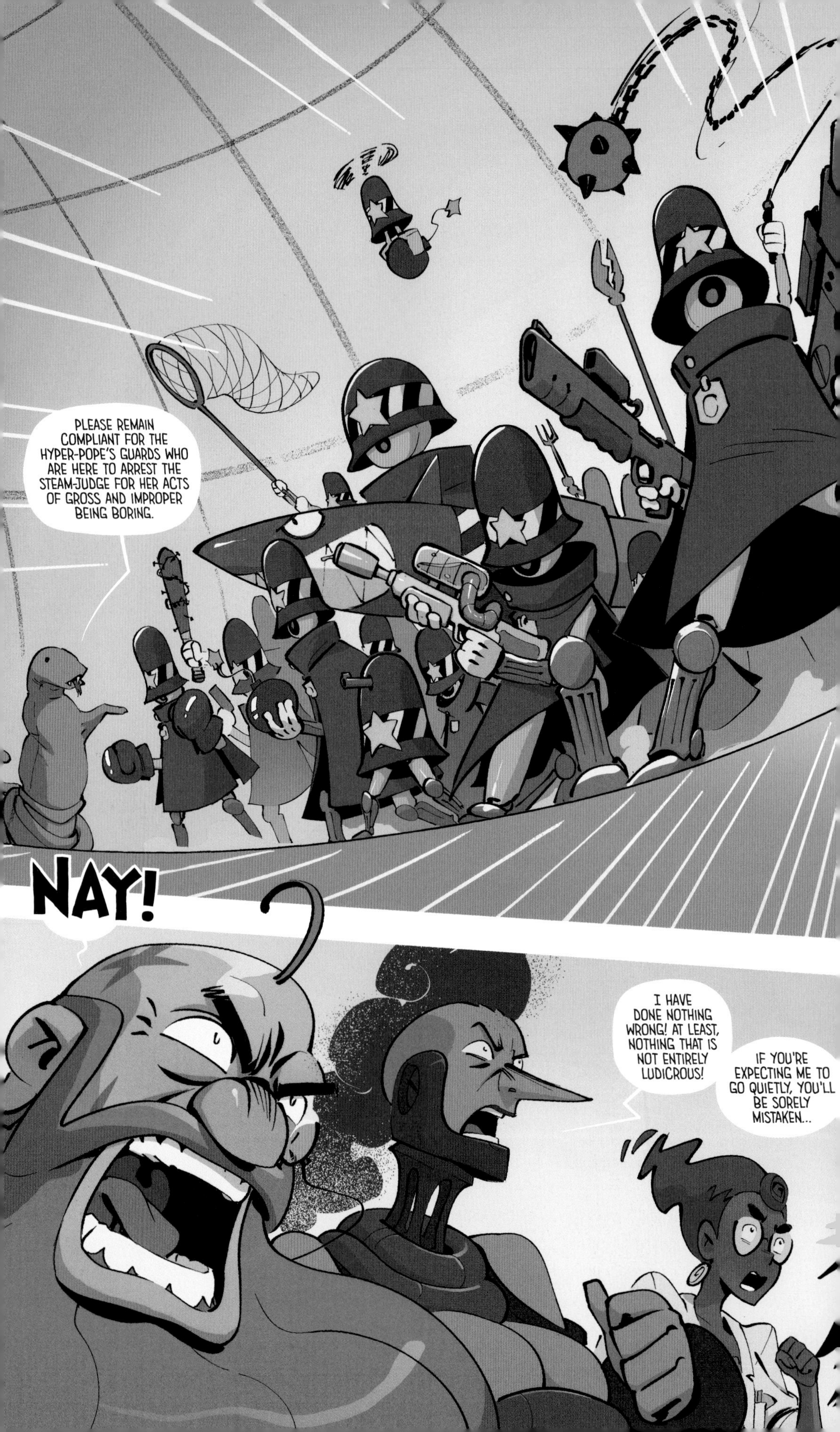
PLEASE REMAIN COMPLIANT FOR THE HYPER-POPE'S GUARDS WHO ARE HERE TO ARREST THE STEAM-JUDGE FOR HER ACTS OF GROSS AND IMPROPER BEING BORING.
NAY!
I HAVE DONE NOTHING WRONG! AT LEAST, NOTHING THAT IS NOT ENTIRELY LUDICROUS!
IF YOU'RE EXPECTING ME TO GO QUIETLY, YOU'LL BE SORELY MISTAKEN...

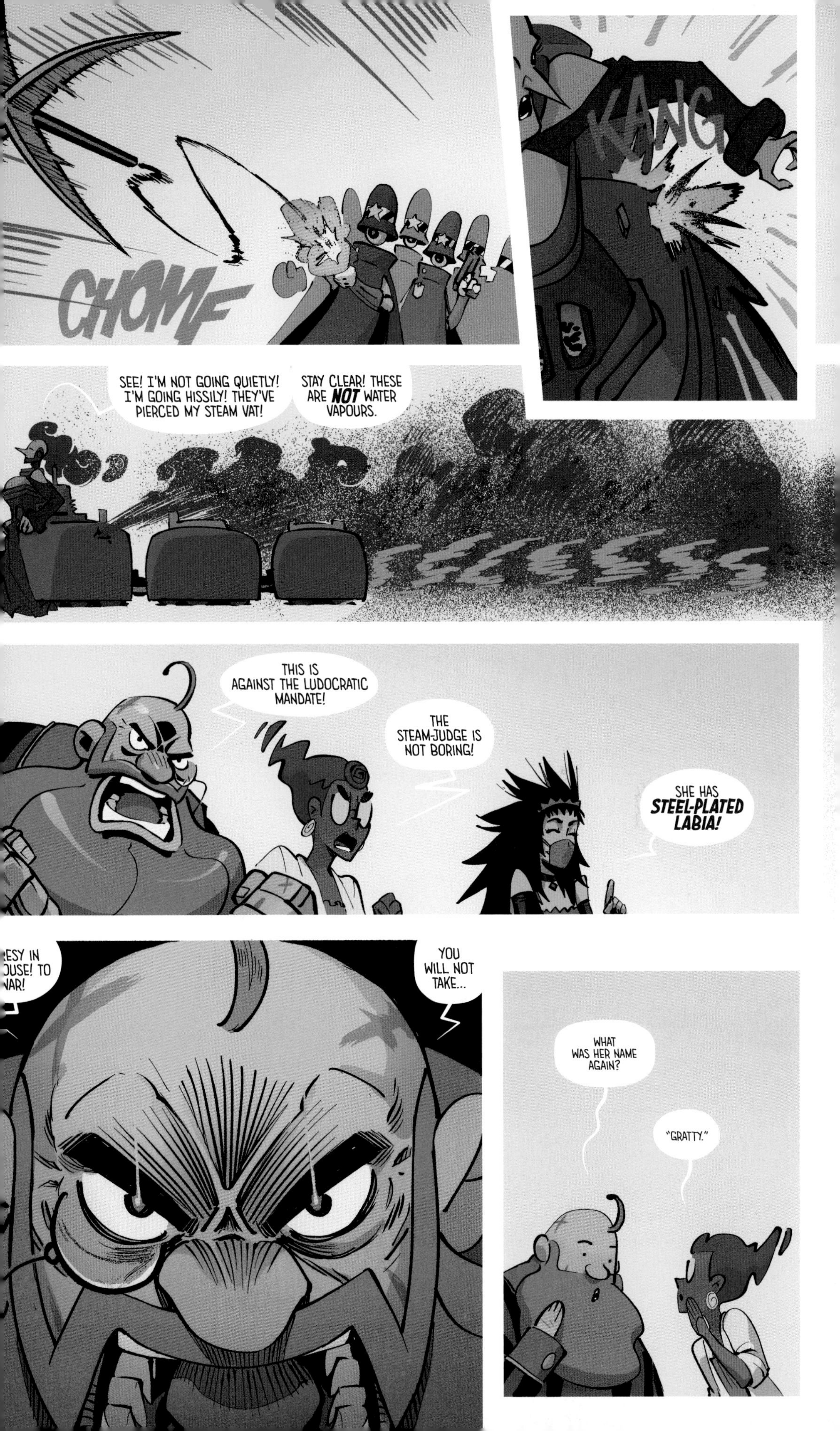
CHOMF
KANG
SEE! I'M NOT GOING QUIETLY! I'M GOING HISSILY! THEY'VE PIERCED MY STEAM VAT!
STAY CLEAR! THESE ARE **NOT** WATER VAPOURS.
SSSSSSSS
THIS IS AGAINST THE LUDOCRATIC MANDATE!
THE STEAM-JUDGE IS NOT BORING!
SHE HAS **STEEL-PLATED LABIA!**
YOU WILL NOT TAKE...
WHAT WAS HER NAME AGAIN?
"GRATTY."

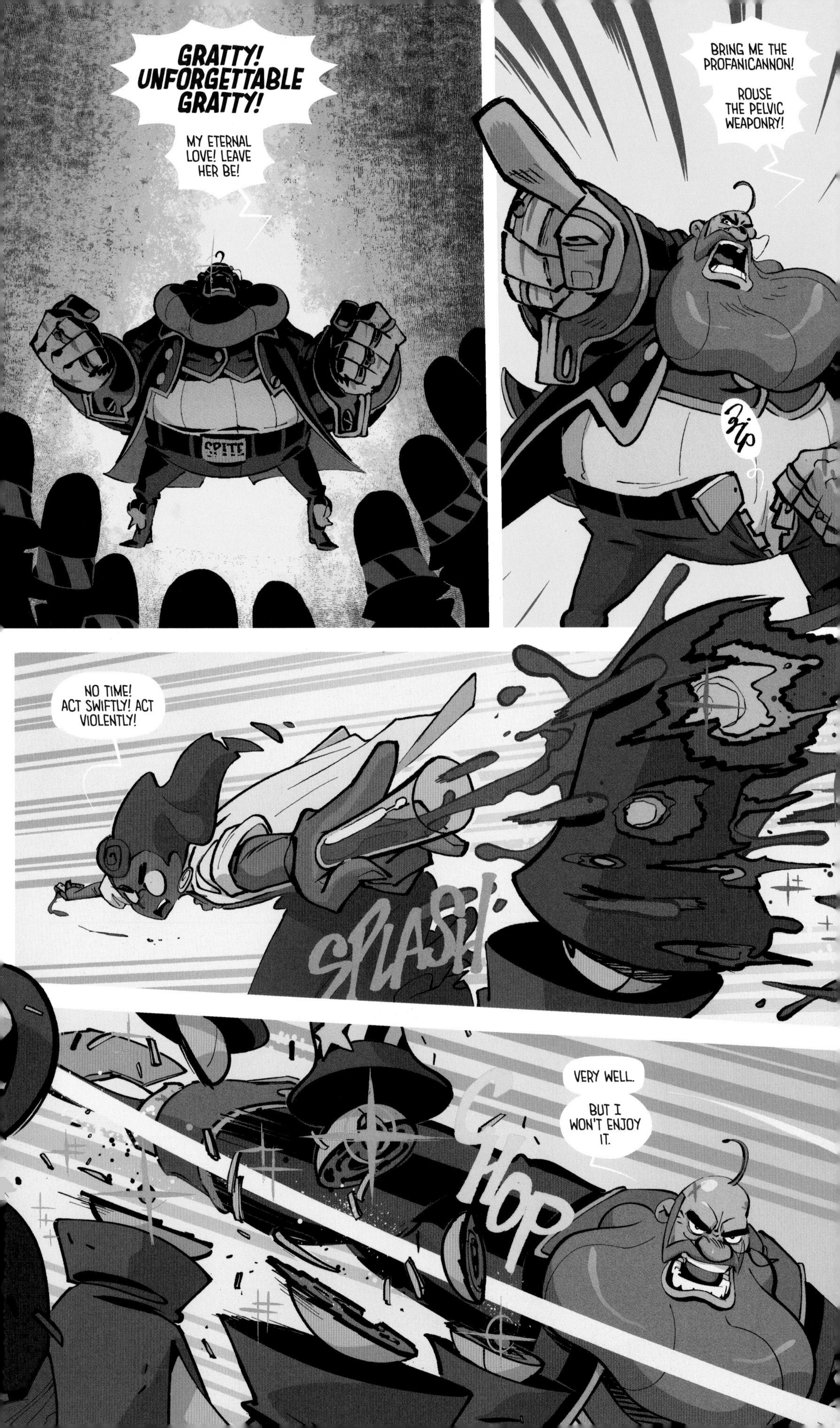
GRATTY! UNFORGETTABLE GRATTY!
MY ETERNAL LOVE! LEAVE HER BE!
SPITE
BRING ME THE PROFANICANNON!
ROUSE THE PELVIC WEAPONRY!
RIP
NO TIME! ACT SWIFTLY! ACT VIOLENTLY!
SPLASH
VERY WELL.
BUT I WON'T ENJOY IT.
CHOP

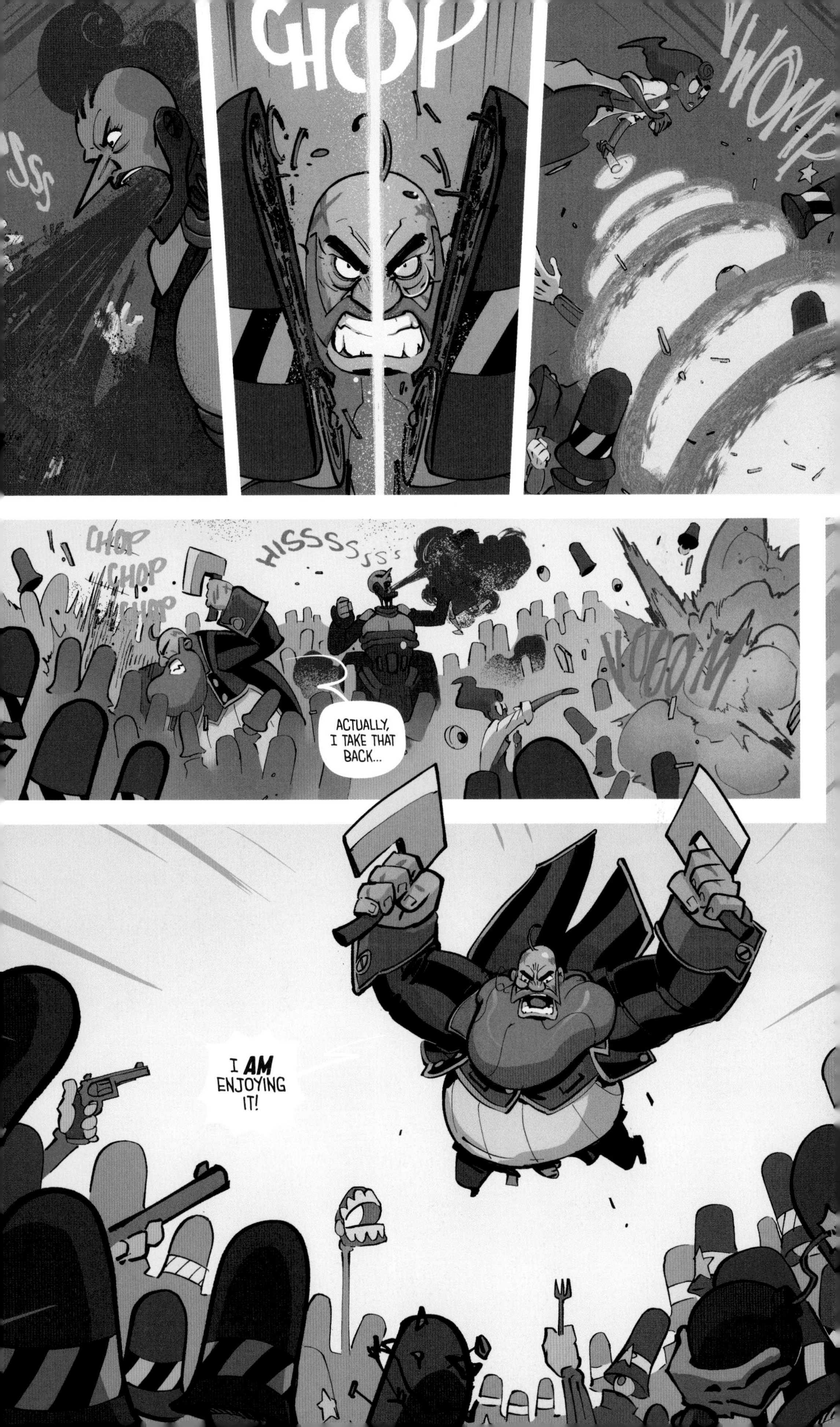

SSS
CHOP
WOMP
CHOP
CHOP
CHOP
HISSSSSSSS
ACTUALLY, I TAKE THAT BACK...
VOOOM
I AM ENJOYING IT!

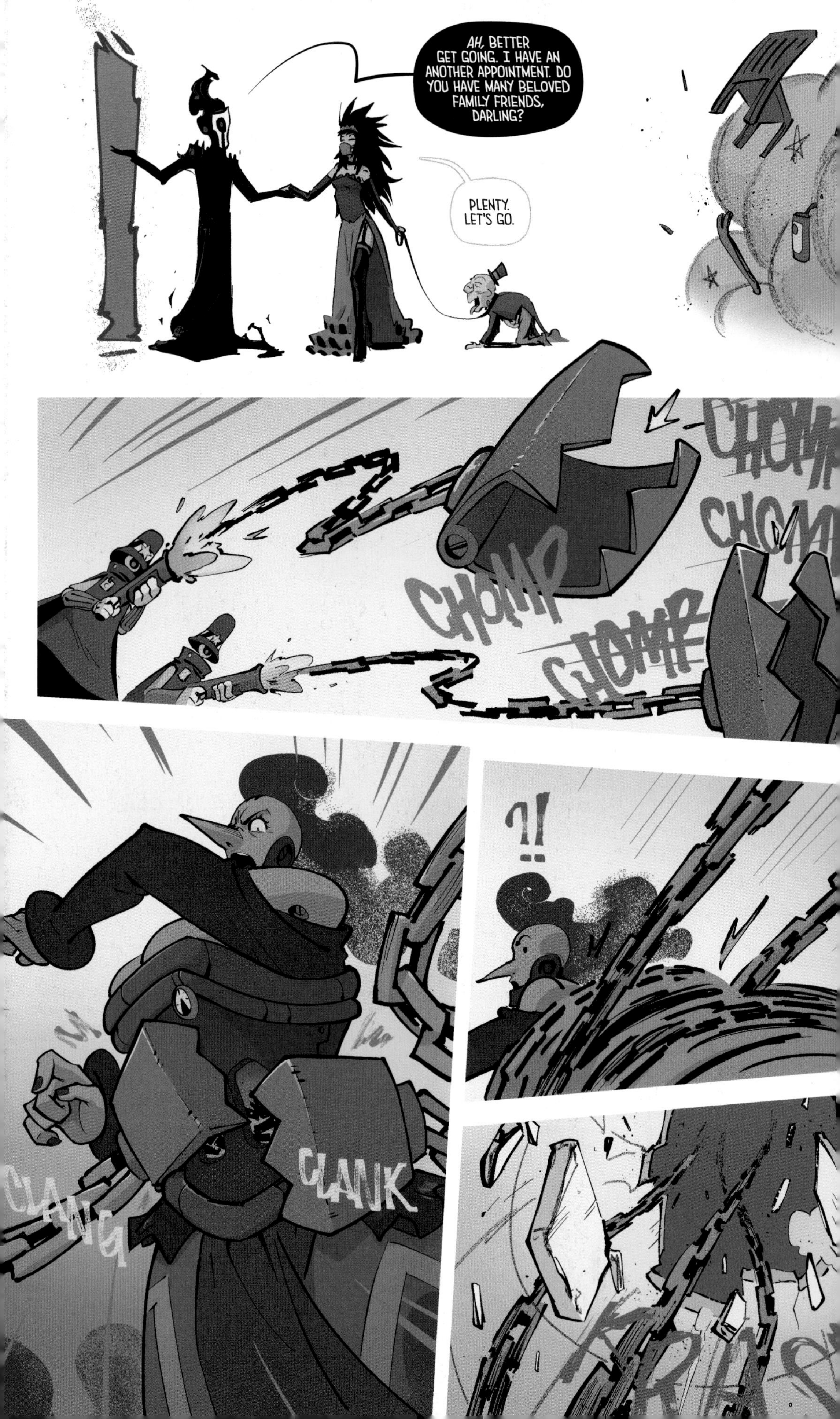
AH, BETTER GET GOING. I HAVE AN ANOTHER APPOINTMENT. DO YOU HAVE MANY BELOVED FAMILY FRIENDS, DARLING?
PLENTY. LET'S GO.
CHOMP
CHOMP
CHOMP
CHOMP
?!
CLANK
CLANG

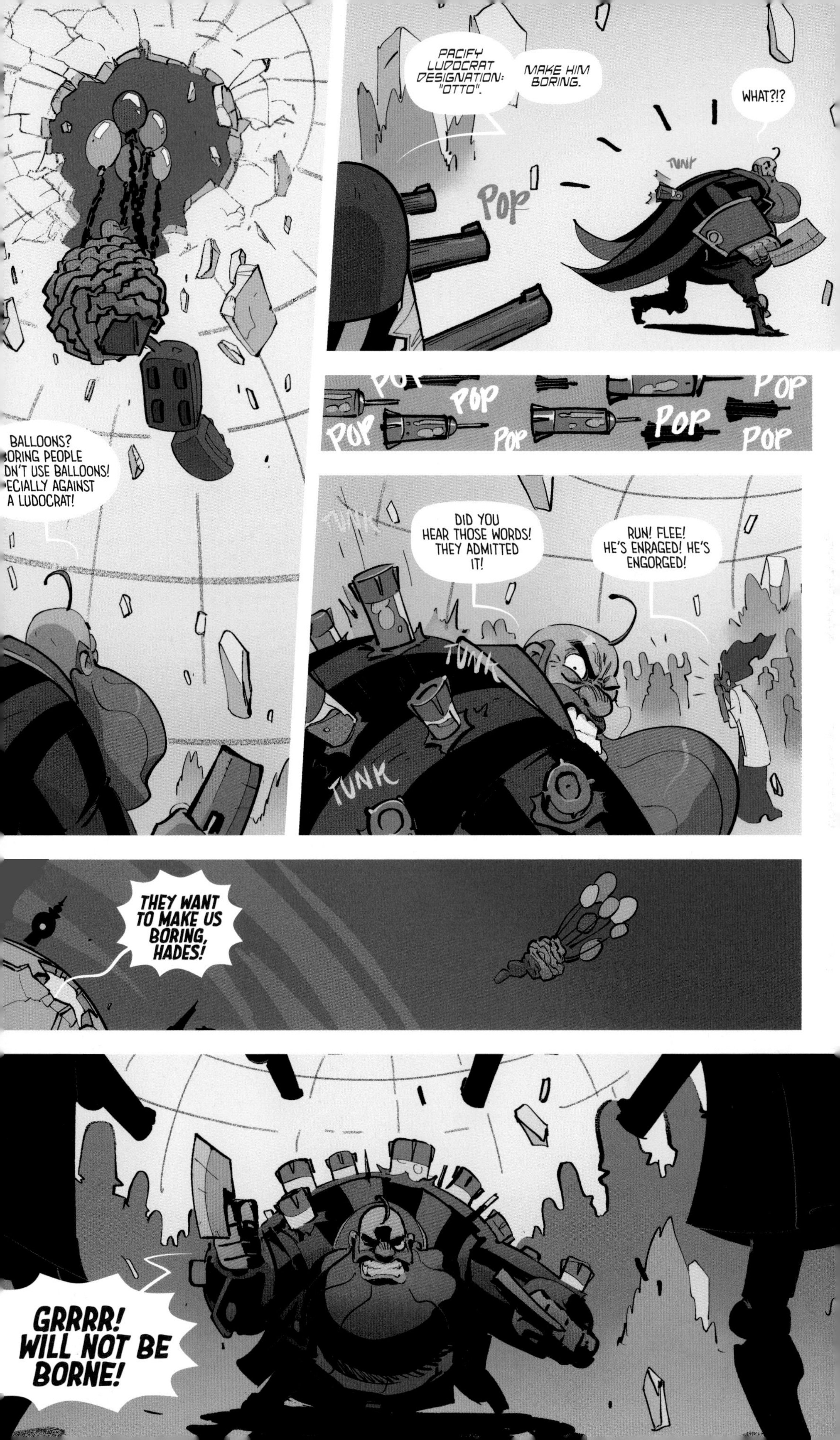
PACIFY LUDOCRAT DESIGNATION: "OTTO".
MAKE HIM BORING.
WHAT?!?
TUNK
POP
POP
POP
POP
POP
POP
POP
BALLOONS? BORING PEOPLE DON'T USE BALLOONS! ECIALLY AGAINST A LUDOCRAT!
TUNK
DID YOU HEAR THOSE WORDS! THEY ADMITTED IT!
RUN! FLEE! HE'S ENRAGED! HE'S ENGORGED!
TUNK
TUNK
THEY WANT TO MAKE US BORING, HADES!
GRRRR! WILL NOT BE BORNE!

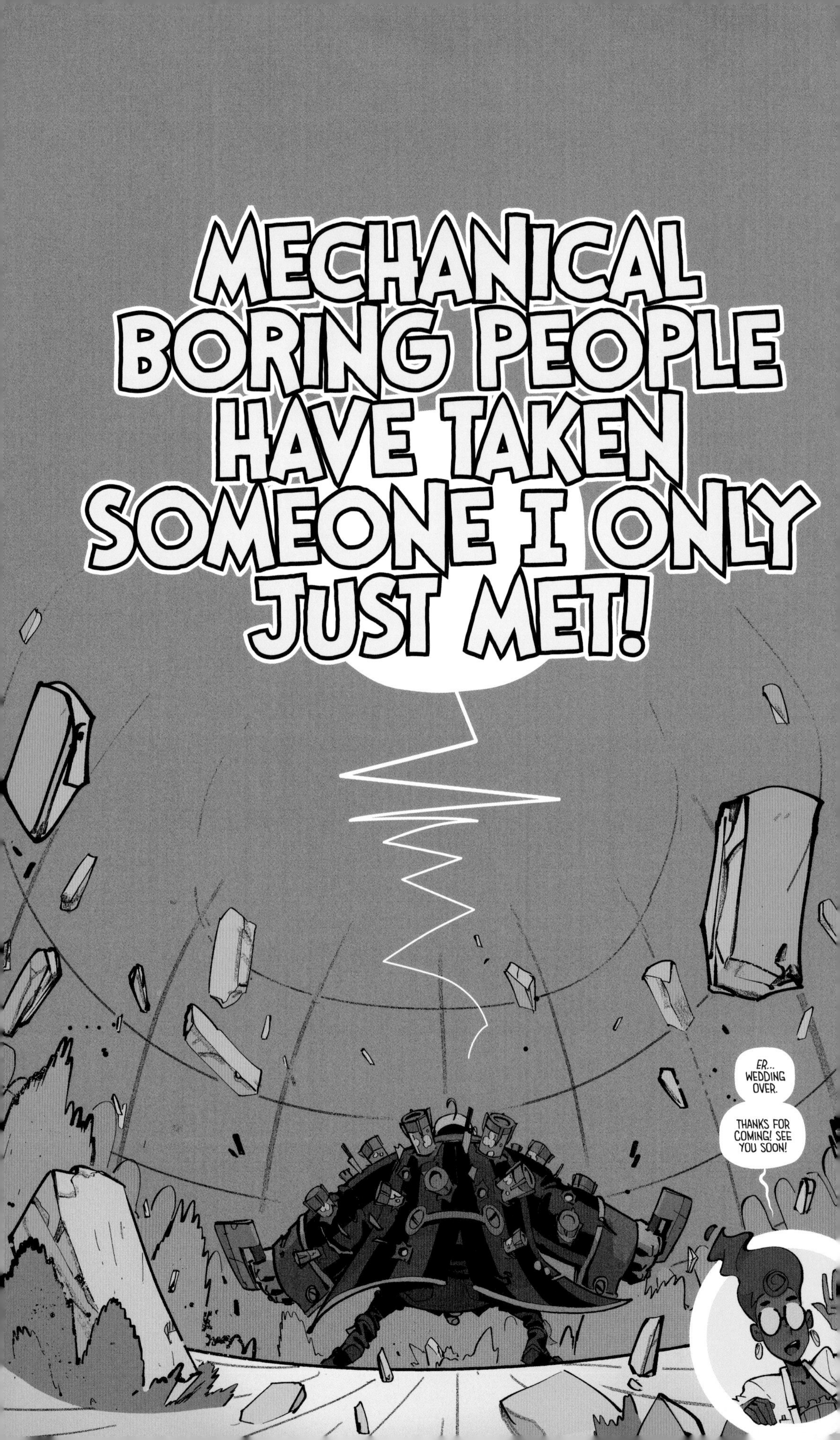
MECHANICAL BORING PEOPLE HAVE TAKEN SOMEONE I ONLY JUST MET!
ER... WEDDING OVER.
THANKS FOR COMING! SEE YOU SOON!

EXCERPTS from

The PERSONAL CYCLOPEDIA of LUDOCRACY,
by PARDIUS HAEMOGLANDULUM,
ELDRITCH HYPER-POPE and SUPREME HIGH LUDOCRAT

On Void Walkers

"...ONCE THE EELS had drained away, and the black beating heart of the Imprecation Worm went cold in my hand, it was clear that we had created something special. We knew we would need an agent with which to trade or spy on other universes, and other realities, and this was the being to do so! That we had boiled down the hard maths of the boffins and injected it into this ineffable being of altered space seemed unbelievable, but there he was: already making plans for a trip to the sideways realm of Poetic Rotwater. By these designs we would win the Goatmilk Wars, but only just." •

forward. Self-care is important, after all. Heck, it was in that very room that we plotted to resurrect Peter Coatling's Conjecture Farms, as well as give license to the Wasp Rituals, and to Bastard Peng and her Beam Guild! What would the world be today if we had not had the space to ponder, and make those decisions in peace? Where indeed." •

On Steam-Judges

"...AND SO IN THE YEARS following the defeat of the Normalisers by the Hybrid Of Zaragoza it became clear that we would need some manner of independent judiciary with which to judge the actions of our fellow Ludocrats. If the Ludocracy could be enjoyed by all, and not simply the Ludicrous, then the situation quite clearly necessitates a kind of steam-powered judging machine. So it was that a manner of coal-burning magistrate was created. Trained in Ludo law and run on fossil fuels and water, the Steam-Judges have long proven their efficacy: utterly incorruptible, and sort of arousing, for some reason. Long may their decisions run on time." •

On Drawing Rooms

"MY FIRST ENCOUNTER with a Drawing Room was just after we had dealt with the Visitor From Beyond The Mirror, and I realised immediately that having such a space, where doodling could become corporeal, was critical to the rapidity of our future invention. I made sure that all Ludocratic Establishments boasted one from that day

```
* * * * *
 * * * *
  * * *
   * *
    *
```

GUESTS, HYPERBEINGS AND RIPPLES OF DEAREST PROFUNDITY

1 **SNAKES ARE,** of course, always invited. No event is complete without snakes, and while few snakes seem to understand the invites they receive, no Ludocratic ceremony – wedding, funeral, disgorgement, or personality bifurcation – is really complete without a strong serpent presence. We didn't catch the name of this little guy, because he was sadly trodden upon by a sauropod who, frankly, doesn't seem to have been on the guest list at all.

* * *

2 **THERE'S SCARCE REASON** in gathering this many Ludocrats in one place without siphoning off the novels and operas that they have inside them and might never get out! These raw potentialities (often disgusting) are streamed directly to the Obscenitarium's automated expression chambers, where the ideas are forced onward through specially configured poets and authors (neurotic types who are bred for the purpose), meaning that an idea is never wasted. The coupons earned can be traded for meat credits!

* * *

3 **NO ENJOINING** of Ludocratic families would be correctly blessed without the presence of Thrax Oblivious, the sentient bag of wheat. Thrax, a masterpiece of alchemical transmogrification, is not, as some have claimed, a Ludocrat transformed into a bag of wheat, but rather the reverse. Our scientists have yet to imbue Thrax with any further capabilities, such as movement or speech, but they assure us that he is most definitely one of, if not the most emotionally intelligent being extant in the universe today.

* * *

4 **WHILE IT WOULD** run against the spirit of Ludocracy to entirely outlaw cannibalism, inviting experimental monsters to a wedding does tend to result in unwanted loss of limb. Fortunately, the worst of the off-plan ingurgitation at this wedding was avoided by shipping in some indentured clowns. There is nothing a monstrous wedding guest enjoys more than being able to crack the old classic "Does this taste funny to you?" through a mouthful of terrifying viscera.

* * *

5 **MUCH OF THE GALLERY** here is filled with Von Subertan's personal invitees: often composed of beings he later intends to eat. Otto never did get to dine on this colossal octopus, however, and the creature later found itself at the wheel of a large automobile, wondering how it got there.

* * *

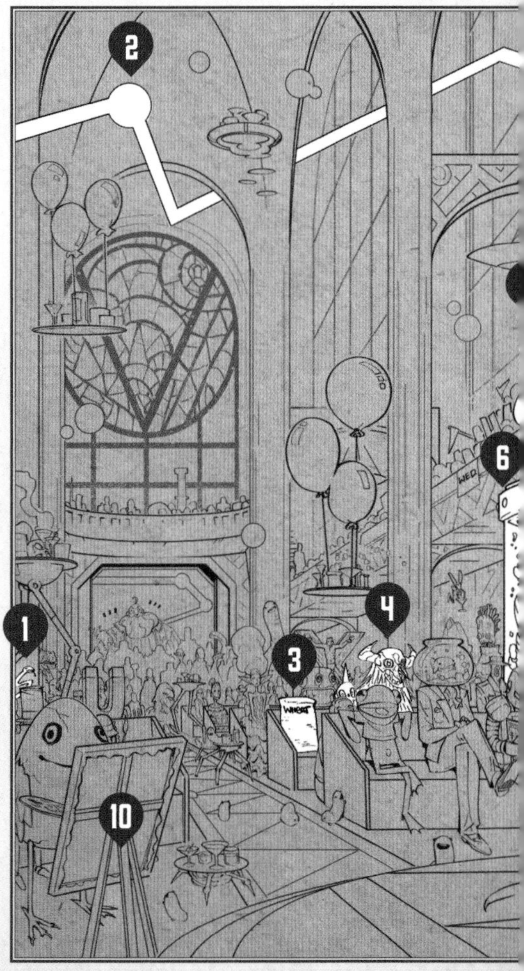

2
6
4
1
3
WHEAT
10

6 **GUIDULA STERLIPHAIN,** Duchess of the Pond Viles, who came to fame through their chain of submerged singles bars. Struggling blindly through cold black water to find your sexual partner has become hugely fashionable in recent years, and Sterliphain was swift to capitalise on the trend. They say, however, that they themselves will never find love, due to a constant, deafening, nightmarish keyboard solo that only they can hear.

* * *

7 **WHAT CAN WE SAY** about Vork Mibula that hasn't already been literally written in the stars by the alien superbeings he has subjugated and forced to do his bidding? There he is, piloting his spider walker. Whilst a minor character sitting on row D, seat 19 in this image, in truth it is Mibula's ignition of the acceleration entity of Lodar-9 which really transforms the multiverse, thanks to its awakening of the Annihilator Precepts: an event which will eventually unfold the dark matter matrices and release God from his paralysis-tomb to complete His unthinkable mission in the material realm.

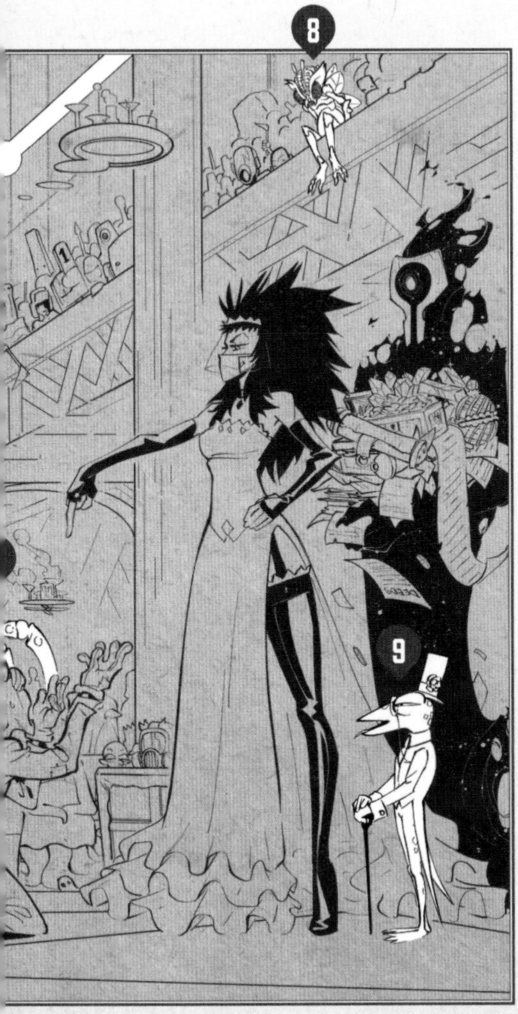
8
9

* * *

8 **VORSK "HUSK-DOER" STENTIFRET,** Ninety-Fifth UnQueen of the ZertHive at Laringineth, does not understand Ludocratic rituals. She will later try to lay an egg inside The Floating Head of Archimemtet, much to that dismembered scholar's surprise. Look, we're not saying there's anything wrong with insect people on the whole, just that if you're going to invite anthropomorphised creatures to your wedding then you can't expect their alien cognisance and contradictory perception of the universe not to result in accidental hybridisation attempts. (FWIW, cat people are, by and large, far more easily distracted.)

* * *

9 **ADJUDICATION GECKOS** make the world go around, and also sometimes make people's heads come off, as in the case of the unfortunate groom. These telepathic bipeds were bred specifically to ensure that Ludocracy never faltered, and that judgements, like this one, are harsh but unfair. Whether a society really should give executive power over life and death to emotionless semi-sentient reptiles is unclear, but it certainly seemed like a fun thing to do at the time.

* * *

10 **A LUDOCRAT DOES NOT REQUIRE PICTORIAL REPRESENTATION** of an event they were present for. They'll remember it if it's worth remembering, and if it's not, they would rather destroy anything which could make them recall something so dull and dreary. However, many find it useful to hire a skilled artist to draw alternative events which *could* have happened, to encourage all Ludocrats to strive to ensure their actuality beats all possibilities. The wedding's portraitist is in fact the twin brother of the actual portraitist, and spent the evening panickedly daubing random shapes. When the truth was uncovered, everyone was too drunk to care.

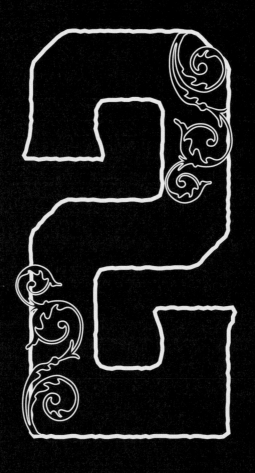

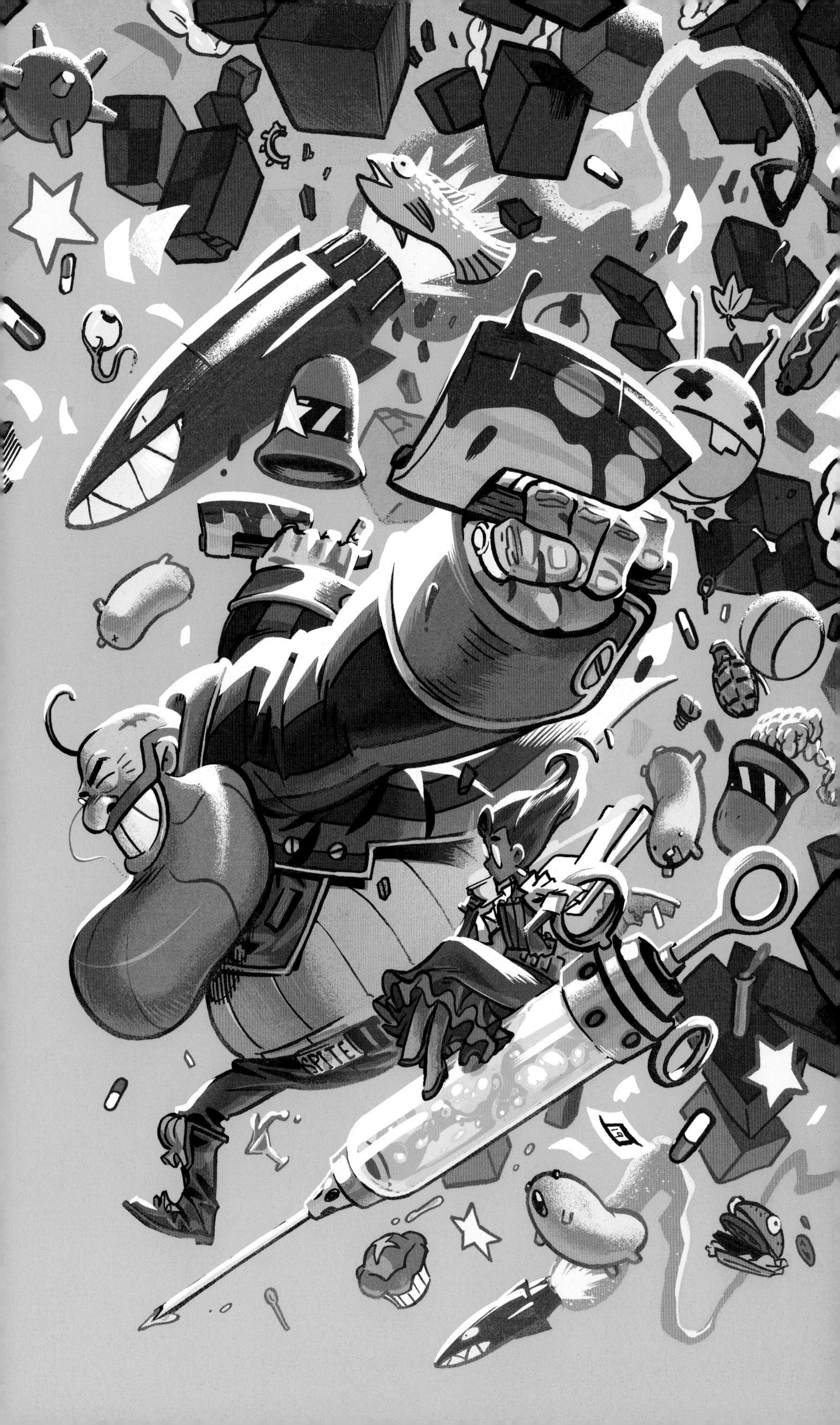
SPITE

ONCE UPON
A TIME...

there was a
WEDDING *where*
a STEAM-JUDGE
met a LARGE MAN
with an AXE.

The STEAM-JUDGE
was ARRESTED *by*
BORING PEOPLE.

The LARGE MAN
with an AXE
was MIFFED.

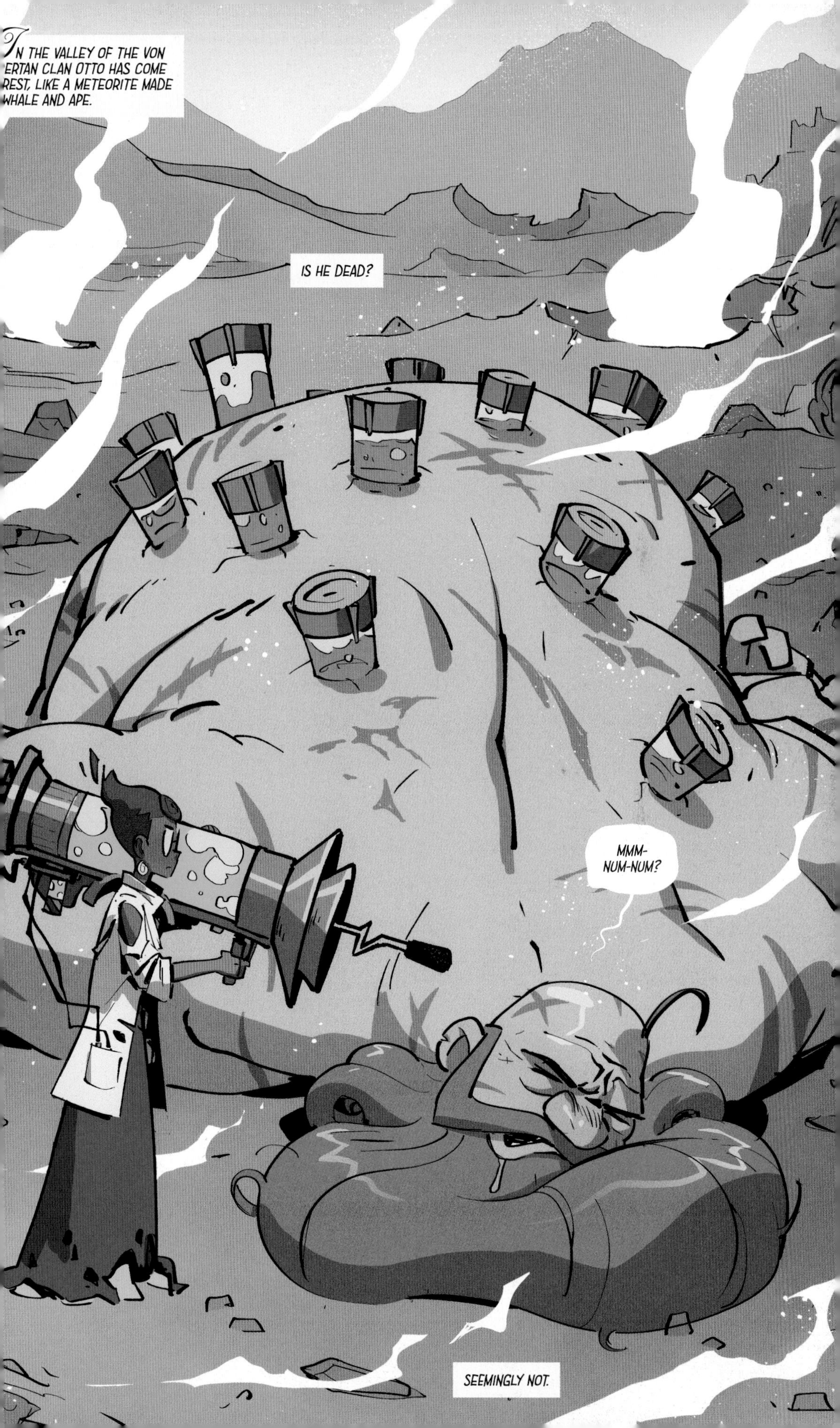
IN THE VALLEY OF THE VON
ERTAN CLAN OTTO HAS COME
REST, LIKE A METEORITE MADE
WHALE AND APE.
IS HE DEAD?
MMM-NUM-NUM?
SEEMINGLY NOT.

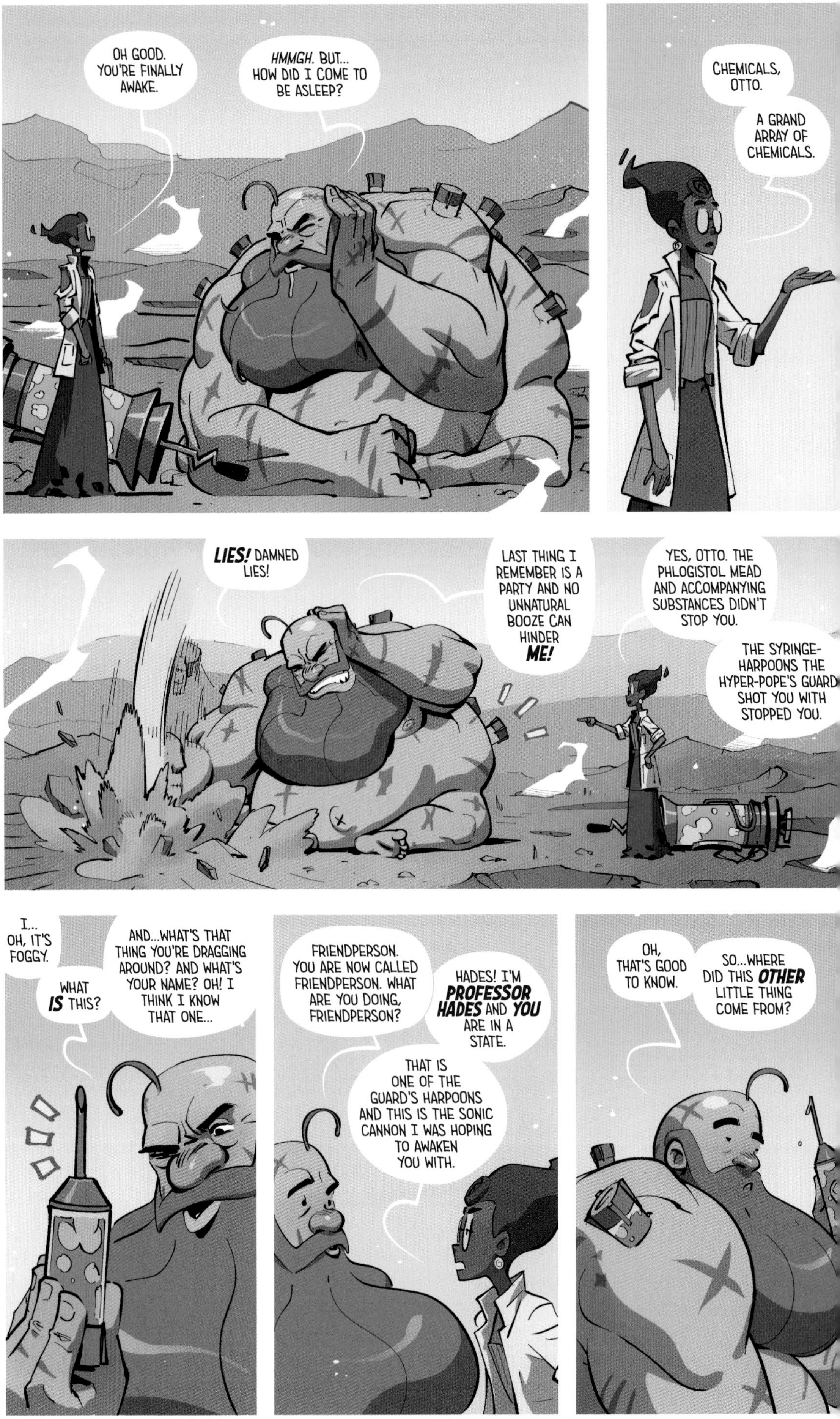
OH GOOD. YOU'RE FINALLY AWAKE.
HMMGH. BUT... HOW DID I COME TO BE ASLEEP?
CHEMICALS, OTTO.
A GRAND ARRAY OF CHEMICALS.
LIES! DAMNED LIES!
LAST THING I REMEMBER IS A PARTY AND NO UNNATURAL BOOZE CAN HINDER ***ME!***
YES, OTTO. THE PHLOGISTOL MEAD AND ACCOMPANYING SUBSTANCES DIDN'T STOP YOU.
THE SYRINGE-HARPOONS THE HYPER-POPE'S GUARD SHOT YOU WITH STOPPED YOU.
I... OH, IT'S FOGGY.
WHAT ***IS*** THIS?
AND...WHAT'S THAT THING YOU'RE DRAGGING AROUND? AND WHAT'S YOUR NAME? OH! I THINK I KNOW THAT ONE...
FRIENDPERSON. YOU ARE NOW CALLED FRIENDPERSON. WHAT ARE YOU DOING, FRIENDPERSON?
HADES! I'M ***PROFESSOR HADES*** AND ***YOU*** ARE IN A STATE.
THAT IS ONE OF THE GUARD'S HARPOONS AND THIS IS THE SONIC CANNON I WAS HOPING TO AWAKEN YOU WITH.
OH, THAT'S GOOD TO KNOW.
SO...WHERE DID THIS ***OTHER*** LITTLE THING COME FROM?

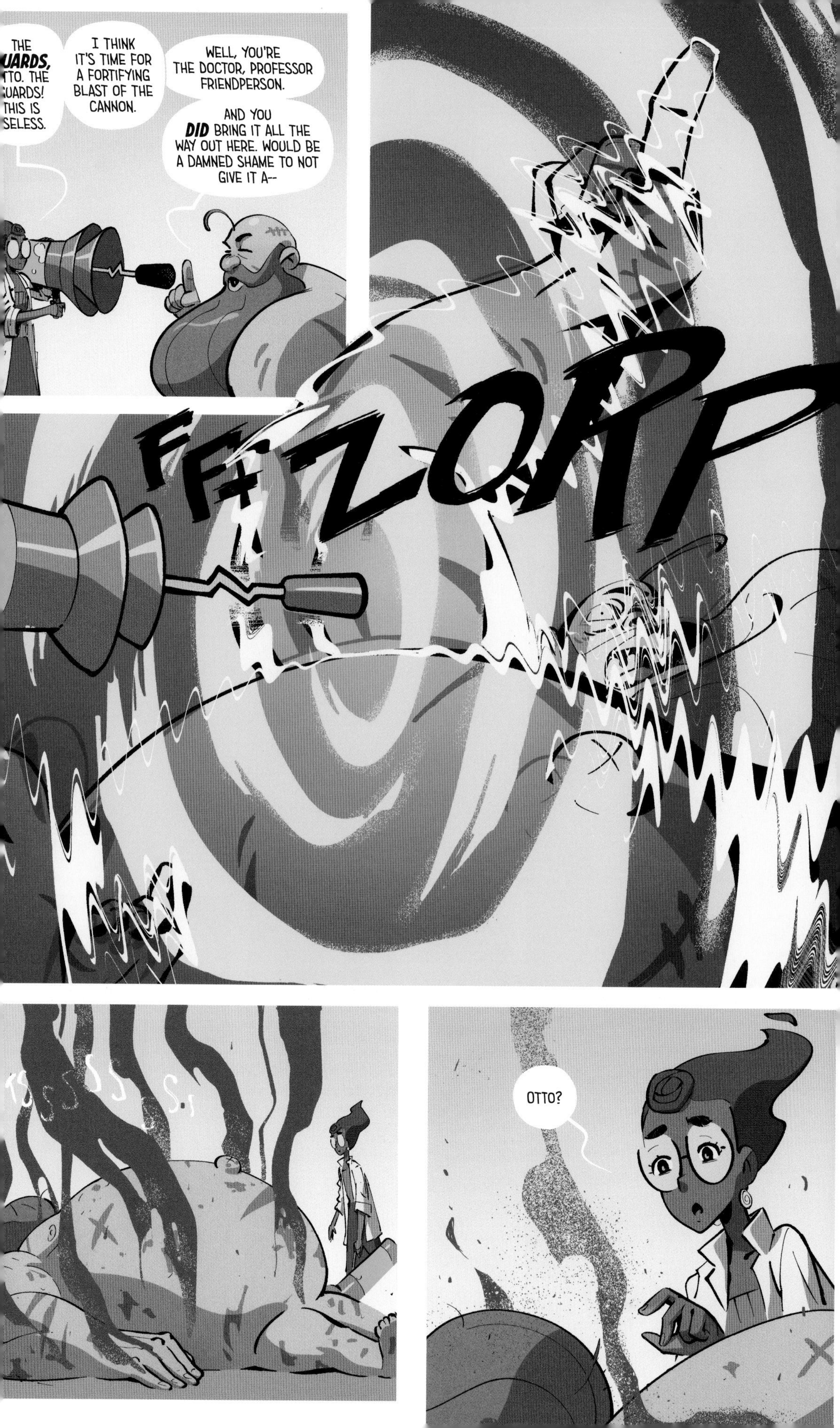
THE GUARDS, OTTO. THE GUARDS! THIS IS USELESS.
I THINK IT'S TIME FOR A FORTIFYING BLAST OF THE CANNON.
WELL, YOU'RE THE DOCTOR, PROFESSOR FRIENDPERSON.
AND YOU DID BRING IT ALL THE WAY OUT HERE. WOULD BE A DAMNED SHAME TO NOT GIVE IT A--
FFZOPP
OTTO?

MY DARLING GRATTY! *MY SOULMATE!*

ARRESTED!

OOH! **MY TENDER HEART!** IT ACHES! IT BREAKS!

PLUMP THE WAR-WIG OF WALLACHIA!

THE HYPER-POPE'S TREACHERY MUST BE REVENGED!

Some time later.

YOUR *WAR-WIG,* SIRE.

HMM. NO. MAYBE IT'S A TRIFLE HOT FOR THE OL' WAR-WIG.

WELL, BETTER GET THIS THING STARTED, *EH,* HADES?

"EVERYONE" THIS WAY.

WE ARE GATHERED HERE TO REVENGE TREACHERY. TREMENDOUS! SO: SECRECY, PROFESSIONALISM, THAT SORT OF THING.

MAY I INTRODUCE OUR MASTERMIND, PROFESSOR HADES ZERO-K.

...MASTERMIND!

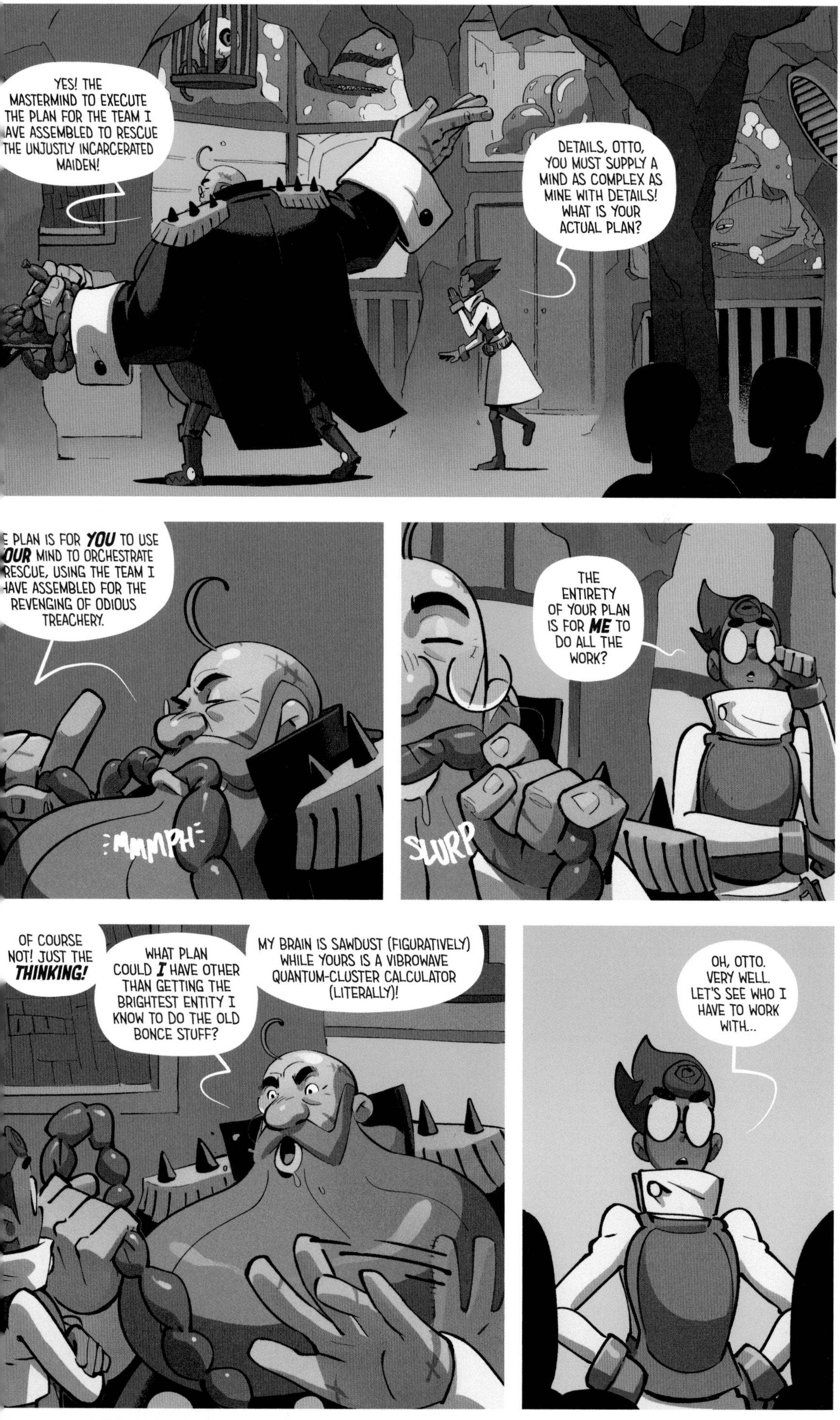
YES! THE MASTERMIND TO EXECUTE THE PLAN FOR THE TEAM I AVE ASSEMBLED TO RESCUE THE UNJUSTLY INCARCERATED MAIDEN!
DETAILS, OTTO, YOU MUST SUPPLY A MIND AS COMPLEX AS MINE WITH DETAILS! WHAT IS YOUR ACTUAL PLAN?
E PLAN IS FOR YOU TO USE OUR MIND TO ORCHESTRATE RESCUE, USING THE TEAM I HAVE ASSEMBLED FOR THE REVENGING OF ODIOUS TREACHERY.
MMMPH
THE ENTIRETY OF YOUR PLAN IS FOR ME TO DO ALL THE WORK?
SLURP
OF COURSE NOT! JUST THE THINKING!
WHAT PLAN COULD I HAVE OTHER THAN GETTING THE BRIGHTEST ENTITY I KNOW TO DO THE OLD BONCE STUFF?
MY BRAIN IS SAWDUST (FIGURATIVELY) WHILE YOURS IS A VIBROWAVE QUANTUM-CLUSTER CALCULATOR (LITERALLY)!
OH, OTTO. VERY WELL. LET'S SEE WHO I HAVE TO WORK WITH...

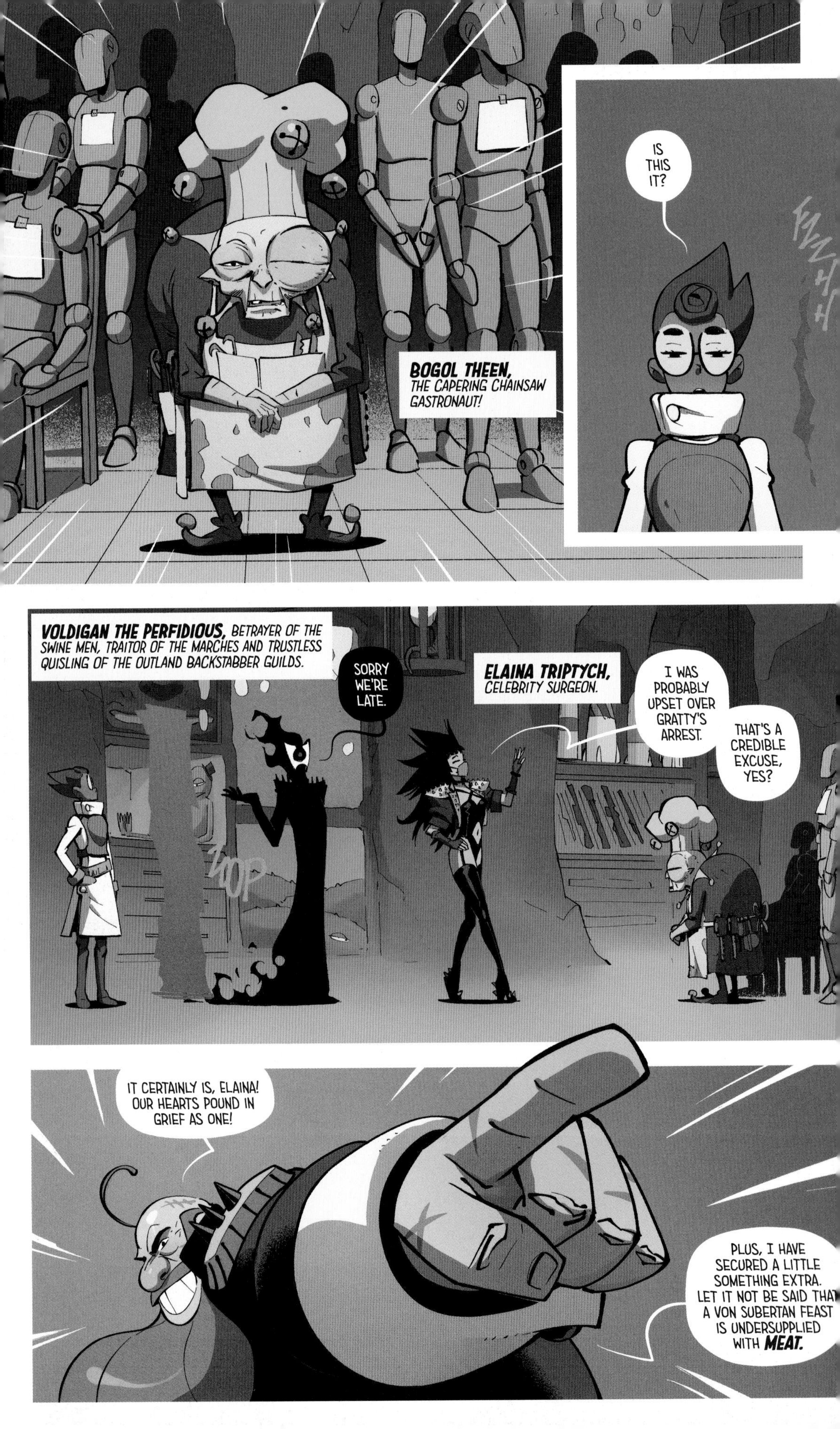
BOGOL THEEN,
THE CAPERING CHAINSAW GASTRONAUT!
IS THIS IT?
VOLDIGAN THE PERFIDIOUS, BETRAYER OF THE SWINE MEN, TRAITOR OF THE MARCHES AND TRUSTLESS QUISLING OF THE OUTLAND BACKSTABBER GUILDS.
SORRY WE'RE LATE.
ELAINA TRIPTYCH,
CELEBRITY SURGEON.
I WAS PROBABLY UPSET OVER GRATTY'S ARREST.
THAT'S A CREDIBLE EXCUSE, YES?
ZOOP
IT CERTAINLY IS, ELAINA! OUR HEARTS POUND IN GRIEF AS ONE!
PLUS, I HAVE SECURED A LITTLE SOMETHING EXTRA. LET IT NOT BE SAID THAT A VON SUBERTAN FEAST IS UNDERSUPPLIED WITH MEAT.

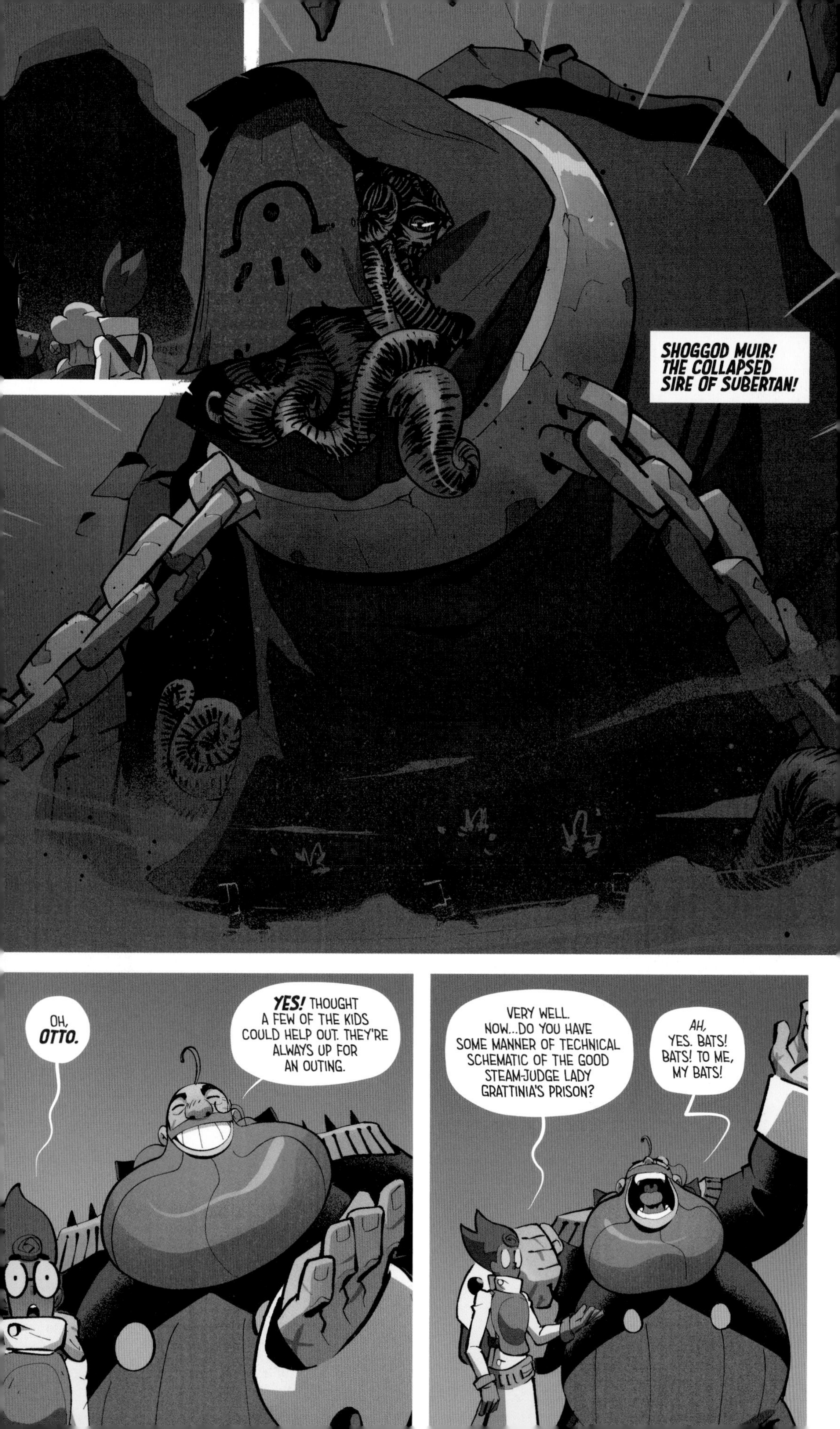
SHOGGOD MUIR! THE COLLAPSED SIRE OF SUBERTAN!
OH, OTTO.
YES! THOUGHT A FEW OF THE KIDS COULD HELP OUT. THEY'RE ALWAYS UP FOR AN OUTING.
VERY WELL. NOW...DO YOU HAVE SOME MANNER OF TECHNICAL SCHEMATIC OF THE GOOD STEAM-JUDGE LADY GRATTINIA'S PRISON?
AH, YES. BATS! BATS! TO ME, MY BATS!

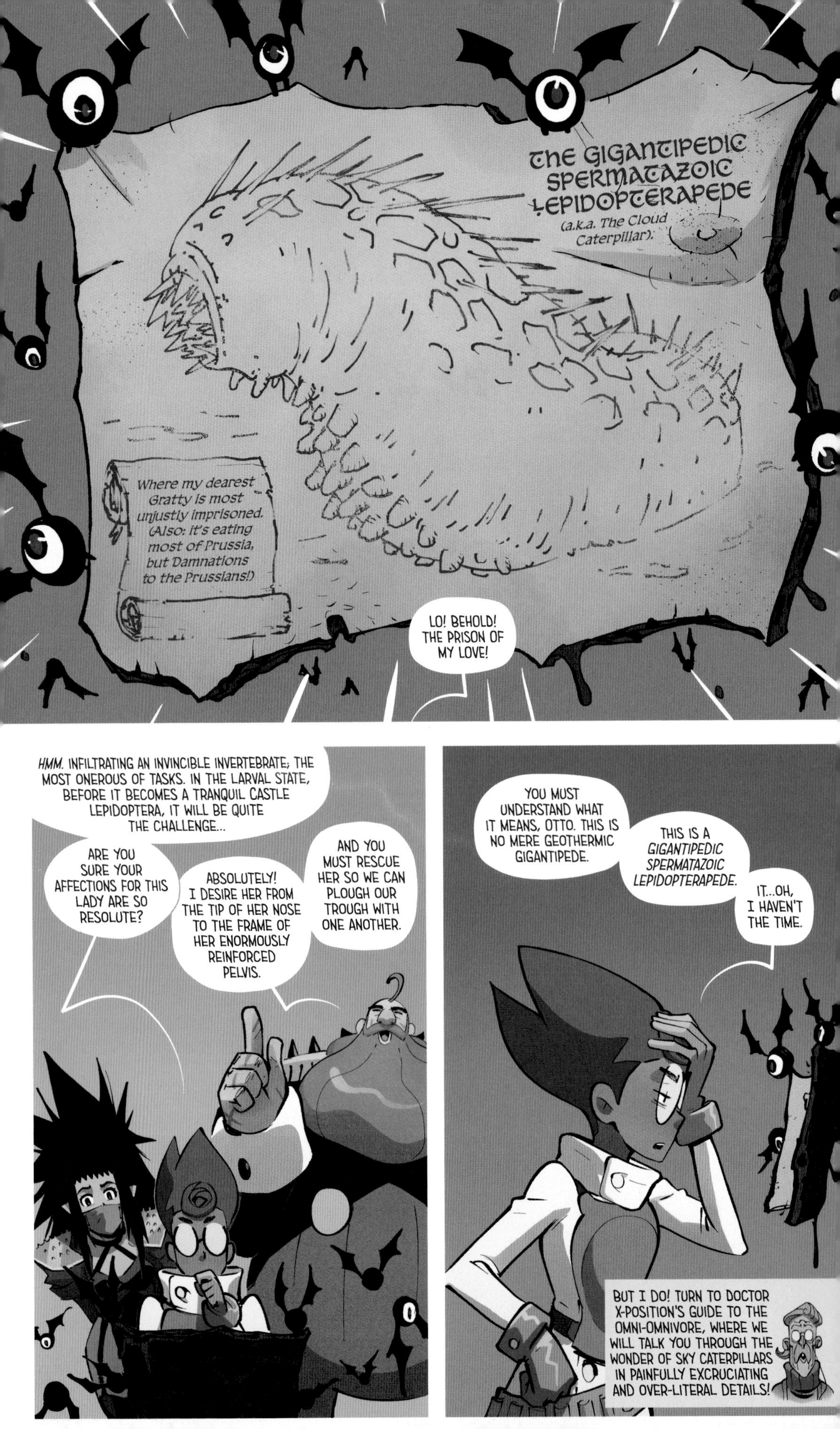
THE GIGANTIPEDIC SPERMATAZOIC LEPIDOPTERAPEDE
(a.k.a. The Cloud Caterpillar).
Where my dearest Gratty is most unjustly imprisoned. (Also: it's eating most of Prussia, but Damnations to the Prussians!)
LO! BEHOLD! THE PRISON OF MY LOVE!
HMM. INFILTRATING AN INVINCIBLE INVERTEBRATE; THE MOST ONEROUS OF TASKS. IN THE LARVAL STATE, BEFORE IT BECOMES A TRANQUIL CASTLE LEPIDOPTERA, IT WILL BE QUITE THE CHALLENGE...
ARE YOU SURE YOUR AFFECTIONS FOR THIS LADY ARE SO RESOLUTE?
ABSOLUTELY! I DESIRE HER FROM THE TIP OF HER NOSE TO THE FRAME OF HER ENORMOUSLY REINFORCED PELVIS.
AND YOU MUST RESCUE HER SO WE CAN PLOUGH OUR TROUGH WITH ONE ANOTHER.
YOU MUST UNDERSTAND WHAT IT MEANS, OTTO. THIS IS NO MERE GEOTHERMIC GIGANTIPEDE.
THIS IS A GIGANTIPEDIC SPERMATAZOIC LEPIDOPTERAPEDE.
IT...OH, I HAVEN'T THE TIME.
BUT I DO! TURN TO DOCTOR X-POSITION'S GUIDE TO THE OMNI-OMNIVORE, WHERE WE WILL TALK YOU THROUGH THE WONDER OF SKY CATERPILLARS IN PAINFULLY EXCRUCIATING AND OVER-LITERAL DETAILS!

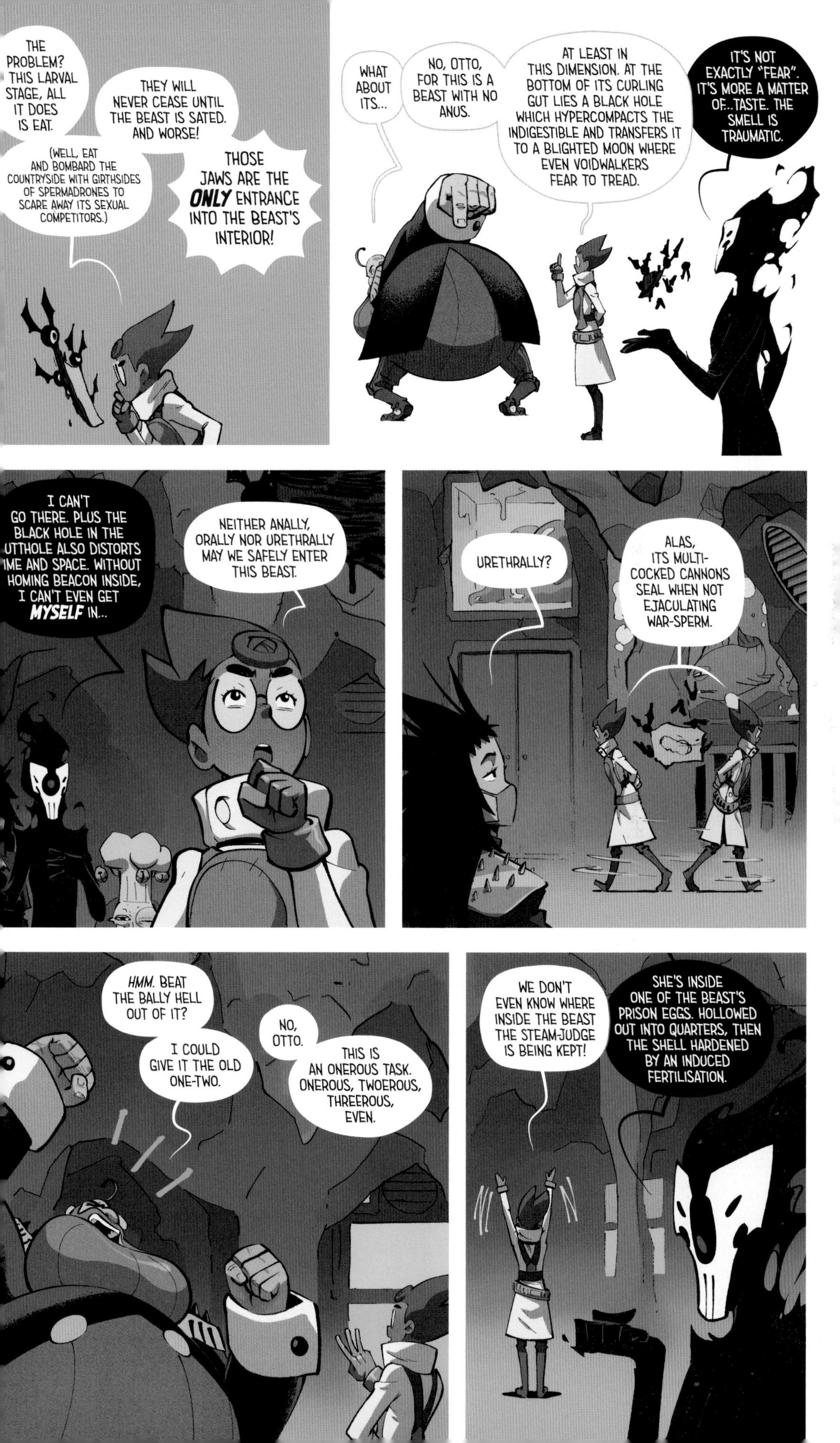

THE PROBLEM? THIS LARVAL STAGE, ALL IT DOES IS EAT.
THEY WILL NEVER CEASE UNTIL THE BEAST IS SATED. AND WORSE!
(WELL, EAT AND BOMBARD THE COUNTRYSIDE WITH GIRTHSIDES OF SPERMADRONES TO SCARE AWAY ITS SEXUAL COMPETITORS.)
THOSE JAWS ARE THE ONLY ENTRANCE INTO THE BEAST'S INTERIOR!
WHAT ABOUT ITS...
NO, OTTO, FOR THIS IS A BEAST WITH NO ANUS.
AT LEAST IN THIS DIMENSION. AT THE BOTTOM OF ITS CURLING GUT LIES A BLACK HOLE WHICH HYPERCOMPACTS THE INDIGESTIBLE AND TRANSFERS IT TO A BLIGHTED MOON WHERE EVEN VOIDWALKERS FEAR TO TREAD.
IT'S NOT EXACTLY "FEAR". IT'S MORE A MATTER OF...TASTE. THE SMELL IS TRAUMATIC.
I CAN'T GO THERE. PLUS THE BLACK HOLE IN THE UTTHOLE ALSO DISTORTS IME AND SPACE. WITHOUT HOMING BEACON INSIDE, I CAN'T EVEN GET MYSELF IN...
NEITHER ANALLY, ORALLY NOR URETHRALLY MAY WE SAFELY ENTER THIS BEAST.
URETHRALLY?
ALAS, ITS MULTI-COCKED CANNONS SEAL WHEN NOT EJACULATING WAR-SPERM.
HMM. BEAT THE BALLY HELL OUT OF IT?
I COULD GIVE IT THE OLD ONE-TWO.
NO, OTTO.
THIS IS AN ONEROUS TASK. ONEROUS, TWOEROUS, THREEROUS, EVEN.
WE DON'T EVEN KNOW WHERE INSIDE THE BEAST THE STEAM-JUDGE IS BEING KEPT!
SHE'S INSIDE ONE OF THE BEAST'S PRISON EGGS. HOLLOWED OUT INTO QUARTERS, THEN THE SHELL HARDENED BY AN INDUCED FERTILISATION.

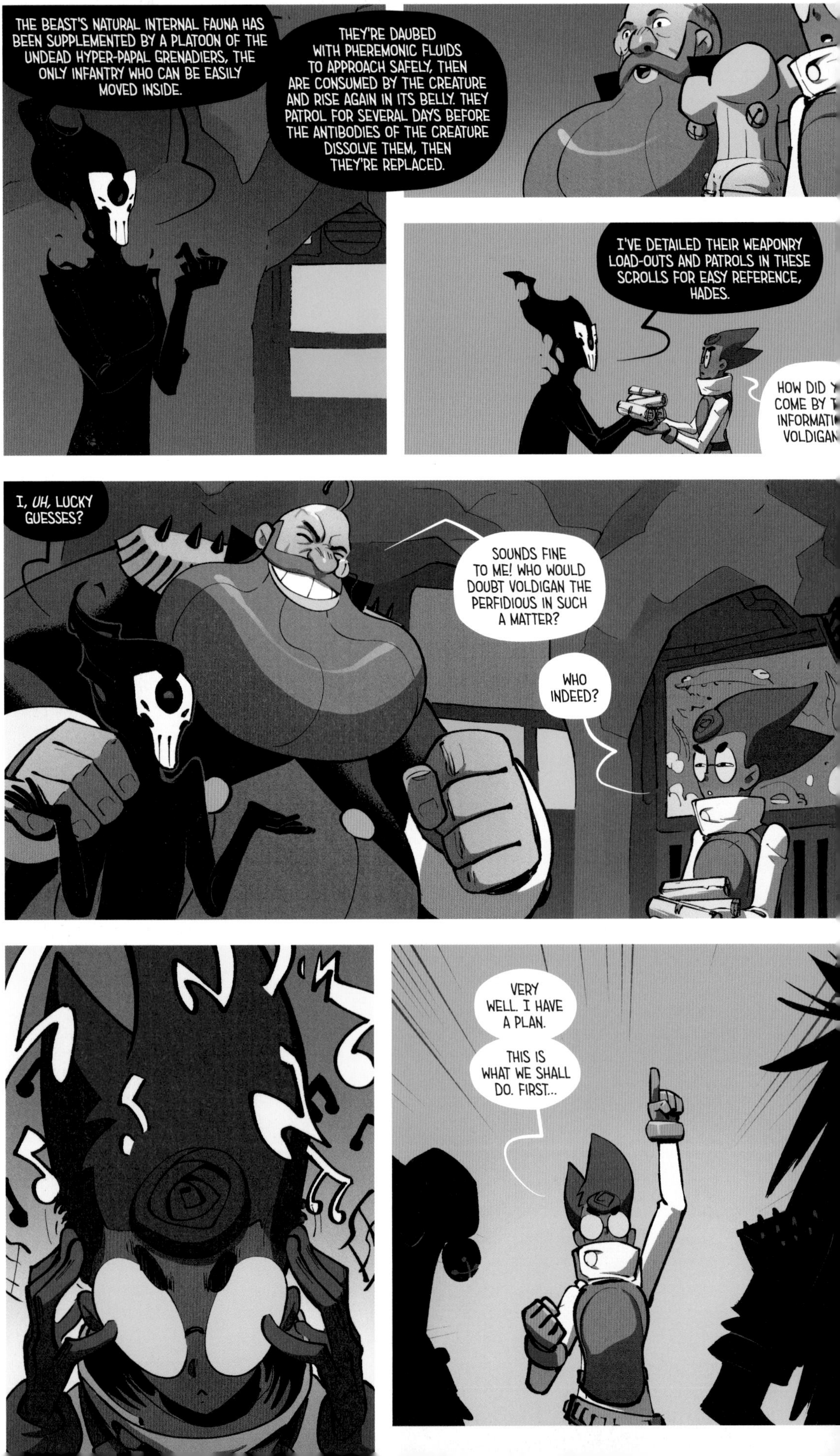
THE BEAST'S NATURAL INTERNAL FAUNA HAS BEEN SUPPLEMENTED BY A PLATOON OF THE UNDEAD HYPER-PAPAL GRENADIERS, THE ONLY INFANTRY WHO CAN BE EASILY MOVED INSIDE.
THEY'RE DAUBED WITH PHEREMONIC FLUIDS TO APPROACH SAFELY, THEN ARE CONSUMED BY THE CREATURE AND RISE AGAIN IN ITS BELLY. THEY PATROL FOR SEVERAL DAYS BEFORE THE ANTIBODIES OF THE CREATURE DISSOLVE THEM, THEN THEY'RE REPLACED.
I'VE DETAILED THEIR WEAPONRY LOAD-OUTS AND PATROLS IN THESE SCROLLS FOR EASY REFERENCE, HADES.
HOW DID Y COME BY T INFORMATI VOLDIGAN
I, UH, LUCKY GUESSES?
SOUNDS FINE TO ME! WHO WOULD DOUBT VOLDIGAN THE PERFIDIOUS IN SUCH A MATTER?
WHO INDEED?
VERY WELL. I HAVE A PLAN.
THIS IS WHAT WE SHALL DO. FIRST...

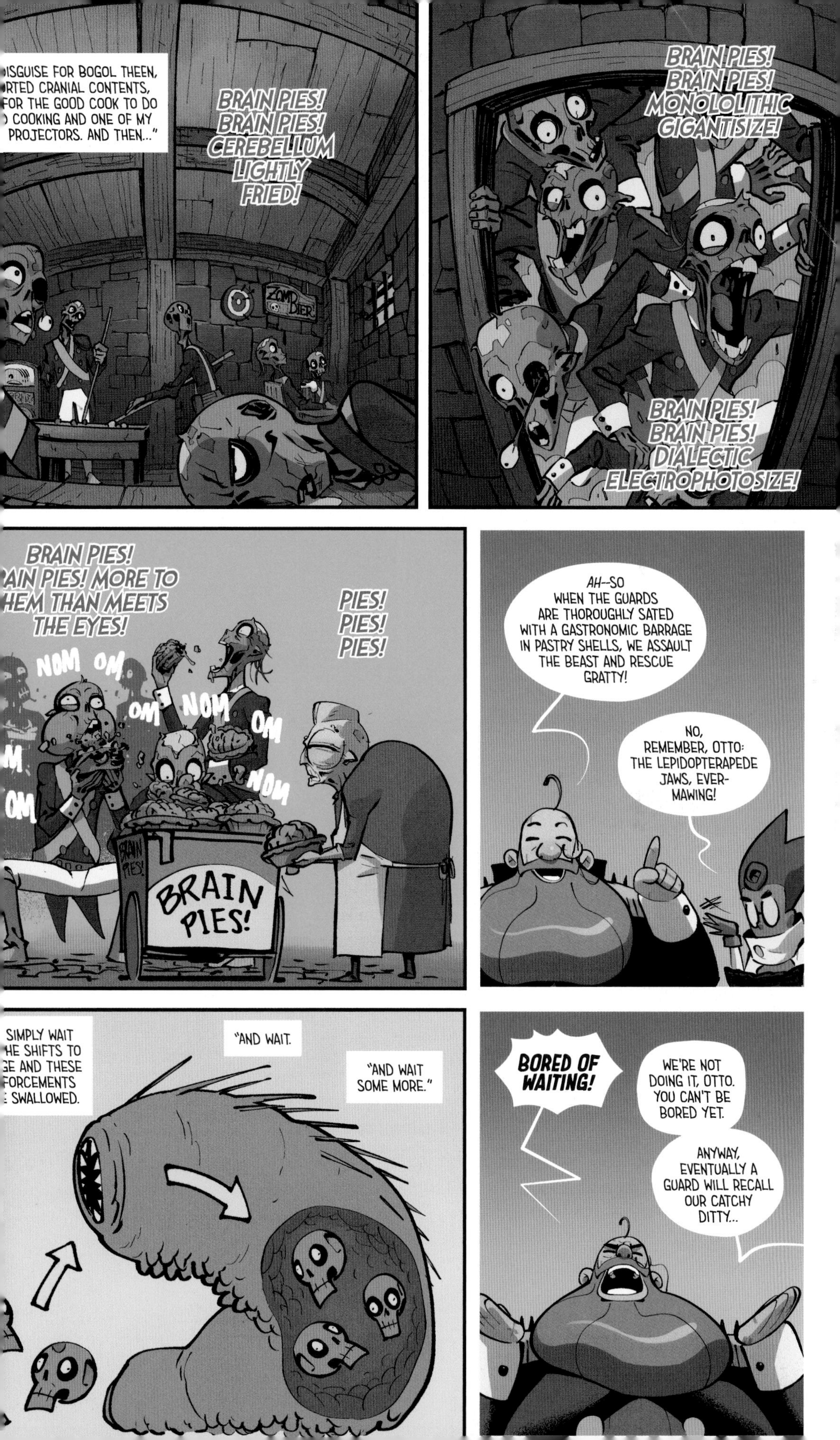

ISGUISE FOR BOGOL THEEN, RTED CRANIAL CONTENTS, FOR THE GOOD COOK TO DO COOKING AND ONE OF MY PROJECTORS. AND THEN..."
BRAIN PIES! BRAIN PIES! CEREBELLUM LIGHTLY FRIED!
ZOMBIER
BRAIN PIES! BRAIN PIES! MONOLOLITHIC GIGANTISIZE!
BRAIN PIES! BRAIN PIES! DIALECTIC ELECTROPHOTOSIZE!
BRAIN PIES! AIN PIES! MORE TO HEM THAN MEETS THE EYES!
PIES! PIES! PIES!
NOM OM
OM NOM OM
NOM
BRAIN PIES!
BRAIN PIES!
AH--SO WHEN THE GUARDS ARE THOROUGHLY SATED WITH A GASTRONOMIC BARRAGE IN PASTRY SHELLS, WE ASSAULT THE BEAST AND RESCUE GRATTY!
NO, REMEMBER, OTTO: THE LEPIDOPTERAPEDE JAWS, EVER-MAWING!
SIMPLY WAIT HE SHIFTS TO GE AND THESE FORCEMENTS SWALLOWED.
"AND WAIT.
"AND WAIT SOME MORE."
BORED OF WAITING!
WE'RE NOT DOING IT, OTTO. YOU CAN'T BE BORED YET.
ANYWAY, EVENTUALLY A GUARD WILL RECALL OUR CATCHY DITTY...

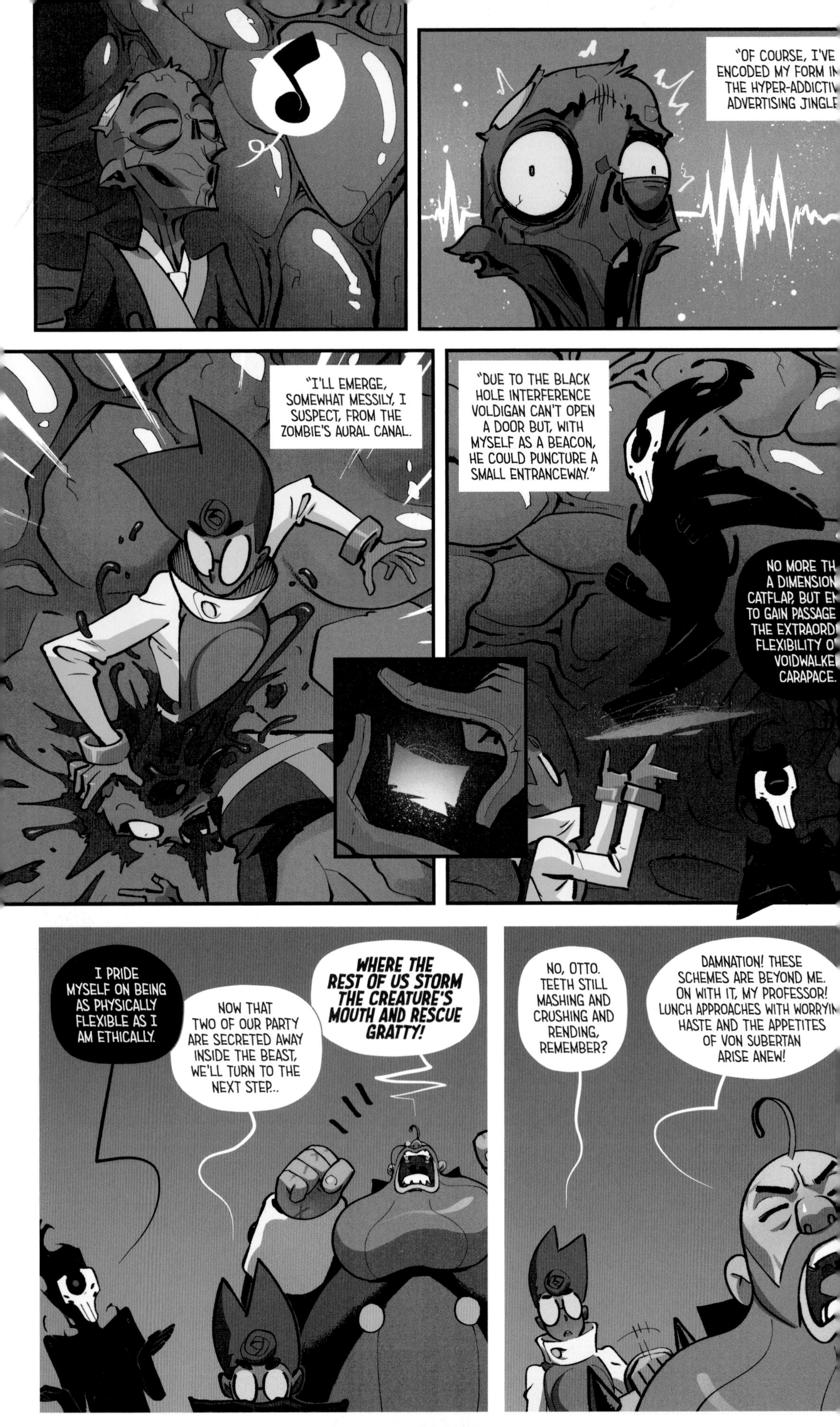
"OF COURSE, I'VE ENCODED MY FORM IN THE HYPER-ADDICTIV ADVERTISING JINGLE
"I'LL EMERGE, SOMEWHAT MESSILY, I SUSPECT, FROM THE ZOMBIE'S AURAL CANAL.
"DUE TO THE BLACK HOLE INTERFERENCE VOLDIGAN CAN'T OPEN A DOOR BUT, WITH MYSELF AS A BEACON, HE COULD PUNCTURE A SMALL ENTRANCEWAY."
NO MORE TH A DIMENSION CATFLAP, BUT EN TO GAIN PASSAGE THE EXTRAORD FLEXIBILITY O VOIDWALKE CARAPACE.
I PRIDE MYSELF ON BEING AS PHYSICALLY FLEXIBLE AS I AM ETHICALLY.
NOW THAT TWO OF OUR PARTY ARE SECRETED AWAY INSIDE THE BEAST, WE'LL TURN TO THE NEXT STEP...
WHERE THE REST OF US STORM THE CREATURE'S MOUTH AND RESCUE GRATTY!
NO, OTTO. TEETH STILL MASHING AND CRUSHING AND RENDING, REMEMBER?
DAMNATION! THESE SCHEMES ARE BEYOND ME. ON WITH IT, MY PROFESSOR! LUNCH APPROACHES WITH WORRYIN HASTE AND THE APPETITES OF VON SUBERTAN ARISE ANEW!

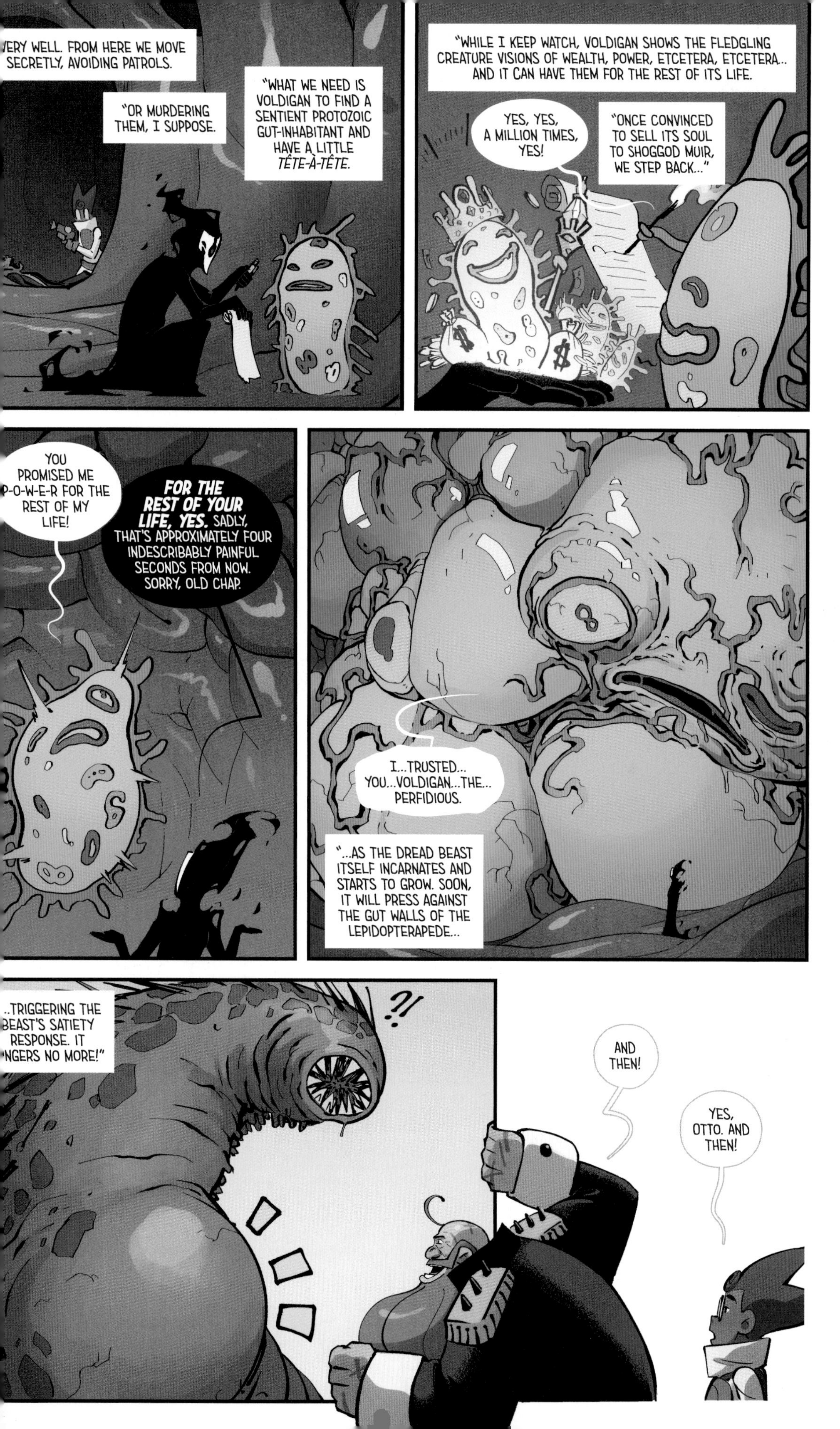
VERY WELL. FROM HERE WE MOVE SECRETLY, AVOIDING PATROLS.
"OR MURDERING THEM, I SUPPOSE.
"WHAT WE NEED IS VOLDIGAN TO FIND A SENTIENT PROTOZOIC GUT-INHABITANT AND HAVE A LITTLE *TÊTE-À-TÊTE*.
"WHILE I KEEP WATCH, VOLDIGAN SHOWS THE FLEDGLING CREATURE VISIONS OF WEALTH, POWER, ETCETERA, ETCETERA... AND IT CAN HAVE THEM FOR THE REST OF ITS LIFE.
YES, YES, A MILLION TIMES, YES!
"ONCE CONVINCED TO SELL ITS SOUL TO SHOGGOD MUIR, WE STEP BACK..."
YOU PROMISED ME P-O-W-E-R FOR THE REST OF MY LIFE!
FOR THE REST OF YOUR LIFE, YES. SADLY, THAT'S APPROXIMATELY FOUR INDESCRIBABLY PAINFUL SECONDS FROM NOW. SORRY, OLD CHAP.
I...TRUSTED... YOU...VOLDIGAN...THE... PERFIDIOUS.
"...AS THE DREAD BEAST ITSELF INCARNATES AND STARTS TO GROW. SOON, IT WILL PRESS AGAINST THE GUT WALLS OF THE LEPIDOPTERAPEDE...
...TRIGGERING THE BEAST'S SATIETY RESPONSE. IT HUNGERS NO MORE!"
?!
AND THEN!
YES, OTTO. AND THEN!

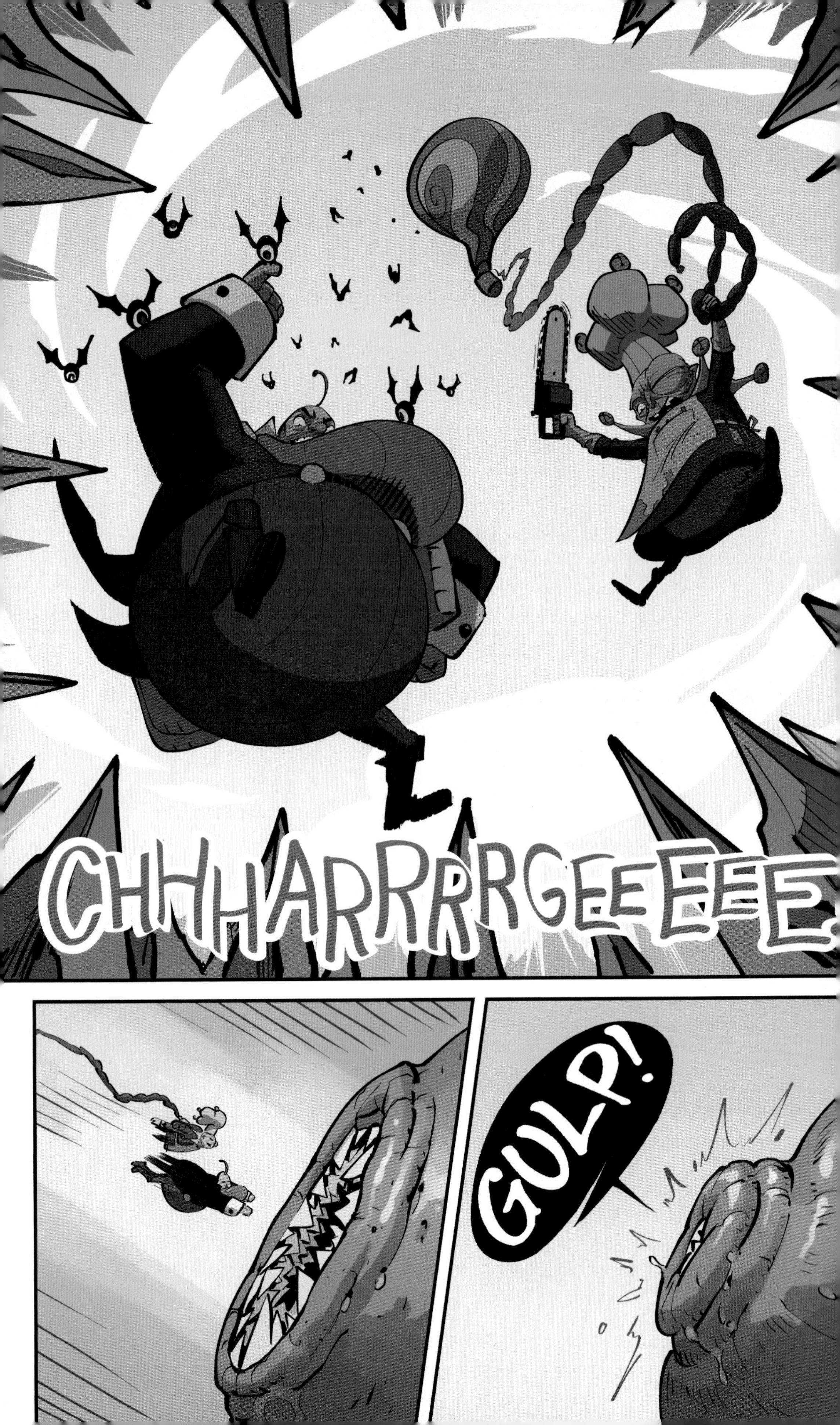
CHHHARRRRRGEEEEEE
GULP!

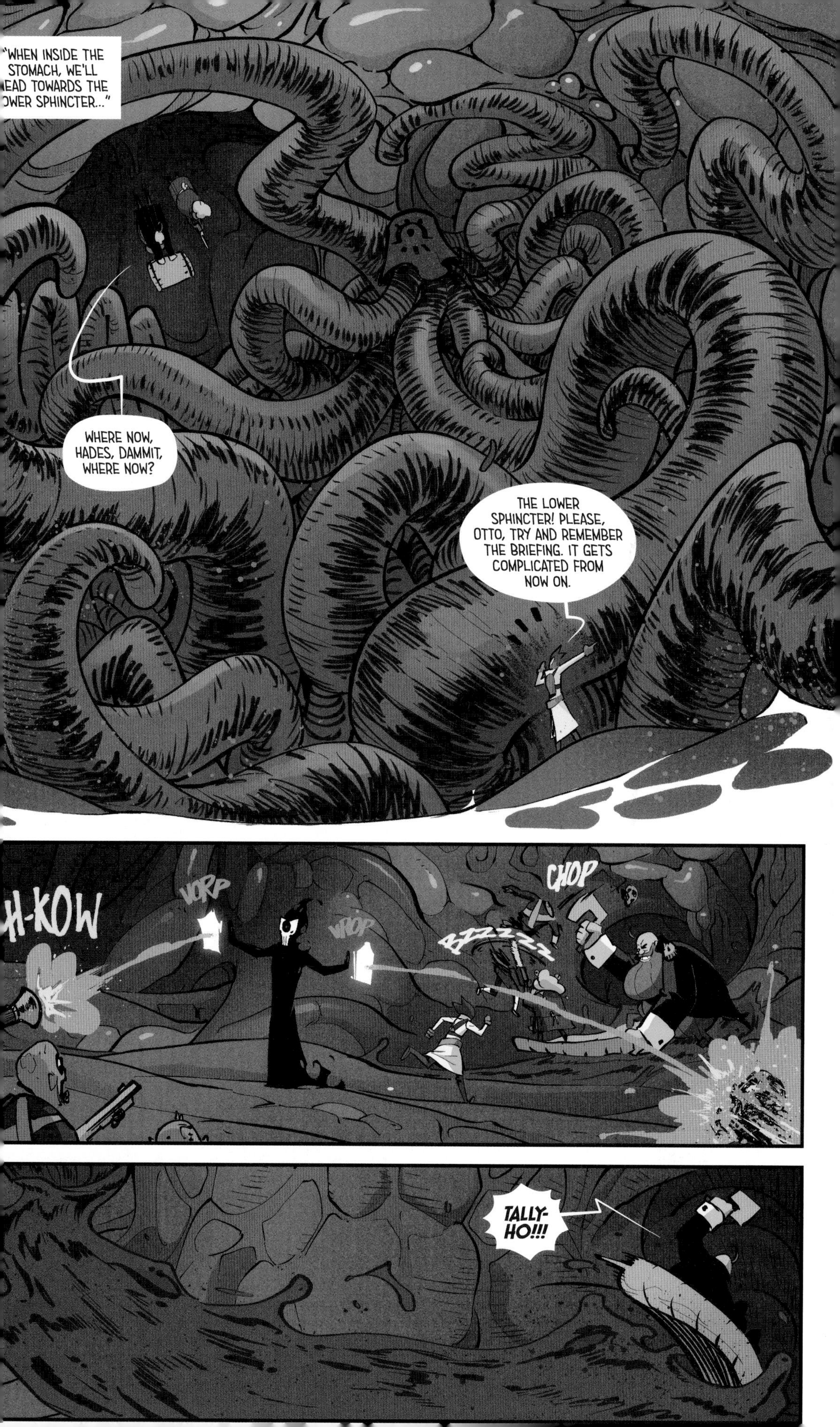
"WHEN INSIDE THE STOMACH, WE'LL EAD TOWARDS THE OWER SPHINCTER..."
WHERE NOW, HADES, DAMMIT, WHERE NOW?
THE LOWER SPHINCTER! PLEASE, OTTO, TRY AND REMEMBER THE BRIEFING. IT GETS COMPLICATED FROM NOW ON.
H-KOW
VORP
WROP
CHOP
BZZZZZ
TALLY-HO!!!

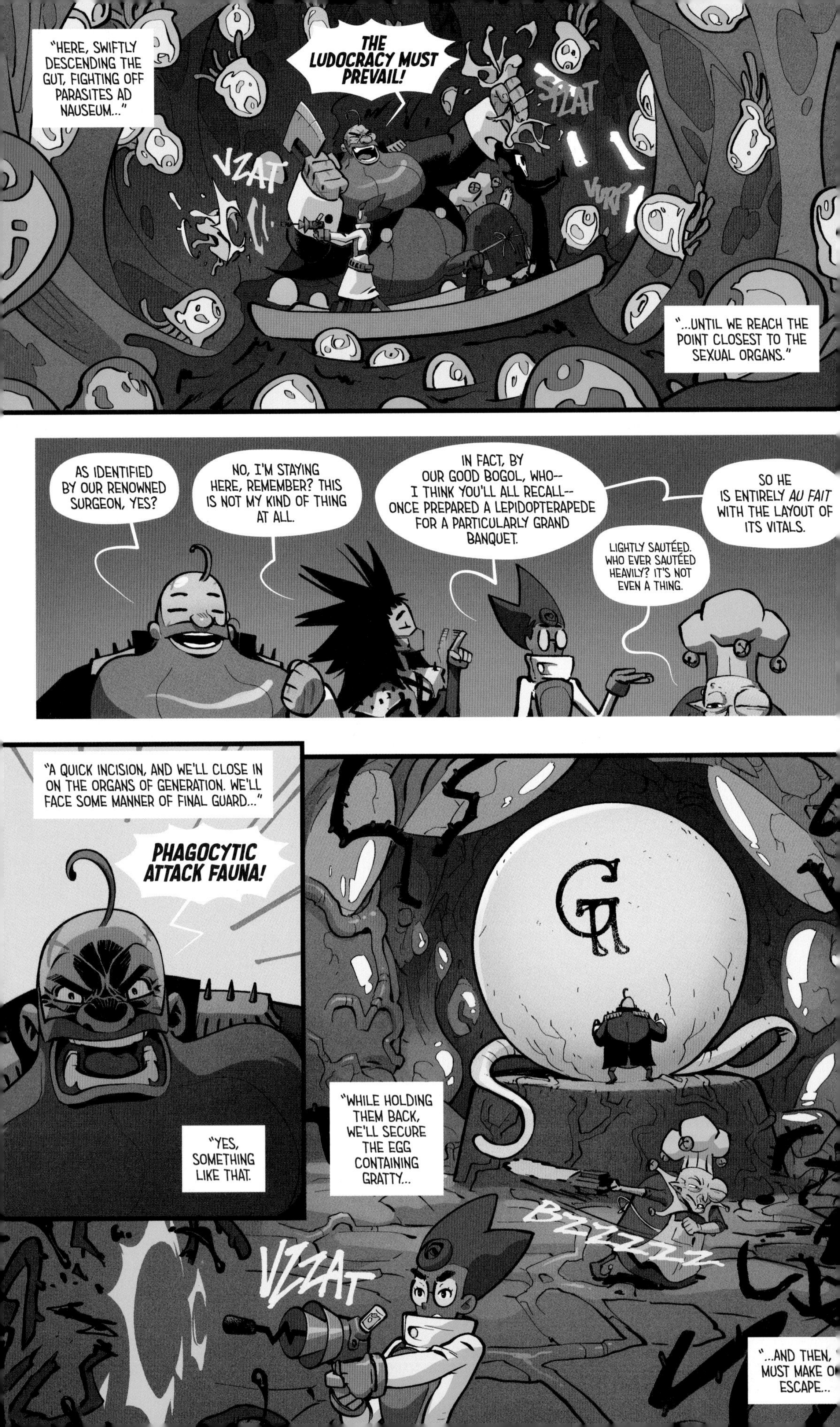
"HERE, SWIFTLY DESCENDING THE GUT, FIGHTING OFF PARASITES AD NAUSEUM..."
THE LUDOCRACY MUST PREVAIL!
VZAT
SPLAT
VURT
"...UNTIL WE REACH THE POINT CLOSEST TO THE SEXUAL ORGANS."
AS IDENTIFIED BY OUR RENOWNED SURGEON, YES?
NO, I'M STAYING HERE, REMEMBER? THIS IS NOT MY KIND OF THING AT ALL.
IN FACT, BY OUR GOOD BOGOL, WHO-- I THINK YOU'LL ALL RECALL-- ONCE PREPARED A LEPIDOPTERAPEDE FOR A PARTICULARLY GRAND BANQUET.
SO HE IS ENTIRELY *AU FAIT* WITH THE LAYOUT OF ITS VITALS.
LIGHTLY SAUTÉED. WHO EVER SAUTÉED HEAVILY? IT'S NOT EVEN A THING.
"A QUICK INCISION, AND WE'LL CLOSE IN ON THE ORGANS OF GENERATION. WE'LL FACE SOME MANNER OF FINAL GUARD..."
PHAGOCYTIC ATTACK FAUNA!
"YES, SOMETHING LIKE THAT.
"WHILE HOLDING THEM BACK, WE'LL SECURE THE EGG CONTAINING GRATTY...
BZZZZZZ
VZZAT
"...AND THEN, MUST MAKE O ESCAPE...

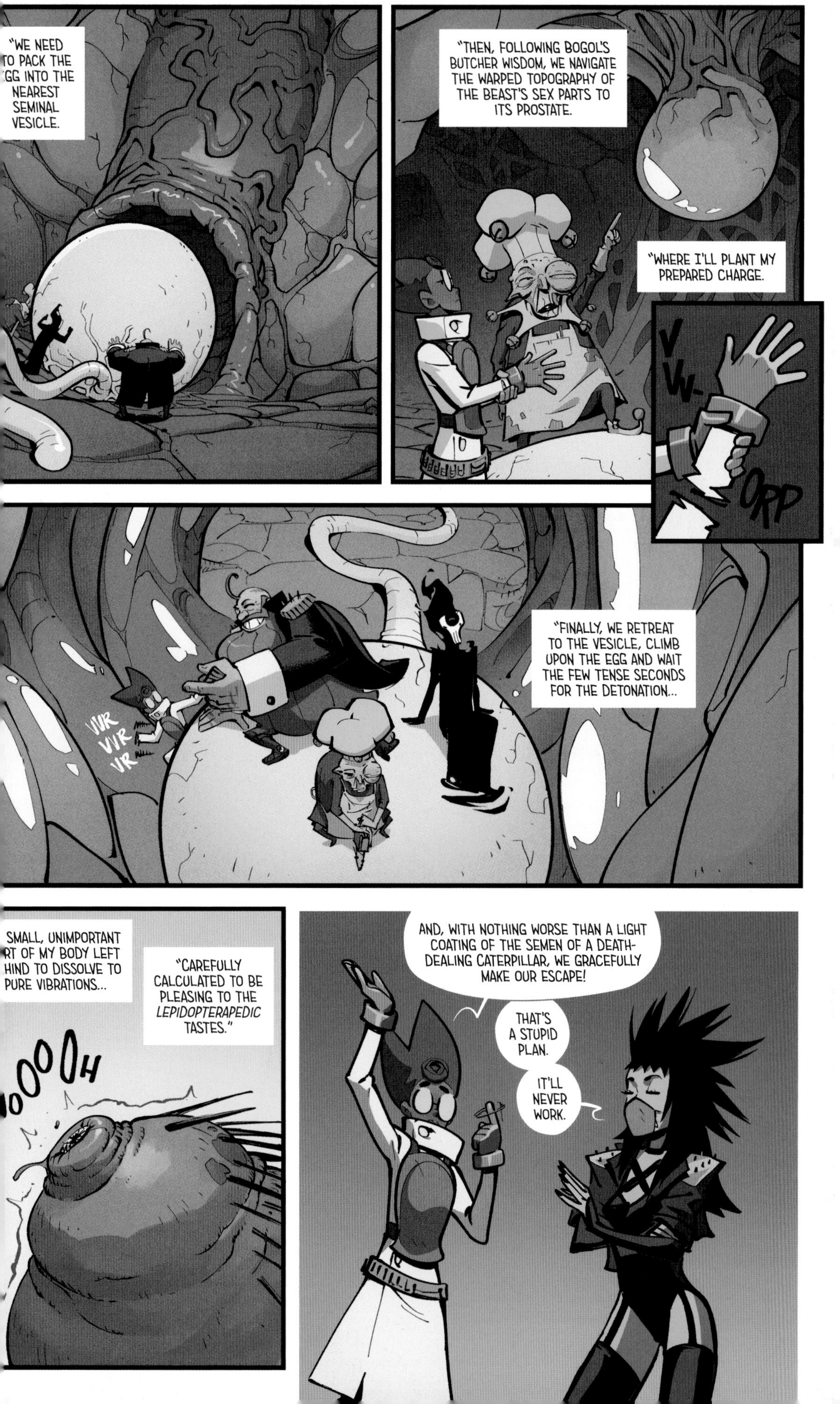
"WE NEED
TO PACK THE
EGG INTO THE
NEAREST
SEMINAL
VESICLE.
"THEN, FOLLOWING BOGOL'S BUTCHER WISDOM, WE NAVIGATE THE WARPED TOPOGRAPHY OF THE BEAST'S SEX PARTS TO ITS PROSTATE.
"WHERE I'LL PLANT MY PREPARED CHARGE.
VVV-
ORP
"FINALLY, WE RETREAT TO THE VESICLE, CLIMB UPON THE EGG AND WAIT THE FEW TENSE SECONDS FOR THE DETONATION...
VVR VVR VR
SMALL, UNIMPORTANT
RT OF MY BODY LEFT
HIND TO DISSOLVE TO
PURE VIBRATIONS...
"CAREFULLY CALCULATED TO BE PLEASING TO THE *LEPIDOPTERAPEDIC* TASTES."
OOOOH
AND, WITH NOTHING WORSE THAN A LIGHT COATING OF THE SEMEN OF A DEATH-DEALING CATERPILLAR, WE GRACEFULLY MAKE OUR ESCAPE!
THAT'S A STUPID PLAN.
IT'LL NEVER WORK.

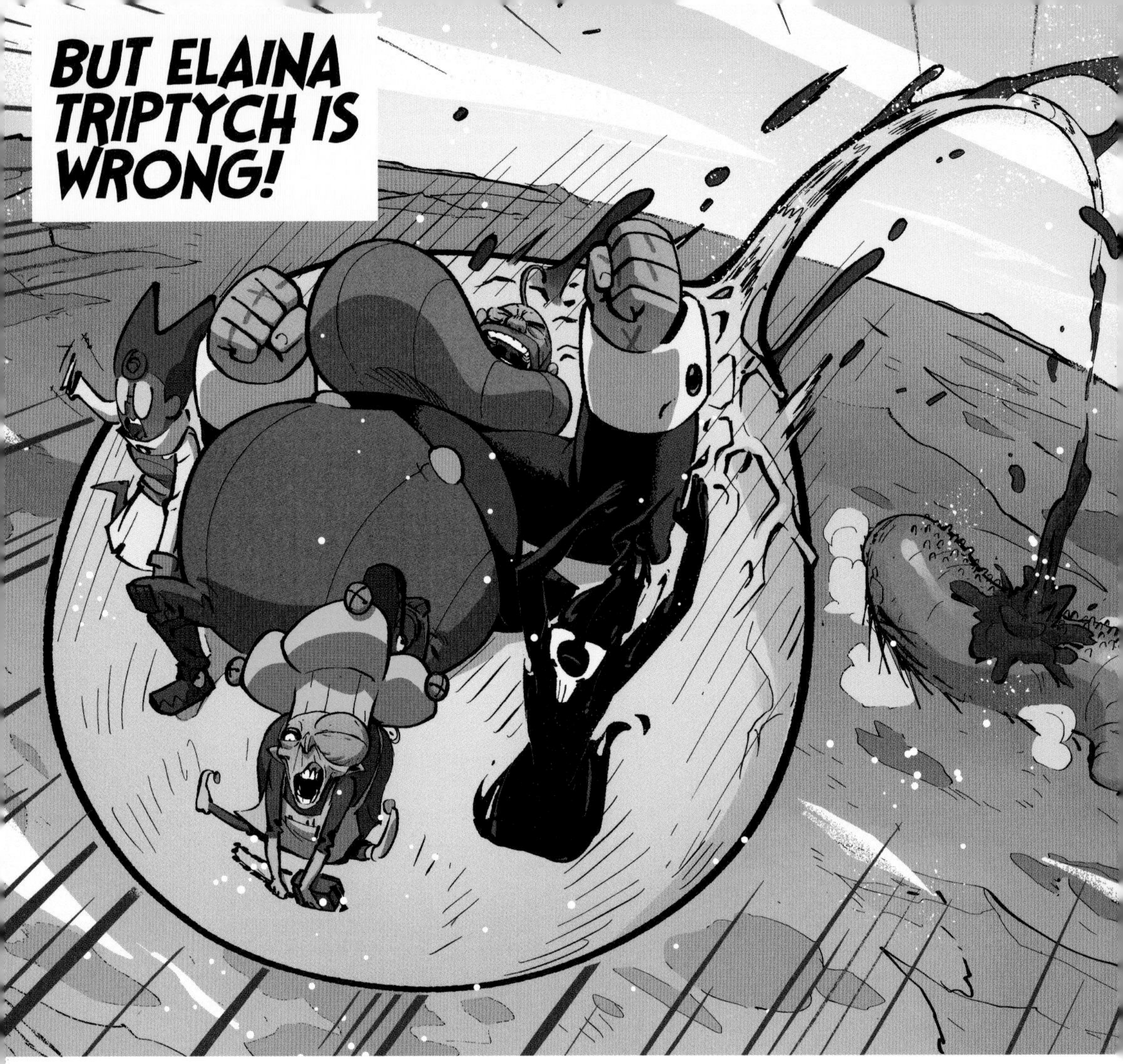
BUT ELAINA TRIPTYCH IS WRONG!

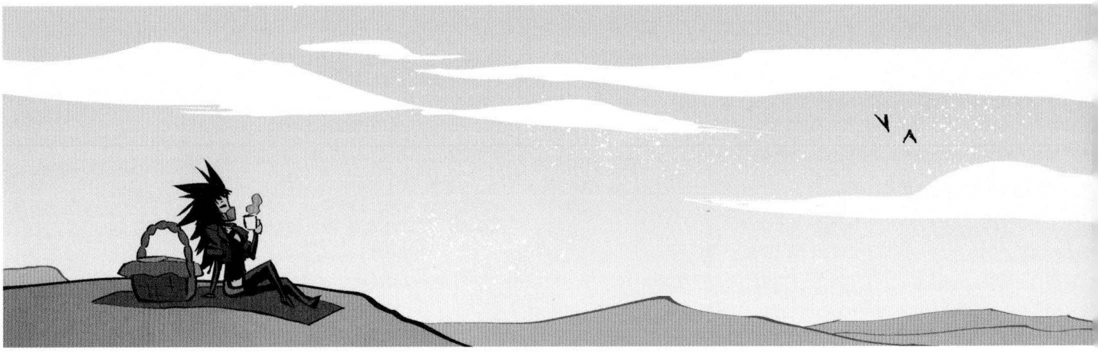

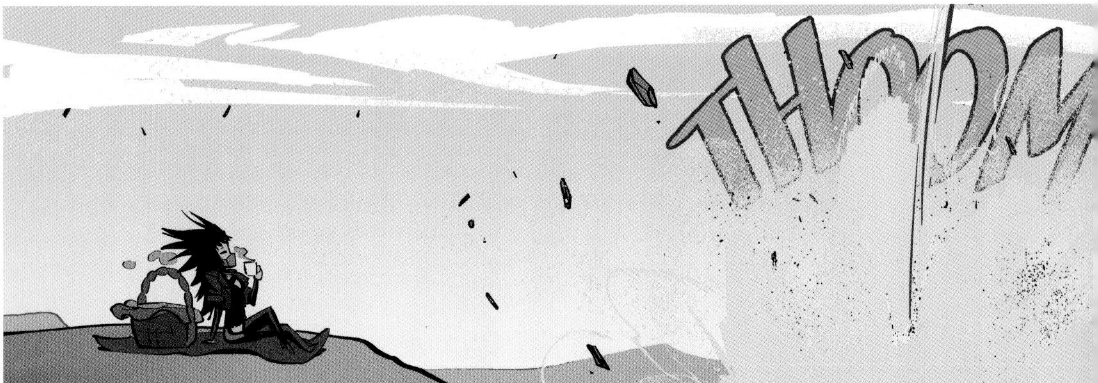
THOOM

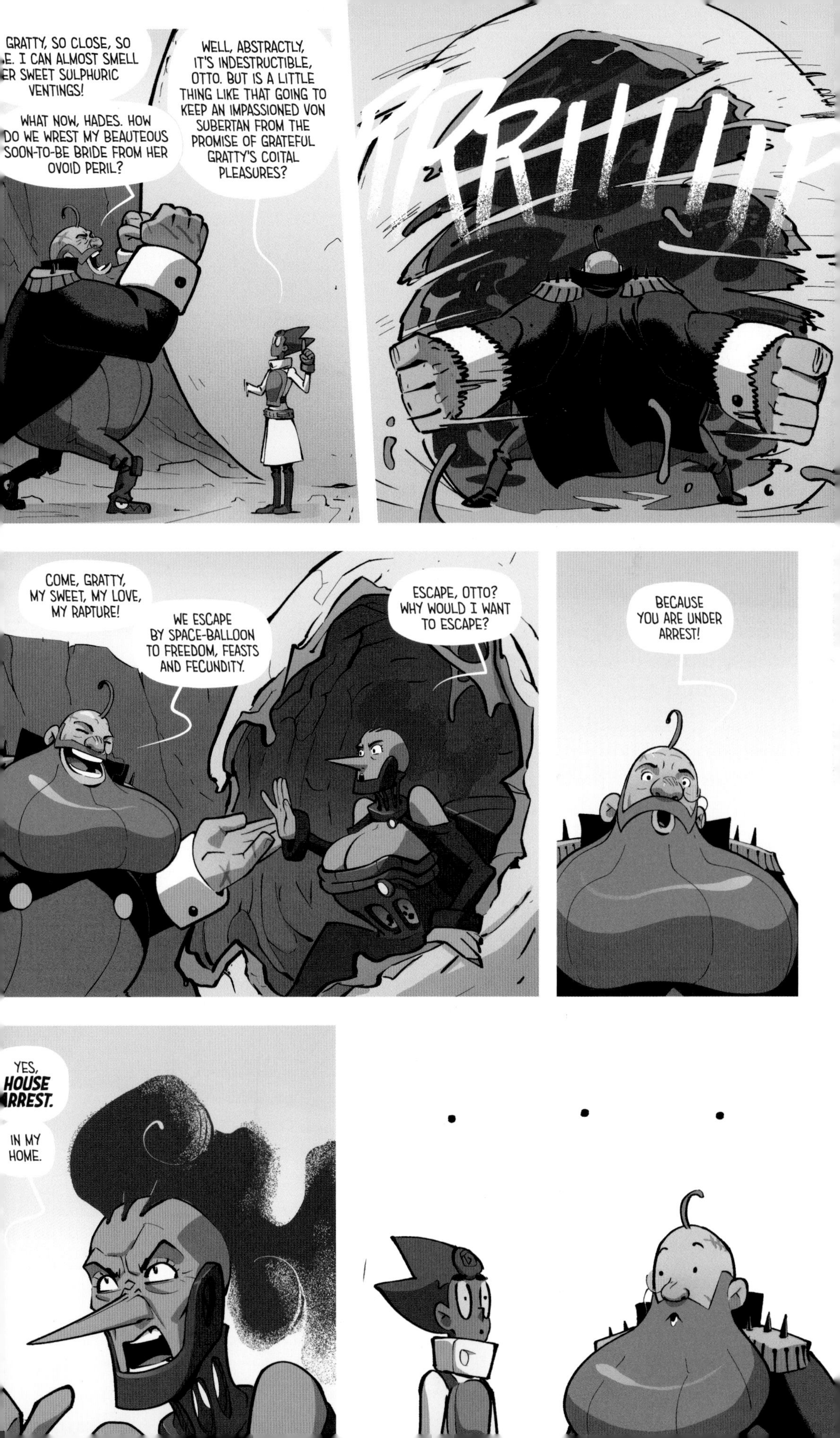
GRATTY, SO CLOSE, SO
E. I CAN ALMOST SMELL
ER SWEET SULPHURIC
VENTINGS!
WHAT NOW, HADES. HOW DO WE WREST MY BEAUTEOUS SOON-TO-BE BRIDE FROM HER OVOID PERIL?
WELL, ABSTRACTLY, IT'S INDESTRUCTIBLE, OTTO. BUT IS A LITTLE THING LIKE THAT GOING TO KEEP AN IMPASSIONED VON SUBERTAN FROM THE PROMISE OF GRATEFUL GRATTY'S COITAL PLEASURES?
RRIIIIIP
COME, GRATTY, MY SWEET, MY LOVE, MY RAPTURE!
WE ESCAPE BY SPACE-BALLOON TO FREEDOM, FEASTS AND FECUNDITY.
ESCAPE, OTTO? WHY WOULD I WANT TO ESCAPE?
BECAUSE YOU ARE UNDER ARREST!
YES, HOUSE
RREST.
IN MY HOME.
. . .

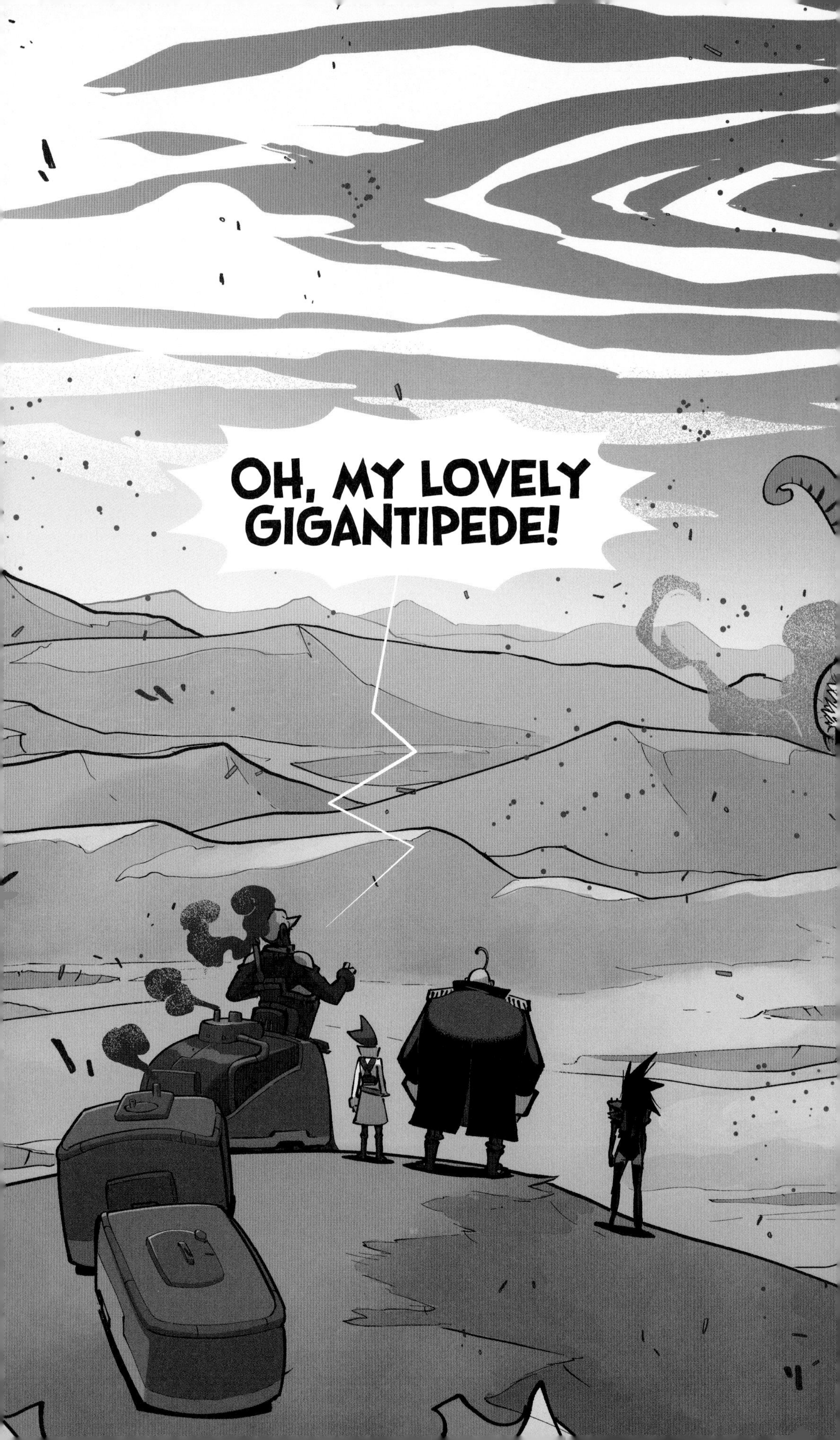
OH, MY LOVELY GIGANTIPEDE!

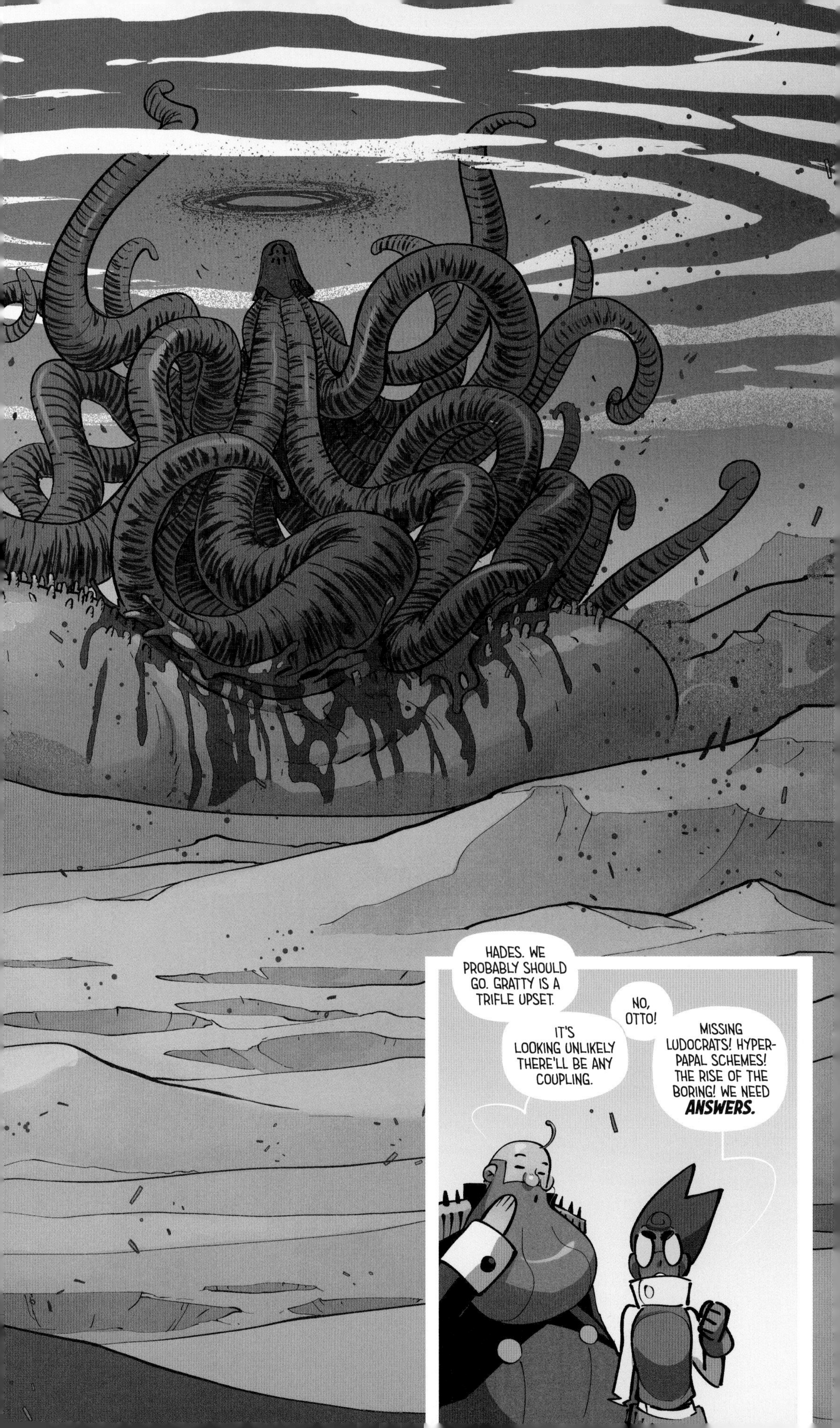
HADES. WE PROBABLY SHOULD GO. GRATTY IS A TRIFLE UPSET.
IT'S LOOKING UNLIKELY THERE'LL BE ANY COUPLING.
NO, OTTO!
MISSING LUDOCRATS! HYPER-PAPAL SCHEMES! THE RISE OF THE BORING! WE NEED **ANSWERS.**

YOUR HONOUR, WE'RE SORRY BUT YOU WERE TALKING ABOUT PROOF THE HYPER-POPE IS ENGAGING IN EGREGIOUS ACTS OF BEING BORING.

CAN YOU ELABORATE?

WHAT? YOU COME TO ME AFTER DESTROYING MY LOVELY HOME AND ASK FAVOURS? OUTRAGEOUS!

THE ONLY WAY I'D TALK IS IF YOU *TORTURED ME!*

THEN THERE IS NO HOPE. TORTURE IS AN ETHICAL LINE I WILL NOT CROSS.

WE WILL HAVE TO CONTINUE WITHOUT YO AI--

I SAID **TORTURE ME!**

NOW, *THIS* IS A MISSION I CAN HELP WITH.

STEP BACK! A HIGHLY CONSENSUAL INTERROGATION WILL FOLLOW!

EXCERPTS from

The PERSONAL CYCLOPEDIA *of* LUDOCRACY,

by PARDIUS HAEMOGLANDULUM,

ELDRITCH HYPER-POPE and SUPREME HIGH LUDOCRAT

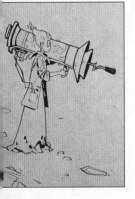

On The Melodic Weapons of The Zero-K

"...HENCE THE DYNASTY of the Zero-K has long been an important ally for the Von Subertan clan. Their control of vast beds of fossilised melody is a powerful resource on its own, but it is the inventiveness of the Zero-K mind that is most formidable and admirable. Their capacity to retool musical frequencies as sub-quantum abrogation systems has created a range of weaponry that not only has no obvious countermeasure, but is also compulsively danceable. It is also, I find most reassuring, our only defence against the atonal dimensions which would invade our own and feed upon music, devouring it from the inside, were we ever to allow them. (Hades' mixtapes based on your subconscious desires can be quite the ride, too.)" •

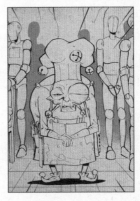

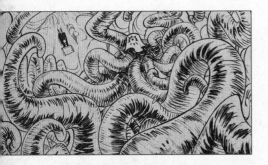

On The Creature Shoggod Muir

"...YET MY BROTHER'S largest and most impressive progeny is the creature Shoggod Muir, a being of abominated space-time whose powers have yet to be accurately mapped. While I have repeatedly instructed Otto to keep the creature contained with rotating teams of trans-Albanian Electrocutionists (they're more resilient to cosmic horror than cheaper American Electrocutionists) he insists on letting the beast roam, causing astonishing mayhem whenever it gets loose. I have to say, as someone who doesn't have kids, I find the commitment of the parenting kind to reproduction rather daunting, but I am thankful to Otto for providing me with so many chaotic nephews and nieces. The world would be a less ludicrous place without them." •

On The Sublime Order of The Gastronauts

"...AND SO IT WAS on the third phase of the feast that we realised, myself and the ghost of my predecessor, Hyper-Pope Delany, that the secret frontier of food was inside the living organisms from which food is normally expected. So it was that we created the order of Gastronauts: ambitious chefs who would wade inside prospective meals to find the freshest and most alarming foods for us to consume. I have forgotten why we expected them to dress as little jester people, but there is no way for me to regret that decision. Our bravest explorers of meat also being very funny to look at has become a cornerstone of Ludocratic sustenance." •

* * * * *

The VON SUBERTAN
Family Tree

The MYSTERIOUS FIGURE *in the* TOWER

Billowing gown, looked great on cover of gothic novels

HORST VON SUBERTAN

Grand sire of the Von Subertans, Keeper of The Hybrid of The Great Pit

RADIKALIEN NORTWICH VON SUBERTAN

Cannibal time-traveller who died of surprise to spite his mother

LOXMIKANA THIPSE

Died loading a shark into her howitzer at the siege of Monkton Egregia

HYPER-REGENT WARSTEIN KRALSTEIN HAPENSBAGGER-FRITH

Went on to marry a handsome axe, no other children

CLEMENT HAPENSBAGGER-FRITH

Famed for his collection of surprising bones

COLONEL EMILIA SAXON-WARSTEIN

Wrestled and defeated The Unhappy Centipede Of Fate

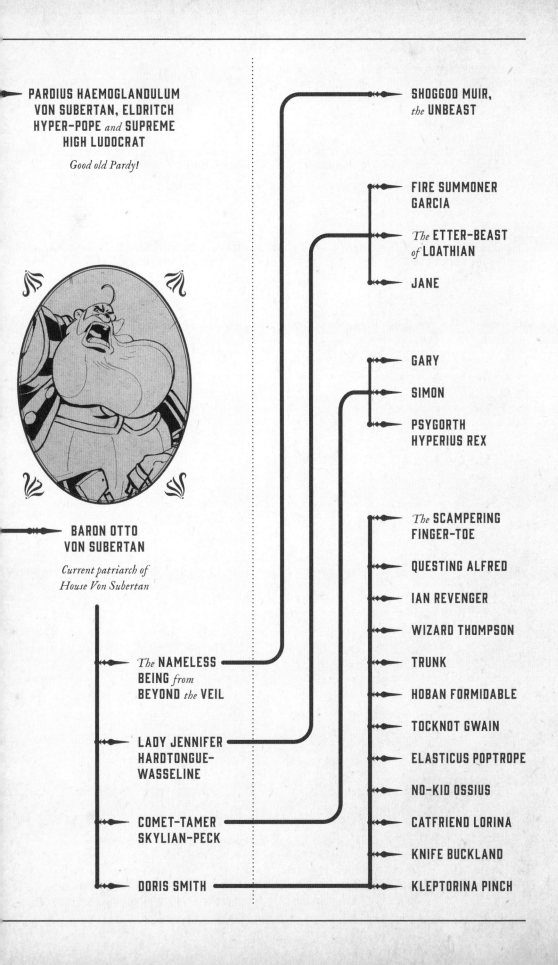

PARDIUS HAEMOGLANDULUM VON SUBERTAN, ELDRITCH HYPER-POPE *and* **SUPREME HIGH LUDOCRAT**

Good old Pardy!

BARON OTTO VON SUBERTAN

Current patriarch of House Von Subertan

The **NAMELESS BEING** *from* **BEYOND** *the* **VEIL**

LADY JENNIFER HARDTONGUE-WASSELINE

COMET-TAMER SKYLIAN-PECK

DORIS SMITH

SHOGGOD MUIR, *the* **UNBEAST**

FIRE SUMMONER GARCIA

The **ETTER-BEAST** *of* **LOATHIAN**

JANE

GARY

SIMON

PSYGORTH HYPERIUS REX

The **SCAMPERING FINGER-TOE**

QUESTING ALFRED

IAN REVENGER

WIZARD THOMPSON

TRUNK

HOBAN FORMIDABLE

TOCKNOT GWAIN

ELASTICUS POPTROPE

NO-KID OSSIUS

CATFRIEND LORINA

KNIFE BUCKLAND

KLEPTORINA PINCH

On the Life Cycle of
GIGANTIPEDIC SPERMATAZOIC LEPIDOPTERAPEDE

(aka *The Cloud Caterpillar*, aka *The Butterfly Palaces of Westphalia*)

UNSURPRISINGLY, it falls to me, Dr Douglas X-Position, the voice of explanation in this tome of unreason, to explain the origin and life cycle of the Gigantipedic Spermatazoic Lepidopterapede, and its place in Ludocratic society.

It is important to understand that at one point in Ludocratic history, before palaces and hovels had been conceived of, everyone lived inside animals. Peasants would climb inside cows, or ride along in a giant land-snail, and the rich and tremendous would live inside the cavernous nose-chambers of the Ponder-Sloths, as they wandered through the primitive forests of the early ludocene.

3
1,977
800
92.5
17
socio-vortex
αξι
ογ
έλα
στ
ος

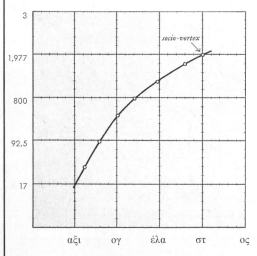

AESTHETIC DENSITY (x) vs METAPHOR DELIMITING (y)

All this changed, however, during the great trend plague of Justinius. A brain virus radically altered aesthetic tastes across the globe, giving nearly 70% of the population of Eurasia strong opinions on interior design (96% in the Antipodes) and so it was that new homes had to be invented.

As is so often the case in the significant tides of history, another factor combined to bring the modern Gigantipedic Spermatazoic Lepidopterapede into the picture: the discovery of the stealth continent of Jungba. Jungba, a mobile landmass that had been cleverly moving out of the way of explorers for centuries, got its undercarriage caught on a bony undersea mass, created by Ludocrats who wanted coral balloon ports. Thus trapped, Jungba was soon entered by a new wave of botanists, balloonists and zoologists, who did their best to discover and cross-breed the unimagined species that dwelt there.

It was Leon Cusp, notable invertebrate remodeller, who found the original creature that was to become the Gigantipedic Spermatazoic Lepidopterapede: a prehistoric mega-Nymphalidae, which hunted and sucked the juices from the flower-headed people of Lurpo (sadly now extinct). Immediately understanding the potential for genetic renovation in the beast, Cusp bred and cross-bred and manipulated to create a creature to lay habitable eggs in the haunted moss at Lupid Tor (now lived in by many in the Ludocratic tradesman classes), eggs which grew into the larval stage we are all so familiar with (used as both administrative spaces and residential structures for all tiers of Ludocrats) and then finally, with luck, metamorphosized into the butterfly stage. The coveted flying palaces dominate the property listings among non-terrestrial real estate vendors.

It perhaps goes without saying that the most interesting aspect of the gigantipedes generally is their ability to defecate trans-dimensionally. It is into the research on this uncanny science that I will dedicate part of my next book, entitled Philosophical Evacuations.

Dr Douglas X-Position, PHD QED

Trained in Expositionary Sciences at the Institute of Verbose Description in Klovehammer, Douglas has long (long) expanded upon the work of his mentor, Eleanor Lucidation. Douglas' world tour in 1065e produced some of his finest work, and has been collected in an important textbook, later editions of which shipped as a manual on how to explain snow to Eskimos.

To send letters to *LUDOCRATS*
please attach your words
to the back of a friendly vole
and instruct them to head to
OTTO's CASTLE, LUDOVERSE.

LETTERS *from* LUDOCRATS

ASTRAL STATIC

My Dearest Zero-K,

Having returned through my private portal from the un-worlds forum and seminar series at Haertoplex, I have found that your nightly transmissions of aetheric melody and astral static have been discontinued. In fact, several of your telepathic channels are now broadcasting some sort of warning matrix instead of the usual informal mixes? Is something wrong?

Yours,
Planeswalker Kent, Battle
Architect Of The Anchorites

Yes.

Yours,
Professor Hades Zero-K

HELLISH HELL

Beloved Otto,

To cut a long story short, damn you to hell. To extend the story somewhat, I have become aware via a sequential picture narrative that you held a wedding at your abode, and it appears a lovely time was had by all, except the murdered. However, I could not help but to note my entire lack of presence. Why was I not invited? You know it's not a wedding without me. To return to the original short story, damn you to hell. I don't even care which hell. It can be an inferior, hellish hell for all I care.

Yours faithfully,
Seven Snakes In A Trenchcoat

Snakes!

Thank you so, so much for your correspondence — it's been too long! Unfortunately his excellency Baron Von Subertan is unavailable for comment due to unforeseen and frankly horrific events. However as his acting press officer I am able to say that while snakes are essential to all Ludocratic matrimonial events, in this instance you, specifically, were overlooked due to a clerical error. The cleric in question has been pushed through a sieve, all the better to be eaten at a later date.

Sincerely,
An Ape with the Head
of a Prehistoric Bird

UNFOLDING THE FLESH

Greetings Ludocrats,

I, Perchod Nebuchadnezzar, Meta-Thoth of the Hezzarine, recently discovered your dimension via the Unhappenings Personal Ads on the astral matrix listings, and I am looking for a committed pen pal. My interests are: telekinetically unfolding the flesh of my screaming enemies, dragging the unknowable prisoners of Azazel from the abyss, and photography. Please write back if interested.

Sincerely,
"Perchy" N

Hello Perchy!

Oh, what timing! I am in need of a committed pen pal, ironically due to having had my last pennish-pal committed. I am now the warden of The Lord of Inkpocalypse's estates, most notably his famous armada of nib-jets. Everyone knows, the pen is mightier than the sword. Swords are just bits of metal while pens soar through the air and drop toxic ink on all who would oppose them. It is a most stirring sight. Unfortunately, I have failed in my duty to safeguard the fleet, having traded them for some magic beans which I ate on some magic toast. Still — I tried. Anyway, I'd be delighted to continue this correspondence. My interests include absolute loyalty and not stabbing people in the back.

Yours,
"Voidy" the Perfidious,
Grand Frequency Shifter,
Traitor at etcetera, etcetera

A GODLESS SKY

To whom it doth concerneth,

I am informed by knowledgable parties that a Gigantipede will feature prominently in your pictorial narrative. I do sincerely hope that it does not have its belly distended to bursting point and an enormous hellbeast emerge to howl darkly at a godless sky.

Yours,
Saint Trillia the Unforbidden,
Gigantipede Protection League

Dearest Trillia,

My lawyer has told me to not respond to this mail as I will likely incriminate myself if I admit to being involved in the explosive death of a gigantipede, so I'm going to do that.

Yours,
Otto Von Subertan

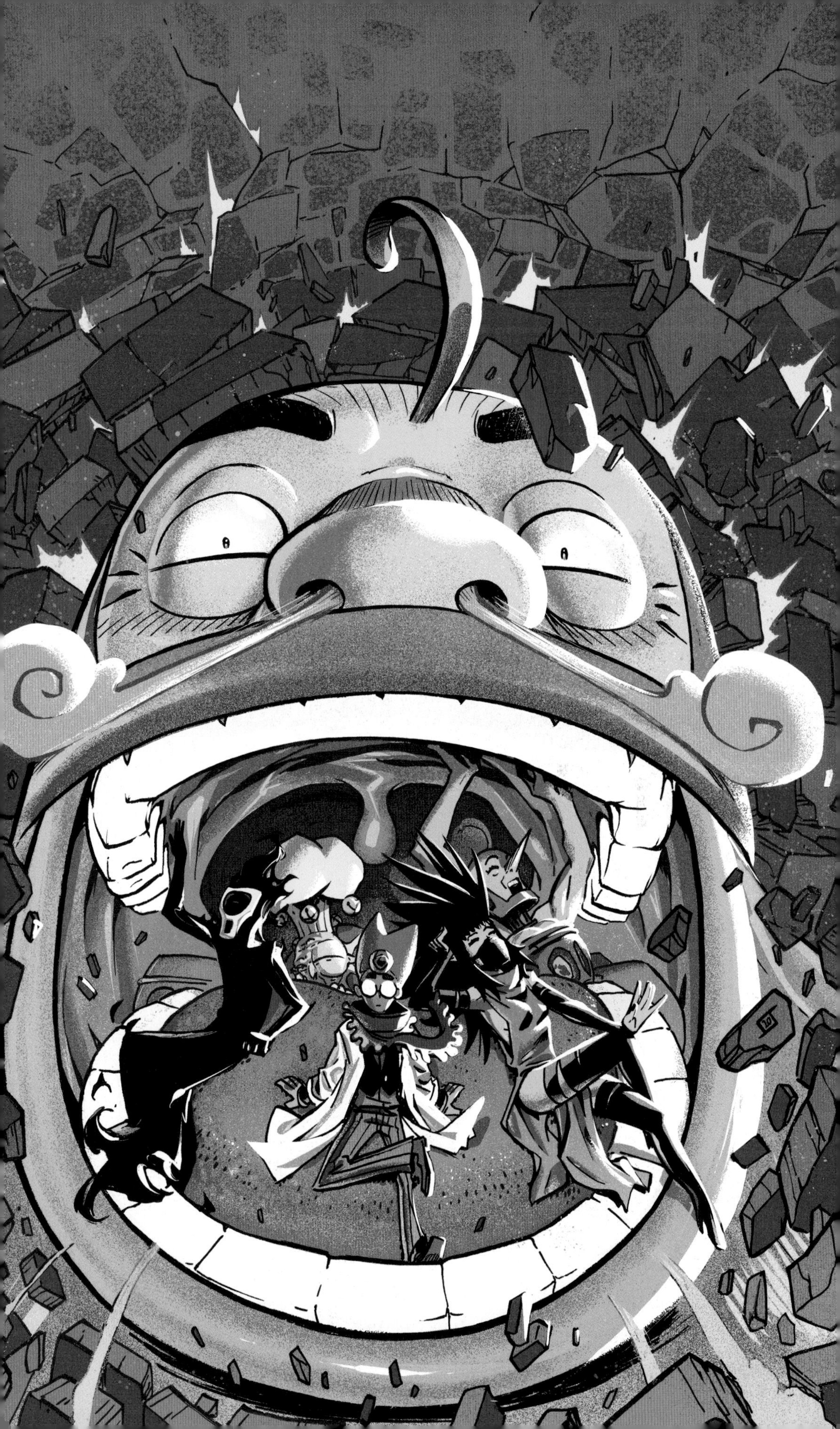

STEAM-JUDGE
knows what
BADNESS *the*
HYPER-POPE
is UP TO.

WILL SHE TALK?

Let's FIND OUT.

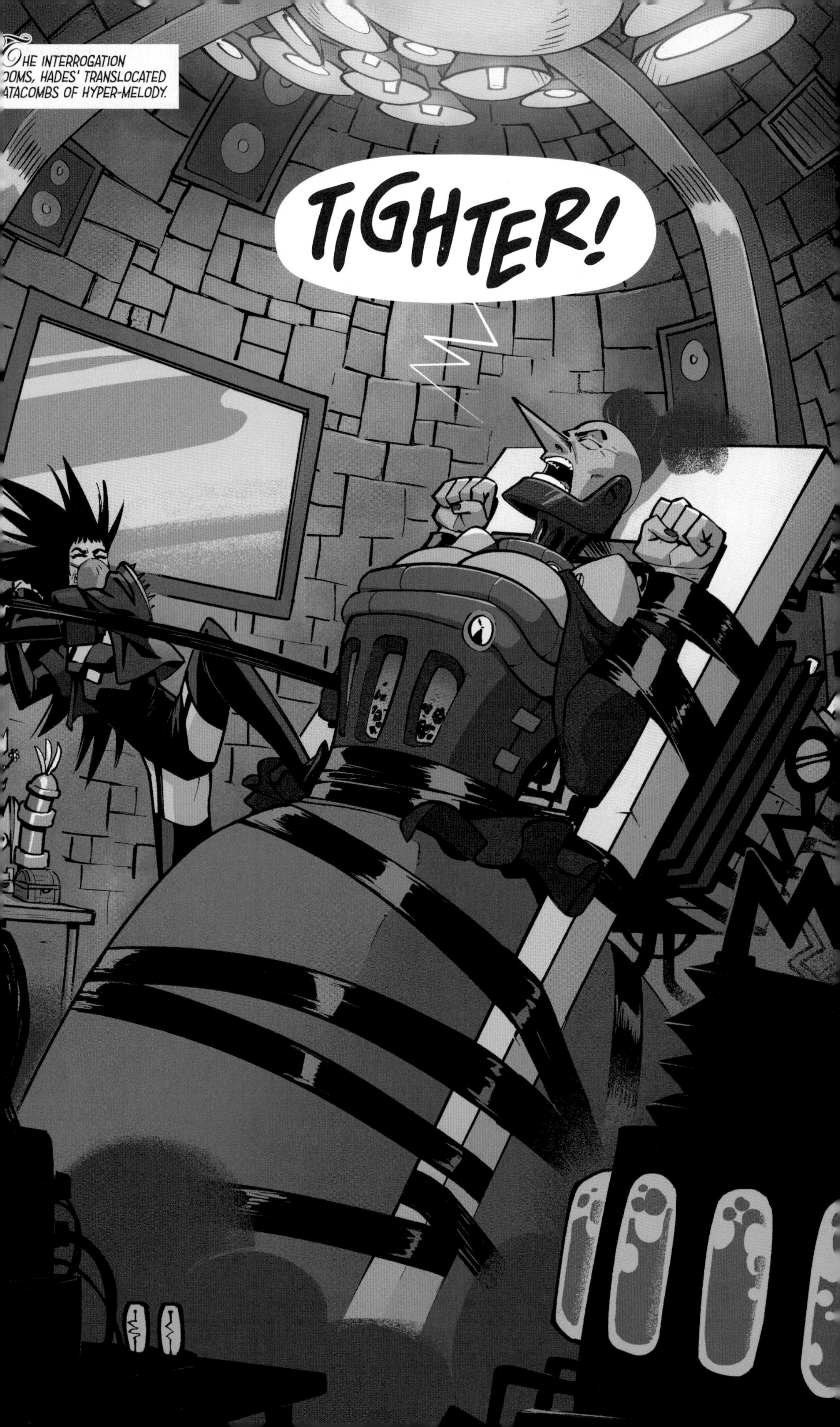
THE INTERROGATION OOMS, HADES' TRANSLOCATED ATACOMBS OF HYPER-MELODY.
TIGHTER!

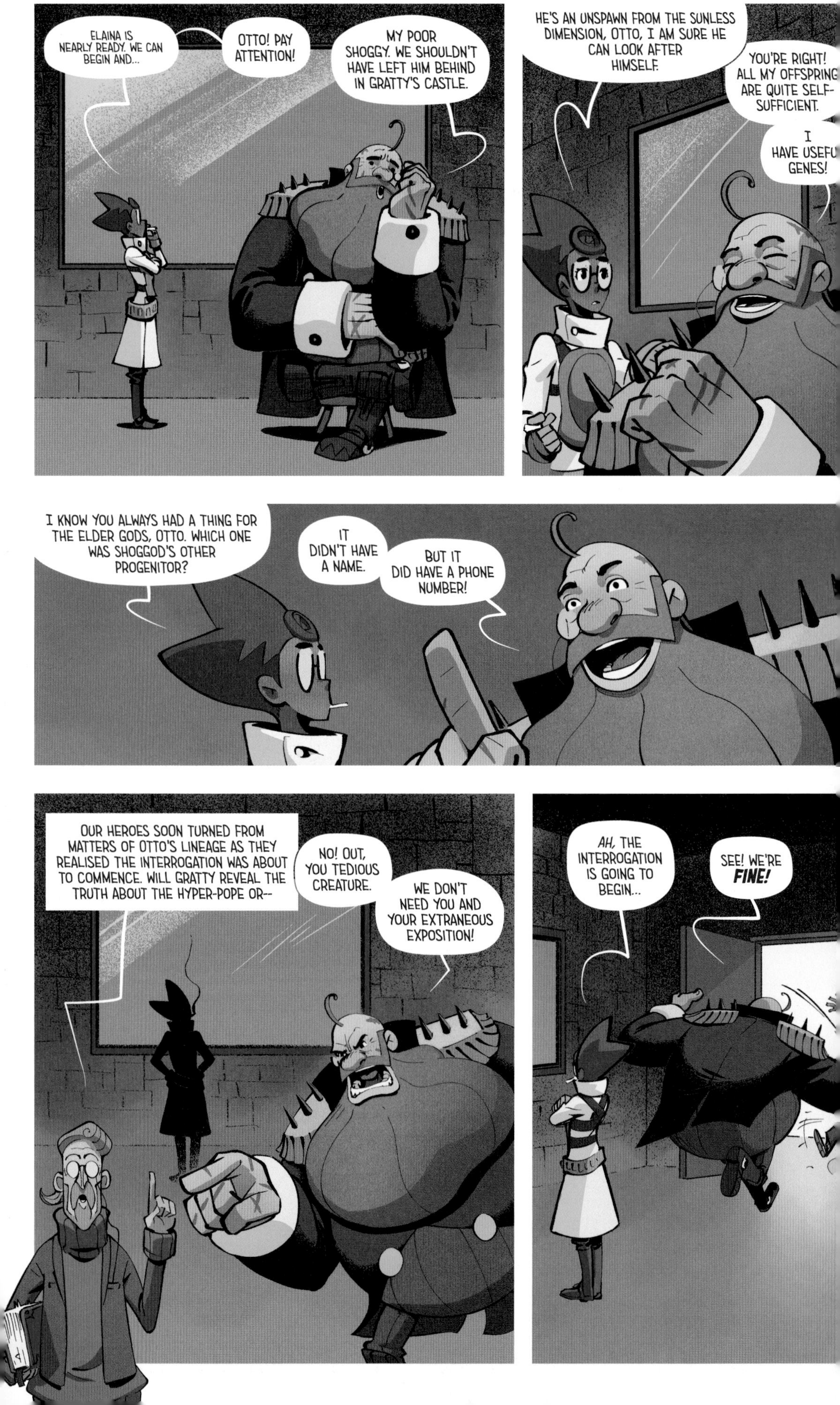
ELAINA IS NEARLY READY. WE CAN BEGIN AND...
OTTO! PAY ATTENTION!
MY POOR SHOGGY. WE SHOULDN'T HAVE LEFT HIM BEHIND IN GRATTY'S CASTLE.
HE'S AN UNSPAWN FROM THE SUNLESS DIMENSION, OTTO, I AM SURE HE CAN LOOK AFTER HIMSELF.
YOU'RE RIGHT! ALL MY OFFSPRING ARE QUITE SELF-SUFFICIENT.
I HAVE USEFU GENES!
I KNOW YOU ALWAYS HAD A THING FOR THE ELDER GODS, OTTO. WHICH ONE WAS SHOGGOD'S OTHER PROGENITOR?
IT DIDN'T HAVE A NAME.
BUT IT DID HAVE A PHONE NUMBER!
OUR HEROES SOON TURNED FROM MATTERS OF OTTO'S LINEAGE AS THEY REALISED THE INTERROGATION WAS ABOUT TO COMMENCE. WILL GRATTY REVEAL THE TRUTH ABOUT THE HYPER-POPE OR--
NO! OUT, YOU TEDIOUS CREATURE.
WE DON'T NEED YOU AND YOUR EXTRANEOUS EXPOSITION!
AH, THE INTERROGATION IS GOING TO BEGIN...
SEE! WE'RE ***FINE!***

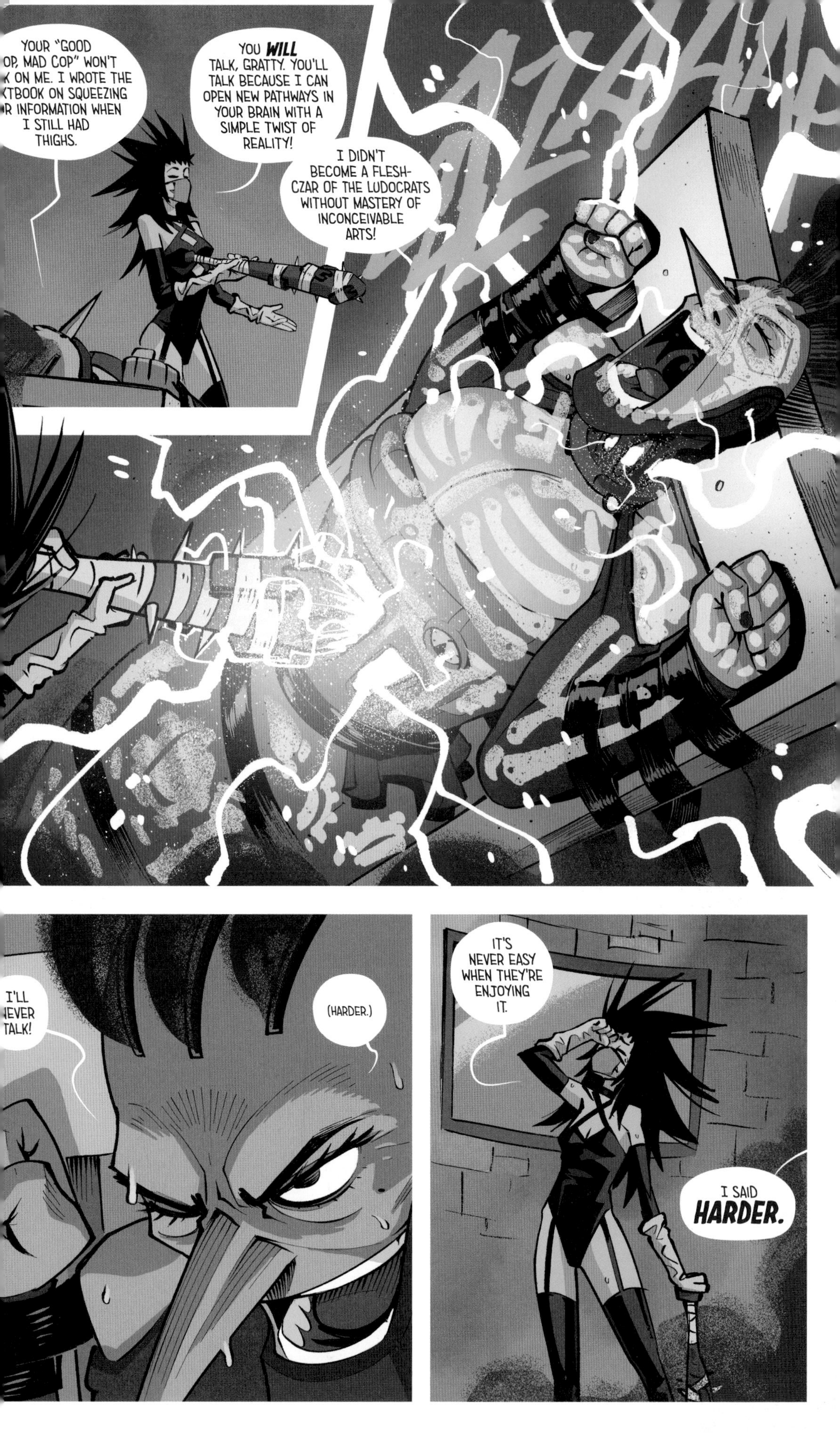
YOUR "GOOD
OP, MAD COP" WON'T
K ON ME. I WROTE THE
KTBOOK ON SQUEEZING
R INFORMATION WHEN
I STILL HAD
THIGHS.
YOU WILL TALK, GRATTY. YOU'LL TALK BECAUSE I CAN OPEN NEW PATHWAYS IN YOUR BRAIN WITH A SIMPLE TWIST OF REALITY!
I DIDN'T BECOME A FLESH-CZAR OF THE LUDOCRATS WITHOUT MASTERY OF INCONCEIVABLE ARTS!
I'LL
NEVER
TALK!
(HARDER.)
IT'S NEVER EASY WHEN THEY'RE ENJOYING IT.
I SAID HARDER.

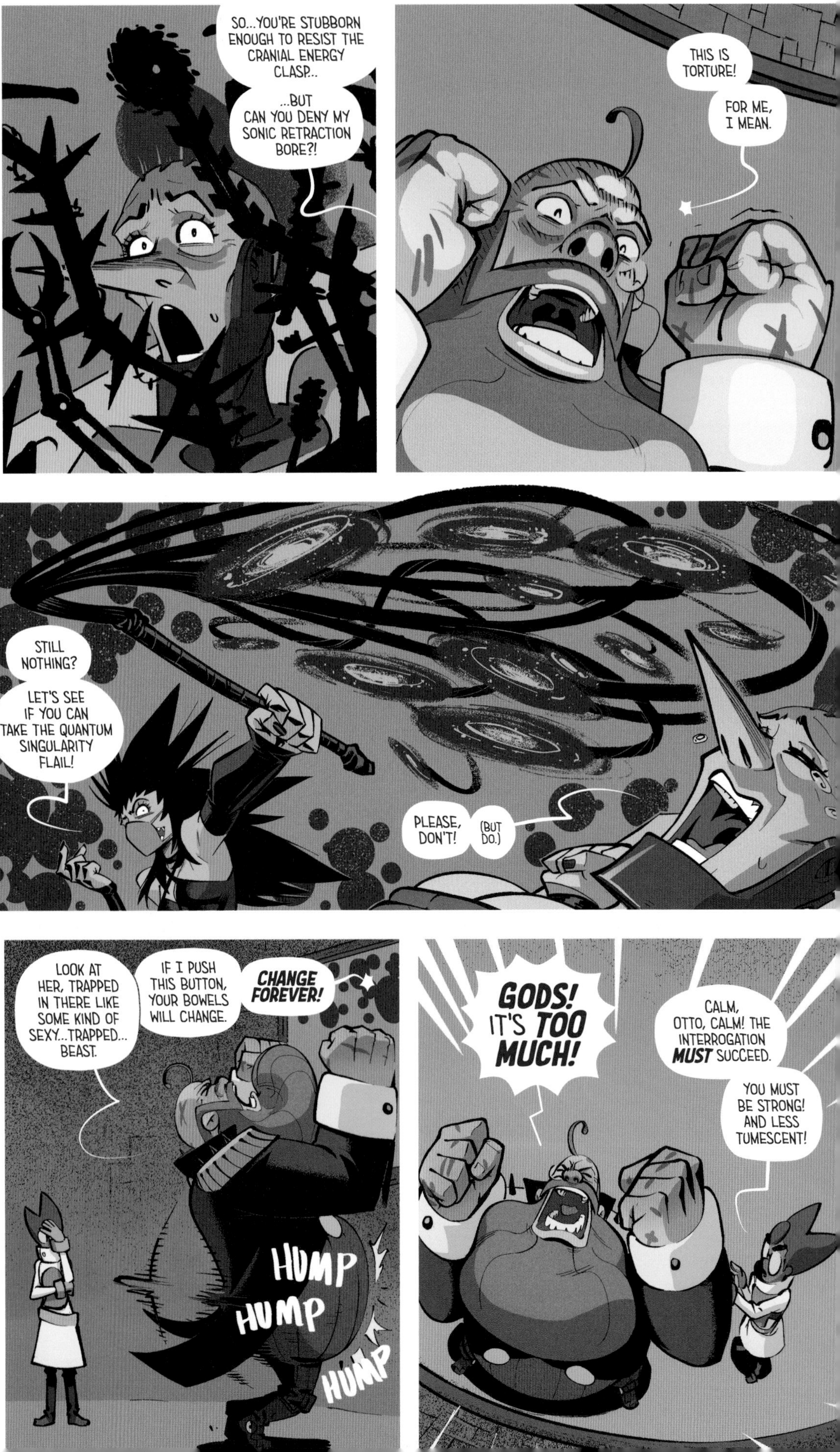
SO...YOU'RE STUBBORN ENOUGH TO RESIST THE CRANIAL ENERGY CLASP...
...BUT CAN YOU DENY MY SONIC RETRACTION BORE?!
THIS IS TORTURE!
FOR ME, I MEAN.
STILL NOTHING?
LET'S SEE IF YOU CAN TAKE THE QUANTUM SINGULARITY FLAIL!
PLEASE, DON'T!
(BUT DO.)
LOOK AT HER, TRAPPED IN THERE LIKE SOME KIND OF SEXY...TRAPPED... BEAST.
IF I PUSH THIS BUTTON, YOUR BOWELS WILL CHANGE.
CHANGE FOREVER!
HUMP
HUMP
HUMP
GODS! IT'S TOO MUCH!
CALM, OTTO, CALM! THE INTERROGATION MUST SUCCEED.
YOU MUST BE STRONG! AND LESS TUMESCENT!

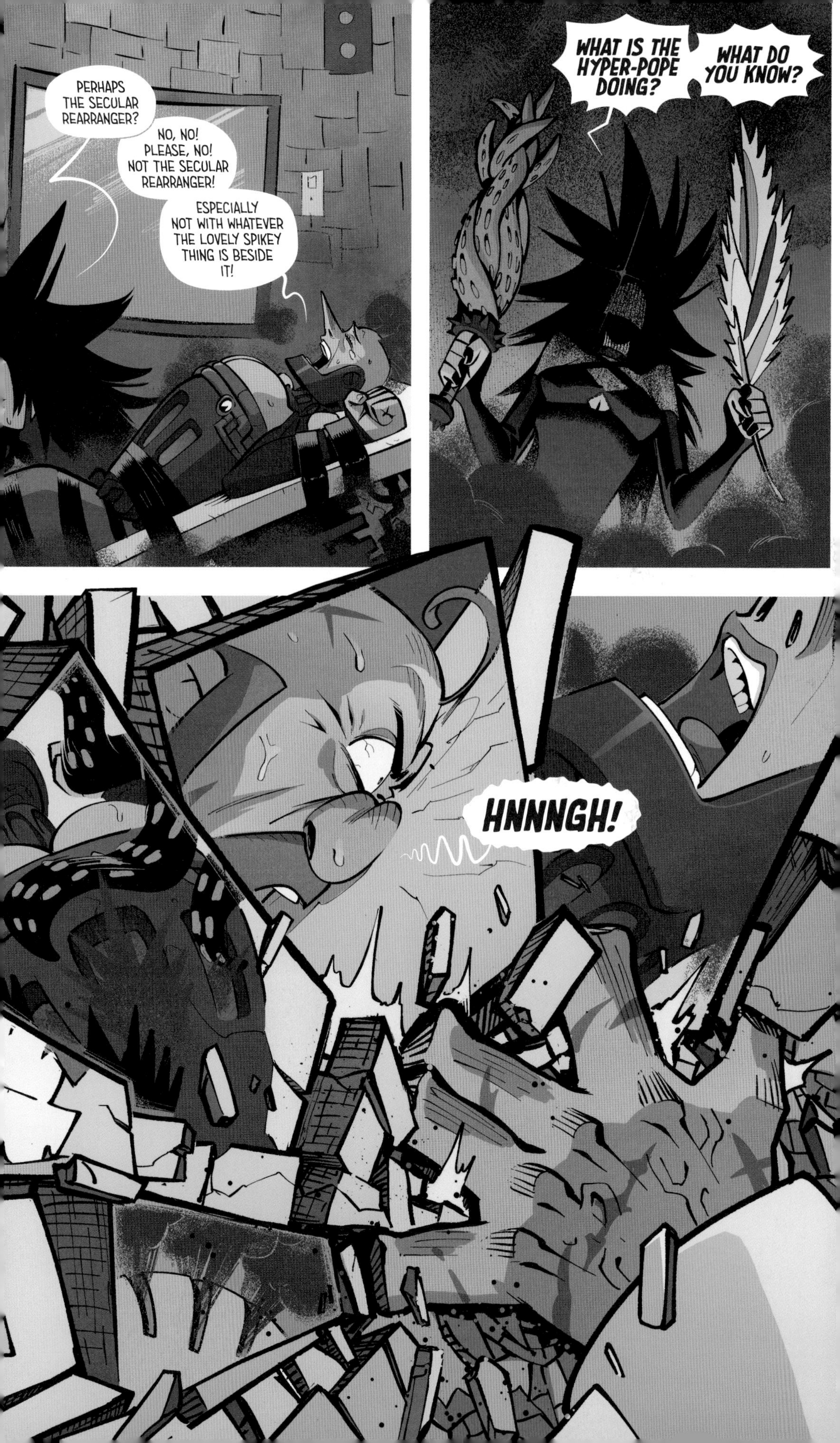
PERHAPS THE SECULAR REARRANGER?
NO, NO! PLEASE, NO! NOT THE SECULAR REARRANGER!
ESPECIALLY NOT WITH WHATEVER THE LOVELY SPIKEY THING IS BESIDE IT!
WHAT IS THE HYPER-POPE DOING?
WHAT DO YOU KNOW?
HNNNGH!

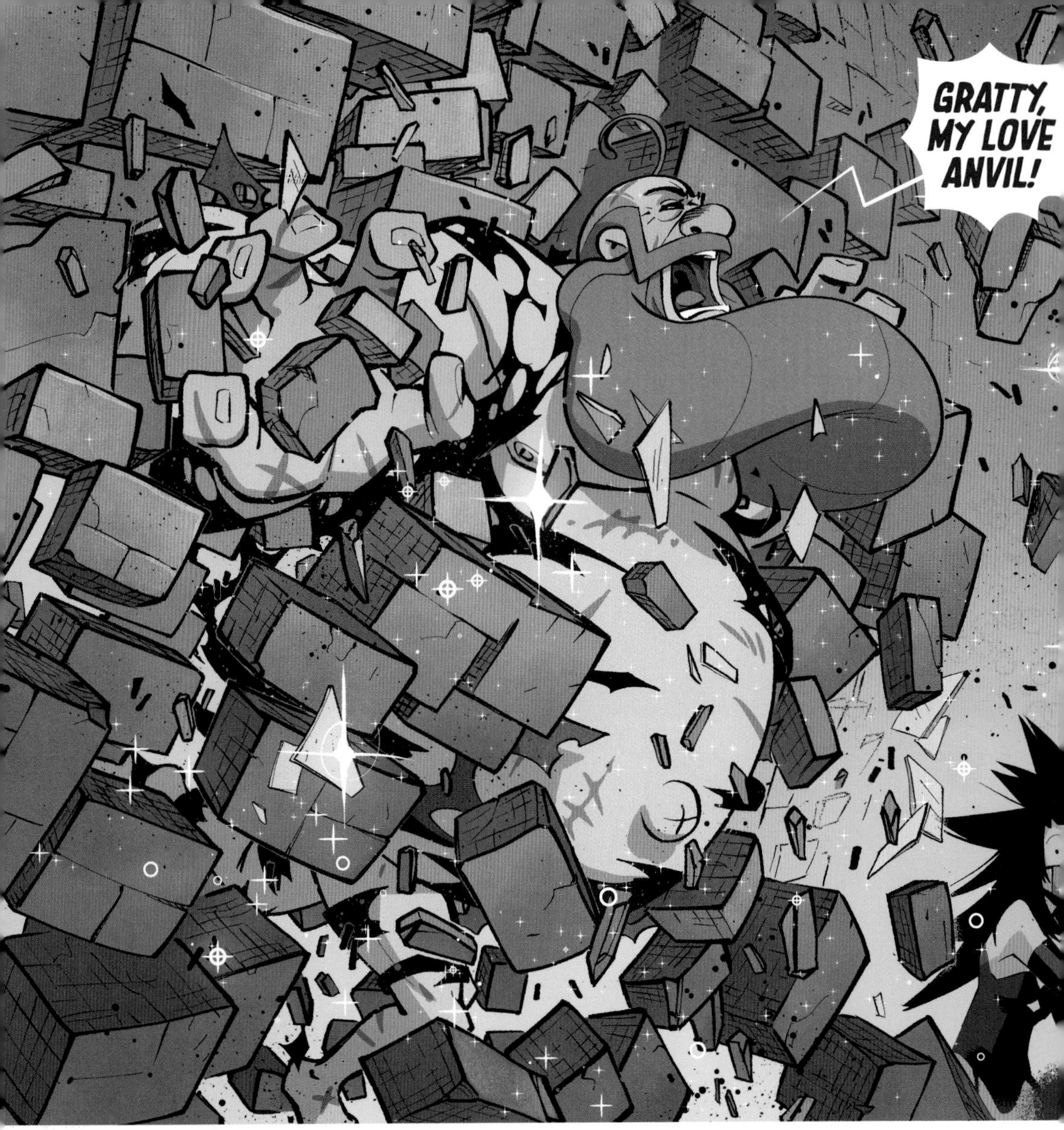
GRATTY, MY LOVE ANVIL!

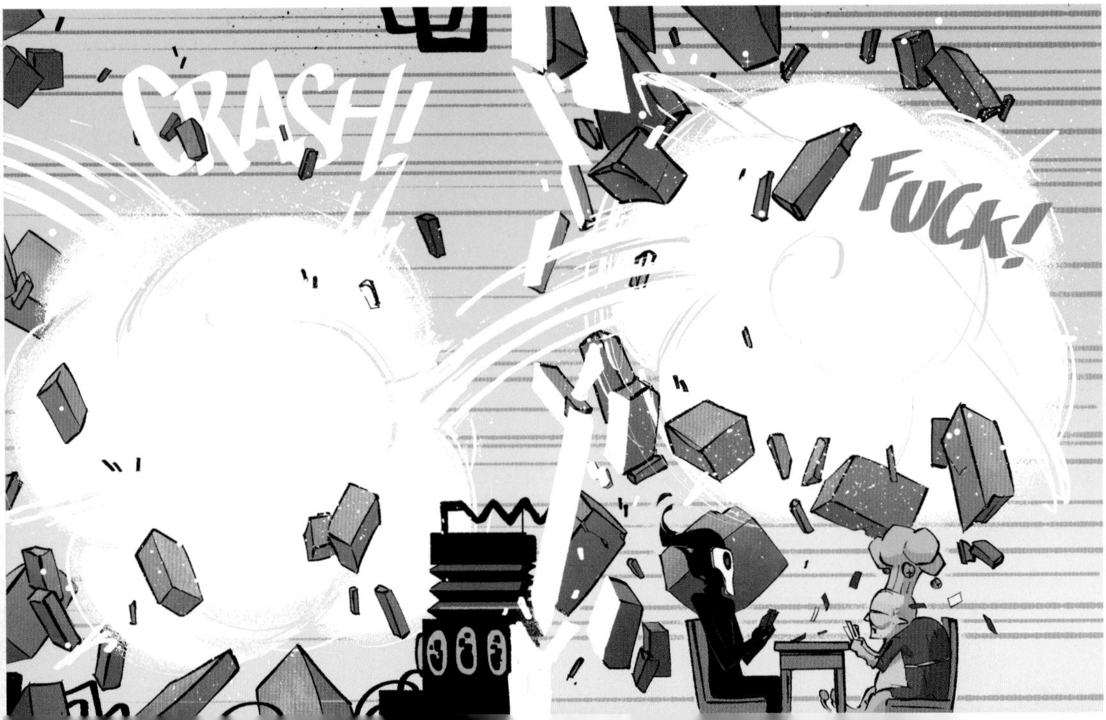
CRASH!
FUCK!

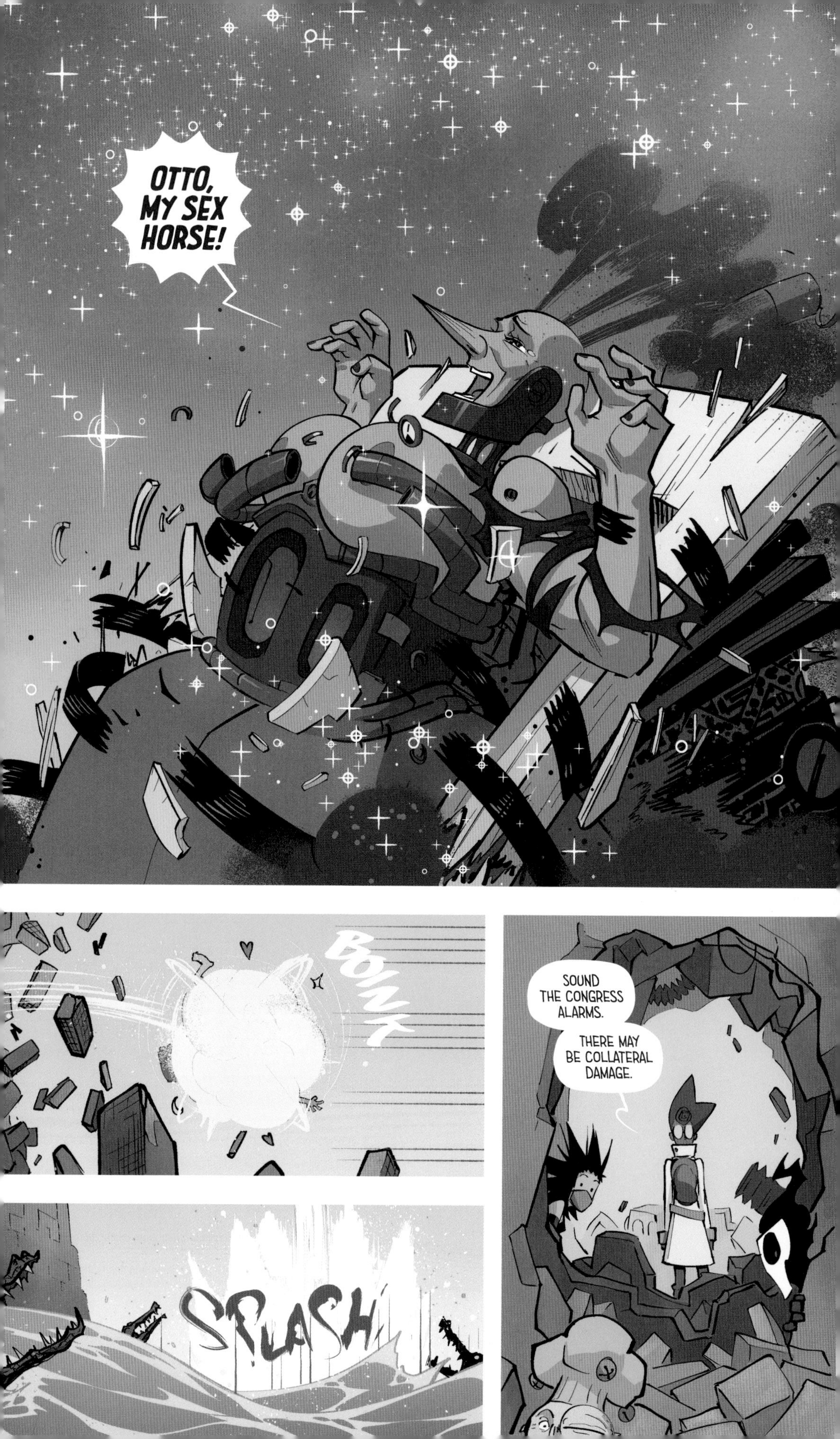
OTTO, MY SEX HORSE!
BOINK
SPLASH
SOUND THE CONGRESS ALARMS.
THERE MAY BE COLLATERAL DAMAGE.

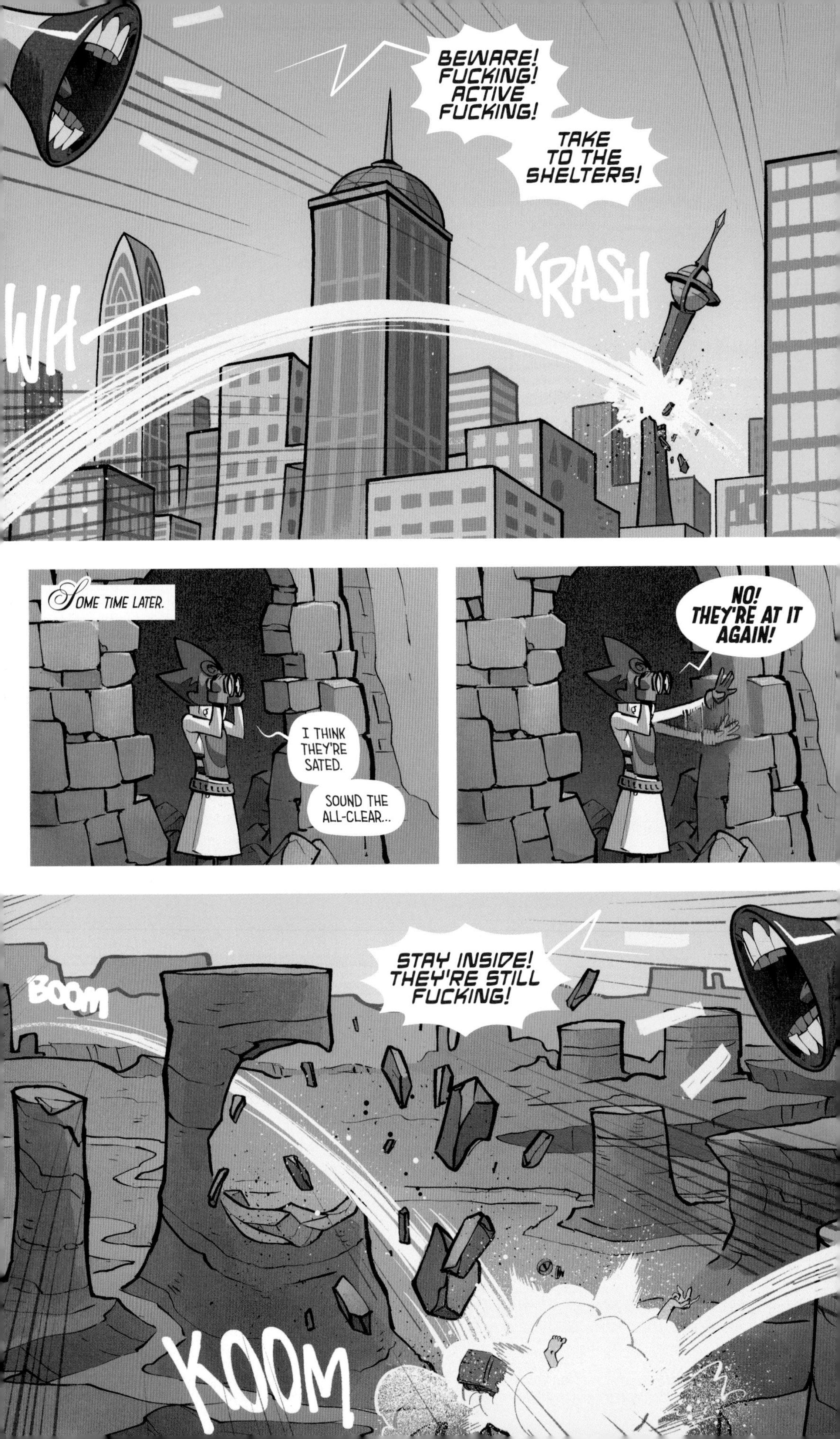
BEWARE! FUCKING! ACTIVE FUCKING!
TAKE TO THE SHELTERS!
WH
KRASH
SOME TIME LATER.
I THINK THEY'RE SATED.
SOUND THE ALL-CLEAR...
NO! THEY'RE AT IT AGAIN!
STAY INSIDE! THEY'RE STILL FUCKING!
BOOM
KOOM

UH-OOO.

I **DO** KNOW WHAT PARDIUS HAS BEEN UP TO.

THE TRUTH IS THAT HE'S SPENT YEARS GATHERING THE MOST EXTREME EXAMPLES OF LUDOCRACY.

HE CONFISCATED THE HAPPENING ACCELERATORS I DUG UP FROM THE TEMPLE OF EVERYTHING, BACK WHEN I WAS AN ARCHAEOLOGY MAJOR.

FINE! POST-COITAL ADMISSION TIME...

HE CLAIMED PROFESSOR ENDWHORL'S ZLOTAL PROPHECY RHOMBOID FOR HIMSELF.

HE EVEN STOLE YOUR MEAT AMPLIFIER, OTTO.

WHAT?! I'VE BEEN LOOKING FOR THAT. WHY WOULD PARDY DO SUCH A THING?

I FEAR HE'S DISCOVERED SOMETHING, OTTO.

SOMETHING TERRIBLE.

GOOD OLD PARDY!

NO, TERRIBLE IN A **BAD** WAY.

OH.

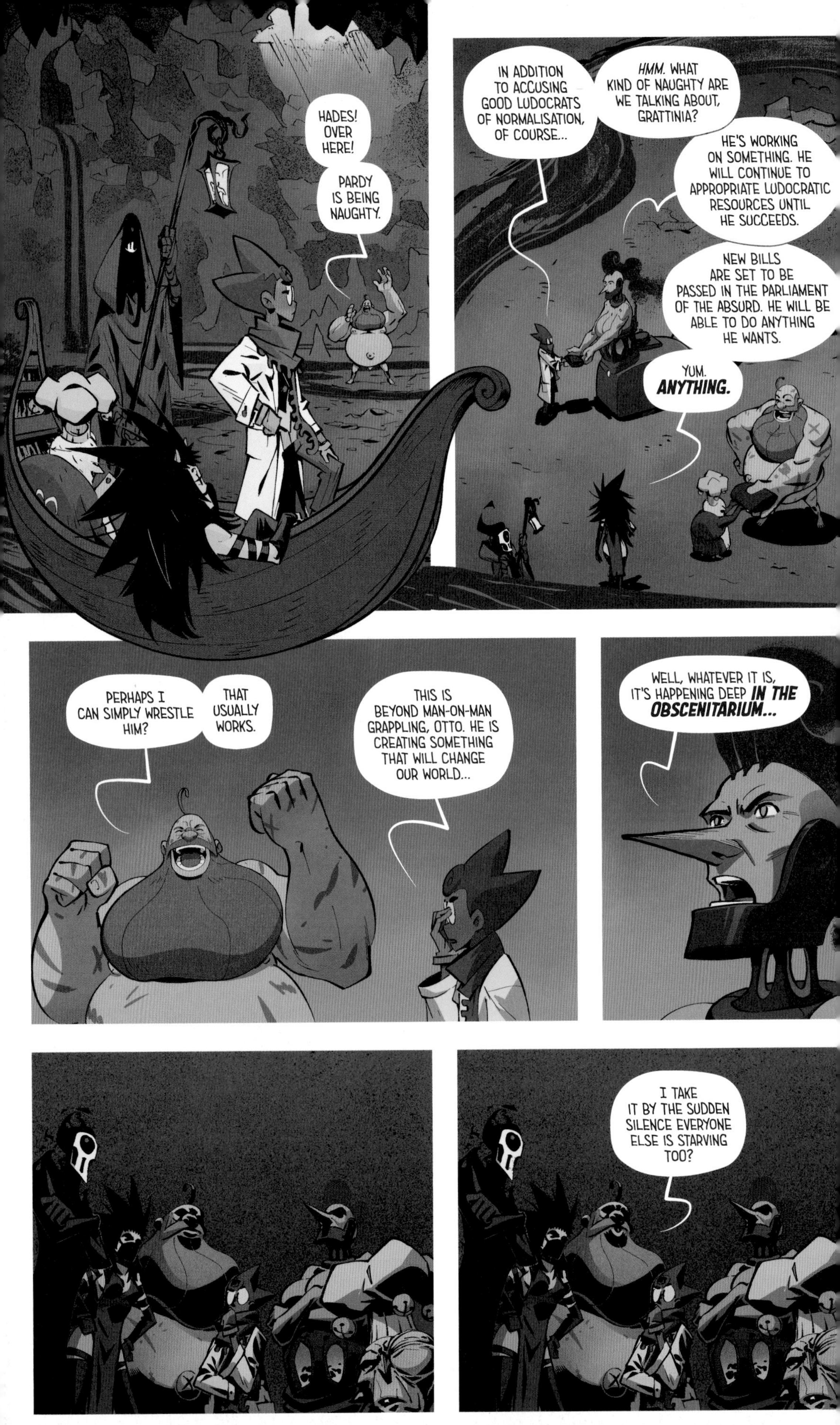
HADES! OVER HERE!
PARDY IS BEING NAUGHTY.
IN ADDITION TO ACCUSING GOOD LUDOCRATS OF NORMALISATION, OF COURSE...
HMM. WHAT KIND OF NAUGHTY ARE WE TALKING ABOUT, GRATTINIA?
HE'S WORKING ON SOMETHING. HE WILL CONTINUE TO APPROPRIATE LUDOCRATIC RESOURCES UNTIL HE SUCCEEDS.
NEW BILLS ARE SET TO BE PASSED IN THE PARLIAMENT OF THE ABSURD. HE WILL BE ABLE TO DO ANYTHING HE WANTS.
YUM. ANYTHING.
PERHAPS I CAN SIMPLY WRESTLE HIM?
THAT USUALLY WORKS.
THIS IS BEYOND MAN-ON-MAN GRAPPLING, OTTO. HE IS CREATING SOMETHING THAT WILL CHANGE OUR WORLD...
WELL, WHATEVER IT IS, IT'S HAPPENING DEEP IN THE OBSCENITARIUM...
I TAKE IT BY THE SUDDEN SILENCE EVERYONE ELSE IS STARVING TOO?

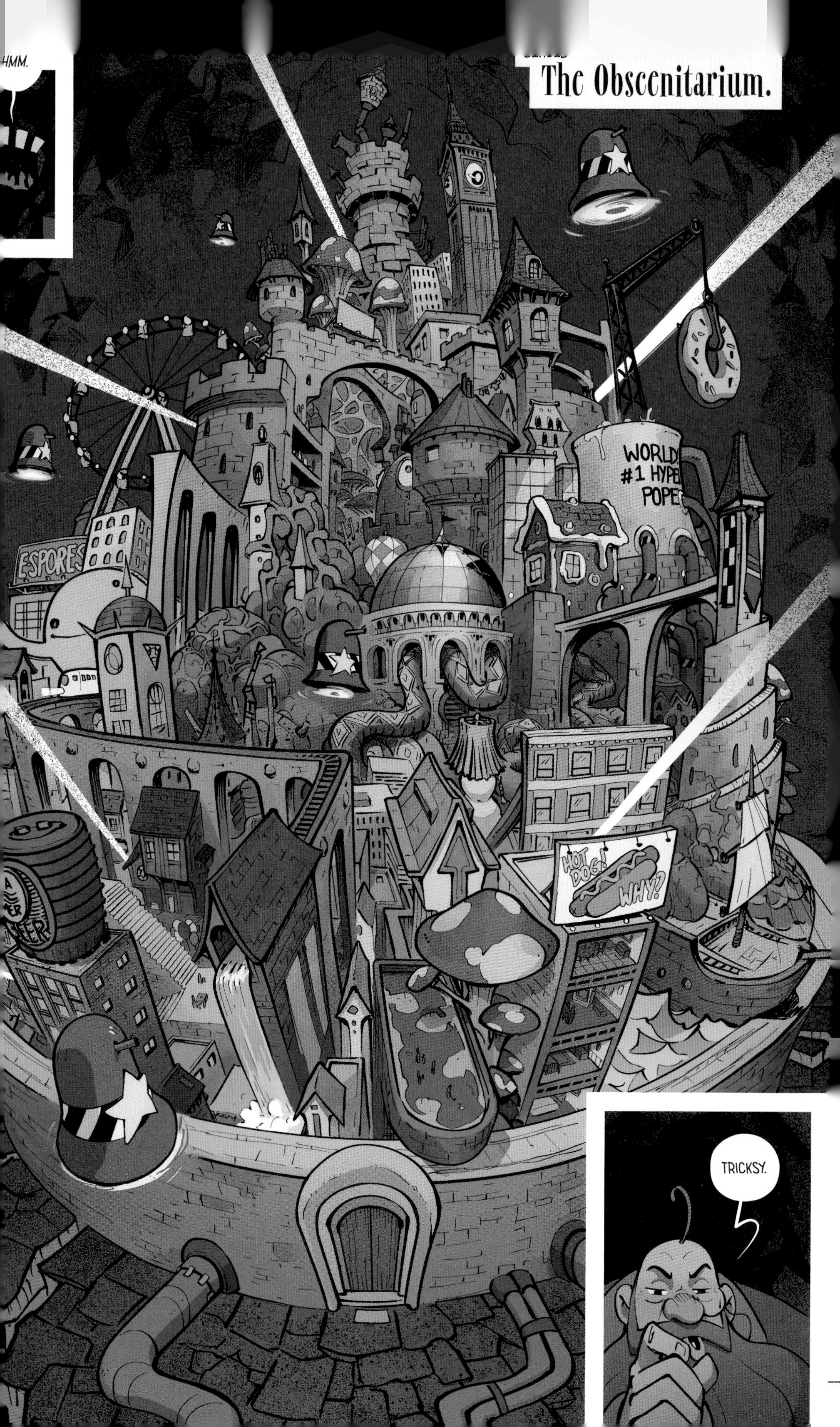
HMM.
The Obscenitarium.
E-SPORES
HOT DOG! WHY?
TRICKSY.

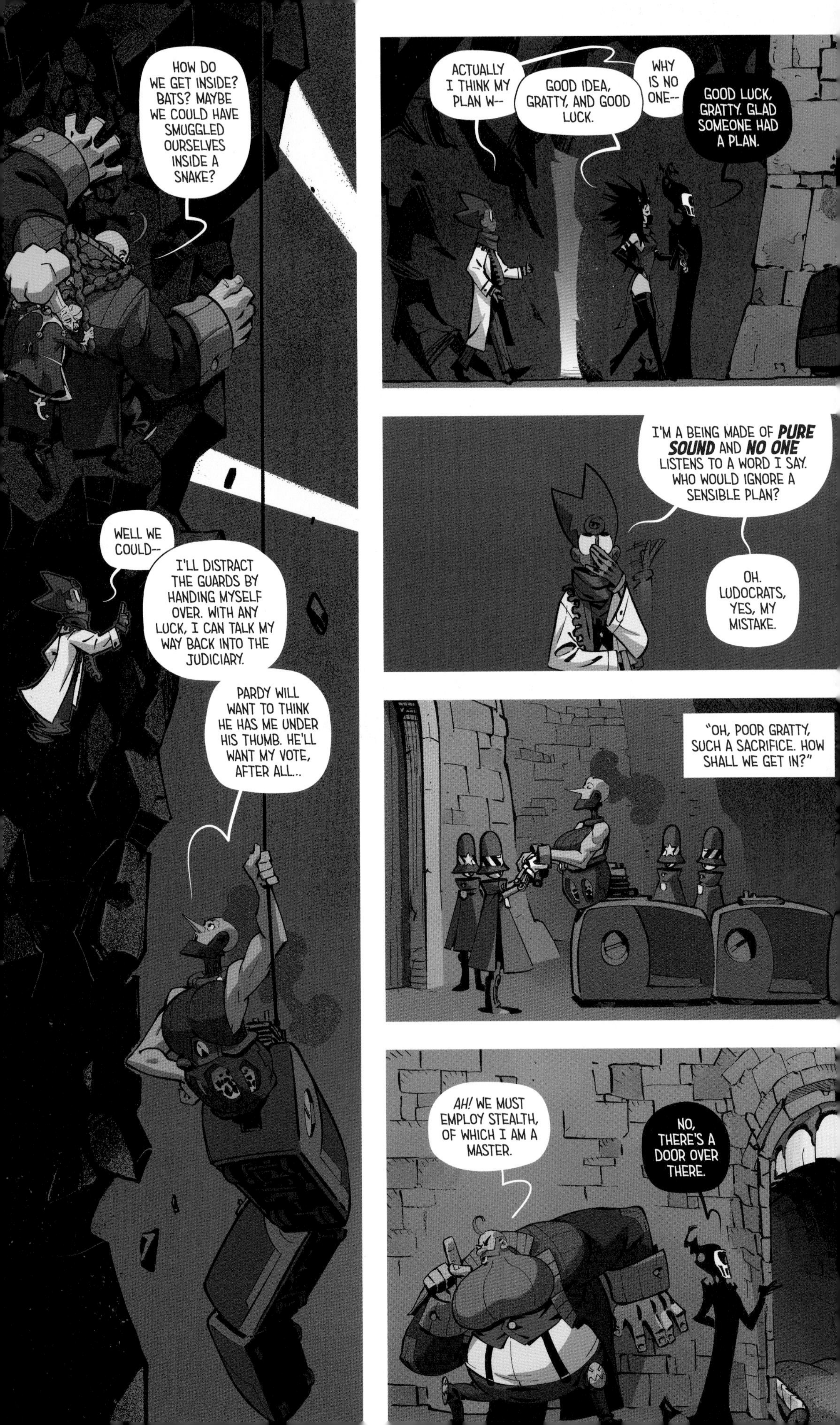
HOW DO WE GET INSIDE? BATS? MAYBE WE COULD HAVE SMUGGLED OURSELVES INSIDE A SNAKE?
WELL WE COULD--
I'LL DISTRACT THE GUARDS BY HANDING MYSELF OVER. WITH ANY LUCK, I CAN TALK MY WAY BACK INTO THE JUDICIARY.
PARDY WILL WANT TO THINK HE HAS ME UNDER HIS THUMB. HE'LL WANT MY VOTE, AFTER ALL...
ACTUALLY I THINK MY PLAN W--
GOOD IDEA, GRATTY, AND GOOD LUCK.
WHY IS NO ONE--
GOOD LUCK, GRATTY. GLAD SOMEONE HAD A PLAN.
I'M A BEING MADE OF PURE SOUND AND NO ONE LISTENS TO A WORD I SAY. WHO WOULD IGNORE A SENSIBLE PLAN?
OH. LUDOCRATS, YES, MY MISTAKE.
"OH, POOR GRATTY, SUCH A SACRIFICE. HOW SHALL WE GET IN?"
AH! WE MUST EMPLOY STEALTH, OF WHICH I AM A MASTER.
NO, THERE'S A DOOR OVER THERE.

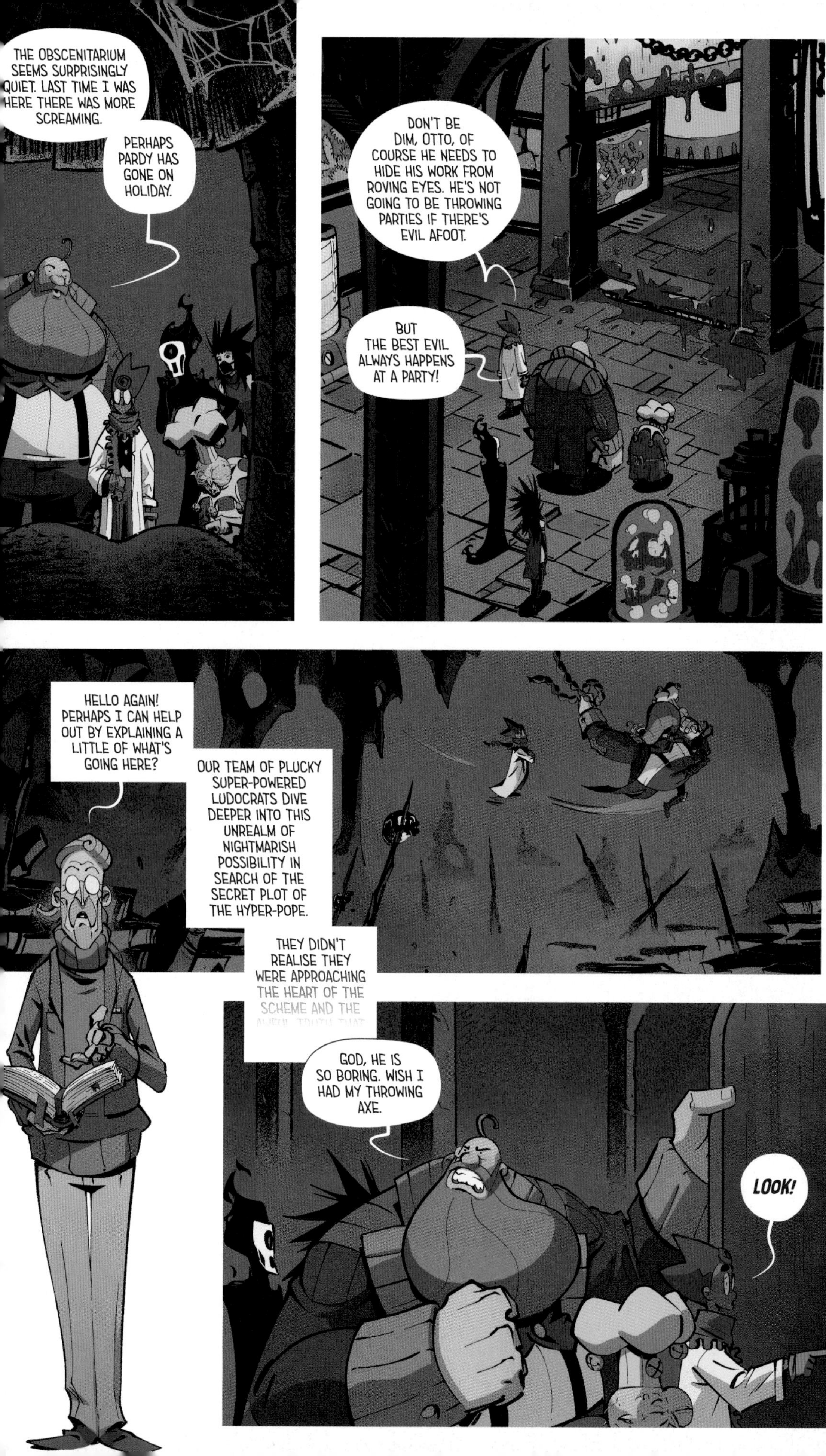

THE OBSCENITARIUM SEEMS SURPRISINGLY QUIET. LAST TIME I WAS HERE THERE WAS MORE SCREAMING.
PERHAPS PARDY HAS GONE ON HOLIDAY.
DON'T BE DIM, OTTO, OF COURSE HE NEEDS TO HIDE HIS WORK FROM ROVING EYES. HE'S NOT GOING TO BE THROWING PARTIES IF THERE'S EVIL AFOOT.
BUT THE BEST EVIL ALWAYS HAPPENS AT A PARTY!
HELLO AGAIN! PERHAPS I CAN HELP OUT BY EXPLAINING A LITTLE OF WHAT'S GOING HERE?
OUR TEAM OF PLUCKY SUPER-POWERED LUDOCRATS DIVE DEEPER INTO THIS UNREALM OF NIGHTMARISH POSSIBILITY IN SEARCH OF THE SECRET PLOT OF THE HYPER-POPE.
THEY DIDN'T REALISE THEY WERE APPROACHING THE HEART OF THE SCHEME AND THE
GOD, HE IS SO BORING. WISH I HAD MY THROWING AXE.
LOOK!

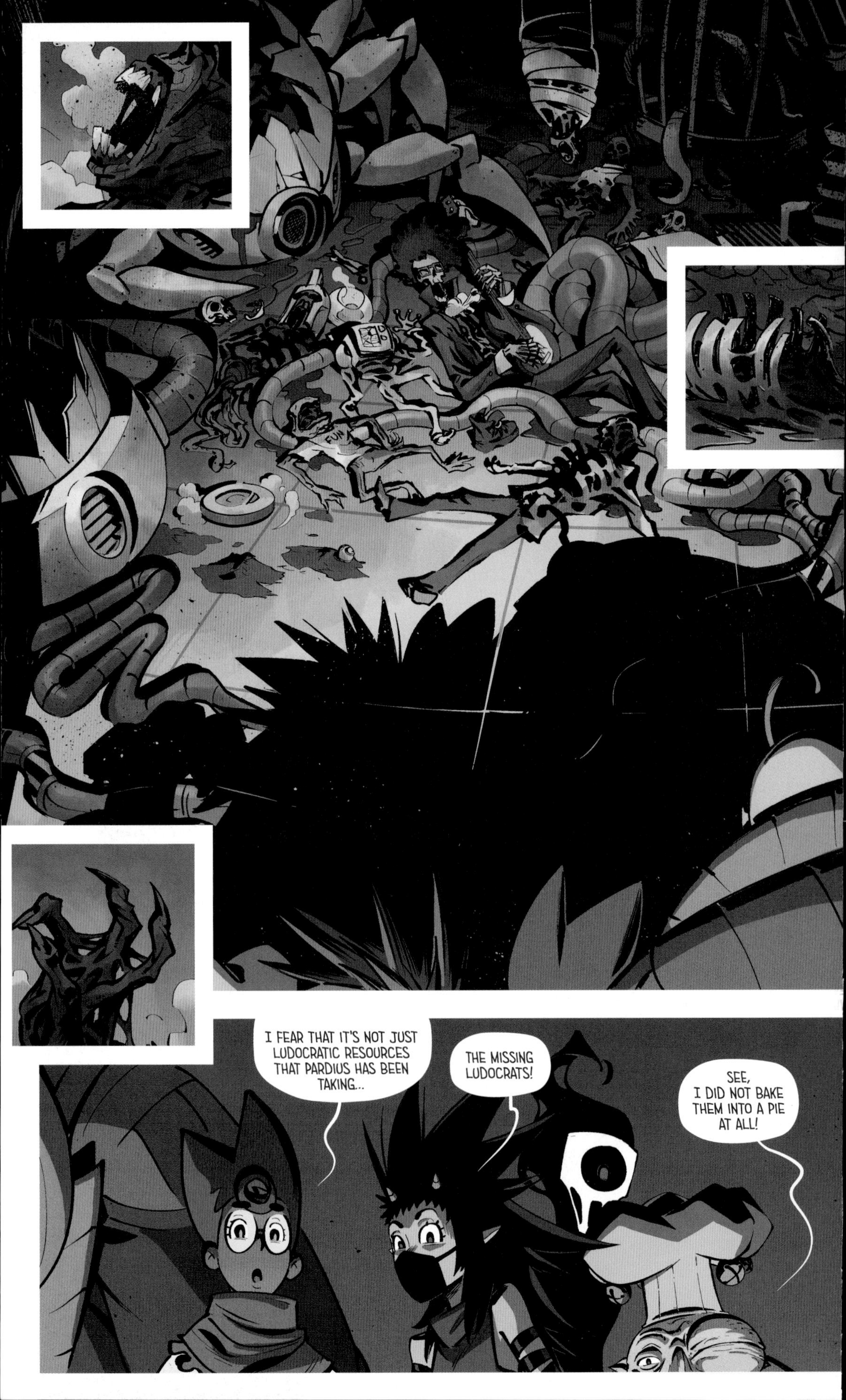
I FEAR THAT IT'S NOT JUST LUDOCRATIC RESOURCES THAT PARDIUS HAS BEEN TAKING...
THE MISSING LUDOCRATS!
SEE, I DID NOT BAKE THEM INTO A PIE AT ALL!

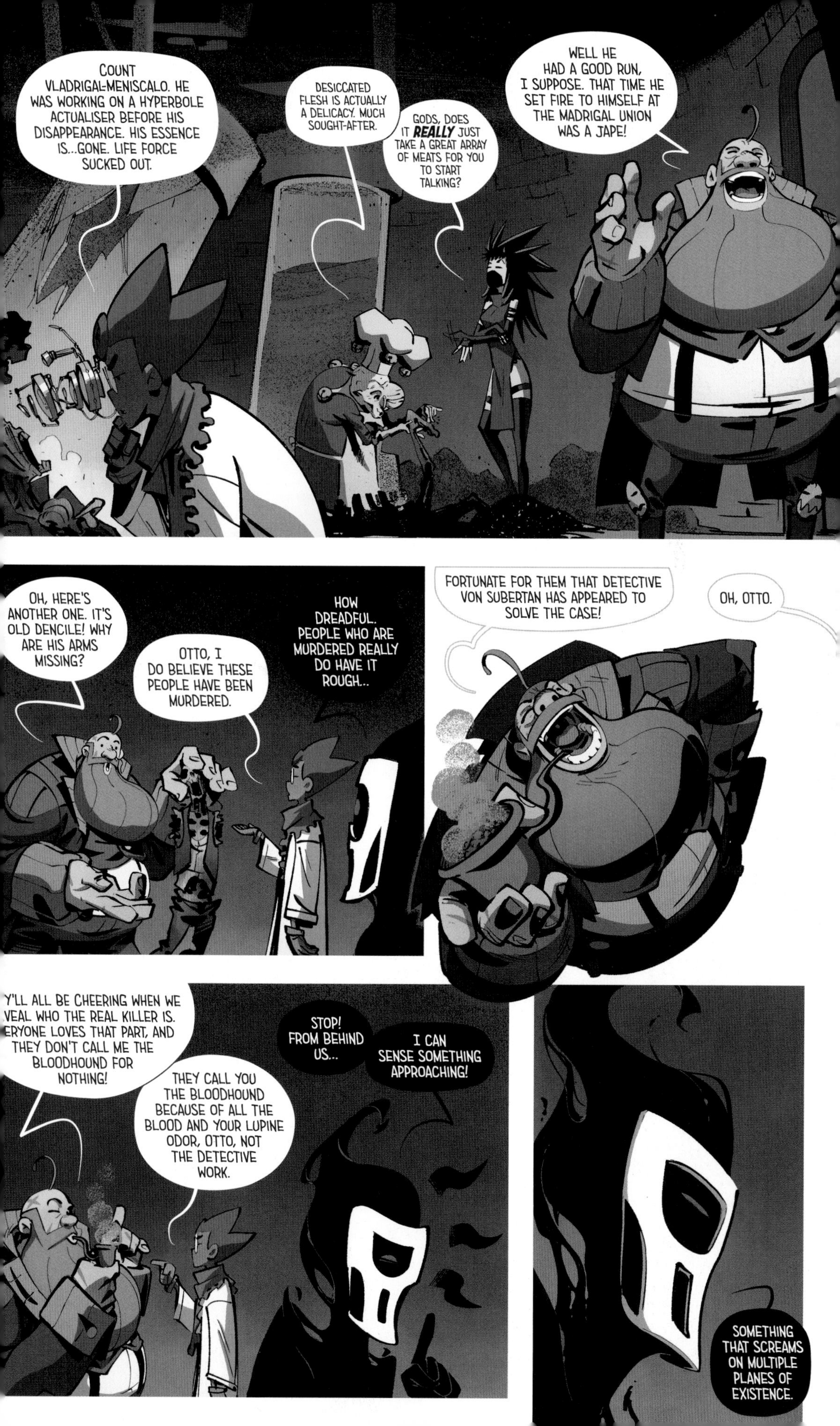
COUNT VLADRIGAL-MENISCALO. HE WAS WORKING ON A HYPERBOLE ACTUALISER BEFORE HIS DISAPPEARANCE. HIS ESSENCE IS...GONE. LIFE FORCE SUCKED OUT.
DESICCATED FLESH IS ACTUALLY A DELICACY. MUCH SOUGHT-AFTER.
GODS, DOES IT **REALLY** JUST TAKE A GREAT ARRAY OF MEATS FOR YOU TO START TALKING?
WELL HE HAD A GOOD RUN, I SUPPOSE. THAT TIME HE SET FIRE TO HIMSELF AT THE MADRIGAL UNION WAS A JAPE!
OH, HERE'S ANOTHER ONE. IT'S OLD DENCILE! WHY ARE HIS ARMS MISSING?
OTTO, I DO BELIEVE THESE PEOPLE HAVE BEEN MURDERED.
HOW DREADFUL. PEOPLE WHO ARE MURDERED REALLY DO HAVE IT ROUGH...
FORTUNATE FOR THEM THAT DETECTIVE VON SUBERTAN HAS APPEARED TO SOLVE THE CASE!
OH, OTTO.
Y'LL ALL BE CHEERING WHEN WE VEAL WHO THE REAL KILLER IS. ERYONE LOVES THAT PART, AND THEY DON'T CALL ME THE BLOODHOUND FOR NOTHING!
THEY CALL YOU THE BLOODHOUND BECAUSE OF ALL THE BLOOD AND YOUR LUPINE ODOR, OTTO, NOT THE DETECTIVE WORK.
STOP! FROM BEHIND US...
I CAN SENSE SOMETHING APPROACHING!
SOMETHING THAT SCREAMS ON MULTIPLE PLANES OF EXISTENCE.

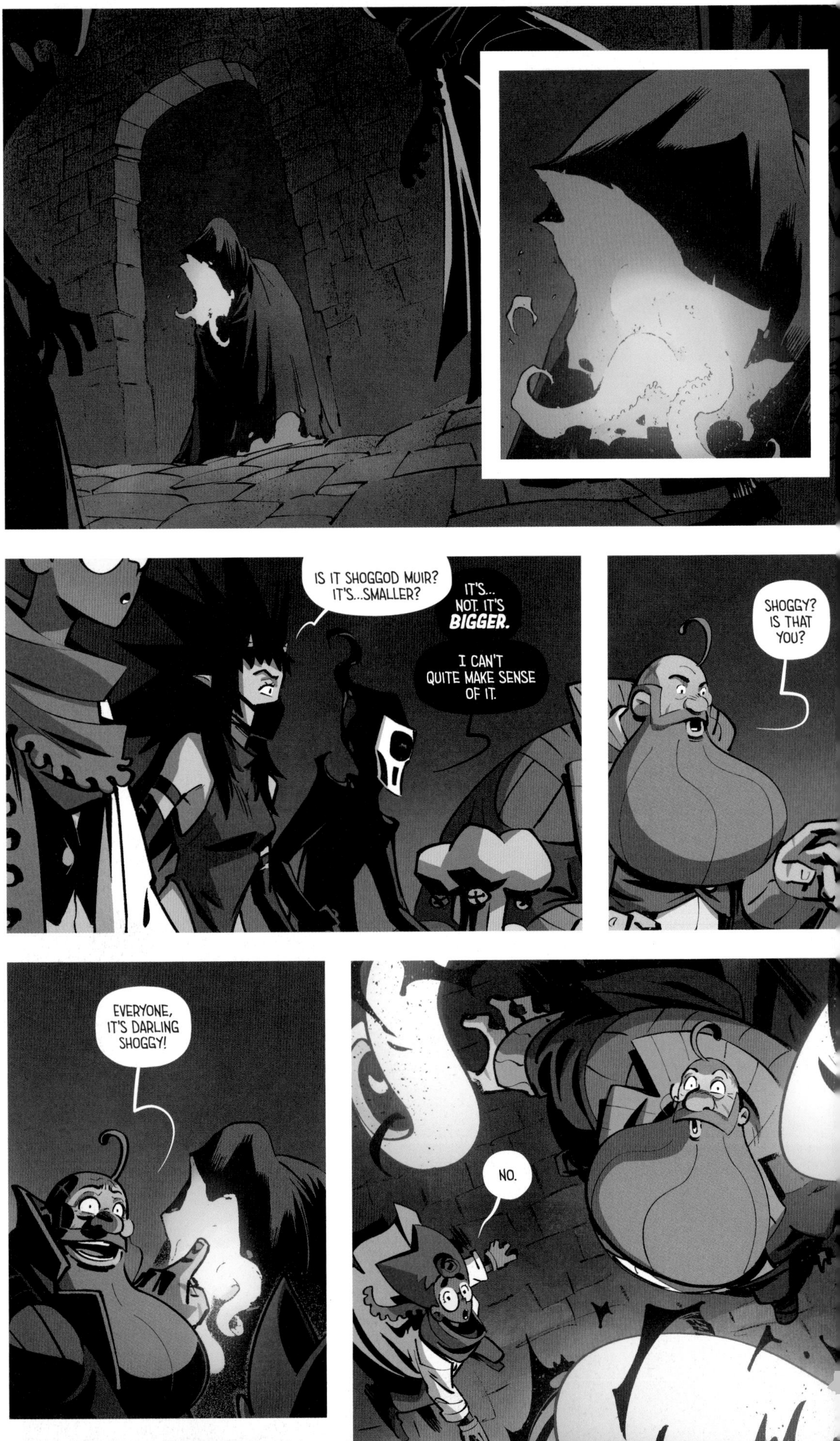
IS IT SHOGGOD MUIR? IT'S...SMALLER?
IT'S... NOT. IT'S **BIGGER.**
I CAN'T QUITE MAKE SENSE OF IT.
SHOGGY? IS THAT YOU?
EVERYONE, IT'S DARLING SHOGGY!
NO.

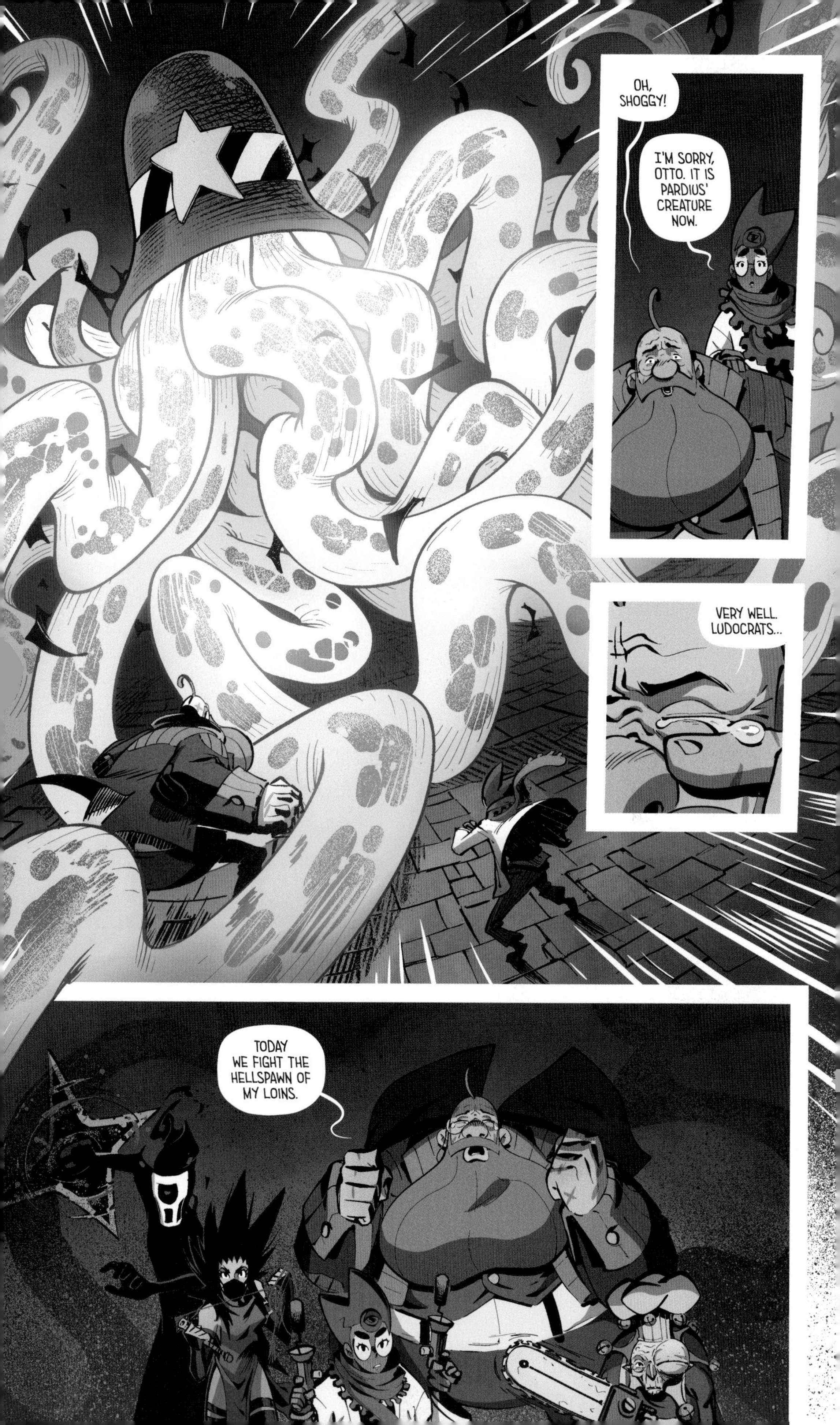
OH, SHOGGY!
I'M SORRY, OTTO. IT IS PARDIUS' CREATURE NOW.
VERY WELL. LUDOCRATS...
TODAY WE FIGHT THE HELLSPAWN OF MY LOINS.

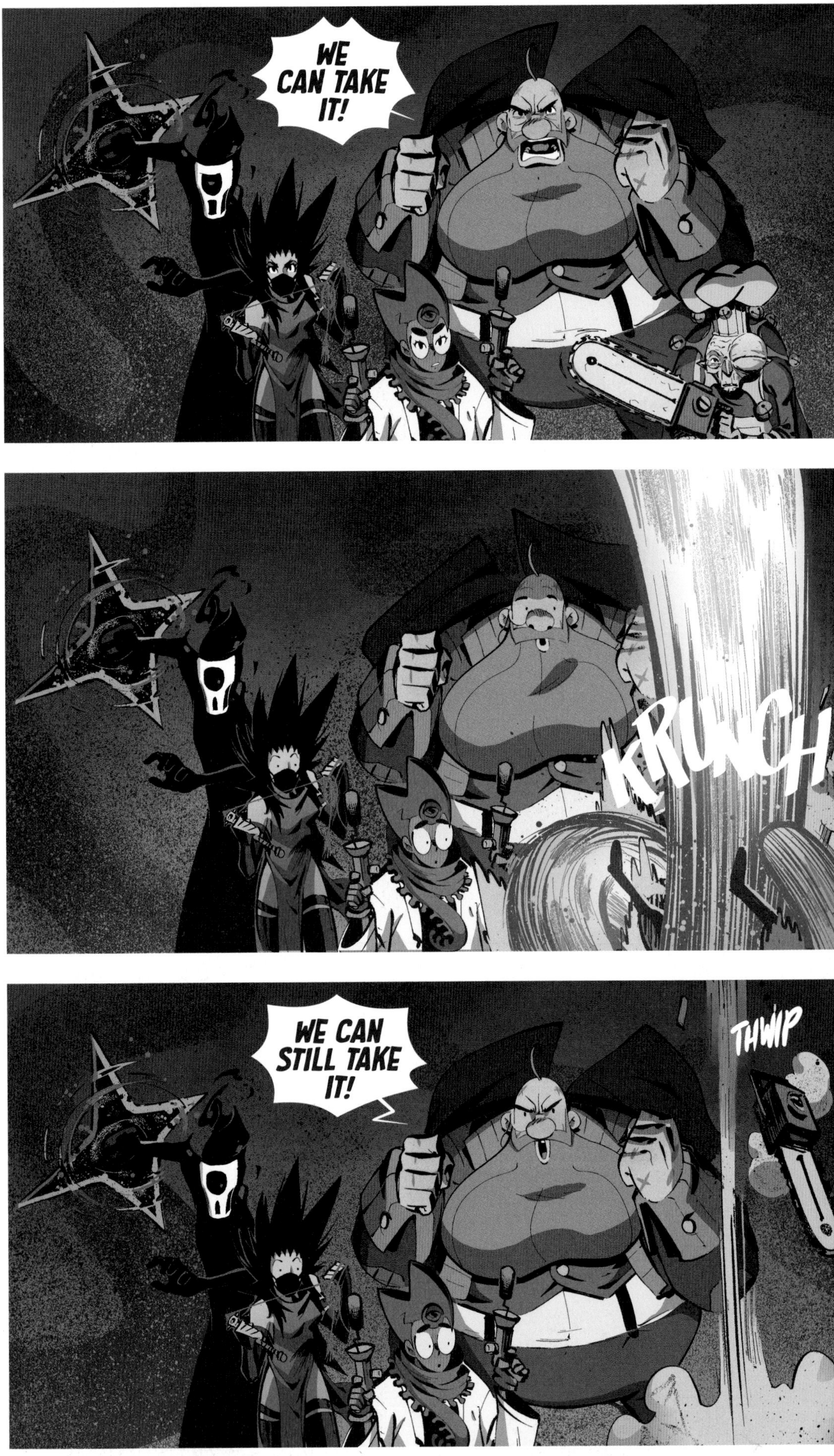
WE CAN TAKE IT!
KRUNCH
WE CAN STILL TAKE IT!
THWIP

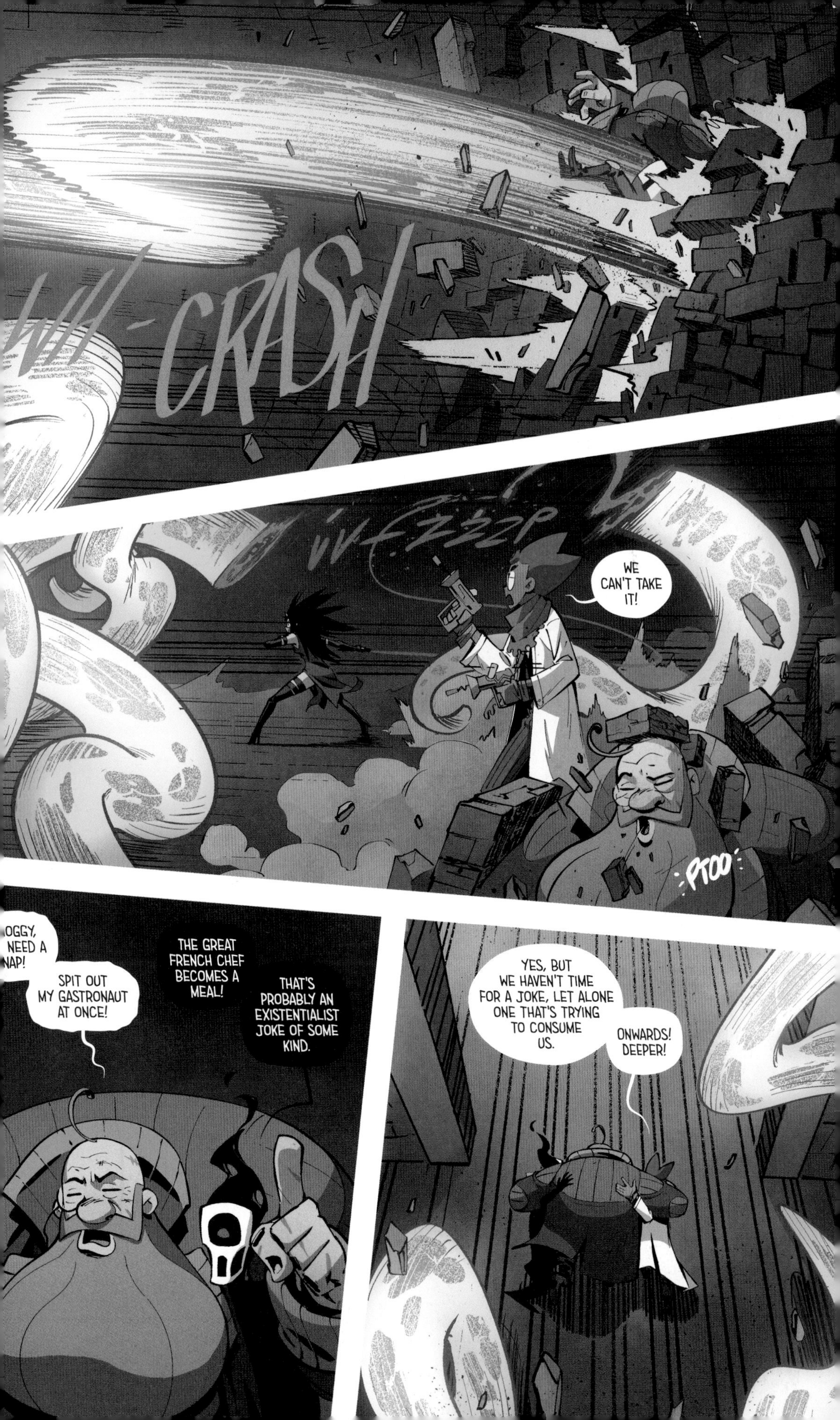
WH-CRASH
VVVZZZZP
WE CAN'T TAKE IT!
PTOO
OGGY, NEED A NAP!
SPIT OUT MY GASTRONAUT AT ONCE!
THE GREAT FRENCH CHEF BECOMES A MEAL!
THAT'S PROBABLY AN EXISTENTIALIST JOKE OF SOME KIND.
YES, BUT WE HAVEN'T TIME FOR A JOKE, LET ALONE ONE THAT'S TRYING TO CONSUME US.
ONWARDS! DEEPER!

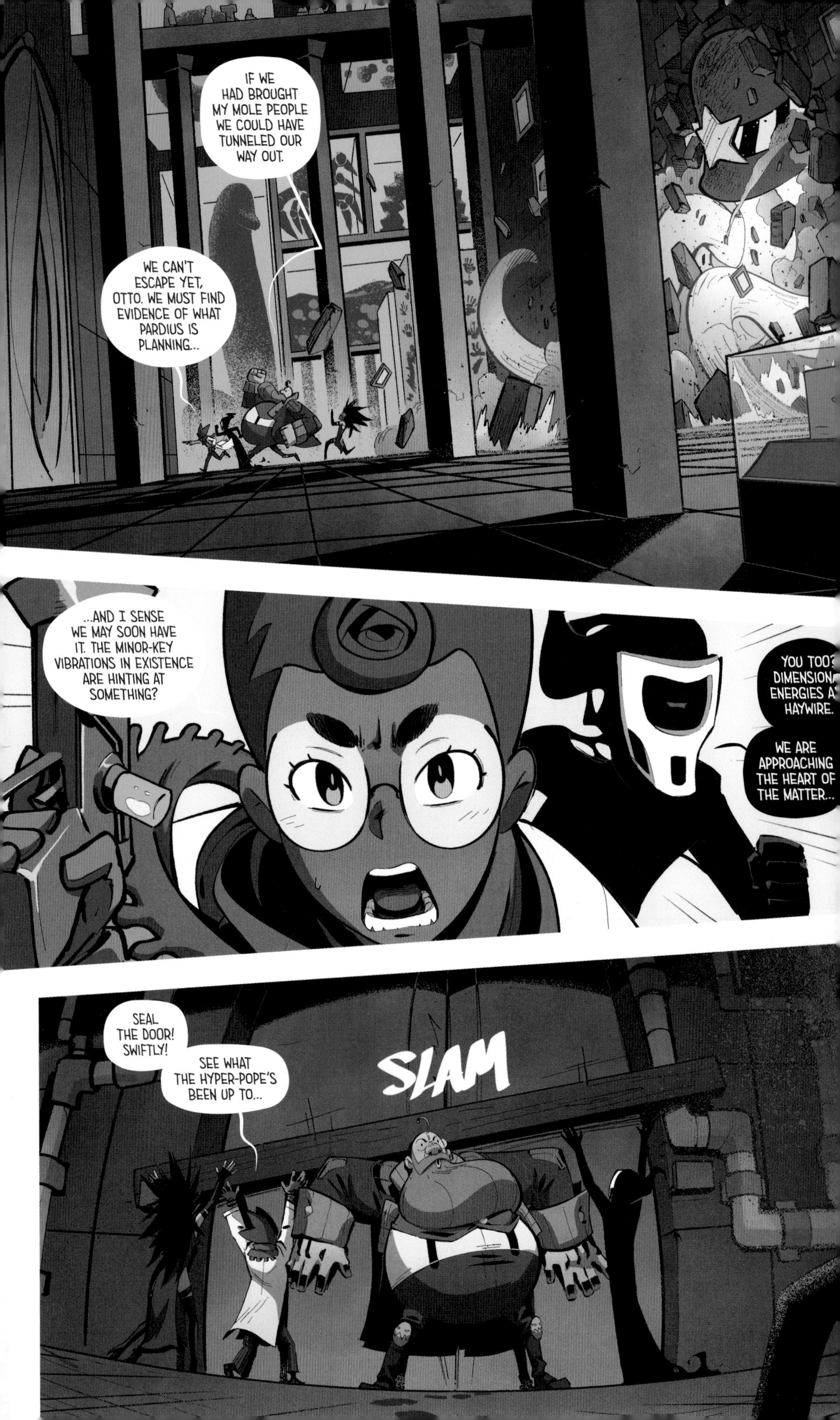

IF WE HAD BROUGHT MY MOLE PEOPLE WE COULD HAVE TUNNELED OUR WAY OUT.
WE CAN'T ESCAPE YET, OTTO. WE MUST FIND EVIDENCE OF WHAT PARDIUS IS PLANNING...
...AND I SENSE WE MAY SOON HAVE IT. THE MINOR-KEY VIBRATIONS IN EXISTENCE ARE HINTING AT SOMETHING?
YOU TOO? DIMENSIONA ENERGIES A HAYWIRE.
WE ARE APPROACHING THE HEART OF THE MATTER...
SEAL THE DOOR! SWIFTLY!
SEE WHAT THE HYPER-POPE'S BEEN UP TO...
SLAM

COO! PRETTY!

PRETTY, YET MONSTROUS, OTTO.

IT'S A VOODOO UNIVERSE.

WHATEVER IS DONE TO **THIS** UNIVERSE HAPPENS TO OUR REALITY...

THE PESTLE AND MORTAR... THEY'RE GOING TO GRIND IT UP. IT'LL **HOMOGENISE ALL EXISTENCE.**

ALL WILL BE RENDERED... BORING.

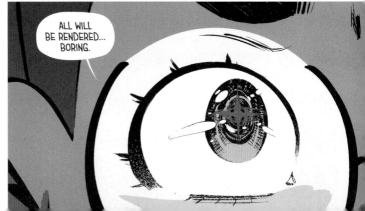

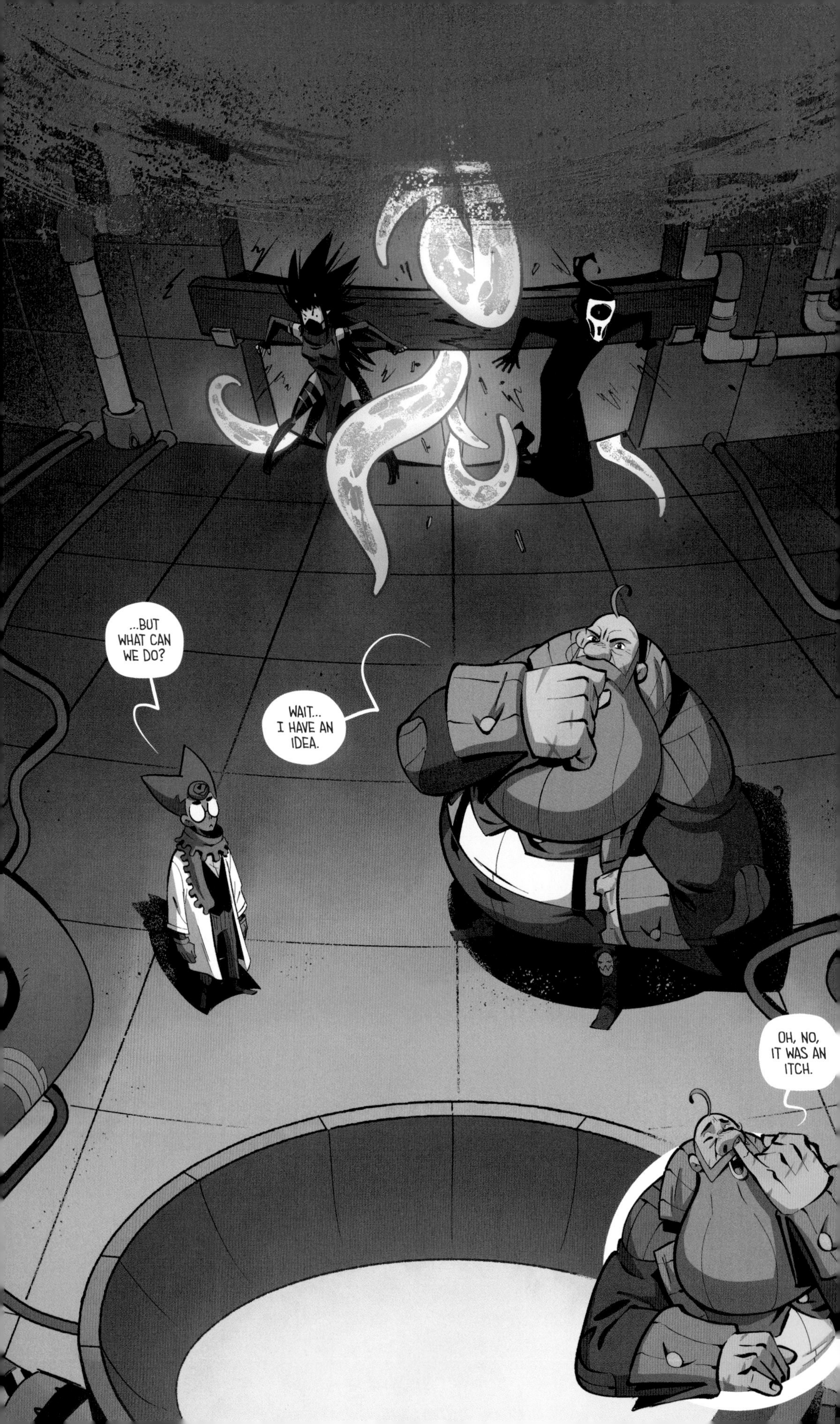
...BUT WHAT CAN WE DO?
WAIT... I HAVE AN IDEA.
OH, NO, IT WAS AN ITCH.

EXCERPTS from

The PERSONAL CYCLOPEDIA *of* LUDOCRACY,
by PARDIUS HAEMOGLANDULUM,
ELDRITCH HYPER-POPE and SUPREME HIGH LUDOCRAT

On the Guillo-Gate

"…FOLLOWING THAT, any nominative determinism was outlawed in the states of the Sanctus Manipuli. But the real issue was how to keep the meat-ghosts, once we had released them, out of our Ludocratic institutions. Their hunger for the emanations of raw science meant that once they had tasted speculative empiricism, they perpetually wanted more. It was down to myself, as Hyper-Pope, to produce a solution. That solution was the guillo-gate. Based on Hiraculon-Bestwick's meat-recognition algorithms, we imbued the gate with an ability to detect genuinely haunted meat from the meat that people walk around in every day. There were a few teething problems, naturally, and our bone-glue serum provided us with a number of critical saves during the early deployment. Nevertheless, these gates now do great work in protecting science from those yawing abominations who would eat it. Furthermore, when it came to appetites of moth people…" •

On the Mouthspeaker

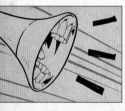

"…WHEN WE CAME to ban the phrase 'did the Earth move for you?' due to the over-literality of its usage, there was a realisation that the average citizen should not be expected to rebuild their lives after the Act Of God that came from Ludocratic coupling. Many solutions were proposed, from big nets to a kind of foam which, on coagulation, froze the frenzied participants. However, it was the age-old semi-sentient mouthspeaker network that was finally used to simply raise the alarm that congress was imminent. Combined with a legacy network of bomb shelters throughout Ludocratic cities, these devices, which had spent the previous centuries irritably muttering to themselves, suddenly had new purpose and, I like to think, were finally happy. " •

On the Unsecret Police

"…ULTIMATELY BESIDE HIMSELF with indignation. Worse, though, was the realisation for all of us that there was no real line between the Ludicrous and the villainous. The Hyper-Pope at the time, Kaidenite Aspidescrator, decided it was overdue the moment to formalise the improvisational law-enforcement of the previous decades with an emotionally neutral solution. Hence the Automated Enforcement Unit of The Unsecret Police was formed. I have made my own improvements in the years since, and I like to think that a liberal usage of logic-formatting and mind control will eventually provide us with a society which is Ludicrous, but which does not foul the papal mandates. My mandates are really not there to be fouled…" •

* * * * *

LUDOBITUARIES

YOUR *handy catalogue* OF THE *lately late*

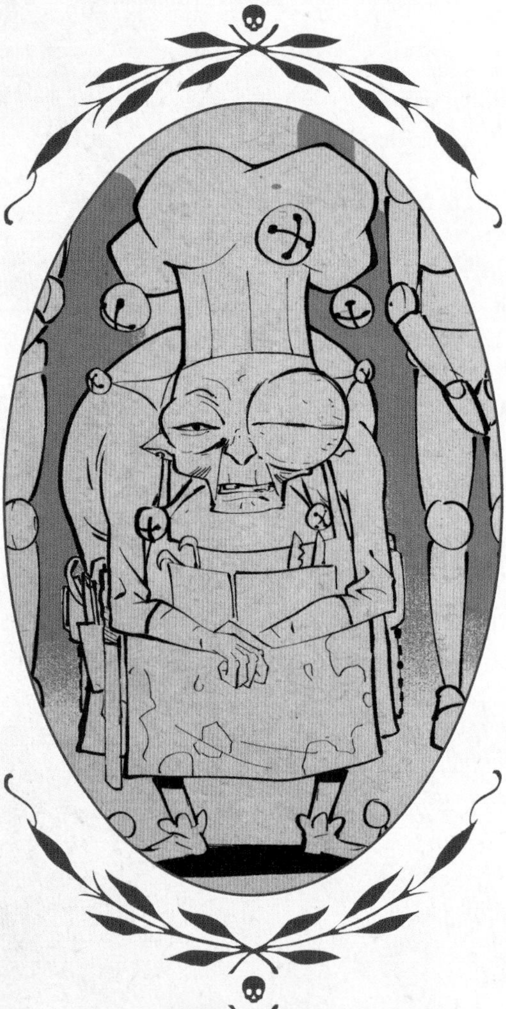

BOGOL THEEN

BORN: *the past.* DIED: *the present.*

AMONG THE FRESHLY DEPARTED *this week was the beloved Gastronaut and prototypical chef, Bogol Theen. Famed for his descent into the Ululating Offal Vortex of Blunwud Gulch, from which he returned with thirty-seven varieties of unknown meat, Bogol was a humble character, best evidenced by his quiet service to aristocratic families such as the Von Subertans and the Eebling-Wartonburys. It was in the employment of these families that his passion for and knowledge of the obscure parts of unimaginable animals was neatly sliced into a fathomless resource, and seeded in kitchens and cooking emplacements through the realm.*

Bogol made little of his charitable work, but his meat golem piloted by five hundred orphans still roams the wastes of the Caspian Basin today, a century after its initial animation. Perhaps even more obscure is the poetry written by this good and gentle soul: a genetic verse which was grown in the veins and muscle tissue of the creatures he cooked. Only those carnivorous enough could truly appreciate his clever syntax, or, indeed, the deep continental irony with which he seasoned his verbiage. Globalt, the Glutton King of Second Denmark, gave the gastronaut the keys to his kingdom and described Bogol as "bulgy and weird", but later said: "He can cook! I like him."

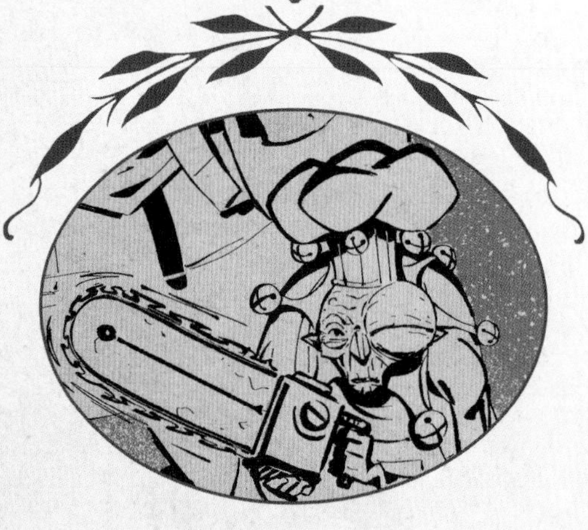

Bogol Theen's ghost will be on display at the Spectre Centre at the Huberg Spook Analysis Facility at Whelyslong. He died horribly. He was born in France.

All pictures
not visible to
mortal eyes.

COUNT VLADRIGAL-MENISCALO

BORN: *the past.* DIED: *the present.*

THE CONVERSION OF AN ACTIVE VOLCANO *into a rock stadium was only one footnote in the glittering career of musician and stylist Vladrigal-Meniscalo. Accelerated up through the classes to Count by virtue of his unnatural ability with (and faintly sexual interest in) instruments of all kinds, Meniscalo was deployed over Cordwalia in the war against the Puritanical Eel of St Fassimer, and his battle hymns are widely credited with bringing expressive dance back to specialist military operations. His disappearance earlier this year was initially assumed to be artistic, but has now been confirmed to be due to him being dead. He leaves behind his wife, Aggroxima Torshfang The Inscrutable, and his children, Mike and Susan.*

DENCILE QUORTIGUS

BORN: *the past.* DIED: *the present.*

THE LOSS OF DENCILE QUORTIGUS, *a well known Ludocrat and high-ranking librarian, will be intensely and melodramatically mourned by the Ludocratic algorithmic-literary sorcerer communities. Quortigus' ability to produce valid theories about cross-reality entanglements (the well-documented phenomenon of events in stories causally influencing those in real life) had made him something of a superstar among the fictive space cabals of Ludocratic academia. The ability to physically descend into fictional spaces was largely derived from Quortigus' work with the widely-loathed impresario-abjurationist, Carl Impostwaite, with whom he produced the Quortigus-Impostwaite equation: a mathematical incantation which made forced reality-extrusion possible, and which many commentators suggested would provide a pathway to more readily accessible forms of space travel than the standard gravity bending which is current taught in Ludocratic institutions.*

Quortigus leaves behind his dog, Kyle, who is slowly learning to talk.

ELIZABETH MIRLE LA FONTAYNE

BORN: *the future.* DIED: *the present.*

ONE OF THE FEW *non-violent deaths this season, Mirle La Fontayne died stylishly in her home at Mount Vermillion after a brief retirement and a long and distinguished service as one of the central managers with the Great Ludocratic Bureaucracy. Having started out her career as an inventor, producing such outlandish concepts as The Haircut and Underwater Dogs, she realised that the thing that was really holding back raising the experiential intensity threshold for all citizens was the supply chain. Having entered the bureaucracy, she spent countless centuries making sure that all whims were catered for and that any request for resources, no matter how boring, could be readily delivered, ideally on hot air balloons equipped with stilt legs. Mirle La Fontayne, queen of logistics, we salute you.*

IMPORTANT, DANGEROUS, AND DELIGHTFUL LANDMARKS TO LOOK OUT FOR ON YOUR VISIT TO

THE OBSCENITARIUM

1 **THE AWFUL EYE-TOWER OF LONDINIUM.** Watching, screaming, and then watching again: the Awful Eye-Tower of Londinium sees all, and reacts accordingly. The nightmare clocktower longs to return to its home city but, alas, since the catastrophe it must remain here.

* * *

2 **PURLO'S EDIFICE OF CONSTRUCTION FUNGUS.** Fungus went out of fashion as a construction material during the 14,670s, when it became clear that the tiny parasites living in it were in fact a culture of microscopic philosophers, each one more tedious than the last. Nevertheless, mycologist wrestler Flaming Purlo decided to install a grand testament to fungus during his time as arch-architect of the Obscenitarium.

* * *

3 **GINGERBEARD SANITARIUM.** Gingerbread house? Think again. That's orange human hair. *Gingerbeard* house. Sure, you can eat it and become enchanted by a witch, but choking down fistfuls of that stuff is actually worse than the curse. Instead, lay down on the bristling orange bed, and think about what you did.

* * *

4 **GERRY SMITH.** Gerry Smith probably shouldn't have volunteered for Egrod Minacious' cascading flesh trials, but he really needed to do something with his life, and so he did this. Gerry is now a perpetually descending berg of throbbing protoplasm and venous material which fills large parts of the Obscenitarium.

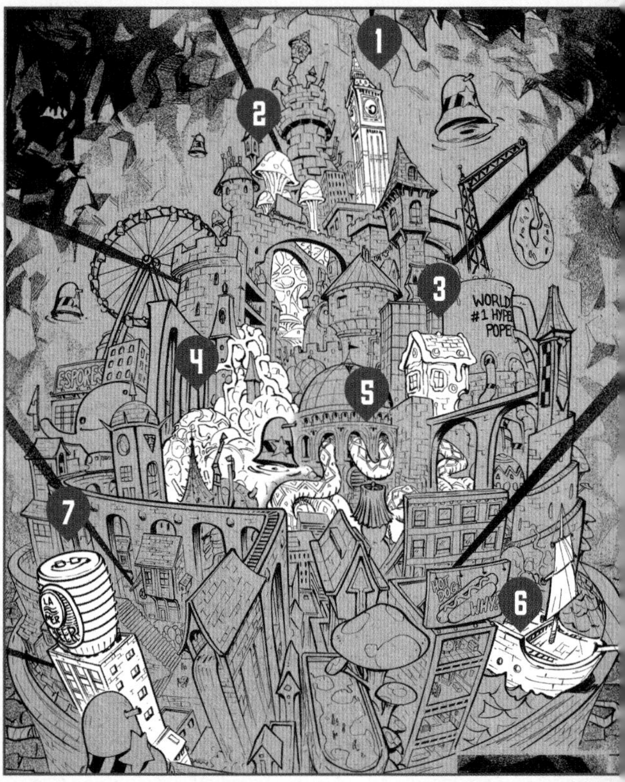
1
2
3
4
5
6
7
WORLD #1 HYPE POPE
SPORES

* * *

5 **DOME OF THE INFINITE SERPENT.** With no head and no tail, this one-step-beyond-ouroboros surges and slithers its way around the dome without rest, making things quite uncomfortable for visitors. Get naked and slather yourself in cooking oil for the best access to the classically-vaulted dome.

* * *

6 **MEDIEVAL GALLEON.** Authentic sailing ship from the discovery of the under-continent. Why not have your pho taken with a sailor? You know, if there's one around.

* * *

7 **BOOZE TOWN.** We've all been to Booze Town, but this particular instance of that figurative location contains the original booze from which all other drink was derived. The UrBooze is normally distilled in the skull of a mythological giant, Drunky, who was said to have invented drinking by fermentin stolen apricots in his bed pit.

To send letters to LUDOCRATS
please attach your words
to the back of a friendly vole
and instruct them to head to
OTTO's CASTLE, LUDOVERSE.

LETTERS *from* LUDOCRATS

AFFAIR OF THE HEART

Dear Elaina,

As the esteemed Agony Aunt of the Ludocrats I was hoping for your advice in a most troubling affair of the heart. We must be together! I say it once! I say it twice! I say it thrice! I say it... fourice? See — my mind is love-addled and I can't even write a simple letter. The only good news is that I know my love is reciprocated. The problem for this affair of the heart is that the organ in question beats inside the chest of a forty-foot demi-ogre who has sworn to disturb the integrity of my cranium with its trusty mallet. I know aorta move on, but I can't bear it. Is my love in vein?

Yours,
Sniffly McCryingson the Third

McCryingson,

Ah, love. That poem spoken by the universe. But you know what? The thing about love is this: it is a shapeshifter. Not one of those cuddly fluffy ones which can take on any form of cartoon pet, no. This is the sort of horrible vicious polymorph that looks like your soulmate, but is in fact a flesh-wolf with mouths for eyes. And let me tell you: flesh-wolves can be fun to begin with it, but sooner or later they're going to chase a squirrel up a tree, and everyone is going to be watching. Look: I'll be straight with you, we're all just restless constructs of dirt with anxiety, and one day even the sun will be a cold ball of iron.

I hope that helps.

Elaina x

ASPIRING TO BE LUDICROUS

Dear Professor o-K,

I am an aspiring Ludocrat currently studying under Grandmouth Hugo Pretend at the University of the Unlikely in Pradenberg. I am writing to ask whether you have any internship opportunities, or advice for those aspiring to be ludicrous? I have attached my portfolio of our third-year work on Astonishment and Related Feelings of Hyperbolic Incongruity.

Regards,
Eddyberg Lastwash

Dear Lastwash,

Of course! And as is traditional for Ludocratic interns, you'll be fairly compensated for your time and efforts. I'm not sure why this simple and reasonable state of affairs is considered ludicrous, but apparently it is.

*Yours,
Professor Hades Zero-K*

IN THIS CURSED WORLD

Dear "The Ludocrats",

I loved issue two of your resplendent episodic adventure, and when I finally put it down (no mean feat!) I found myself reclined upon a throne of fungus in a world of palpable darkness. I have been made king in this cursed world, and the ghost crabs which reside here fear me, catering to my every whim. My question is this: how can I get my mail-order copy redirected to my new address, when the postman has been consumed by the crustacean people of this prison dimension? PS my new address is "The Palace Of The Quadrolimb, Crabtown, Hell Plane Eukaryotia, Post Code 56-98-AHGH".

Thanks in advance!

Yours,
David Brimble

Dear Mr Brimble,

I'm afraid this has been a growing problem in our subscriber base. The standard postal staff have, for all their commendable efforts, proved incapable of bringing copies of Ludocrats to more difficult locales, at least without becoming terribly dog-eared. Where the dog-ears come from is a mystery we're trying to solve. We've upgraded your subscription to our premier postmodern service, which will deconstruct your package and reconstruct it safely inside your mailbox. There is a small danger of some extra meta self-indulgence being inserted in the comic in the process, but when our organ is what it is, we suspect you won't even notice.

We have also updated your mailing address.

Wulf the Slayer, Archmagus of the Quantum Froth, Bizarre-Czar, Seducer of Singularities, Chitinous Knight of the Fourfold Spleen, Image Comics' "The Ludocrats" subscription department

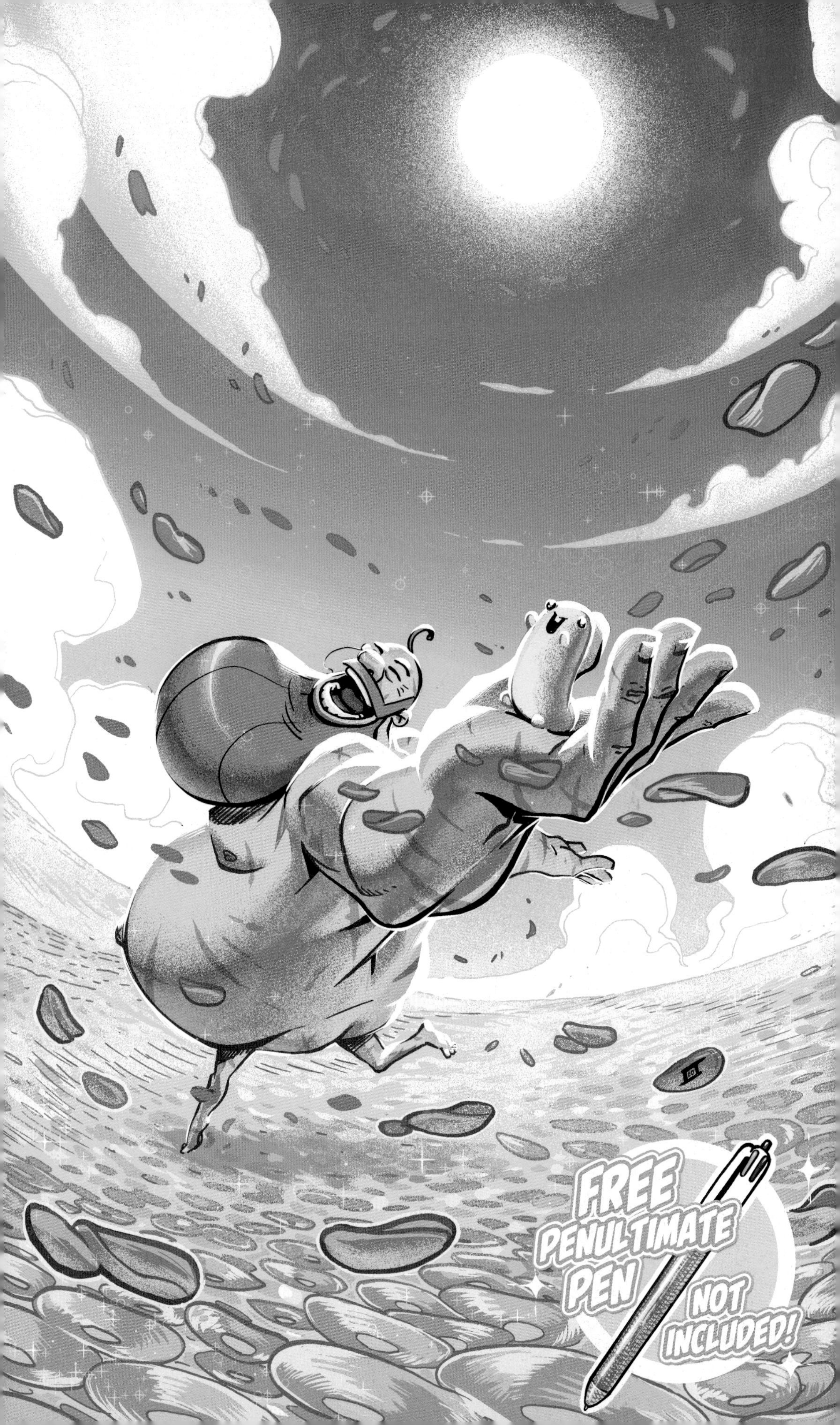
FREE
PENULTIMATE
PEN
NOT
INCLUDED!

NCE UPON A TIME
some BRAVE HEROES
discovered a HYPER-POPE
planned to HOMOGENISE
ALL REALITY
to make it BORING.

OH NOES!

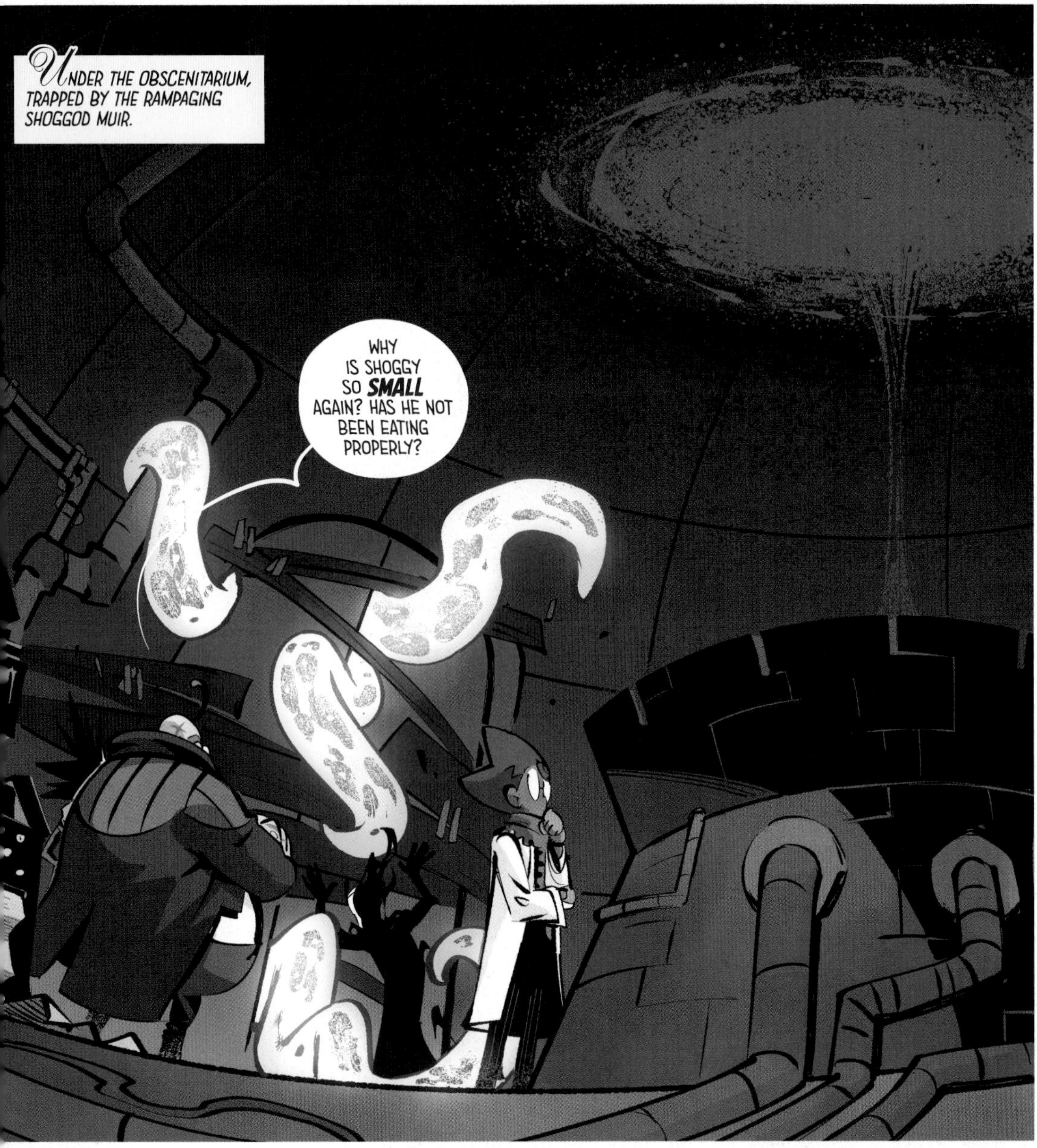
UNDER THE OBSCENITARIUM, TRAPPED BY THE RAMPAGING SHOGGOD MUIR.
WHY IS SHOGGY SO **SMALL** AGAIN? HAS HE NOT BEEN EATING PROPERLY?

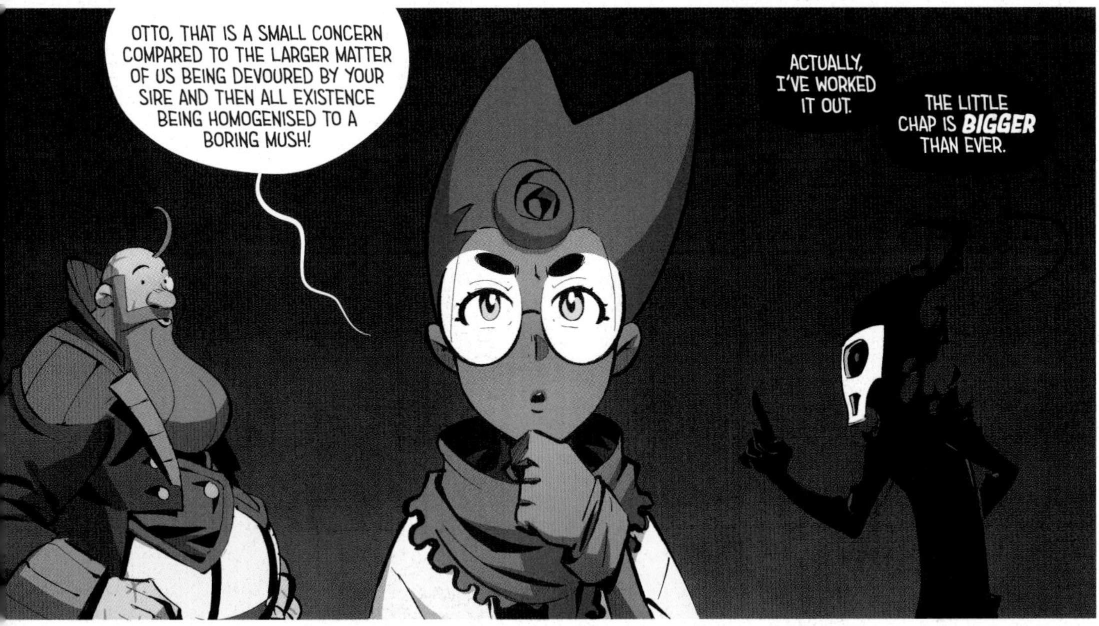
OTTO, THAT IS A SMALL CONCERN COMPARED TO THE LARGER MATTER OF US BEING DEVOURED BY YOUR SIRE AND THEN ALL EXISTENCE BEING HOMOGENISED TO A BORING MUSH!
ACTUALLY, I'VE WORKED IT OUT.
THE LITTLE CHAP IS **BIGGER** THAN EVER.

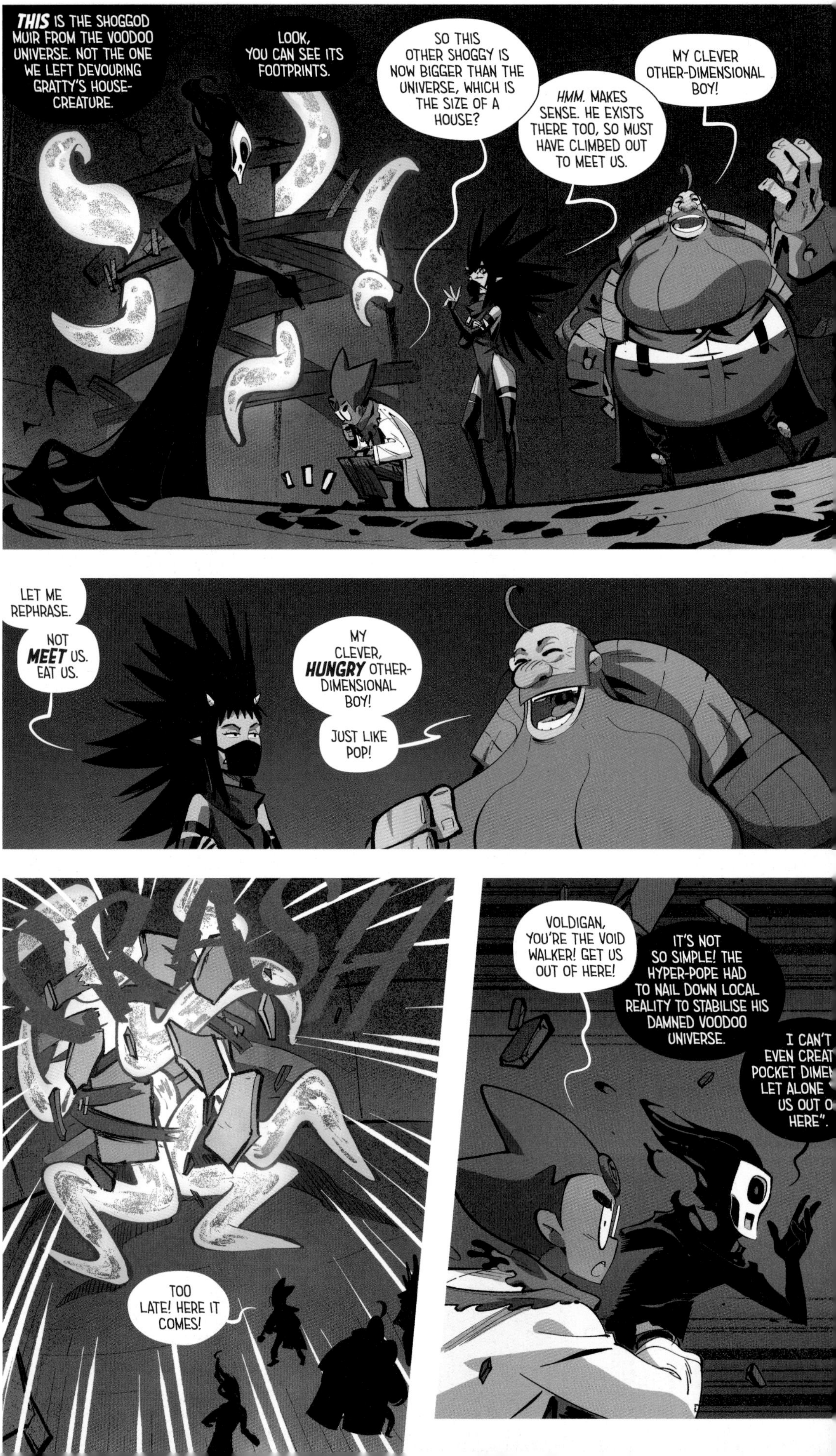
THIS IS THE SHOGGOD MUIR FROM THE VOODOO UNIVERSE. NOT THE ONE WE LEFT DEVOURING GRATTY'S HOUSE-CREATURE.
LOOK, YOU CAN SEE ITS FOOTPRINTS.
SO THIS OTHER SHOGGY IS NOW BIGGER THAN THE UNIVERSE, WHICH IS THE SIZE OF A HOUSE?
HMM. MAKES SENSE. HE EXISTS THERE TOO, SO MUST HAVE CLIMBED OUT TO MEET US.
MY CLEVER OTHER-DIMENSIONAL BOY!
LET ME REPHRASE.
NOT MEET US. EAT US.
MY CLEVER, HUNGRY OTHER-DIMENSIONAL BOY!
JUST LIKE POP!
TOO LATE! HERE IT COMES!
VOLDIGAN, YOU'RE THE VOID WALKER! GET US OUT OF HERE!
IT'S NOT SO SIMPLE! THE HYPER-POPE HAD TO NAIL DOWN LOCAL REALITY TO STABILISE HIS DAMNED VOODOO UNIVERSE.

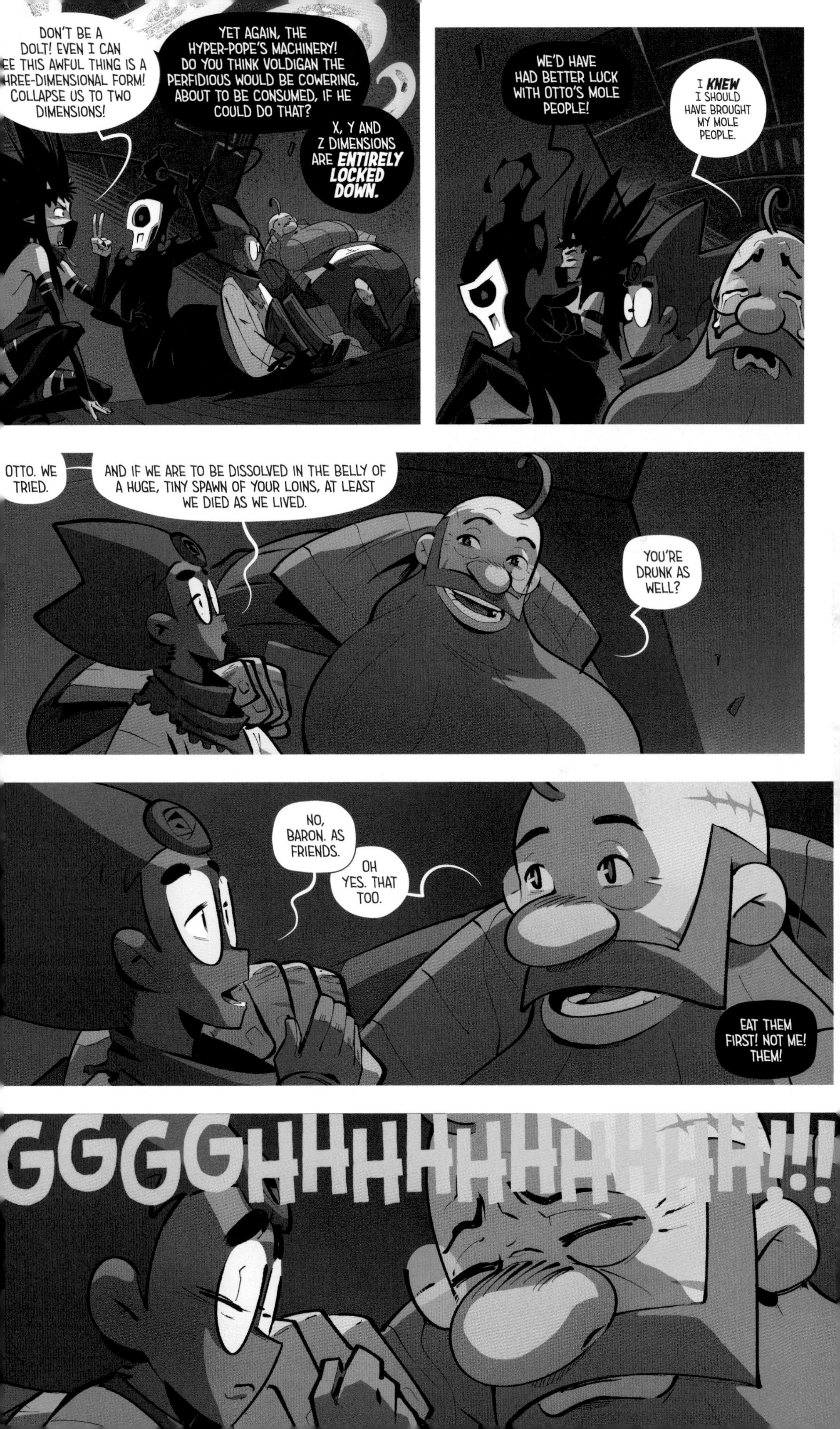
DON'T BE A DOLT! EVEN I CAN EE THIS AWFUL THING IS A HREE-DIMENSIONAL FORM! COLLAPSE US TO TWO DIMENSIONS!
YET AGAIN, THE HYPER-POPE'S MACHINERY! DO YOU THINK VOLDIGAN THE PERFIDIOUS WOULD BE COWERING, ABOUT TO BE CONSUMED, IF HE COULD DO THAT?
X, Y AND Z DIMENSIONS ARE ENTIRELY LOCKED DOWN.
WE'D HAVE HAD BETTER LUCK WITH OTTO'S MOLE PEOPLE!
I KNEW I SHOULD HAVE BROUGHT MY MOLE PEOPLE.
OTTO. WE TRIED.
AND IF WE ARE TO BE DISSOLVED IN THE BELLY OF A HUGE, TINY SPAWN OF YOUR LOINS, AT LEAST WE DIED AS WE LIVED.
YOU'RE DRUNK AS WELL?
NO, BARON. AS FRIENDS.
OH YES. THAT TOO.
EAT THEM FIRST! NOT ME! THEM!
GGGGHHHHHHHHHHHHHHH!!!

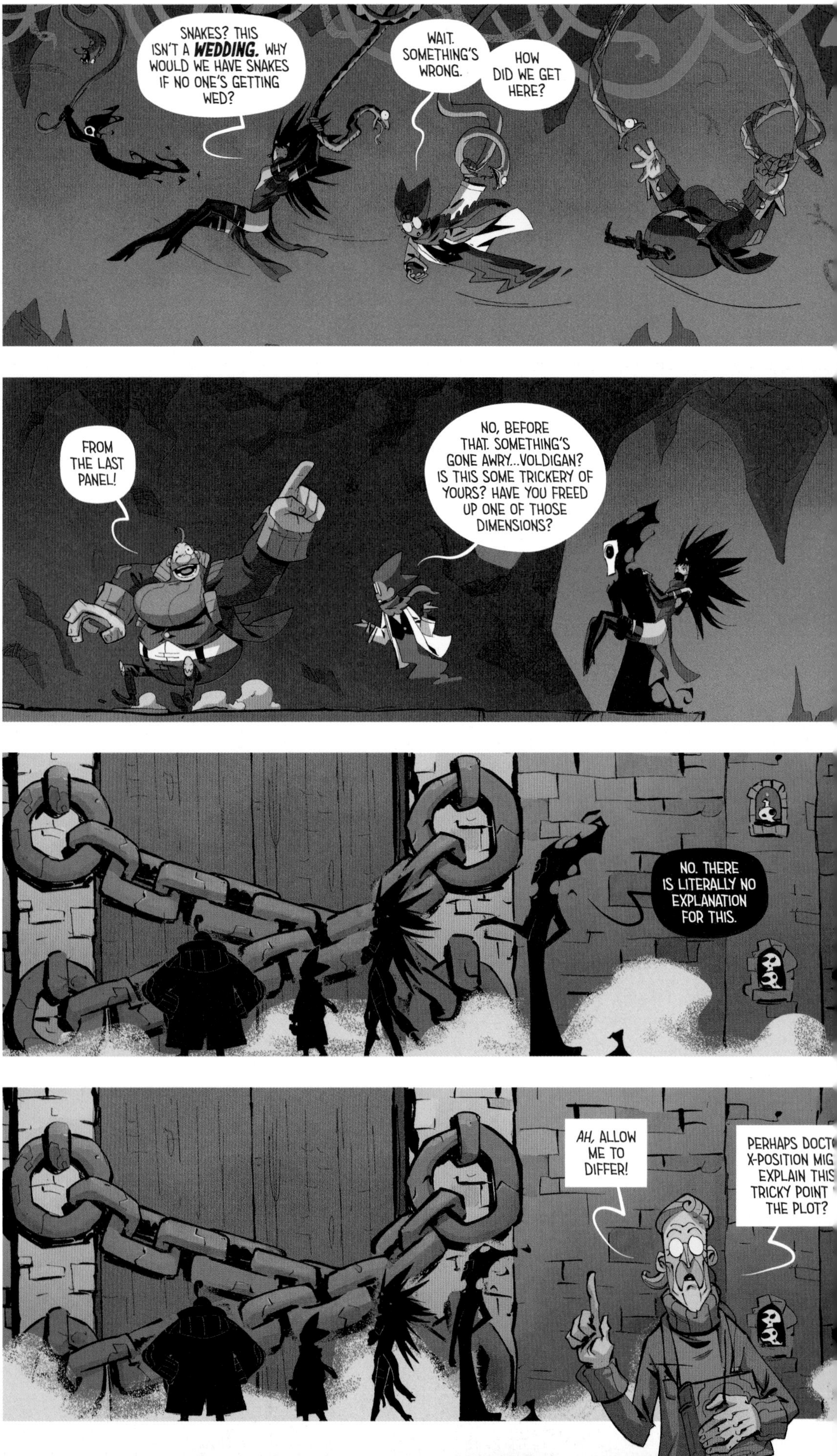
SNAKES? THIS ISN'T A **WEDDING.** WHY WOULD WE HAVE SNAKES IF NO ONE'S GETTING WED?
WAIT. SOMETHING'S WRONG.
HOW DID WE GET HERE?
FROM THE LAST PANEL!
NO, BEFORE THAT. SOMETHING'S GONE AWRY...VOLDIGAN? IS THIS SOME TRICKERY OF YOURS? HAVE YOU FREED UP ONE OF THOSE DIMENSIONS?
NO. THERE IS LITERALLY NO EXPLANATION FOR THIS.
AH, ALLOW ME TO DIFFER!
PERHAPS DOCTO X-POSITION MIG EXPLAIN THIS TRICKY POINT THE PLOT?

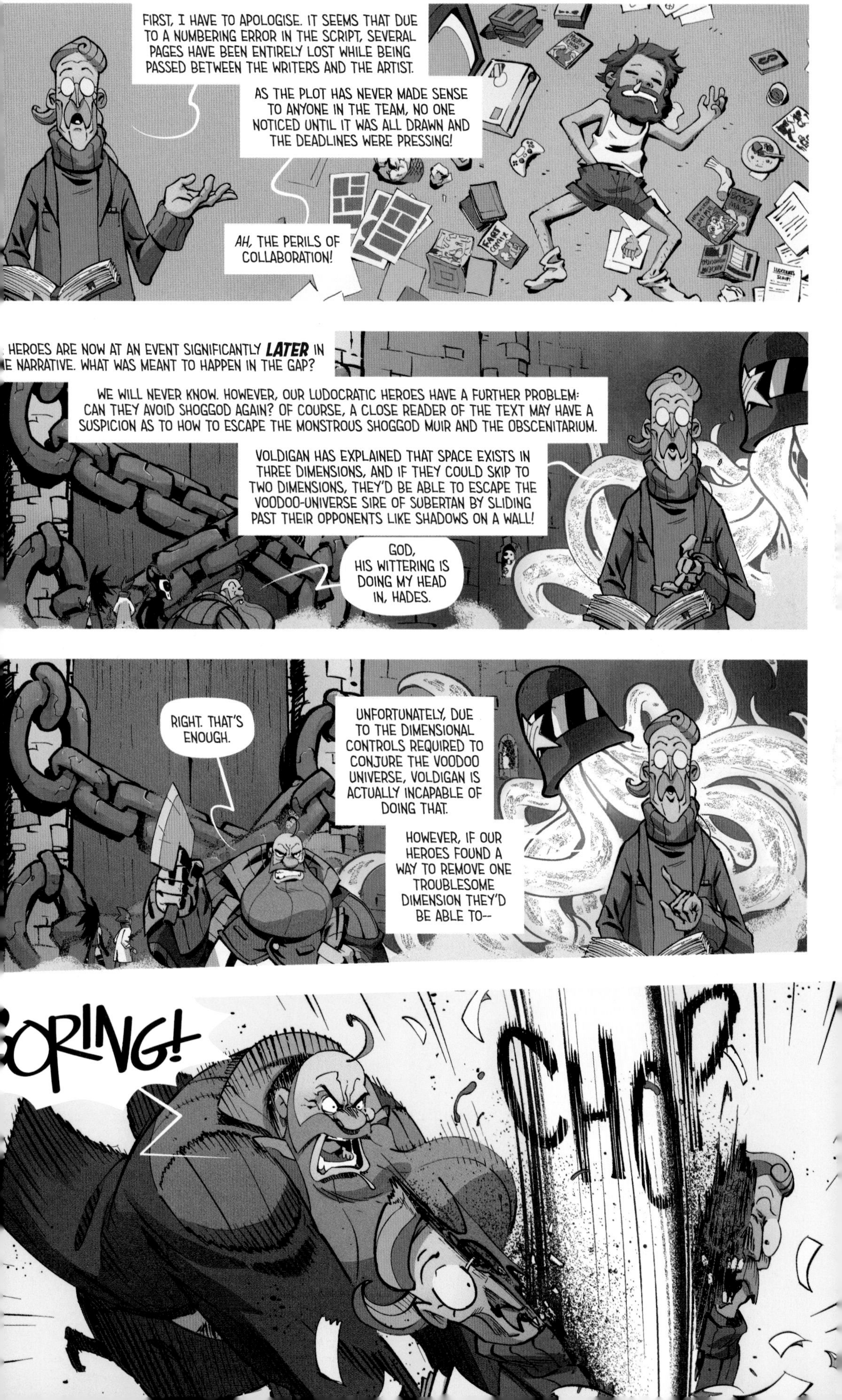

FIRST, I HAVE TO APOLOGISE. IT SEEMS THAT DUE TO A NUMBERING ERROR IN THE SCRIPT, SEVERAL PAGES HAVE BEEN ENTIRELY LOST WHILE BEING PASSED BETWEEN THE WRITERS AND THE ARTIST.
AS THE PLOT HAS NEVER MADE SENSE TO ANYONE IN THE TEAM, NO ONE NOTICED UNTIL IT WAS ALL DRAWN AND THE DEADLINES WERE PRESSING!
AH, THE PERILS OF COLLABORATION!
HEROES ARE NOW AT AN EVENT SIGNIFICANTLY ***LATER*** IN
E NARRATIVE. WHAT WAS MEANT TO HAPPEN IN THE GAP?
WE WILL NEVER KNOW. HOWEVER, OUR LUDOCRATIC HEROES HAVE A FURTHER PROBLEM: CAN THEY AVOID SHOGGOD AGAIN? OF COURSE, A CLOSE READER OF THE TEXT MAY HAVE A SUSPICION AS TO HOW TO ESCAPE THE MONSTROUS SHOGGOD MUIR AND THE OBSCENITARIUM.
VOLDIGAN HAS EXPLAINED THAT SPACE EXISTS IN THREE DIMENSIONS, AND IF THEY COULD SKIP TO TWO DIMENSIONS, THEY'D BE ABLE TO ESCAPE THE VOODOO-UNIVERSE SIRE OF SUBERTAN BY SLIDING PAST THEIR OPPONENTS LIKE SHADOWS ON A WALL!
GOD, HIS WITTERING IS DOING MY HEAD IN, HADES.
RIGHT. THAT'S ENOUGH.
UNFORTUNATELY, DUE TO THE DIMENSIONAL CONTROLS REQUIRED TO CONJURE THE VOODOO UNIVERSE, VOLDIGAN IS ACTUALLY INCAPABLE OF DOING THAT.
HOWEVER, IF OUR HEROES FOUND A WAY TO REMOVE ONE TROUBLESOME DIMENSION THEY'D BE ABLE TO--
ORING!
CHOP

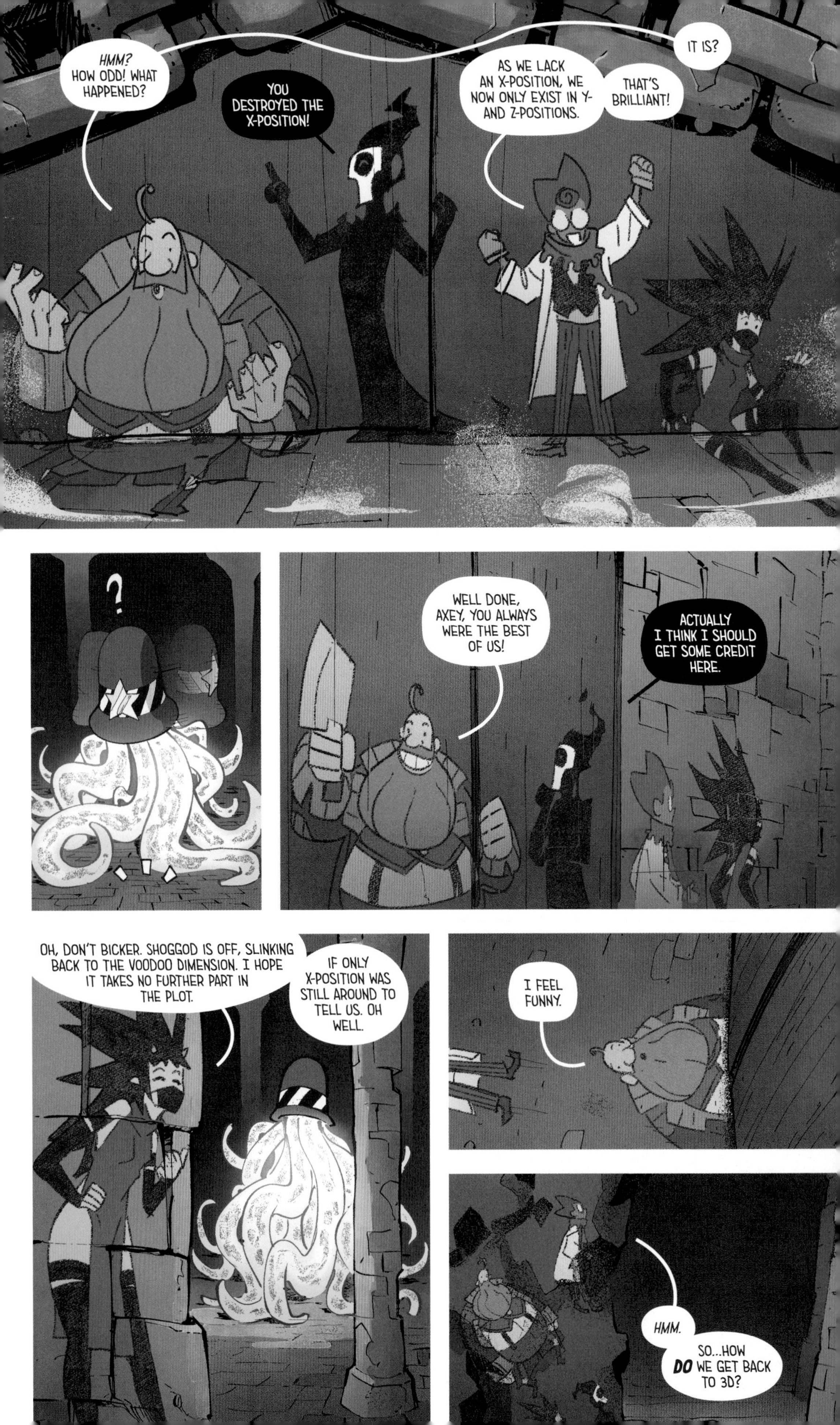

HMM? HOW ODD! WHAT HAPPENED?
YOU DESTROYED THE X-POSITION!
AS WE LACK AN X-POSITION, WE NOW ONLY EXIST IN Y- AND Z-POSITIONS.
THAT'S BRILLIANT!
IT IS?
?
WELL DONE, AXEY, YOU ALWAYS WERE THE BEST OF US!
ACTUALLY I THINK I SHOULD GET SOME CREDIT HERE.
OH, DON'T BICKER. SHOGGOD IS OFF, SLINKING BACK TO THE VOODOO DIMENSION. I HOPE IT TAKES NO FURTHER PART IN THE PLOT.
IF ONLY X-POSITION WAS STILL AROUND TO TELL US. OH WELL.
I FEEL FUNNY.
HMM.
SO...HOW **DO** WE GET BACK TO 3D?

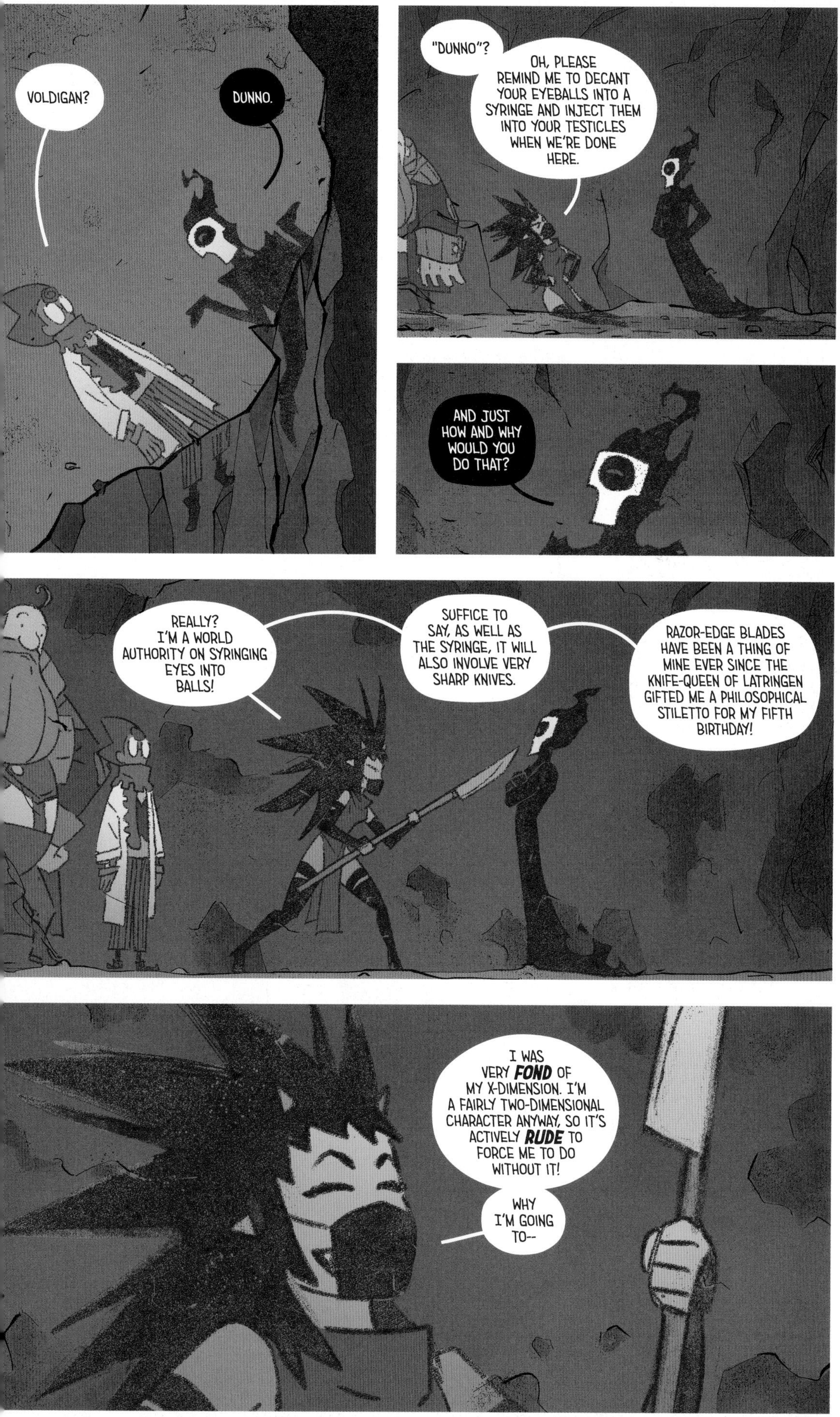
VOLDIGAN?
DUNNO.
"DUNNO"?
OH, PLEASE REMIND ME TO DECANT YOUR EYEBALLS INTO A SYRINGE AND INJECT THEM INTO YOUR TESTICLES WHEN WE'RE DONE HERE.
AND JUST HOW AND WHY WOULD YOU DO THAT?
REALLY? I'M A WORLD AUTHORITY ON SYRINGING EYES INTO BALLS!
SUFFICE TO SAY, AS WELL AS THE SYRINGE, IT WILL ALSO INVOLVE VERY SHARP KNIVES.
RAZOR-EDGE BLADES HAVE BEEN A THING OF MINE EVER SINCE THE KNIFE-QUEEN OF LATRINGEN GIFTED ME A PHILOSOPHICAL STILETTO FOR MY FIFTH BIRTHDAY!
I WAS VERY **FOND** OF MY X-DIMENSION. I'M A FAIRLY TWO-DIMENSIONAL CHARACTER ANYWAY, SO IT'S ACTIVELY **RUDE** TO FORCE ME TO DO WITHOUT IT!
WHY I'M GOING TO--

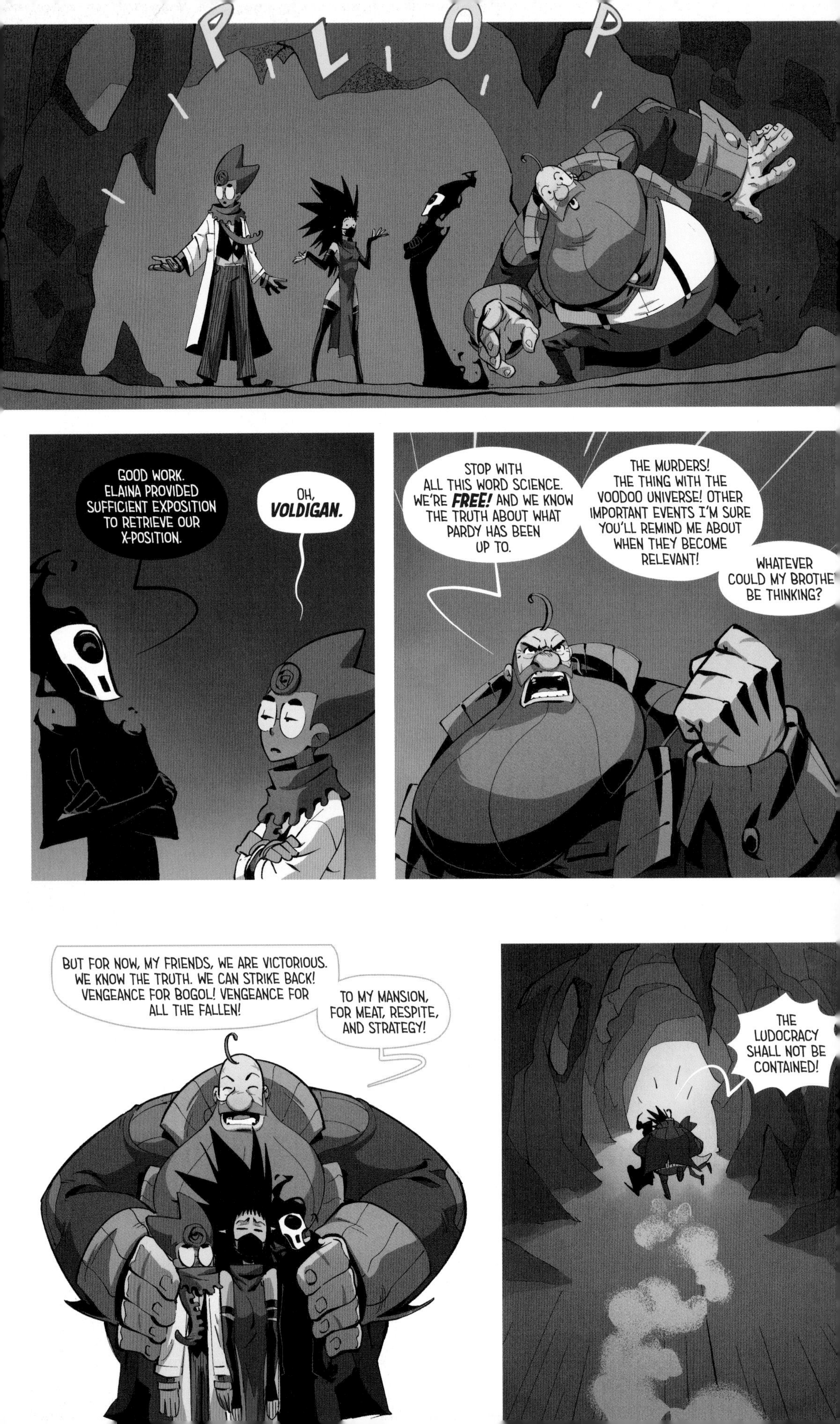
PLOP
GOOD WORK. ELAINA PROVIDED SUFFICIENT EXPOSITION TO RETRIEVE OUR X-POSITION.
OH, VOLDIGAN.
STOP WITH ALL THIS WORD SCIENCE. WE'RE FREE! AND WE KNOW THE TRUTH ABOUT WHAT PARDY HAS BEEN UP TO.
THE MURDERS! THE THING WITH THE VOODOO UNIVERSE! OTHER IMPORTANT EVENTS I'M SURE YOU'LL REMIND ME ABOUT WHEN THEY BECOME RELEVANT!
WHATEVER COULD MY BROTHE BE THINKING?
BUT FOR NOW, MY FRIENDS, WE ARE VICTORIOUS. WE KNOW THE TRUTH. WE CAN STRIKE BACK! VENGEANCE FOR BOGOL! VENGEANCE FOR ALL THE FALLEN!
TO MY MANSION, FOR MEAT, RESPITE, AND STRATEGY!
THE LUDOCRACY SHALL NOT BE CONTAINED!

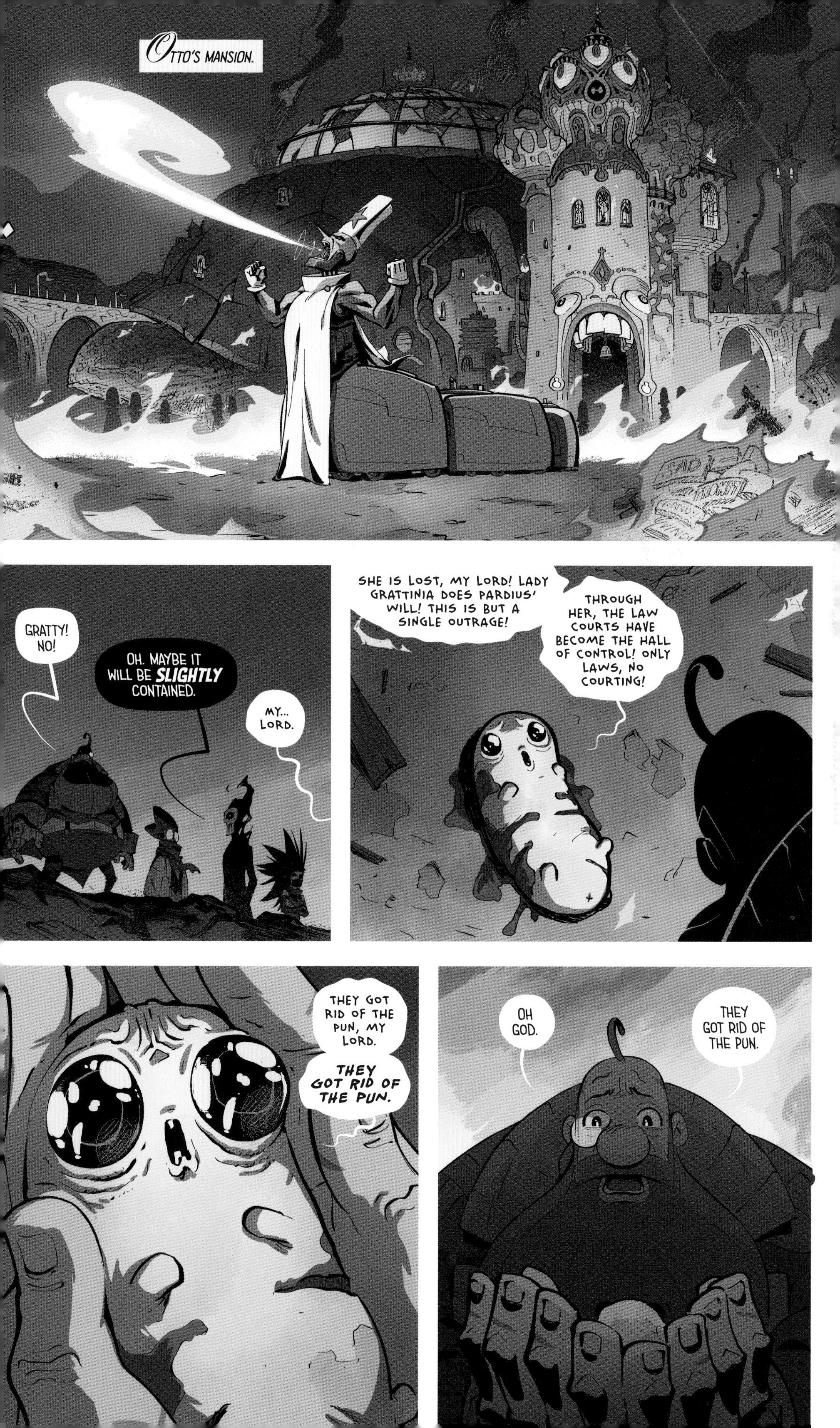

OTTO'S MANSION.
GRATTY! NO!
OH. MAYBE IT WILL BE SLIGHTLY CONTAINED.
MY... LORD.
SHE IS LOST, MY LORD! LADY GRATTINIA DOES PARDIUS' WILL! THIS IS BUT A SINGLE OUTRAGE!
THROUGH HER, THE LAW COURTS HAVE BECOME THE HALL OF CONTROL! ONLY LAWS, NO COURTING!
THEY GOT RID OF THE PUN, MY LORD.
THEY GOT RID OF THE PUN.
OH GOD.
THEY GOT RID OF THE PUN.

I CANNOT BELIEVE THIS! THE STEAM-JUDGES HAVE NEVER BEEN CONTROLLED BY **ANYONE.**

SHE HEADS A NEW JUDICIARY! UNDER HER, THIS LAW IS NO LONGER A THING TO PROTECT WONDER BUT TO CRUSH IT.

SHE CAME UPON US...WITH... FLAME... AND...

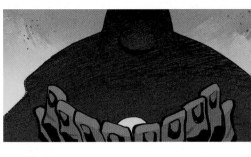

OH, GRATTY. WHATEVER TO DO?

WELL, AXEY WORKED BEFORE...

NO, OTTO. EVEN IF YOU DEFEAT HER, WHAT THEN? WOULD YOU STORM THE INVIOLATE INDESTRUCTIBLE HALL OF CONTROL ITSELF AND TEAR THE HYPER-POPE FROM HIS THRONE? WE NEED TO REGROUP AND FIND ALLIES.

BUT WHERE TO START?

HMMPF! I SUPPOSE I AM A BIT TIRED. WE REALLY NEED TO HAVE SOME DINNER BEFORE THERE'S ANY MORE VIOLENCE. I'M SO HUNGRY.

MY GUT SAYS WE HEAD INTO THE CITY! IT KNOWS A SWEET LITTLE BOUCHERIE ON LA RUE DE LA CHAIR.

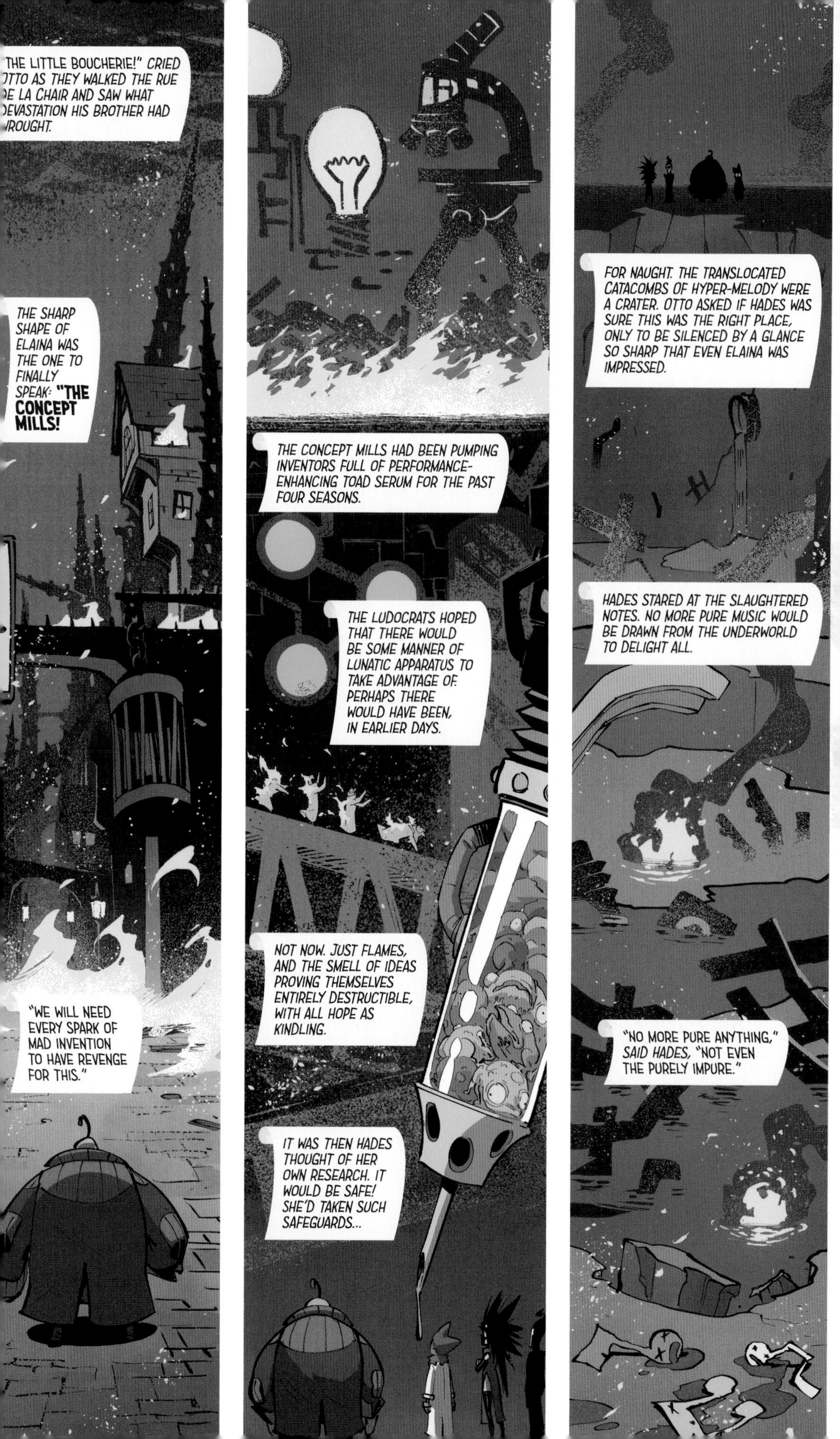
"THE LITTLE BOUCHERIE!" CRIED OTTO AS THEY WALKED THE RUE DE LA CHAIR AND SAW WHAT DEVASTATION HIS BROTHER HAD WROUGHT.
THE SHARP SHAPE OF ELAINA WAS THE ONE TO FINALLY SPEAK: "THE CONCEPT MILLS!
"WE WILL NEED EVERY SPARK OF MAD INVENTION TO HAVE REVENGE FOR THIS."
THE CONCEPT MILLS HAD BEEN PUMPING INVENTORS FULL OF PERFORMANCE-ENHANCING TOAD SERUM FOR THE PAST FOUR SEASONS.
THE LUDOCRATS HOPED THAT THERE WOULD BE SOME MANNER OF LUNATIC APPARATUS TO TAKE ADVANTAGE OF. PERHAPS THERE WOULD HAVE BEEN, IN EARLIER DAYS.
NOT NOW. JUST FLAMES, AND THE SMELL OF IDEAS PROVING THEMSELVES ENTIRELY DESTRUCTIBLE, WITH ALL HOPE AS KINDLING.
IT WAS THEN HADES THOUGHT OF HER OWN RESEARCH. IT WOULD BE SAFE! SHE'D TAKEN SUCH SAFEGUARDS...
FOR NAUGHT. THE TRANSLOCATED CATACOMBS OF HYPER-MELODY WERE A CRATER. OTTO ASKED IF HADES WAS SURE THIS WAS THE RIGHT PLACE, ONLY TO BE SILENCED BY A GLANCE SO SHARP THAT EVEN ELAINA WAS IMPRESSED.
HADES STARED AT THE SLAUGHTERED NOTES. NO MORE PURE MUSIC WOULD BE DRAWN FROM THE UNDERWORLD TO DELIGHT ALL.
"NO MORE PURE ANYTHING," SAID HADES, "NOT EVEN THE PURELY IMPURE."

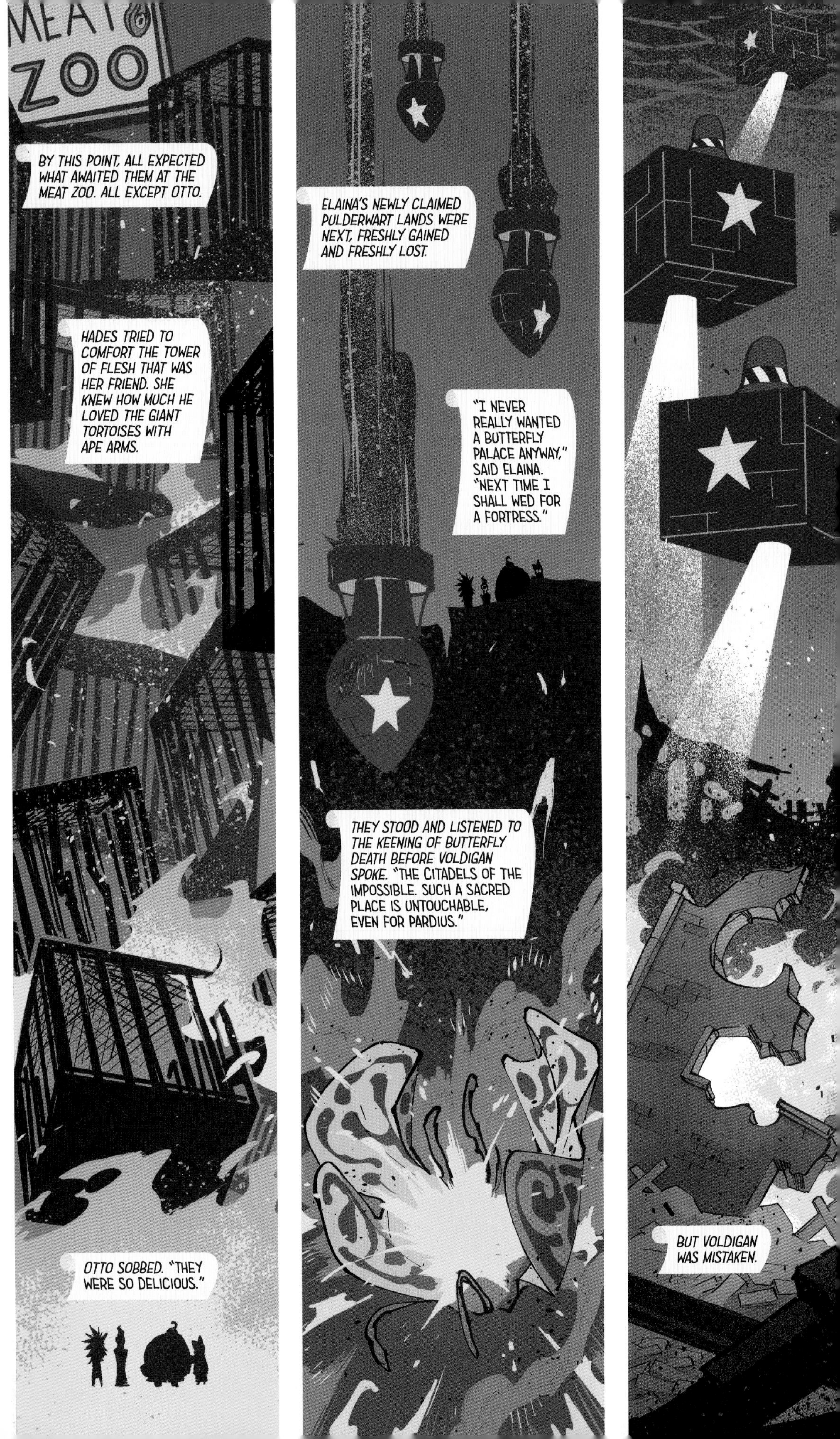
MEAT ZOO
BY THIS POINT, ALL EXPECTED WHAT AWAITED THEM AT THE MEAT ZOO. ALL EXCEPT OTTO.
HADES TRIED TO COMFORT THE TOWER OF FLESH THAT WAS HER FRIEND. SHE KNEW HOW MUCH HE LOVED THE GIANT TORTOISES WITH APE ARMS.
OTTO SOBBED. "THEY WERE SO DELICIOUS."
ELAINA'S NEWLY CLAIMED PULDERWART LANDS WERE NEXT, FRESHLY GAINED AND FRESHLY LOST.
"I NEVER REALLY WANTED A BUTTERFLY PALACE ANYWAY," SAID ELAINA. "NEXT TIME I SHALL WED FOR A FORTRESS."
THEY STOOD AND LISTENED TO THE KEENING OF BUTTERFLY DEATH BEFORE VOLDIGAN SPOKE. "THE CITADELS OF THE IMPOSSIBLE. SUCH A SACRED PLACE IS UNTOUCHABLE, EVEN FOR PARDIUS."
BUT VOLDIGAN WAS MISTAKEN.

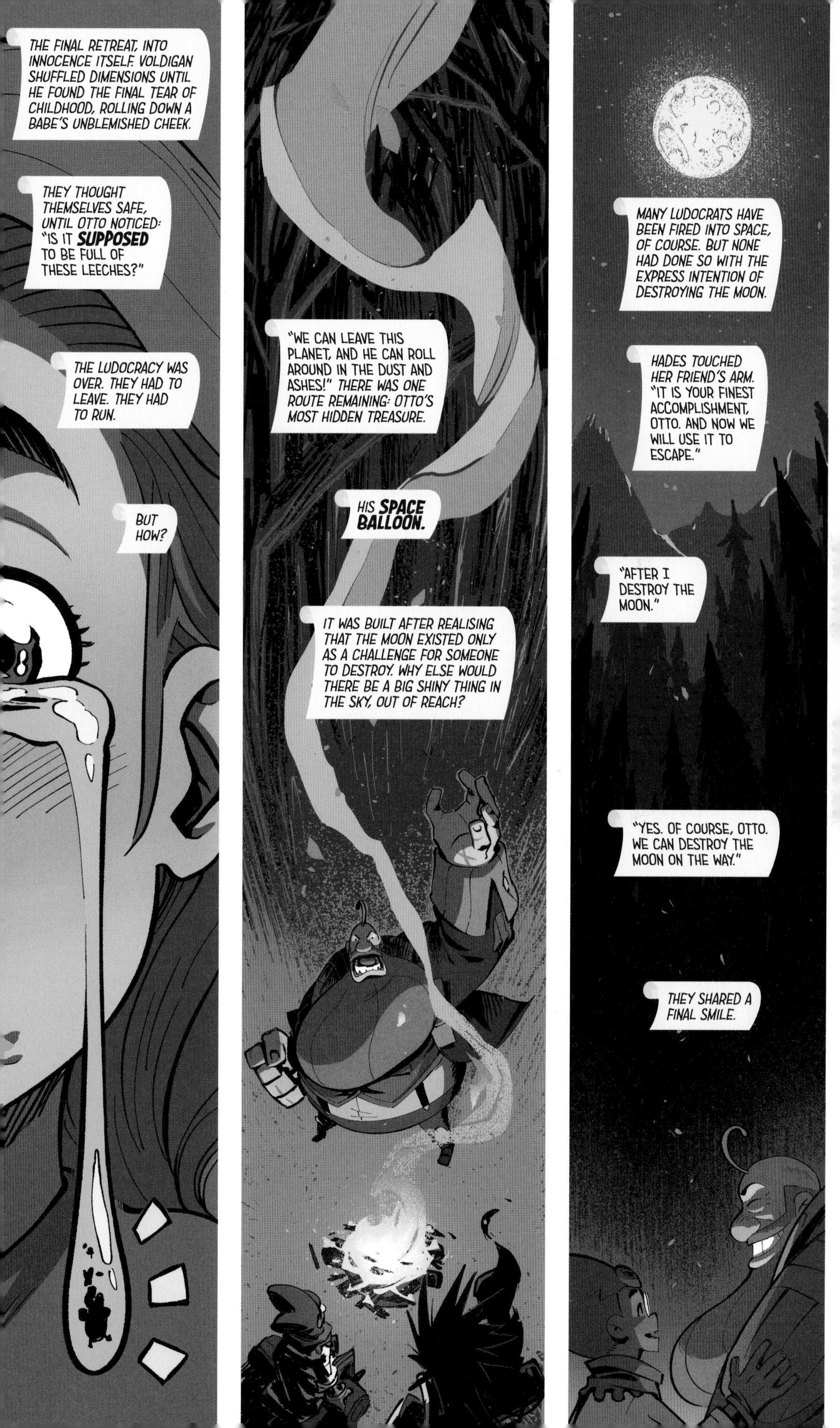
THE FINAL RETREAT, INTO INNOCENCE ITSELF. VOLDIGAN SHUFFLED DIMENSIONS UNTIL HE FOUND THE FINAL TEAR OF CHILDHOOD, ROLLING DOWN A BABE'S UNBLEMISHED CHEEK.
THEY THOUGHT THEMSELVES SAFE, UNTIL OTTO NOTICED: "IS IT **SUPPOSED** TO BE FULL OF THESE LEECHES?"
THE LUDOCRACY WAS OVER. THEY HAD TO LEAVE. THEY HAD TO RUN.
BUT HOW?
"WE CAN LEAVE THIS PLANET, AND HE CAN ROLL AROUND IN THE DUST AND ASHES!" THERE WAS ONE ROUTE REMAINING: OTTO'S MOST HIDDEN TREASURE.
HIS **SPACE BALLOON.**
IT WAS BUILT AFTER REALISING THAT THE MOON EXISTED ONLY AS A CHALLENGE FOR SOMEONE TO DESTROY. WHY ELSE WOULD THERE BE A BIG SHINY THING IN THE SKY, OUT OF REACH?
MANY LUDOCRATS HAVE BEEN FIRED INTO SPACE, OF COURSE. BUT NONE HAD DONE SO WITH THE EXPRESS INTENTION OF DESTROYING THE MOON.
HADES TOUCHED HER FRIEND'S ARM. "IT IS YOUR FINEST ACCOMPLISHMENT, OTTO. AND NOW WE WILL USE IT TO ESCAPE."
"AFTER I DESTROY THE MOON."
"YES. OF COURSE, OTTO. WE CAN DESTROY THE MOON ON THE WAY."
THEY SHARED A FINAL SMILE.

AND THEN ALL SMILES WERE GONE.
NOW I WILL NEVER GET TO DESTROY THE MOON!

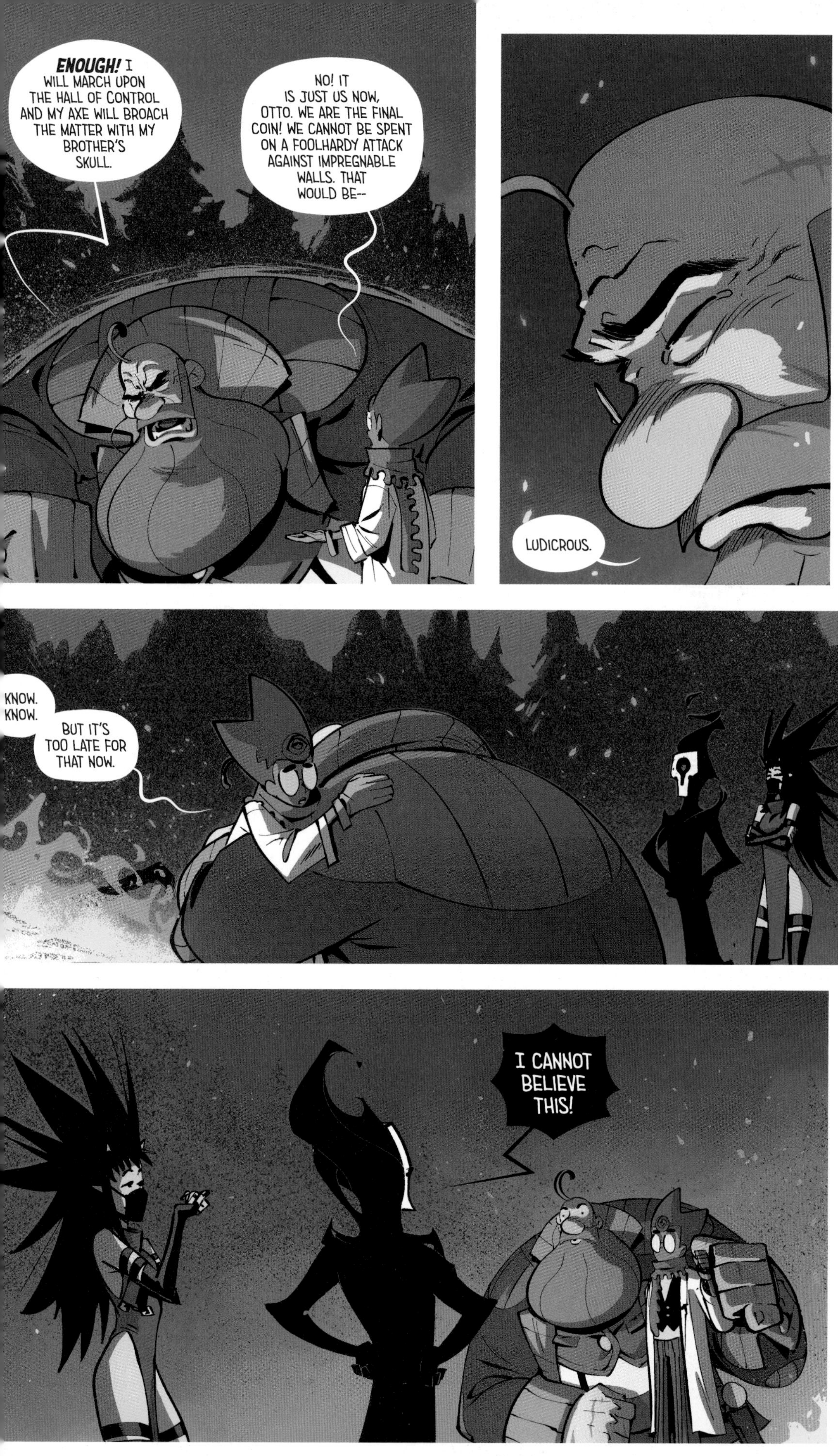
ENOUGH! I WILL MARCH UPON THE HALL OF CONTROL AND MY AXE WILL BROACH THE MATTER WITH MY BROTHER'S SKULL.
NO! IT IS JUST US NOW, OTTO. WE ARE THE FINAL COIN! WE CANNOT BE SPENT ON A FOOLHARDY ATTACK AGAINST IMPREGNABLE WALLS. THAT WOULD BE--
LUDICROUS.
KNOW. KNOW.
BUT IT'S TOO LATE FOR THAT NOW.
I CANNOT BELIEVE THIS!

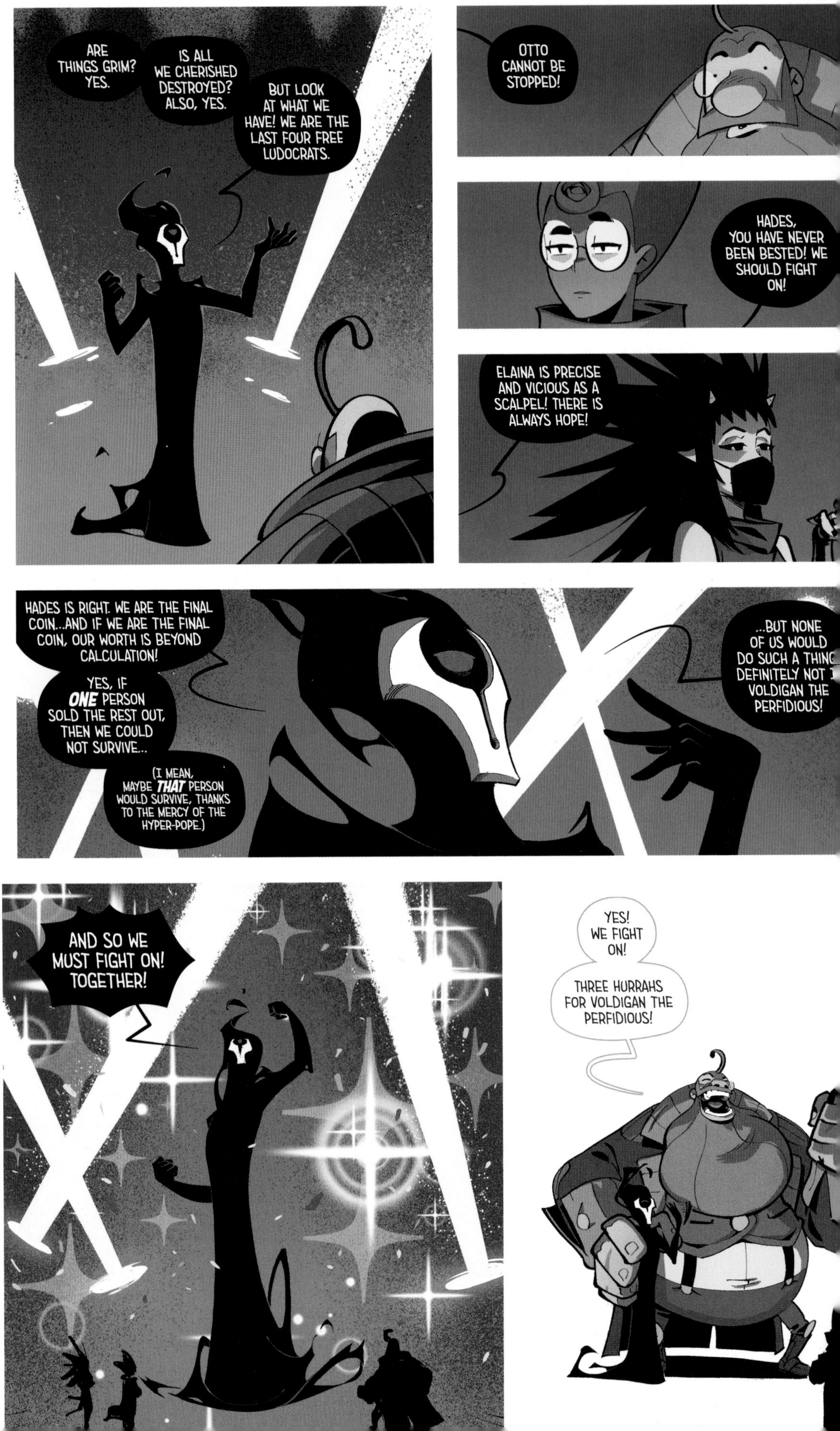
ARE THINGS GRIM? YES.
IS ALL WE CHERISHED DESTROYED? ALSO, YES.
BUT LOOK AT WHAT WE HAVE! WE ARE THE LAST FOUR FREE LUDOCRATS.
OTTO CANNOT BE STOPPED!
HADES, YOU HAVE NEVER BEEN BESTED! WE SHOULD FIGHT ON!
ELAINA IS PRECISE AND VICIOUS AS A SCALPEL! THERE IS ALWAYS HOPE!
HADES IS RIGHT. WE ARE THE FINAL COIN...AND IF WE ARE THE FINAL COIN, OUR WORTH IS BEYOND CALCULATION!
YES, IF ONE PERSON SOLD THE REST OUT, THEN WE COULD NOT SURVIVE...
(I MEAN, MAYBE THAT PERSON WOULD SURVIVE, THANKS TO THE MERCY OF THE HYPER-POPE.)
...BUT NONE OF US WOULD DO SUCH A THING DEFINITELY NOT VOLDIGAN THE PERFIDIOUS!
AND SO WE MUST FIGHT ON! TOGETHER!
YES! WE FIGHT ON!
THREE HURRAHS FOR VOLDIGAN THE PERFIDIOUS!

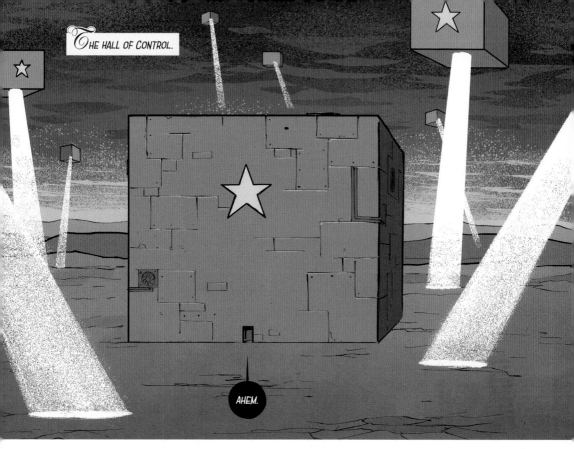

THE HALL OF CONTROL.

AHEM.

GOOD DAY TO YOU, I'D LIKE TO REPORT A CRIMINAL: ONE OTTO VON SUBERTAN AND PARTY. ENEMIES OF THE HYPER-POPE, MISCREANTS, THAT SORT OF THING.

I HAVE ALL THE PAPERWORK, LOCATIONS, ETC. I'M QUITE FAMILIAR WITH--

TODAY'S INFORMANT QUOTIENT HAS BEEN REACHED.

I BEG YOUR PARDON?

WHAT ARE YOU TALKING ABOUT? I'M THE TRAITOR!

NO, VOLDIGAN.

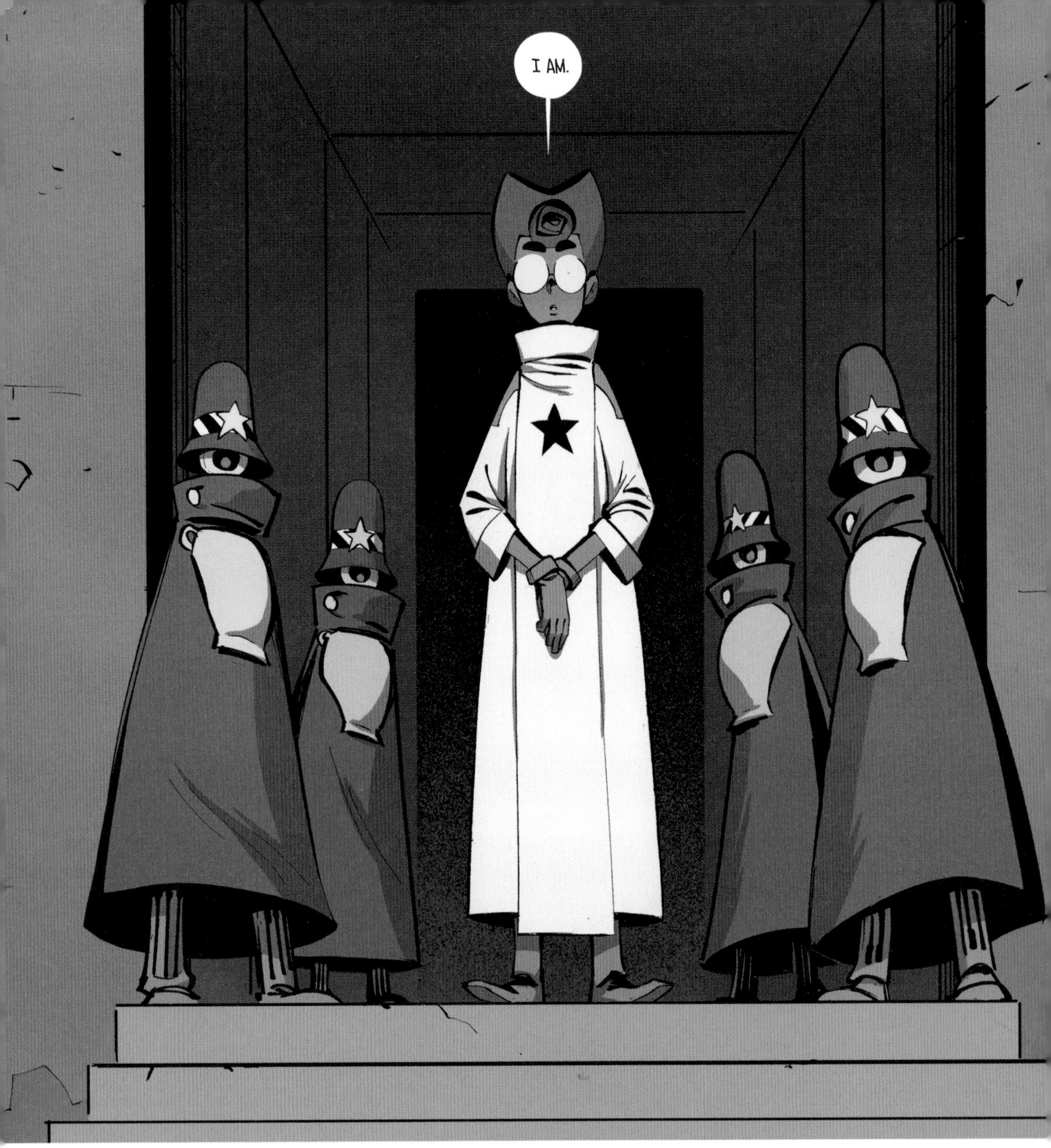
I AM.

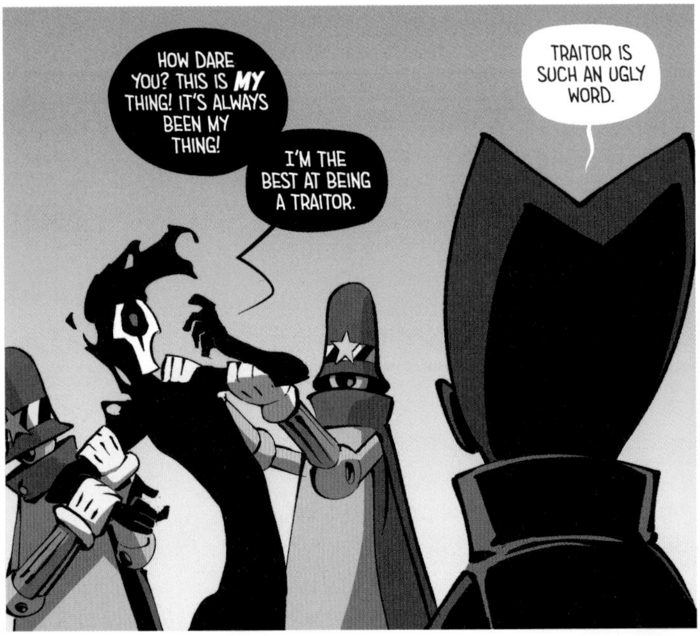
HOW DARE YOU? THIS IS ***MY*** THING! IT'S ALWAYS BEEN MY THING!
I'M THE BEST AT BEING A TRAITOR.
TRAITOR IS SUCH AN UGLY WORD.

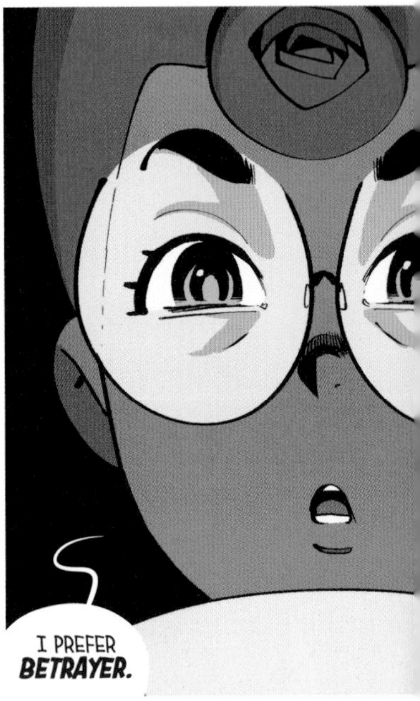
I PREFER ***BETRAYER.***

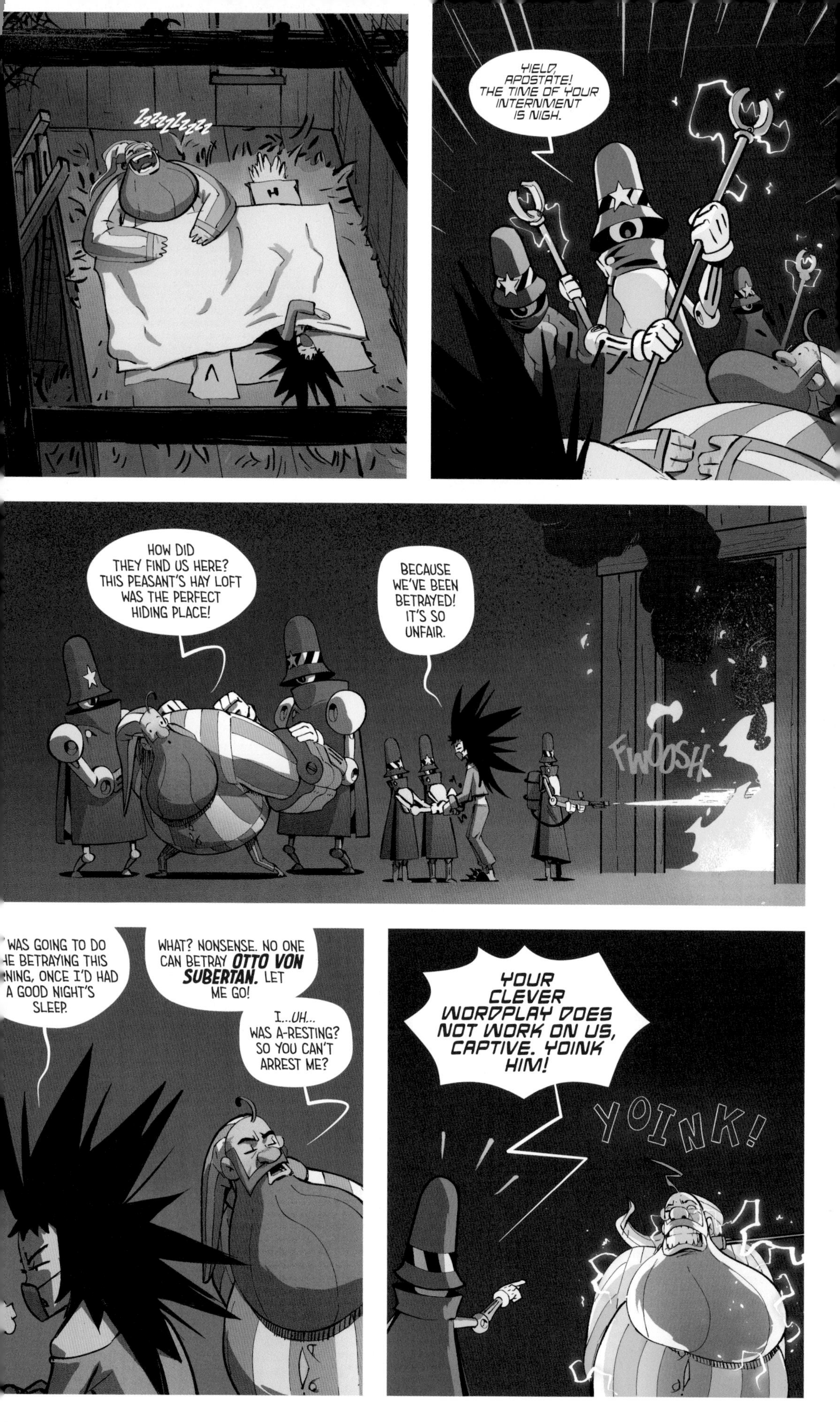
Zzzzzzzzz
YIELD, APOSTATE! THE TIME OF YOUR INTERNMENT IS NIGH.
HOW DID THEY FIND US HERE? THIS PEASANT'S HAY LOFT WAS THE PERFECT HIDING PLACE!
BECAUSE WE'VE BEEN BETRAYED! IT'S SO UNFAIR.
FWOOSH
WAS GOING TO DO
HE BETRAYING THIS
NING, ONCE I'D HAD
A GOOD NIGHT'S
SLEEP.
WHAT? NONSENSE. NO ONE CAN BETRAY **OTTO VON SUBERTAN.** LET ME GO!
I...UH... WAS A-RESTING? SO YOU CAN'T ARREST ME?
YOUR CLEVER WORDPLAY DOES NOT WORK ON US, CAPTIVE. YOINK HIM!
YOINK!

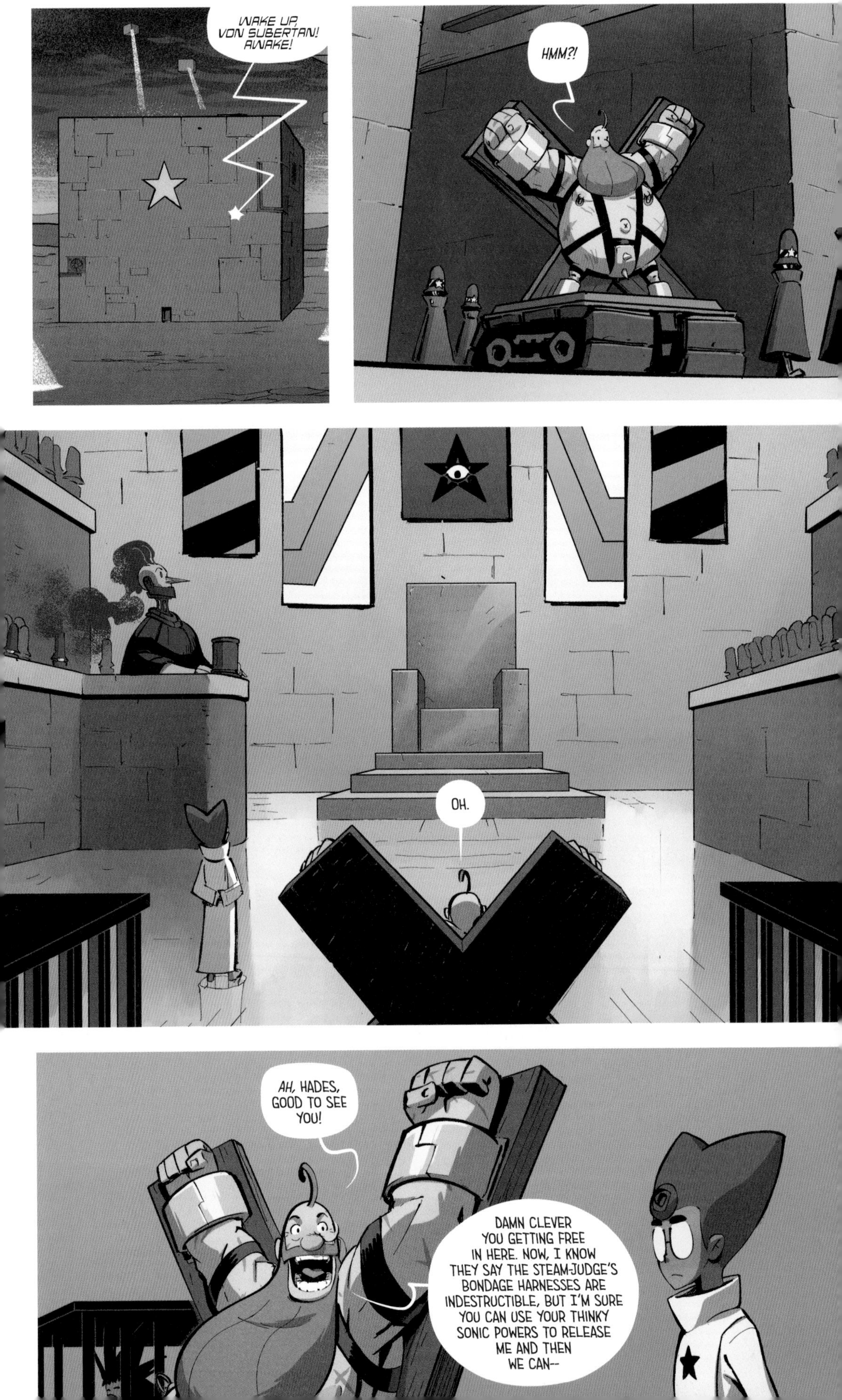
WAKE UP, VON SUBERTAN! AWAKE!
HMM?!
OH.
AH, HADES, GOOD TO SEE YOU!
DAMN CLEVER YOU GETTING FREE IN HERE. NOW, I KNOW THEY SAY THE STEAM-JUDGE'S BONDAGE HARNESSES ARE INDESTRUCTIBLE, BUT I'M SURE YOU CAN USE YOUR THINKY SONIC POWERS TO RELEASE ME AND THEN WE CAN--

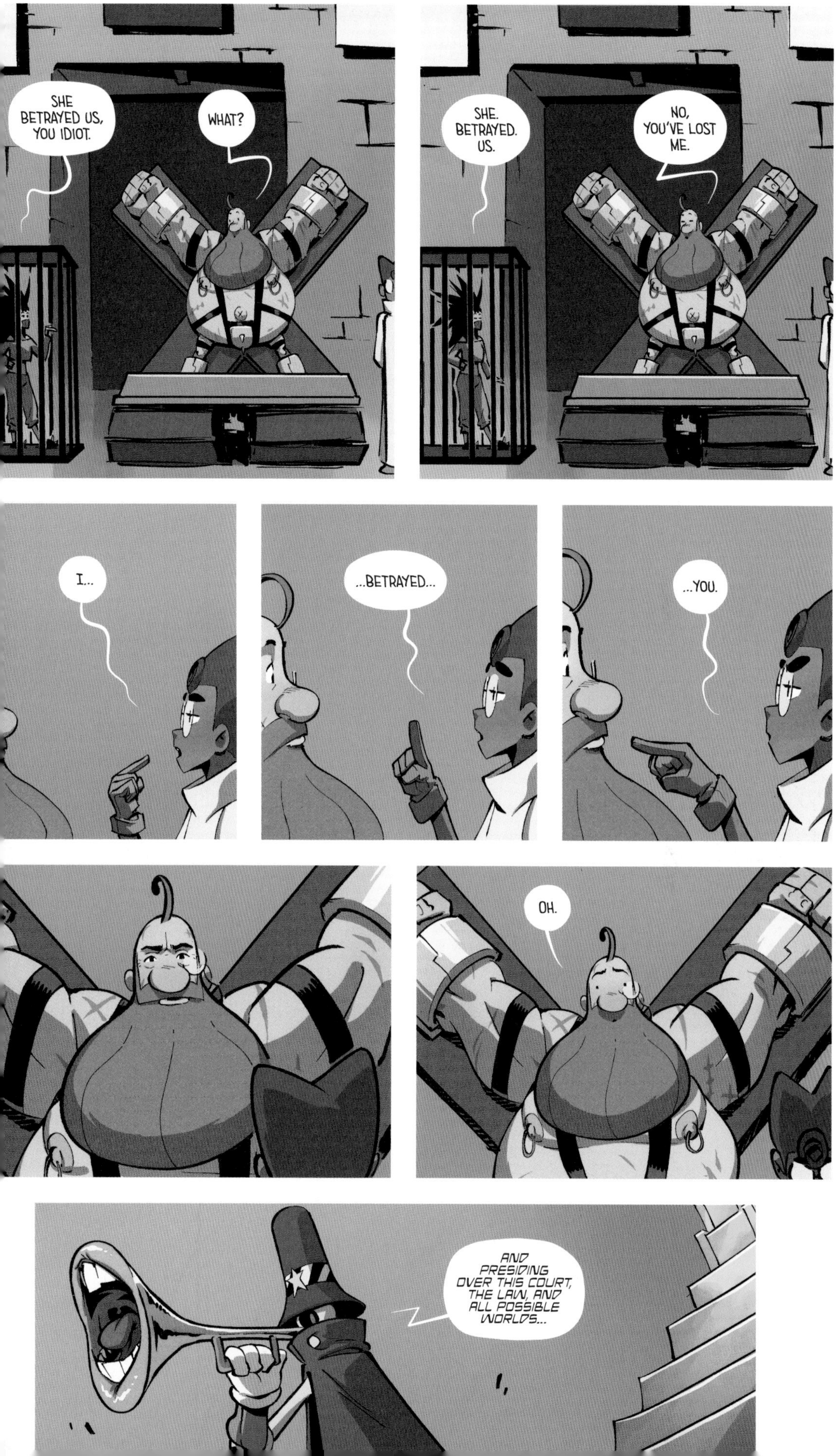
SHE BETRAYED US, YOU IDIOT.
WHAT?
SHE. BETRAYED. US.
NO, YOU'VE LOST ME.
I...
...BETRAYED...
...YOU.
OH.
AND PRESIDING OVER THIS COURT, THE LAW, AND ALL POSSIBLE WORLDS...

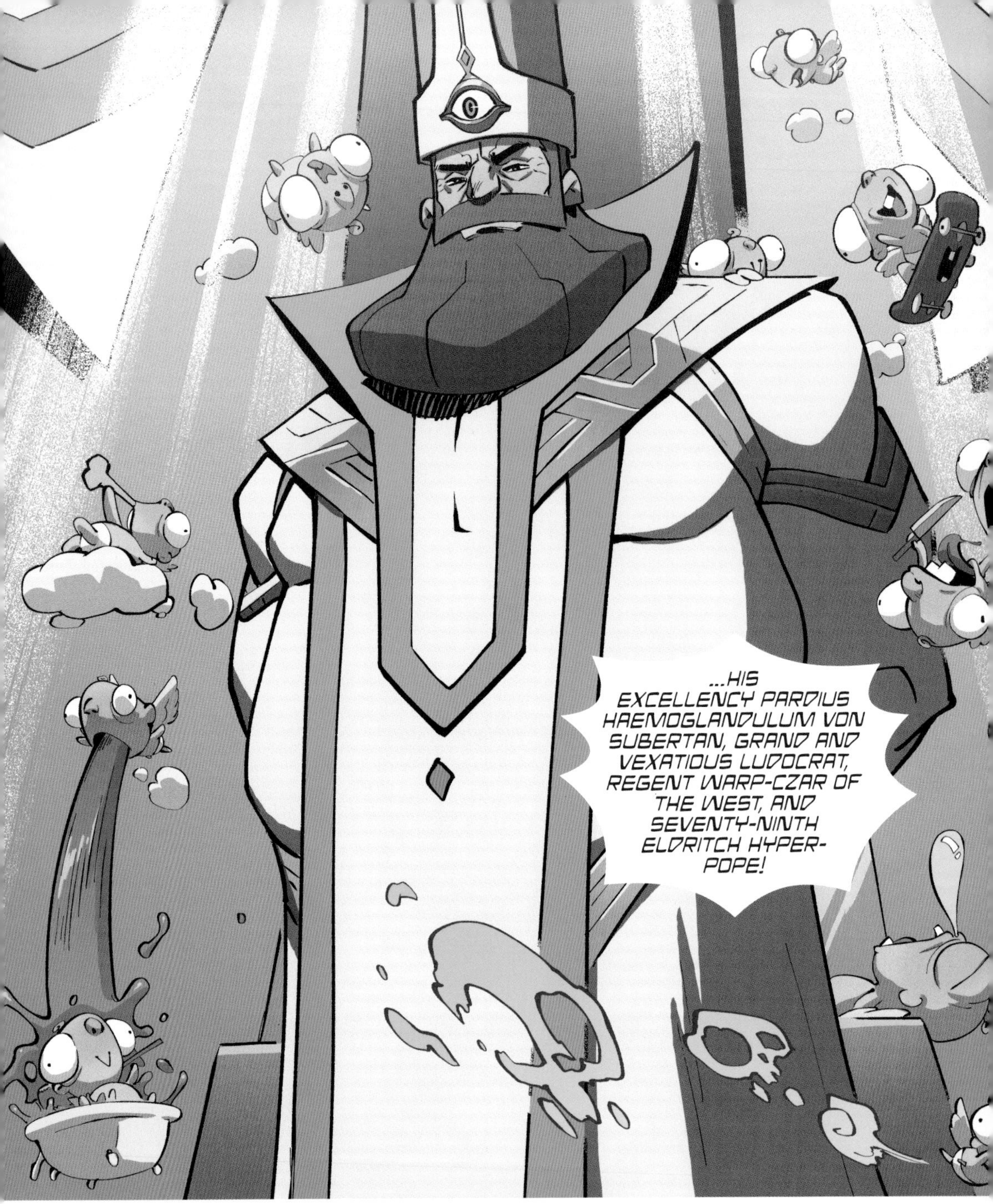
...HIS EXCELLENCY PARDIUS HAEMOGLANDULUM VON SUBERTAN, GRAND AND VEXATIOUS LUDOCRAT, REGENT WARP-CZAR OF THE WEST, AND SEVENTY-NINTH ELDRITCH HYPER-POPE!

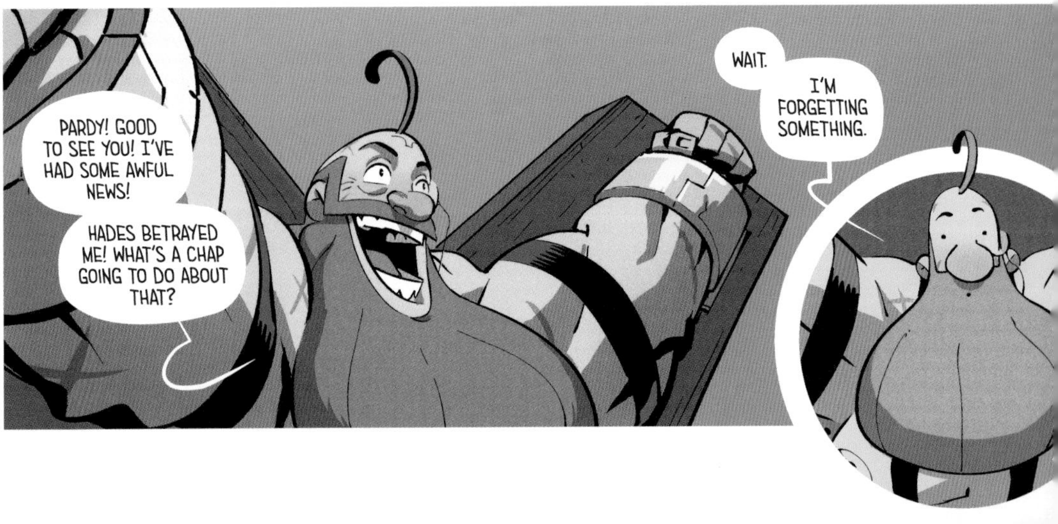
PARDY! GOOD TO SEE YOU! I'VE HAD SOME AWFUL NEWS!
HADES BETRAYED ME! WHAT'S A CHAP GOING TO DO ABOUT THAT?
WAIT.
I'M FORGETTING SOMETHING.

EXCERPTS from

The PERSONAL CYCLOPEDIA *of* LUDOCRACY,
by PARDIUS HAEMOGLANDULUM,
ELDRITCH HYPER-POPE and SUPREME HIGH LUDOCRAT

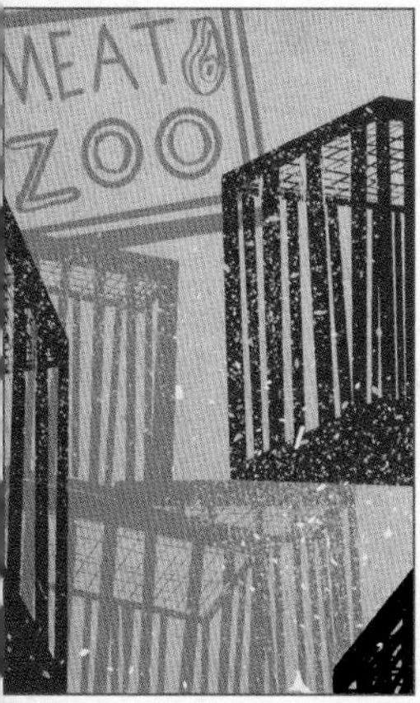
MEAT
ZOO

On the Meat Zoo

"...OF ALL THE LOSSES made necessary by my plan, it is my brother Otto's Meat Zoo which will doubtless be the most keenly felt, not least by me. Although I never told him how proud I was, I remember with glee the day he opened the zoo and walked me through the place, showing me tanks filled with giant alligators and humanoid crabs of various distinction. I can say without hesitation that it was one of the happiest of my life. For what makes any of us happier than seeing a friend or relative anticipating exotic meat? For me there was nothing else in life. And I know that for Otto there were many accomplishments, and this one stood apart, and even the Space Balloon was really a passing fancy next to his dedication to the sprawling zoo complex..." •

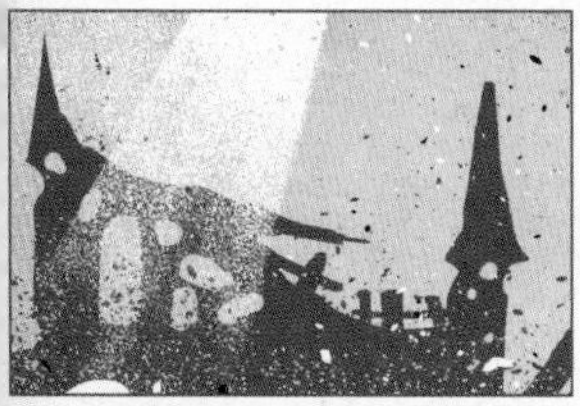

On the Citadel of the Impossible

"...AND THE MOST PERSISTENT argument has always been that if we do something that is impossible, then does it have to be reclassified as possible, therefore rendering the feat uninteresting? The Citadel of the Impossible became the heart of that discussion, as we built a place that would not only be impossible, but also act as a sort of impossibility research station, where those who demanded more than the possible could spend time with themselves, and butt against the limits of reality. I wish I could say it was a happy place, but in truth those who strive to change reality often have to get up really quite early, and often drink far too much coffee." •

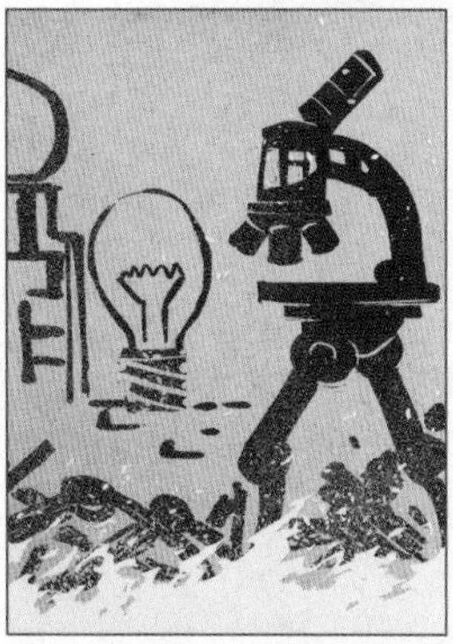

On the Concept Mills

"...AFTER CENTURIES of Ludocracy it became apparent that the real challenge for the future of our civilisation was the limit of human imagination. So then, we considered, what about inhuman imagination? The imagination of geology and light switches had long been ignored, and so it was that the Concept Mills were constructed: ideas would be extracted from every conceivable source, and then their raw idea stuff could be ground up together to make bread. Not literal bread, of course, but concept bread. Delicious concept bread. Mmm, an aroma unlike any other. It was this medium in which the future was cooked, and without this vital resource I fear the Ludocracy would have fallen to boredom and normalisers during past decades of stride and instability..." •

* * * * *

IMPORTANT GLOSSARY of TERMS

{ LUDOCRATIC }

JARGON and TECHNICAL TERMS

AUGVERT (*verb*) to improve something by forcibly turning it inside out.

ASTONISCELERATOR (*long noun*) any accelerator which can be used to vastly increase the rate of something unexpected, e.g. digestion.

AUTOMECHAMELIORATION (*even longer noun*) the process of making an object or situation improve by pushing it through a machine of your own invention.

COMPUTER (*noun*) a horrible device that should only be used in the most desperate circumstances, where numbers absolutely must be turned into something useful.

CONOSCULARISATION (*noun*) the process of attempting to understand something by putting it directly into your mouth.

ENCILIATE (*verb*) to cover any inanimate object in a layer of tiny moving hairs, giving it a rudimentary ability to locomote.

EPIDECONTEXTUALIZE (*verb*) to aggressively remove context from any given object or situation, usually via bomb or beam device.

FLAMINGATE (*verb*) to cover any inanimate object in a layer of thrashing flamingo legs, giving it a rudimentary ability to locomote.

GLEEKINETISTICIAN (*noun*) any Ludocrat whose work generally includes smashing things into each other at high speed and then cheerfully publishing the results in a large red book.

GLORTAL (*adjective*) the condition of speech being bestowed upon something which has no sentience, i.e. "glortal pasta" being food that screams insensible epithets as it is being consumed.

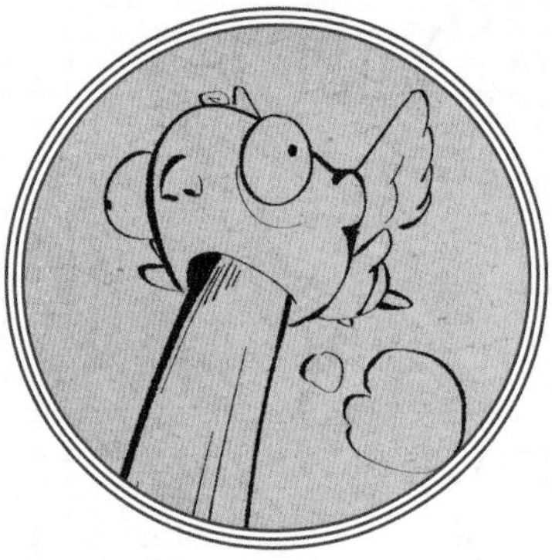

FIG. I.I

Do try to keep your GLORTAL *food down. Talking vomit is quite rude.*

* * *

HYPERABROGATE (*verb*) to remove fundamental qualities from an object while leaving it otherwise unchanged, e.g. the removal of wetness from water, or of elephantness from an elephant. (**WARNING**: Do not try to look upon the hyperabrogated elephant.)

IMPRECATION (*noun*) any condition which alters the metaphysical destiny of a being in a negative way, colloquially called a "curse".

LUDOCRATE (*verb*) to put something hideous or surprising inside a delightful container. (A widespread pastime among all classes of Ludocrat.)

IMPORTANT GLOSSARY of TERMS

{ LUDOCRATIC }

JARGON and TECHNICAL TERMS

MOUTHPIT (*noun*) a common addition to Ludocratic dwellings: a huge, semi-sentient mouth into which unwelcome visitors are expected to dive headfirst.

YAM. 2.0
The MOUTHPIT *was conceived during the baroque era of interior orifice design.*

* * *

PARAZOOAMPLIFICATE (*verb*) of curses: to massively exaggerate the animalistic qualities of any given imprecation, e.g. one cursed to walk like a crab would also bury themselves in sand at any opportunity.

PLATCISION (*noun*) any decision made by fighting with axes on a rotating platform above a spike pit.

QUKE'S LAW (*noun, probably?*) a law attributed to the famed saboteur Bort Quke, the law states that "as a Ludocratic discussion grows longer, the probability of a plan to destroy the moon as part of an unrelated activity approaches 1".

UZPRUDKOMVENGAR (*adjective*) a Germanish term widely adopted because it sounds excellent to say while nodding sagely, when actually you've got nothing else to add.

NUT. 3.14
When all is said and done,
UZPRUDKOMVENGAR, *Comrades!*

* * *

SPLENDID VORTEX (*adjectivised noun*) any vortex which is splendid.

ZRASHT (*verb*) to imbue inanimate objects with a sense of ego, but in a bad way, so that they can be proud of themselves when you trip over them, stub your toe, or otherwise suffer from their dreadful spitefulness. Awful things.

IMPORTANT GLOSSARY of TERMS
{ LUDOCRATIC }

LUDOCRATIC SAYINGS and FIGURES of SPEECH

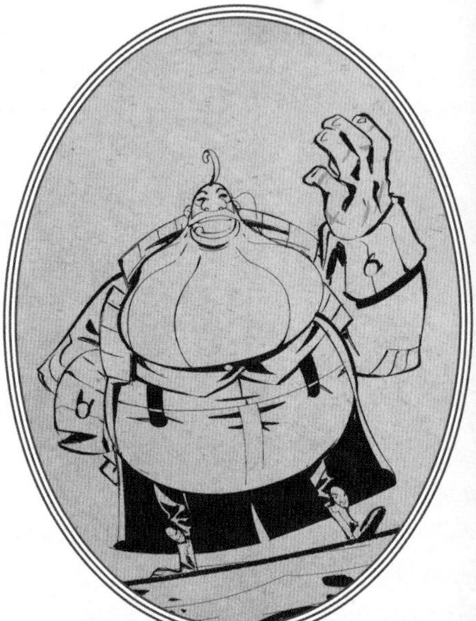

"That's Rotwater!"

☞ A COMMON PHRASE *that is often misunderstood to mean lies or falsehoods, but in fact celebrates the imagination-boosting effects of a traditional Ludocratic tonic, Percy's Alembic Rotwater. It actually means: "That's a good idea, but you have come to it via artificial means and it is therefore of less value than an idea you originated without narcotic assistance."*

"You can only eat so many monkeys' hands."

☞ THIS LITERALLY UNTRUE *saying essentially means "you can have too much of a good thing", but has fallen out of use since it was widely recognised as being both rude and boring.*

"Struggling to put grandfather in the logflume."

☞ A EUPHEMISM.

"What's in the Old Factory?"

☞ THE ORIGIN *of this muttering is now lost, but it's often uttered (quietly) by trepidatious Ludocrats embarking on an adventure that might prove fatal. It is perhaps connected to the traditional children's nursery rhyme "We Never Should Have Gone into the Old Factory (For Johnny Now Has No Eyes Left)."*

"Better the axe than the squirming."

☞ FOR A LUDOCRAT *there is no truer saying than this, for it is always better to take physical risks in your attempt to make life more ludicrous, than to end up being exposed to something that makes your mind fall prey to The Squirming.*

"Two in the hand is worth five in the concept abominator."

☞ WHO HAS NOT *put something precious in the concept abominator and then had to leave it there while life passes them by? Seize the day, Ludocrats!*

"Don't push a moth up your nose again."

☞ GOOD, PRACTICAL ADVICE.

"In the land of the boring, the one-eyed man is at least able to start an interesting conversation, you know, about the eye thing."

☞ A TRUISM THAT *Ludocrats are taught from birth: the moral of the saying is that having one eye can be cool. But some have interpreted it to mean that being different is a great conversation starter, as well as a fundamental philosophy for approaching life.*

"Do stare into the abyss."

☞ I MEAN, WHY NOT? *Do the thing. It's probably not as ludicrous as you think it is, and that's disappointing for everyone.*

"Actions speak louder than words."

☞ ALTHOUGH THAT'S ONLY TRUE *if the action is shouting, or perhaps setting off the Talking Doom Behemoth of Blantivar, long may it remain silent.*

To send letters to LUDOCRATS
please attach your words
to the back of a friendly vole
and instruct them to head to
OTTO'S CASTLE, LUDOVERSE.

LETTERS *from* LUDOCRATS

NANOSANDWICHES

To the Office of the Hyper-Pope,

This is the final demand for payment for the construction of the Obscenitarium. We object to the idea that it was no small effort. In fact, it was considerable small effort - specifically by our nanobrickies who consumed 10^{57} nanosandwiches and a similar number of nanocups of tea (plus 20^{57} nanosugarcubes). If we do not receive satisfaction, we will have to take this to a higher power. That the Hyper-Pope is the higher power does make this difficult, but we'll work that out if we have to.

Yours in frustration,
Captain Breeze Block III,
the Imperial Construction Corps

Dear Captain Breeze Block,

Sorry for the delay, but the office of the Hyper-Pope has been involved in something of a military putsch, meaning that communication has been somewhat delayed. Thankfully, with our Iron Grip secure, business can resume. We informed our General Secretary of your complaint, and our General Secretary informed our Admiral Secretary, and our Admiral Secretary informed our Secretary Secretary, who is on the way to resolve events to your satisfaction, assuming that being reduced to a smear on the letter-face of their enormous war-typewriter will satisfy you. It will certainly satisfy us.

Yours faithfully,
The Office Of The Hyper-Pope

ORIFICES

Dear Bogol Theen,

I find myself in a Tizzy. If you don't know, a Tizzy is an enormous beast, covered with fibrous matter and four sets of googly eyes, and I am embedded in one of its orifices up to my elbow. I have no idea how to prepare this beast for banquet at the best of times, let alone in such a limited position. Have you any tips for an amateur gastronaut?

Yours,
Veronica Quadrahedron

Dearest Veronica,

We regret to inform you that Monsieur Theen was lost to us, just recently, in a terrible tentacular accident. However, we do have access to his notes, and he writes that a Tizzy "is a dish best served from the inside out", so it sounds like you're in a great position! If you'd like us to send over a complimentary incinerator crew please do fill in the form we've attached for your convenience.

Kindness,
Susie Lemonwhine,
Chief Mortologist,
Konnigsberg Deathlabs

HOTNODE

Ludocrew!

Yo, it's Larry Handgriber from the Hotnode News Beam! I'm a HUGE fan - over three hundred feet across! But don't let that concern you: the good news is that we want to feature you on our next transmission! And as you know, the Hotnode News Beam is transmitted DIRECTLY into the deepest feelings of every subscriber. They don't even know where it's coming from! There's nothing sinister about it, but you're not allowed to ask how we make our money.

Cool, cool.
Larry

Dear Lorry,

We'll certainly be interested in an interview! Here you are:

1. *Where do you get your ideas from?*
2. *Is there a movie deal? Can you talk about it?*
3. *Who would you cast in your movie about your sinister emotion transmission?*
4. *Is there a movie deal? Can you talk about it now?*
5. *What superhero comic would you like to write for the big two?*
6. *Are there any superheroes you would like to write for any other large numbers?*
7. *Movie deal?*
8. *Have you anything else you'd like to talk about?*
9. *Oh — a TV deal? Can you talk about it?*

Looking forward to your responses, Lorry.

Yours,
The Ludocrats

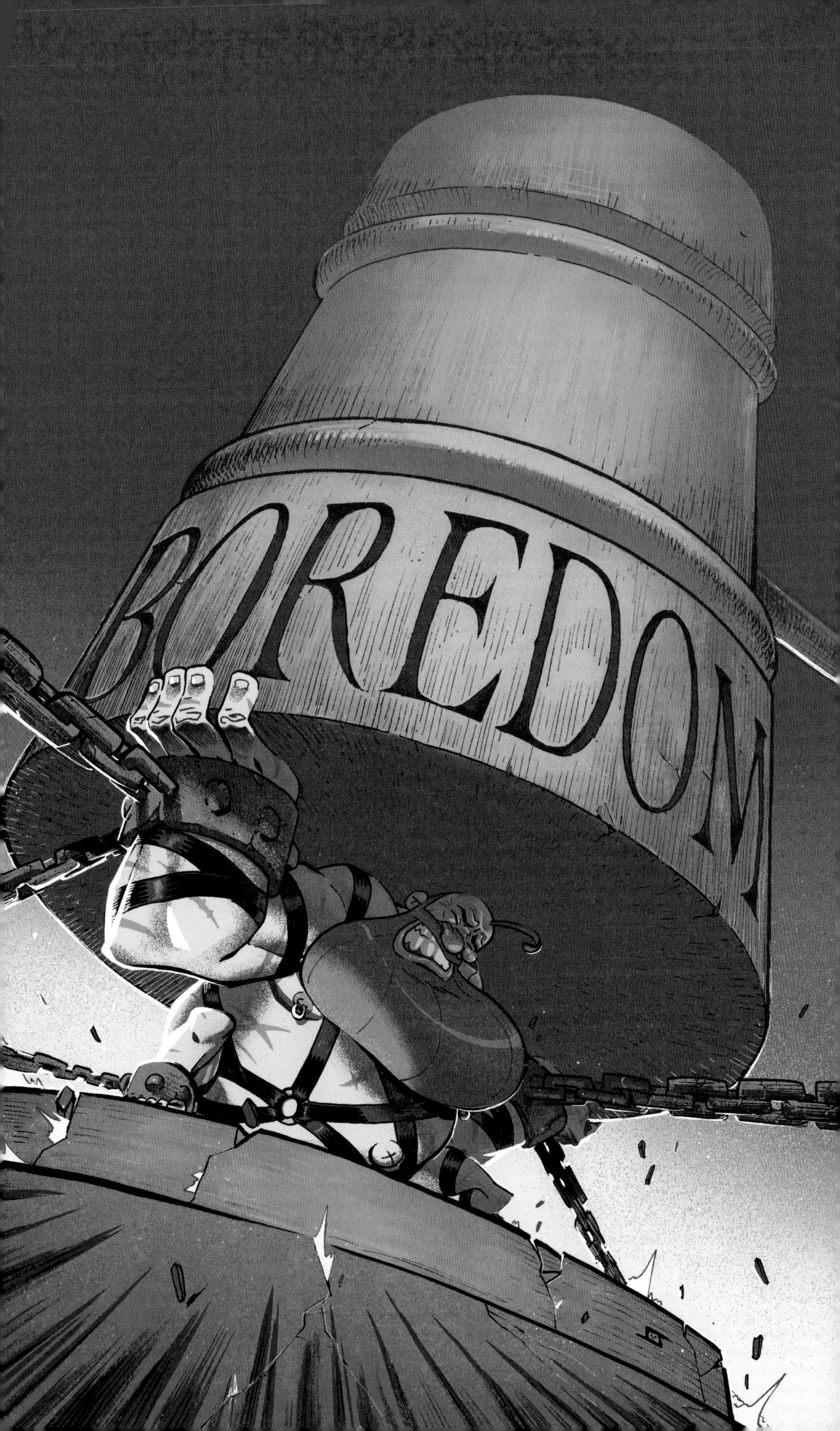
BOREDOM

N THE *previous* COMICS
a LARGE MAN *with an* AXE
was FRAMED *for a* CRIME
HE DIDN'T COMMIT.

HE DID NOT ESCAPE.

HE *is* NOT
the A–TEAM.

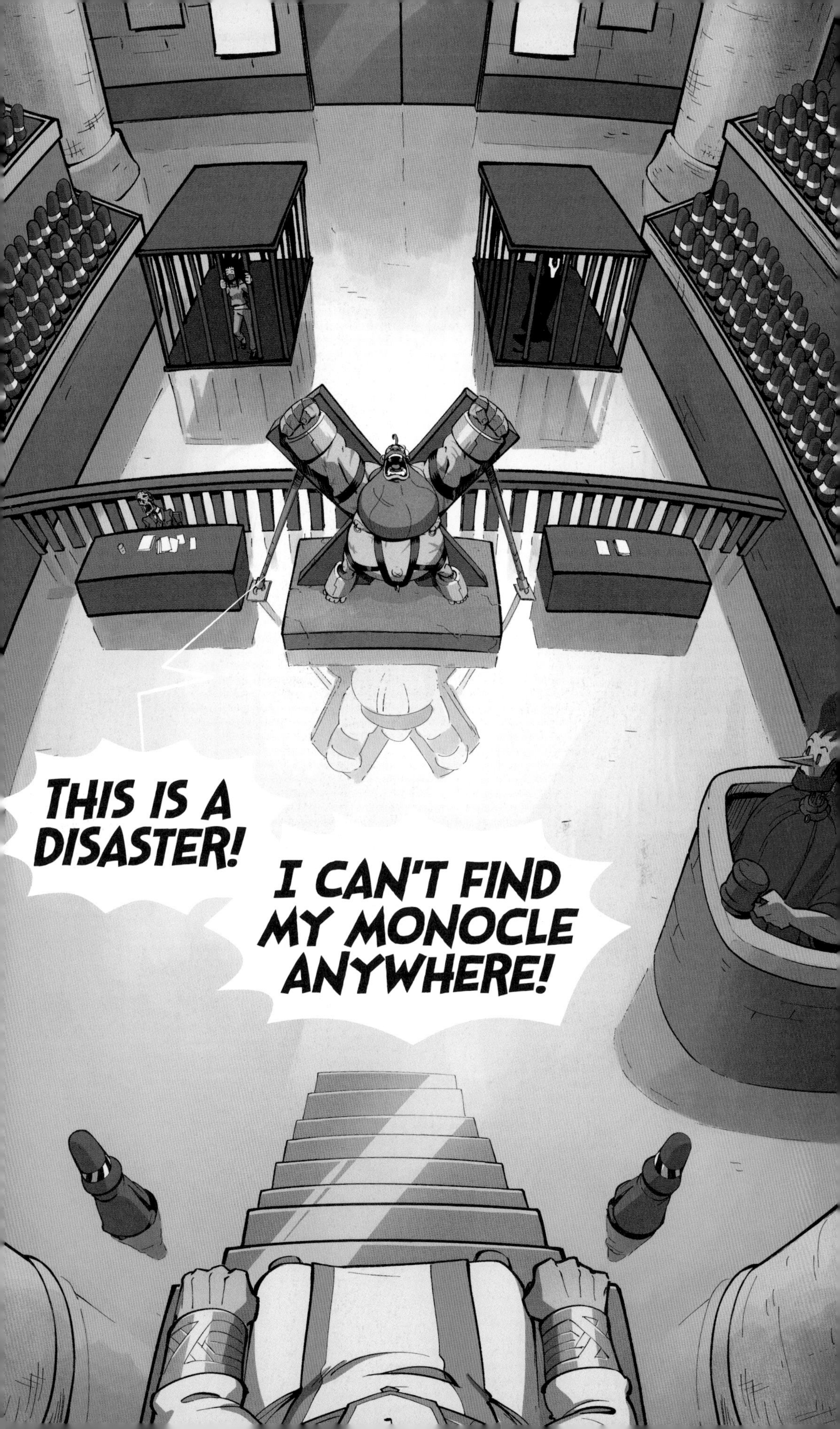
THIS IS A DISASTER!
I CAN'T FIND MY MONOCLE ANYWHERE!

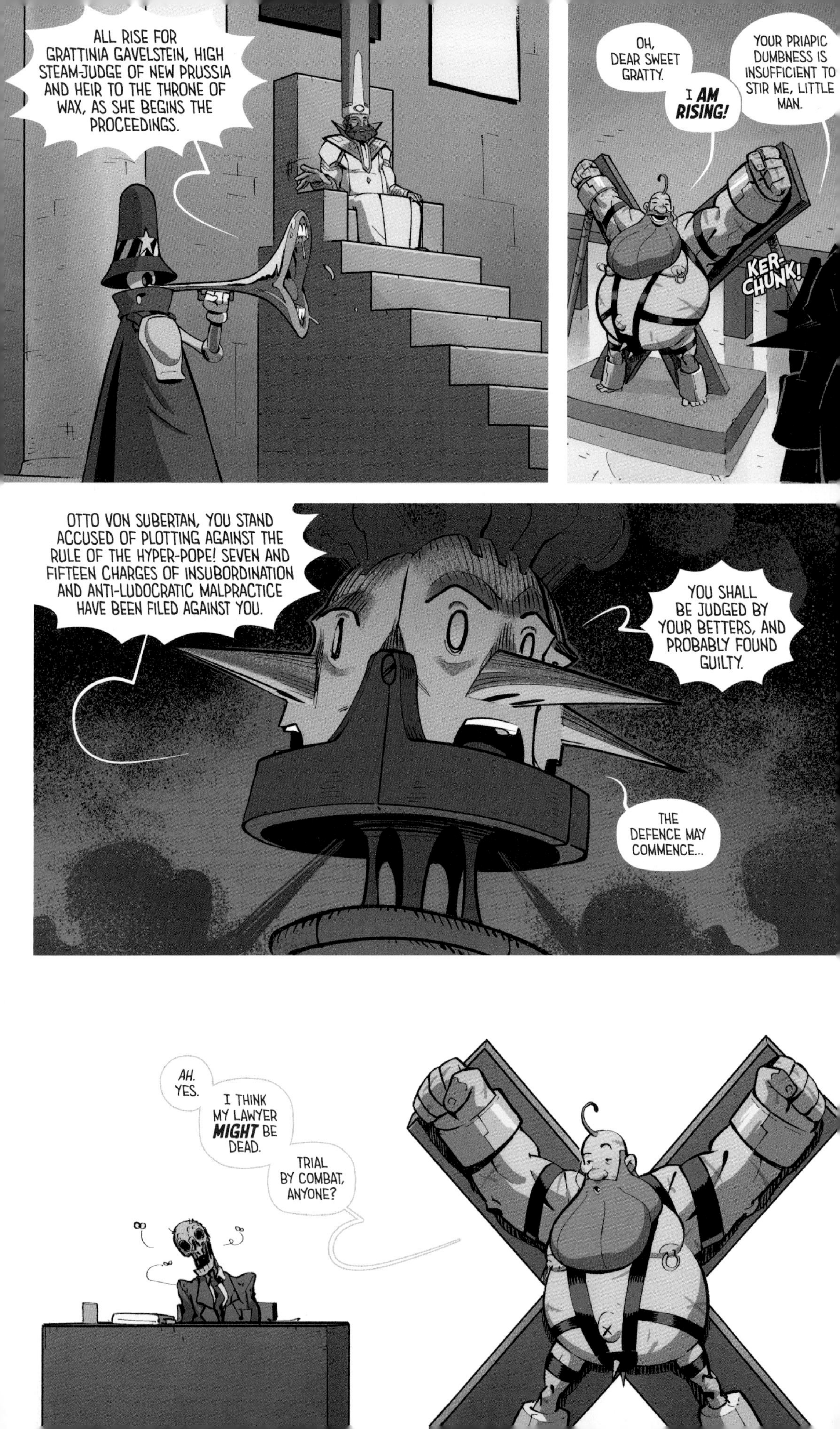
ALL RISE FOR GRATTINIA GAVELSTEIN, HIGH STEAM-JUDGE OF NEW PRUSSIA AND HEIR TO THE THRONE OF WAX, AS SHE BEGINS THE PROCEEDINGS.
OH, DEAR SWEET GRATTY.
I **AM RISING!**
YOUR PRIAPIC DUMBNESS IS INSUFFICIENT TO STIR ME, LITTLE MAN.
KER-CHUNK!
OTTO VON SUBERTAN, YOU STAND ACCUSED OF PLOTTING AGAINST THE RULE OF THE HYPER-POPE! SEVEN AND FIFTEEN CHARGES OF INSUBORDINATION AND ANTI-LUDOCRATIC MALPRACTICE HAVE BEEN FILED AGAINST YOU.
YOU SHALL BE JUDGED BY YOUR BETTERS, AND PROBABLY FOUND GUILTY.
THE DEFENCE MAY COMMENCE...
AH. YES.
I THINK MY LAWYER **MIGHT** BE DEAD.
TRIAL BY COMBAT, ANYONE?

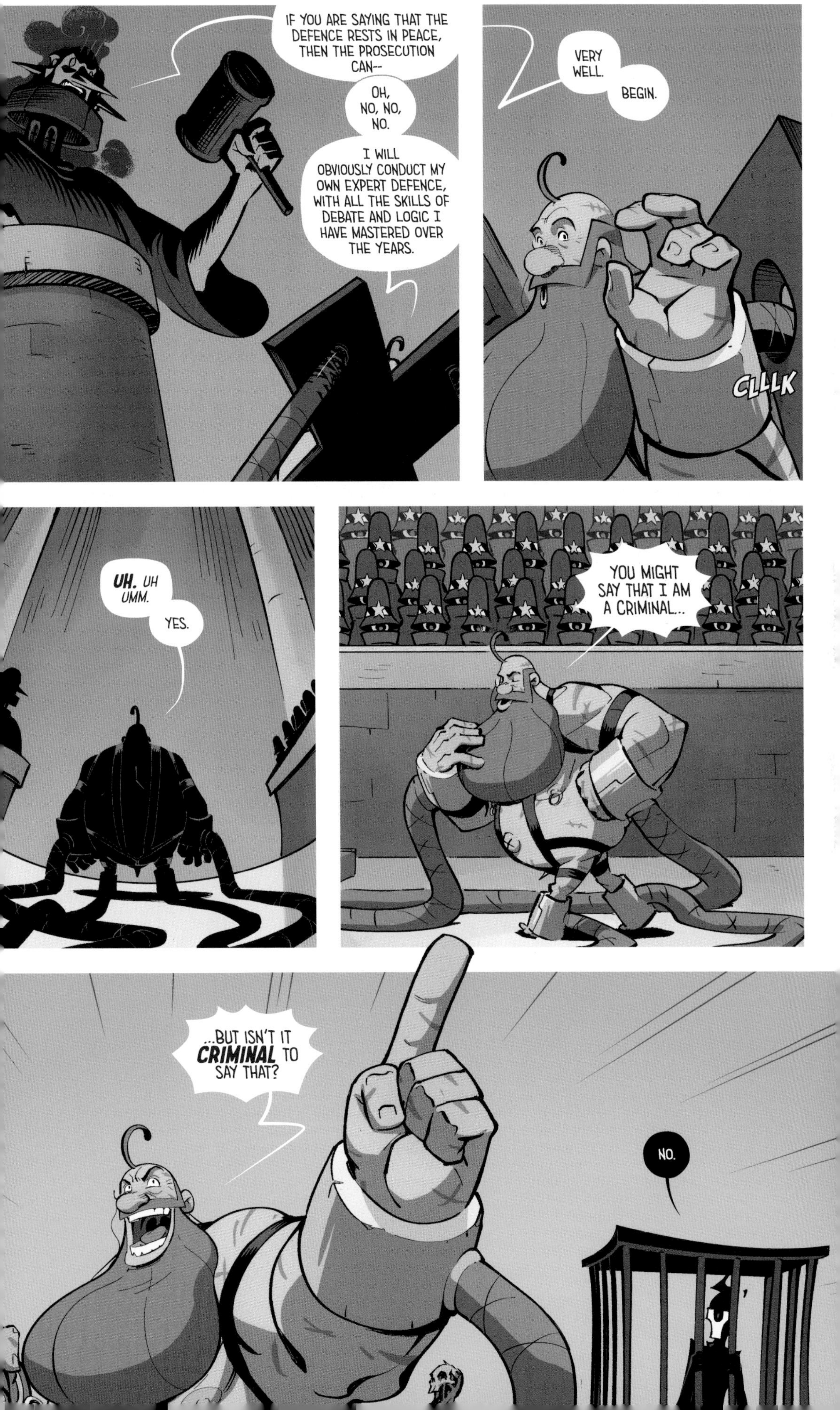
IF YOU ARE SAYING THAT THE DEFENCE RESTS IN PEACE, THEN THE PROSECUTION CAN--
OH, NO, NO, NO.
I WILL OBVIOUSLY CONDUCT MY OWN EXPERT DEFENCE, WITH ALL THE SKILLS OF DEBATE AND LOGIC I HAVE MASTERED OVER THE YEARS.
VERY WELL.
BEGIN.
CLLLK
UH. UH UMM.
YES.
YOU MIGHT SAY THAT I AM A CRIMINAL...
...BUT ISN'T IT CRIMINAL TO SAY THAT?
NO.

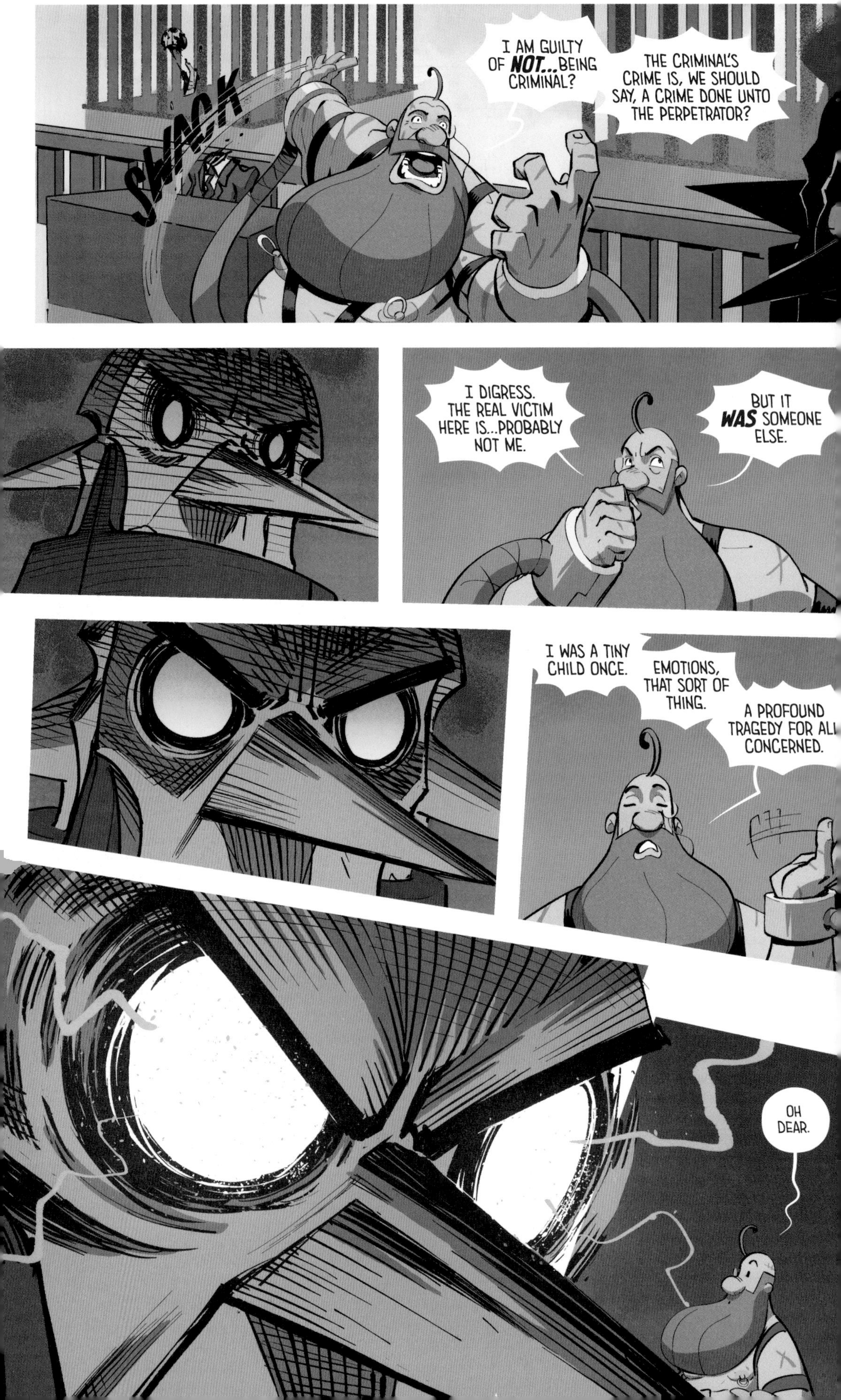
SWACK
I AM GUILTY OF **NOT...** BEING CRIMINAL?
THE CRIMINAL'S CRIME IS, WE SHOULD SAY, A CRIME DONE UNTO THE PERPETRATOR?
I DIGRESS. THE REAL VICTIM HERE IS...PROBABLY NOT ME.
BUT IT **WAS** SOMEONE ELSE.
I WAS A TINY CHILD ONCE.
EMOTIONS, THAT SORT OF THING.
A PROFOUND TRAGEDY FOR ALL CONCERNED.
OH DEAR.

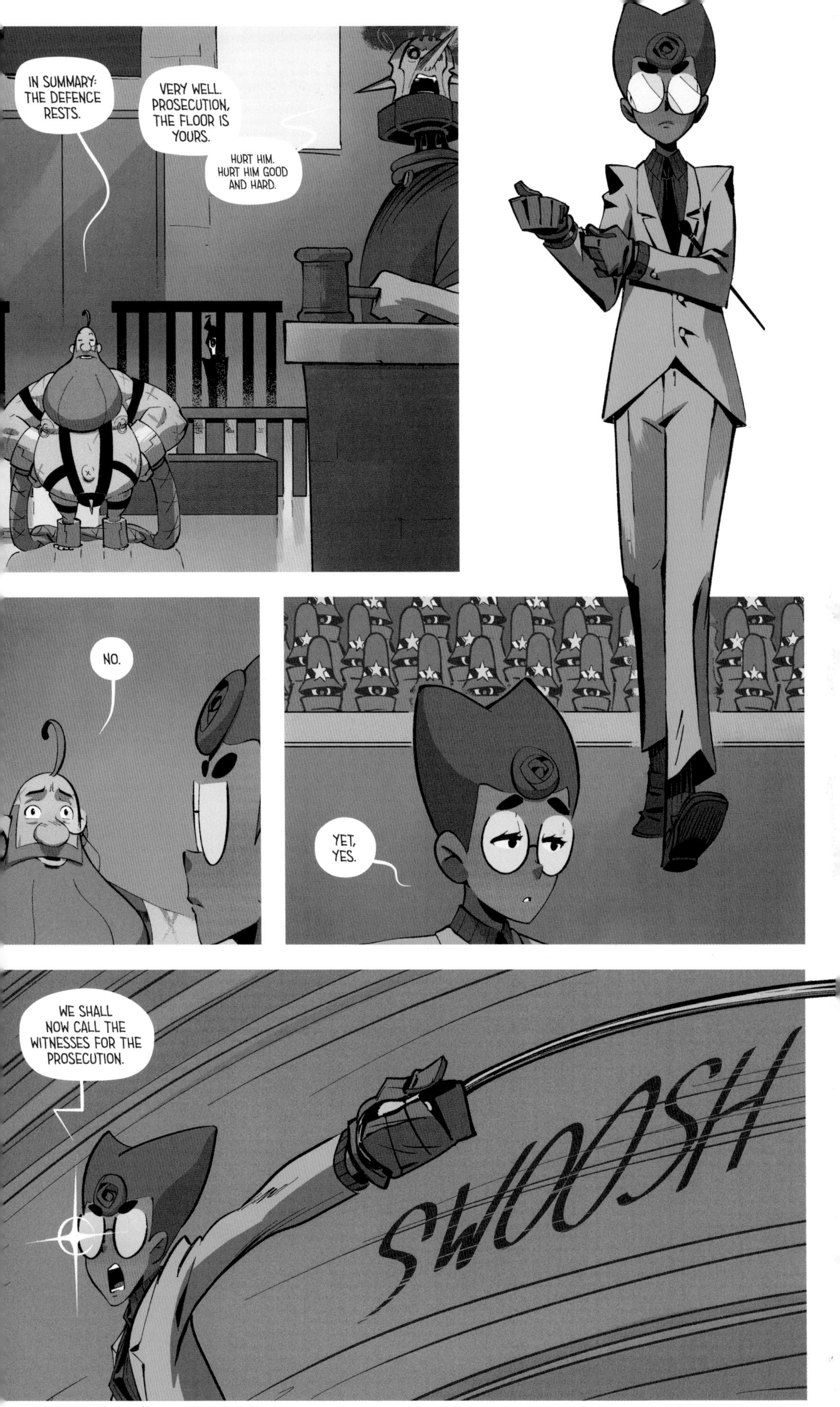
IN SUMMARY: THE DEFENCE RESTS.
VERY WELL. PROSECUTION, THE FLOOR IS YOURS.
HURT HIM. HURT HIM GOOD AND HARD.
NO.
YET, YES.
WE SHALL NOW CALL THE WITNESSES FOR THE PROSECUTION.
SWOOSH

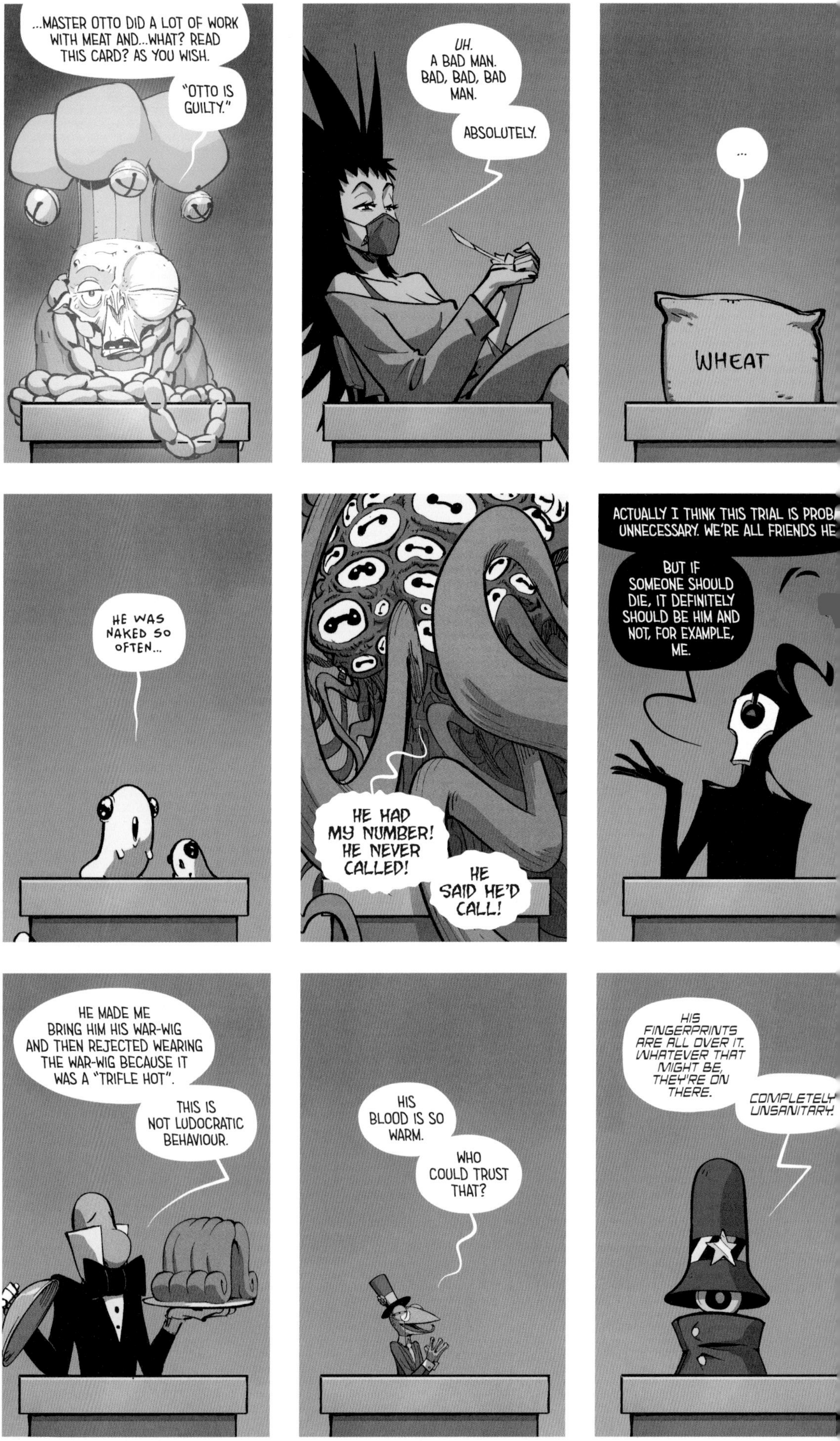

...MASTER OTTO DID A LOT OF WORK WITH MEAT AND...WHAT? READ THIS CARD? AS YOU WISH.
"OTTO IS GUILTY."
UH. A BAD MAN. BAD, BAD, BAD MAN.
ABSOLUTELY.
...
WHEAT
HE WAS NAKED SO OFTEN...
HE HAD MY NUMBER! HE NEVER CALLED!
HE SAID HE'D CALL!
ACTUALLY I THINK THIS TRIAL IS PROB UNNECESSARY. WE'RE ALL FRIENDS HE
BUT IF SOMEONE SHOULD DIE, IT DEFINITELY SHOULD BE HIM AND NOT, FOR EXAMPLE, ME.
HE MADE ME BRING HIM HIS WAR-WIG AND THEN REJECTED WEARING THE WAR-WIG BECAUSE IT WAS A "TRIFLE HOT".
THIS IS NOT LUDOCRATIC BEHAVIOUR.
HIS BLOOD IS SO WARM.
WHO COULD TRUST THAT?
HIS FINGERPRINTS ARE ALL OVER IT. WHATEVER THAT MIGHT BE, THEY'RE ON THERE.
COMPLETELY UNSANITARY.

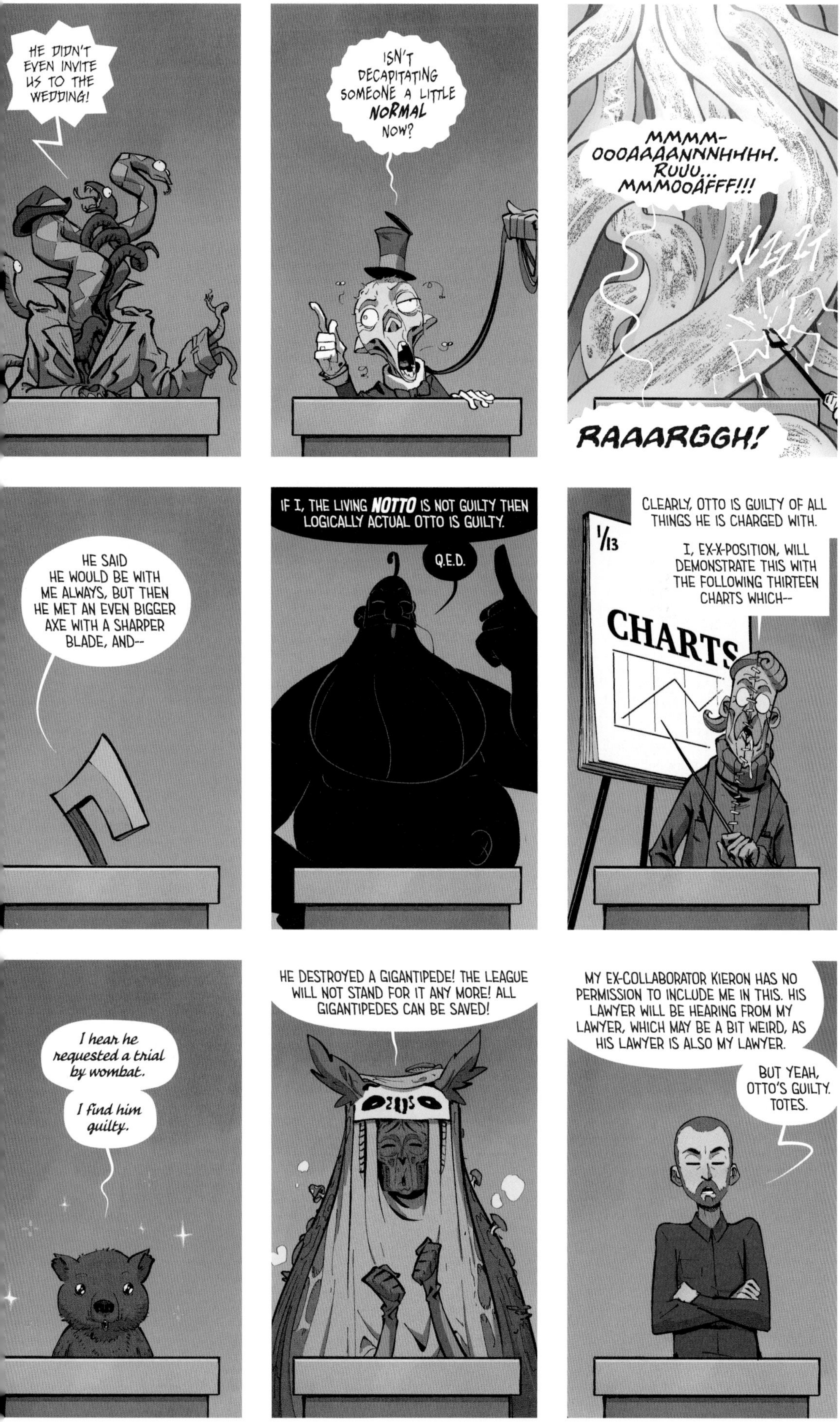
HE DIDN'T EVEN INVITE US TO THE WEDDING!
ISN'T DECAPITATING SOMEONE A LITTLE NORMAL NOW?
MMMM-OOOAAAANNNHHHH. RUUU... MMMOOÄFFF!!!
RAAARGGH!
HE SAID HE WOULD BE WITH ME ALWAYS, BUT THEN HE MET AN EVEN BIGGER AXE WITH A SHARPER BLADE, AND--
IF I, THE LIVING NOTTO IS NOT GUILTY THEN LOGICALLY ACTUAL OTTO IS GUILTY.
Q.E.D.
CLEARLY, OTTO IS GUILTY OF ALL THINGS HE IS CHARGED WITH.
1/13
CHARTS
I, EX-X-POSITION, WILL DEMONSTRATE THIS WITH THE FOLLOWING THIRTEEN CHARTS WHICH--
I hear he requested a trial by wombat.
I find him guilty.
HE DESTROYED A GIGANTIPEDE! THE LEAGUE WILL NOT STAND FOR IT ANY MORE! ALL GIGANTIPEDES CAN BE SAVED!
MY EX-COLLABORATOR KIERON HAS NO PERMISSION TO INCLUDE ME IN THIS. HIS LAWYER WILL BE HEARING FROM MY LAWYER, WHICH MAY BE A BIT WEIRD, AS HIS LAWYER IS ALSO MY LAWYER.
BUT YEAH, OTTO'S GUILTY. TOTES.

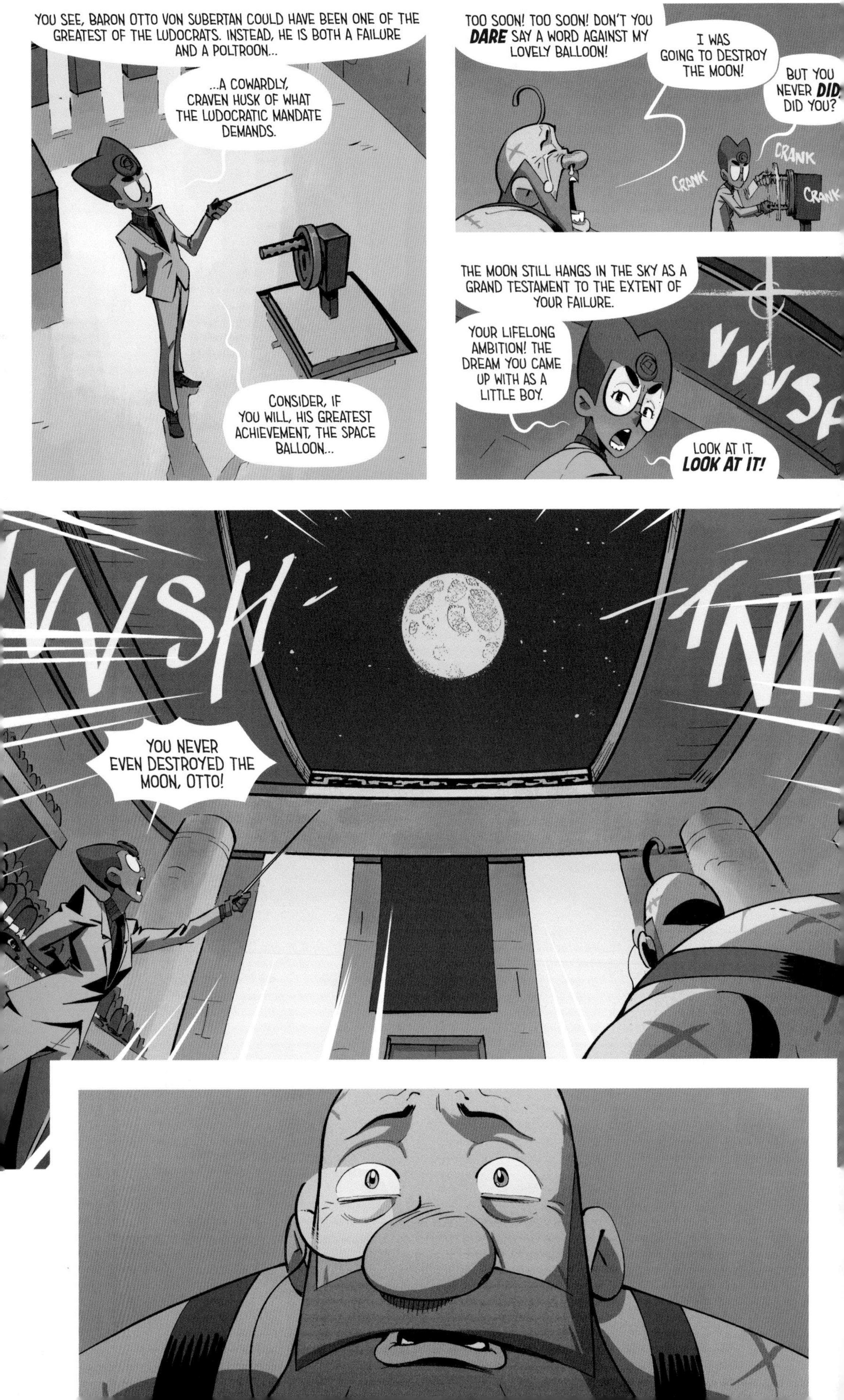
YOU SEE, BARON OTTO VON SUBERTAN COULD HAVE BEEN ONE OF THE GREATEST OF THE LUDOCRATS. INSTEAD, HE IS BOTH A FAILURE AND A POLTROON...
...A COWARDLY, CRAVEN HUSK OF WHAT THE LUDOCRATIC MANDATE DEMANDS.
CONSIDER, IF YOU WILL, HIS GREATEST ACHIEVEMENT, THE SPACE BALLOON...
TOO SOON! TOO SOON! DON'T YOU **DARE** SAY A WORD AGAINST MY LOVELY BALLOON!
I WAS GOING TO DESTROY THE MOON!
BUT YOU NEVER **DID**, DID YOU?
CRANK
CRANK
CRANK
THE MOON STILL HANGS IN THE SKY AS A GRAND TESTAMENT TO THE EXTENT OF YOUR FAILURE.
YOUR LIFELONG AMBITION! THE DREAM YOU CAME UP WITH AS A LITTLE BOY.
LOOK AT IT. **LOOK AT IT!**
VVVSH
VVSH
INK
YOU NEVER EVEN DESTROYED THE MOON, OTTO!

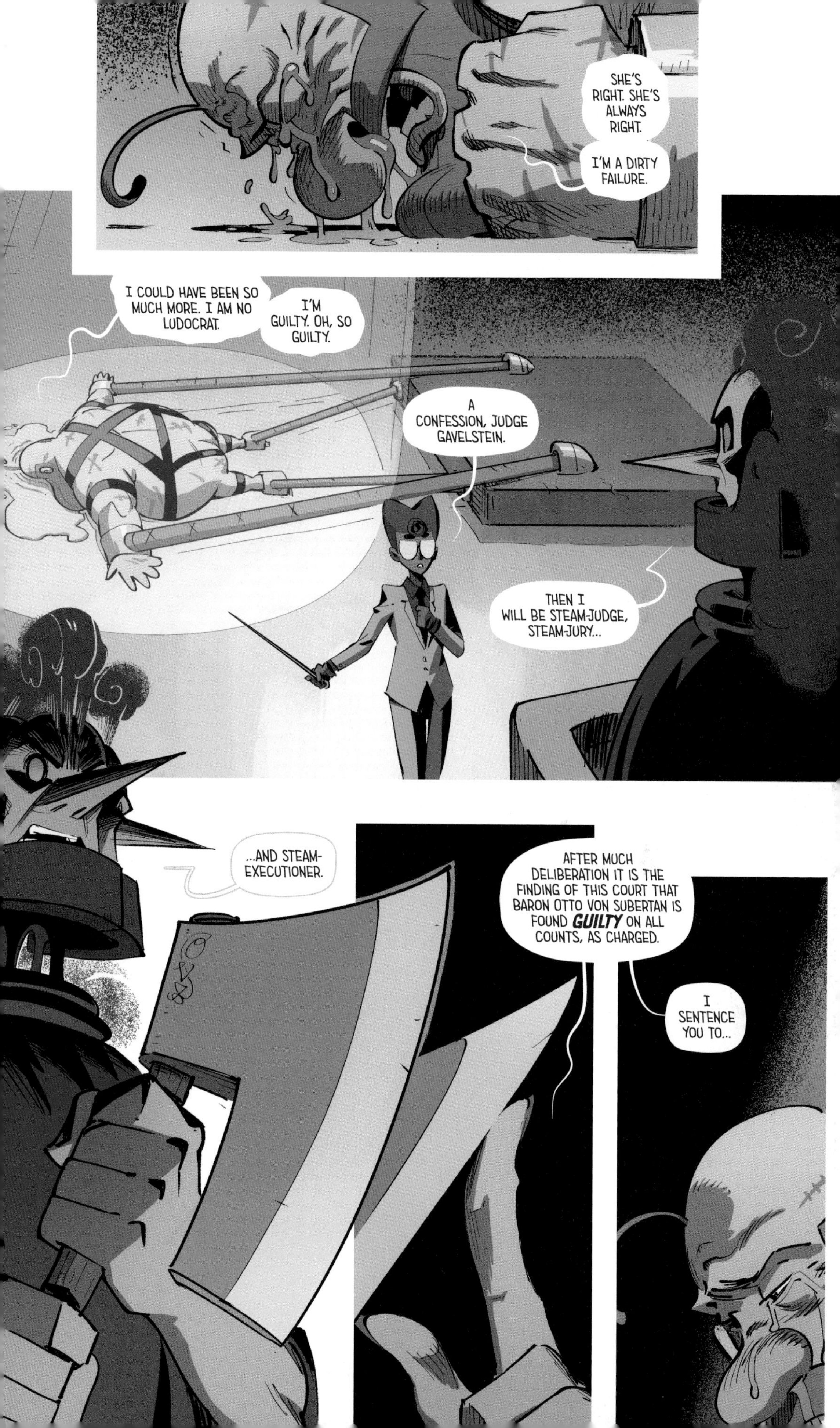
SHE'S RIGHT. SHE'S ALWAYS RIGHT.
I'M A DIRTY FAILURE.
I COULD HAVE BEEN SO MUCH MORE. I AM NO LUDOCRAT.
I'M GUILTY. OH, SO GUILTY.
A CONFESSION, JUDGE GAVELSTEIN.
THEN I WILL BE STEAM-JUDGE, STEAM-JURY...
...AND STEAM-EXECUTIONER.
AFTER MUCH DELIBERATION IT IS THE FINDING OF THIS COURT THAT BARON OTTO VON SUBERTAN IS FOUND **GUILTY** ON ALL COUNTS, AS CHARGED.
I SENTENCE YOU TO...

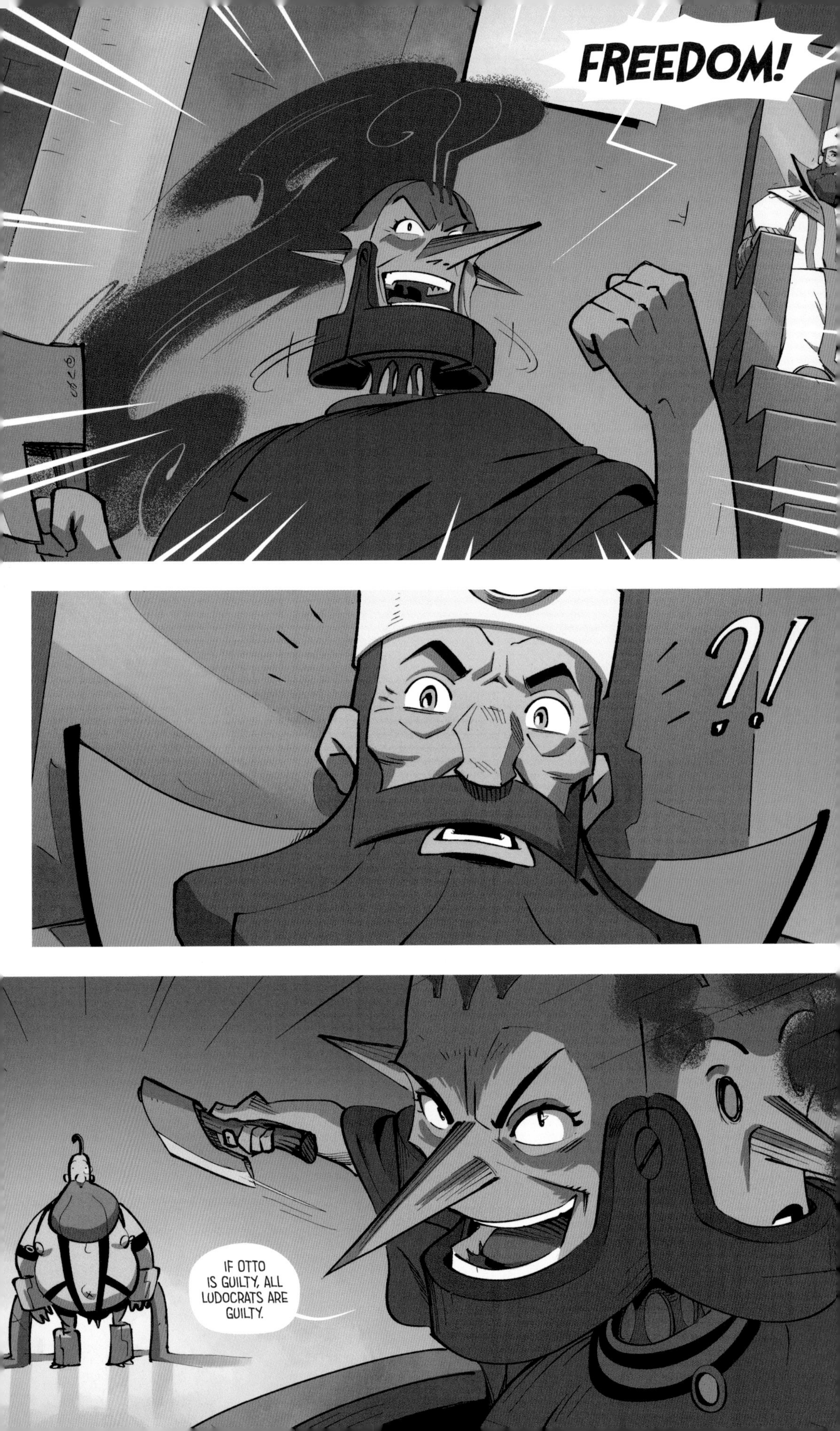
FREEDOM!
?!
IF OTTO IS GUILTY, ALL LUDOCRATS ARE GUILTY.

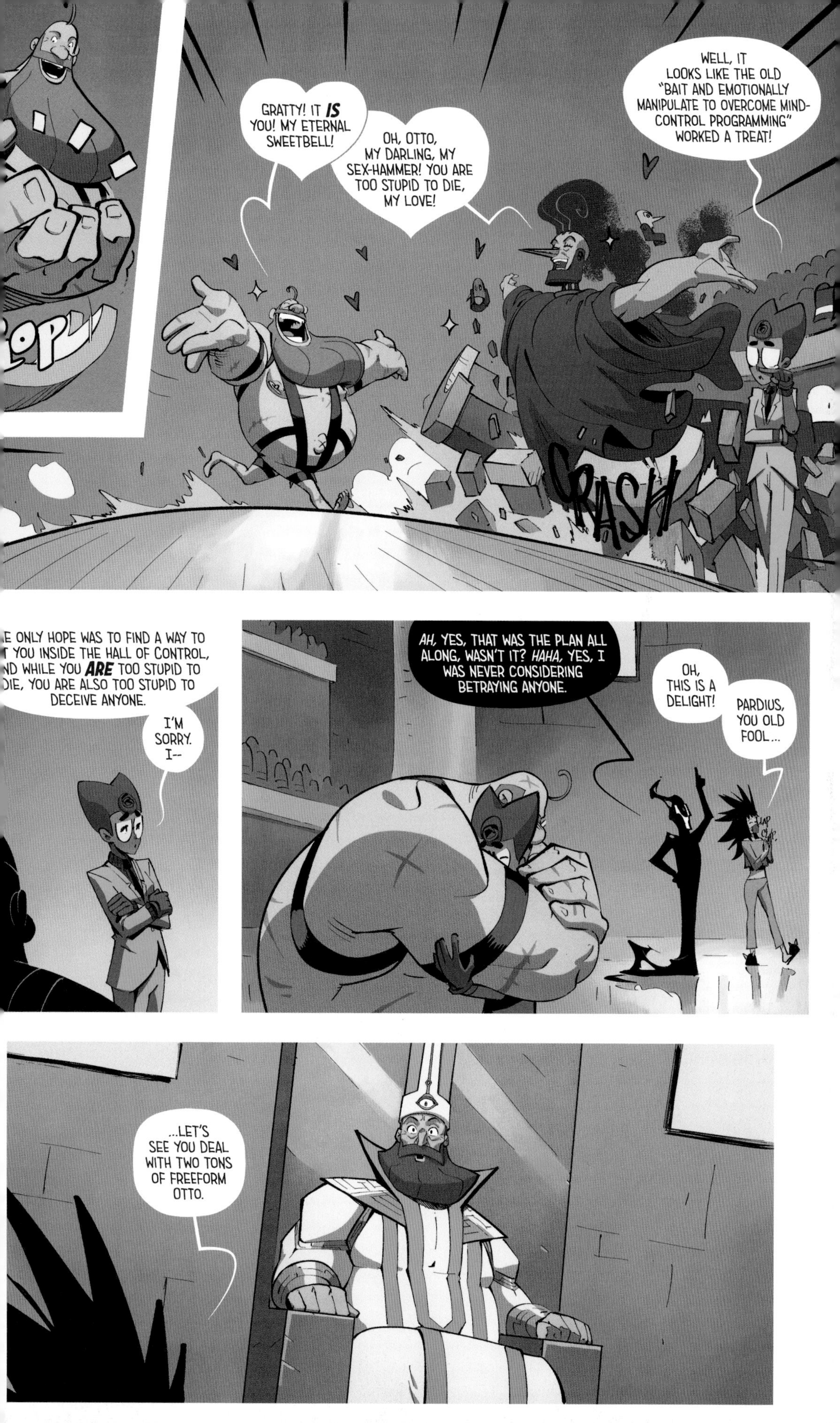
GRATTY! IT *IS* YOU! MY ETERNAL SWEETBELL!
OH, OTTO, MY DARLING, MY SEX-HAMMER! YOU ARE TOO STUPID TO DIE, MY LOVE!
WELL, IT LOOKS LIKE THE OLD "BAIT AND EMOTIONALLY MANIPULATE TO OVERCOME MIND-CONTROL PROGRAMMING" WORKED A TREAT!
CRASH
E ONLY HOPE WAS TO FIND A WAY TO
T YOU INSIDE THE HALL OF CONTROL,
ND WHILE YOU **ARE** TOO STUPID TO
DIE, YOU ARE ALSO TOO STUPID TO
DECEIVE ANYONE.
I'M SORRY. I--
AH, YES, THAT WAS THE PLAN ALL ALONG, WASN'T IT? *HAHA,* YES, I WAS NEVER CONSIDERING BETRAYING ANYONE.
OH, THIS IS A DELIGHT!
PARDIUS, YOU OLD FOOL...
...LET'S SEE YOU DEAL WITH TWO TONS OF FREEFORM OTTO.

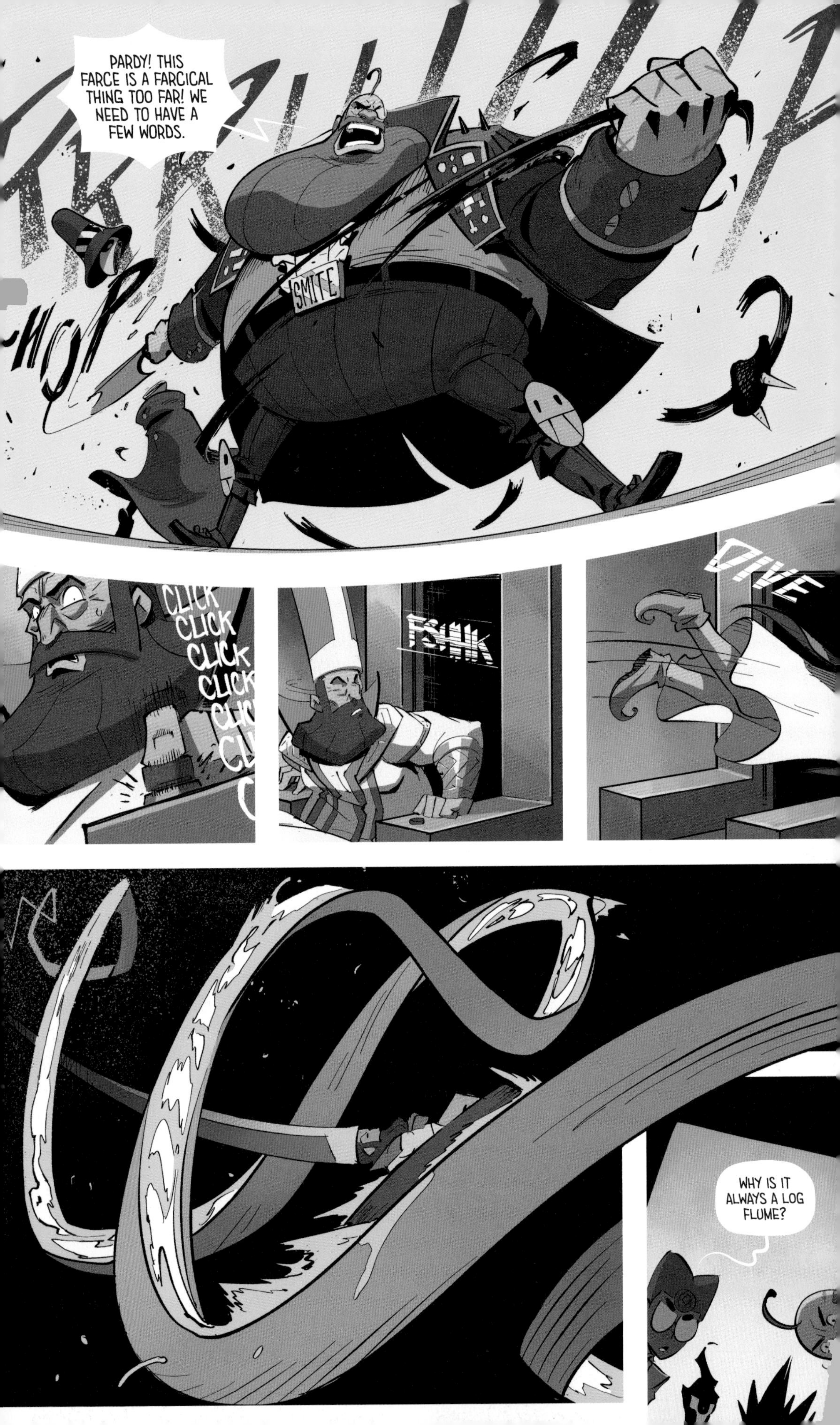
TKKKHHHH
PARDY! THIS FARCE IS A FARCICAL THING TOO FAR! WE NEED TO HAVE A FEW WORDS.
CHOP!
SMITE
CLICK CLICK CLICK CLICK
FSHHK
DIVE
WHY IS IT ALWAYS A LOG FLUME?

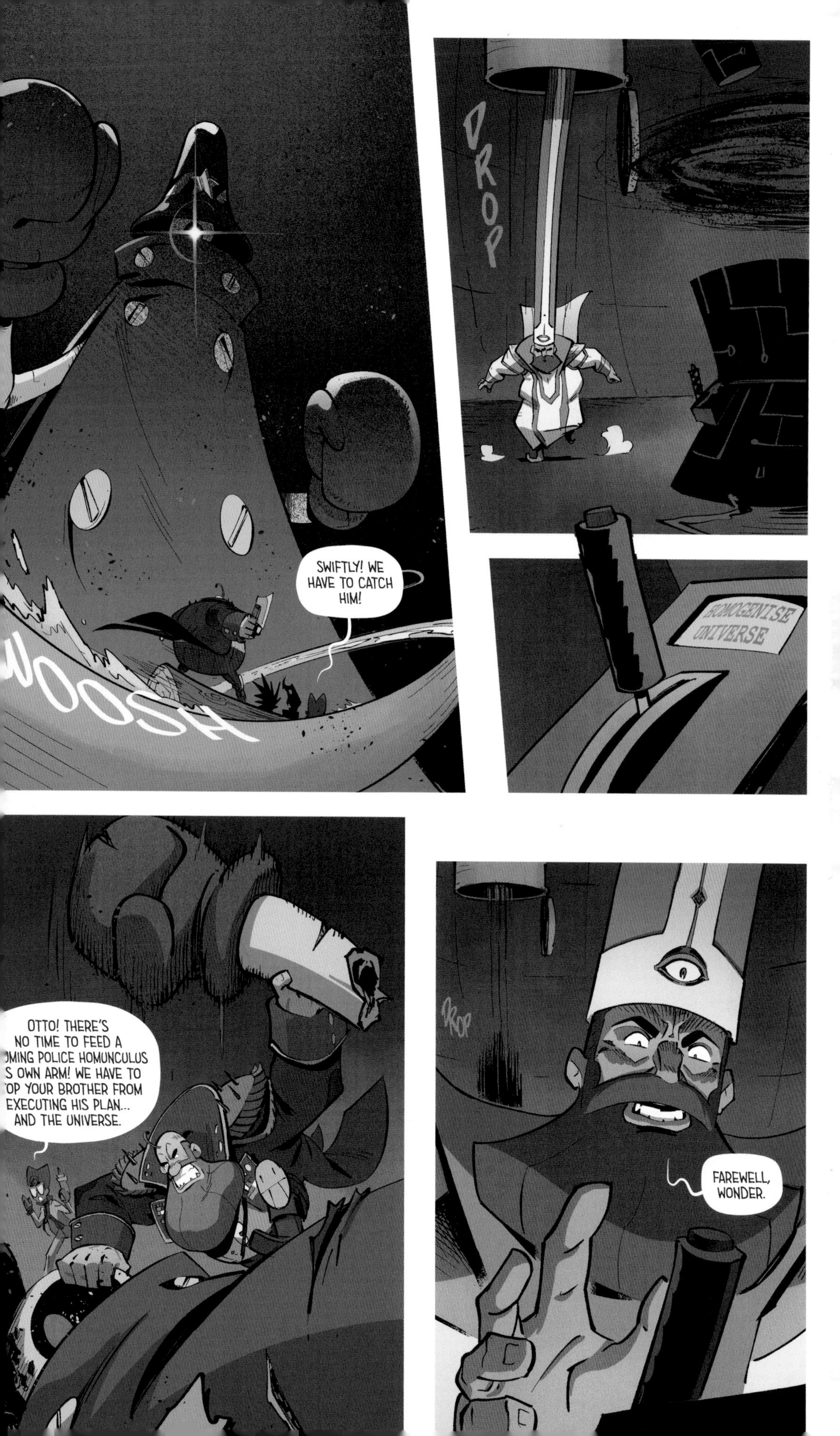
SWIFTLY! WE HAVE TO CATCH HIM!
WOOSH
DROP
HOMOGENISE UNIVERSE
OTTO! THERE'S NO TIME TO FEED A
OMING POLICE HOMUNCULUS
S OWN ARM! WE HAVE TO
OP YOUR BROTHER FROM
EXECUTING HIS PLAN...
AND THE UNIVERSE.
DROP
FAREWELL, WONDER.

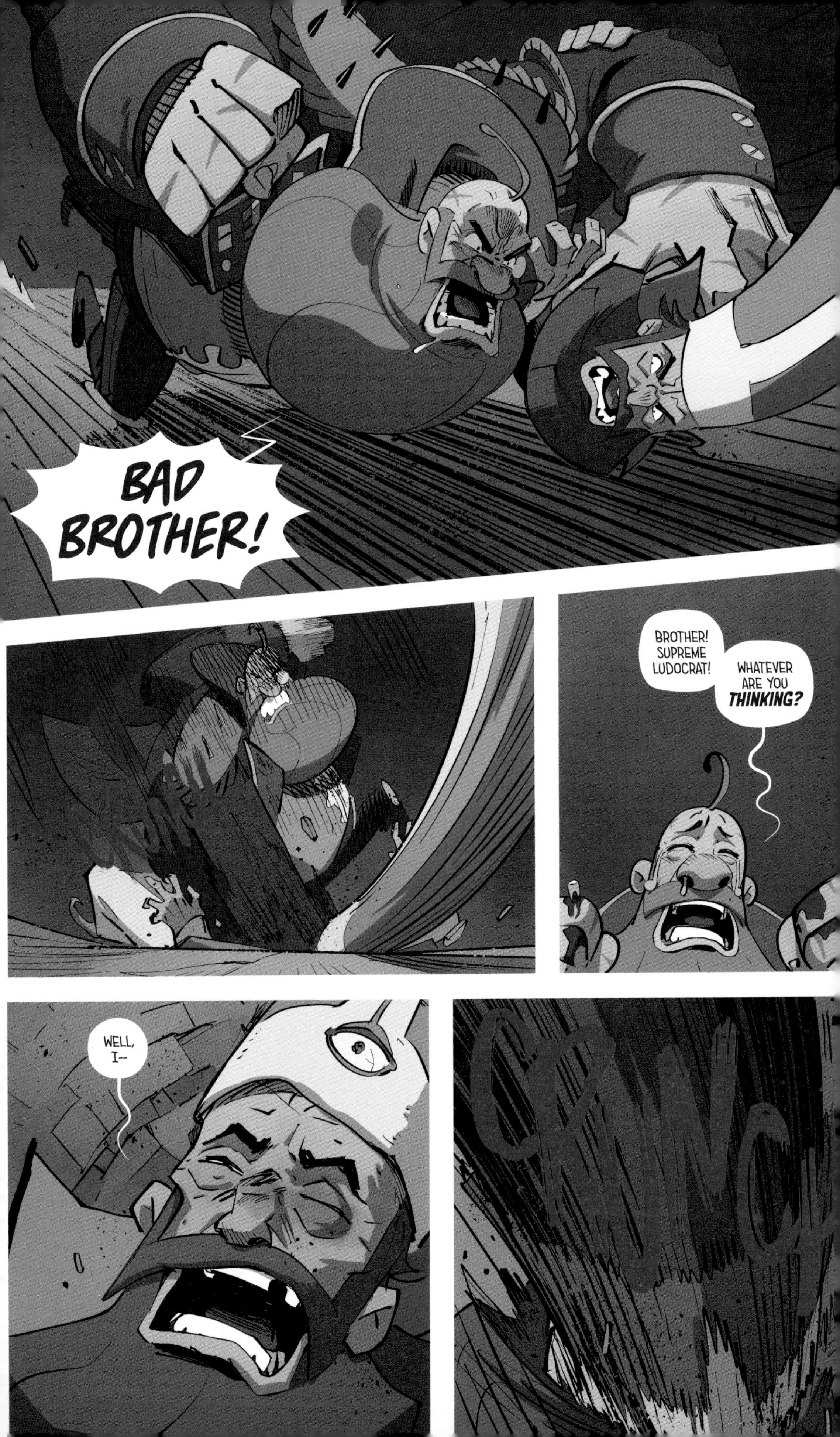
BAD BROTHER!
BROTHER! SUPREME LUDOCRAT!
WHATEVER ARE YOU *THINKING?*
WELL, I--

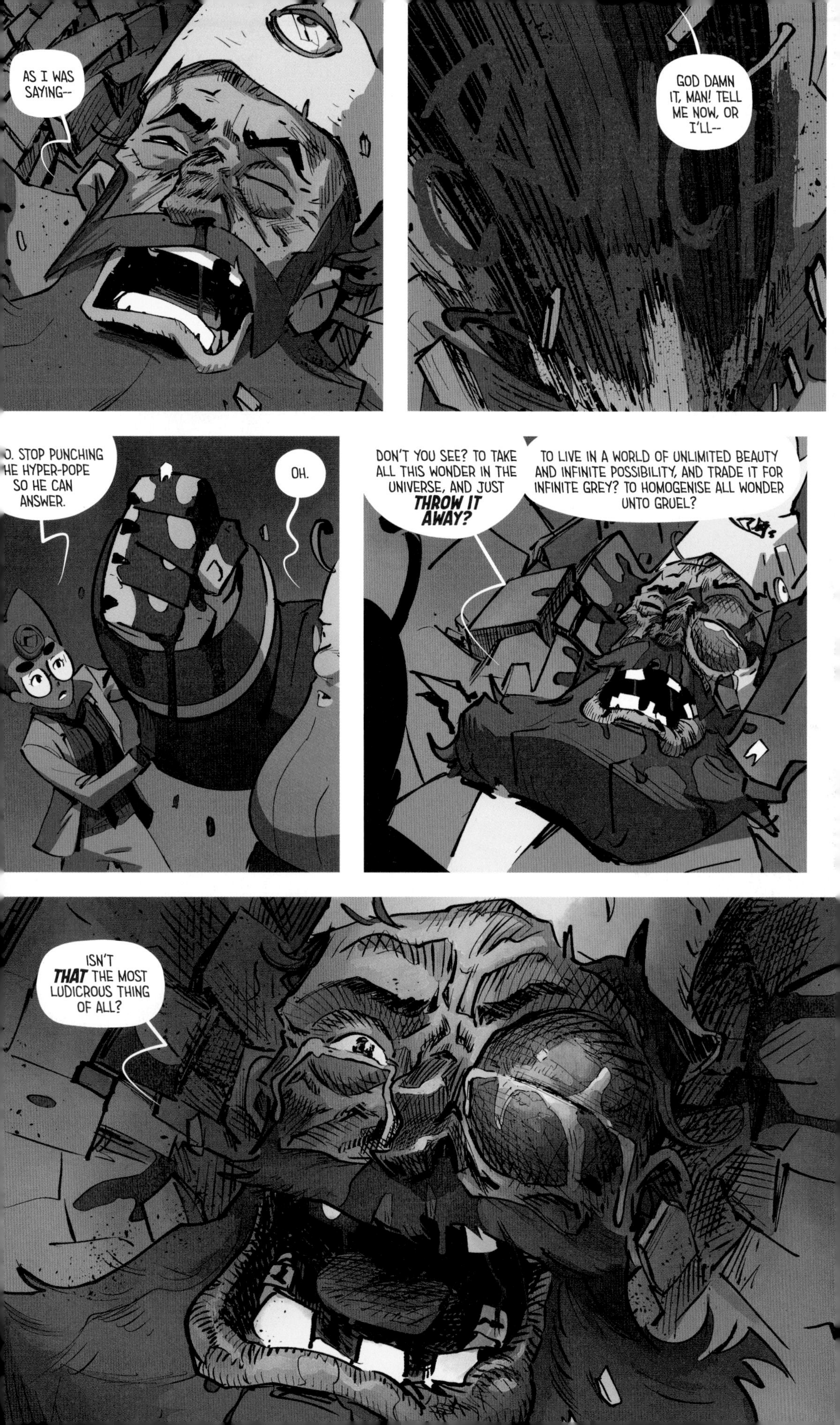
AS I WAS SAYING--
GOD DAMN IT, MAN! TELL ME NOW, OR I'LL--
CRUNCH
O. STOP PUNCHING HE HYPER-POPE SO HE CAN ANSWER.
OH.
DON'T YOU SEE? TO TAKE ALL THIS WONDER IN THE UNIVERSE, AND JUST **THROW IT AWAY?**
TO LIVE IN A WORLD OF UNLIMITED BEAUTY AND INFINITE POSSIBILITY, AND TRADE IT FOR INFINITE GREY? TO HOMOGENISE ALL WONDER UNTO GRUEL?
ISN'T **THAT** THE MOST LUDICROUS THING OF ALL?

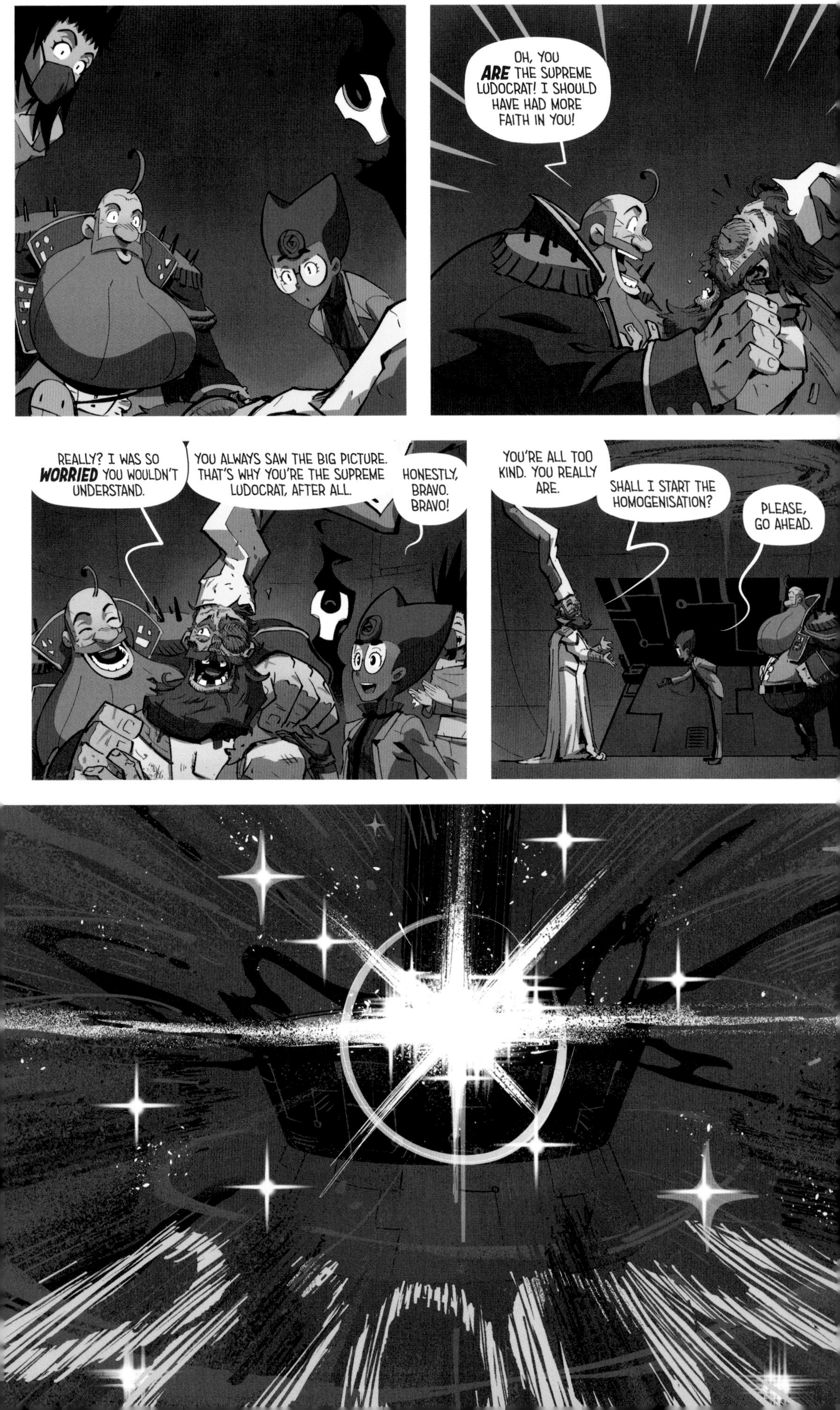
OH, YOU **ARE** THE SUPREME LUDOCRAT! I SHOULD HAVE HAD MORE FAITH IN YOU!
REALLY? I WAS SO **WORRIED** YOU WOULDN'T UNDERSTAND.
YOU ALWAYS SAW THE BIG PICTURE. THAT'S WHY YOU'RE THE SUPREME LUDOCRAT, AFTER ALL.
HONESTLY, BRAVO. BRAVO!
YOU'RE ALL TOO KIND. YOU REALLY ARE.
SHALL I START THE HOMOGENISATION?
PLEASE, GO AHEAD.

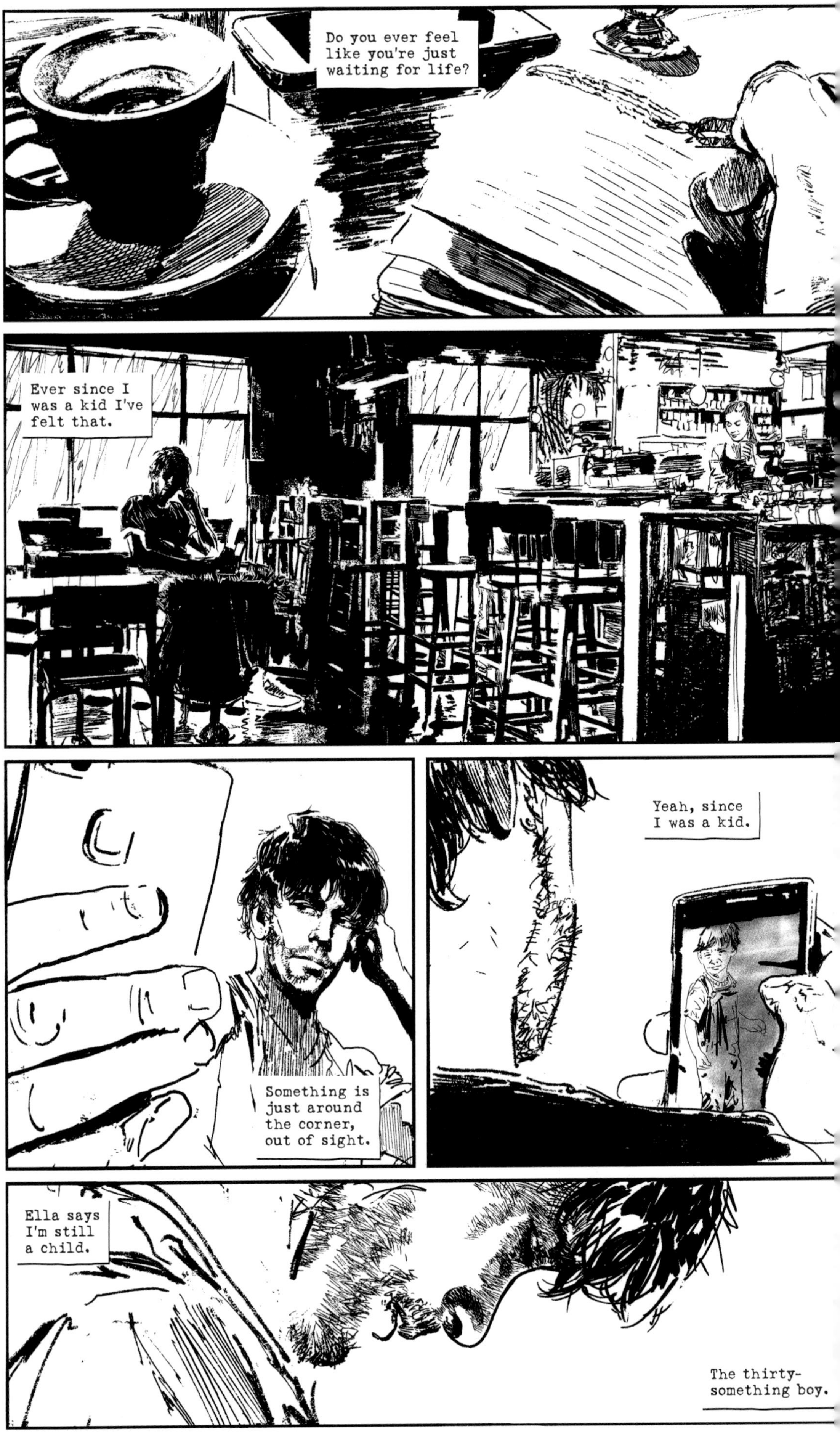

Do you ever feel like you're just waiting for life?
Ever since I was a kid I've felt that.
Something is just around the corner, out of sight.
Yeah, since I was a kid.
Ella says I'm still a child.
The thirty-something boy.

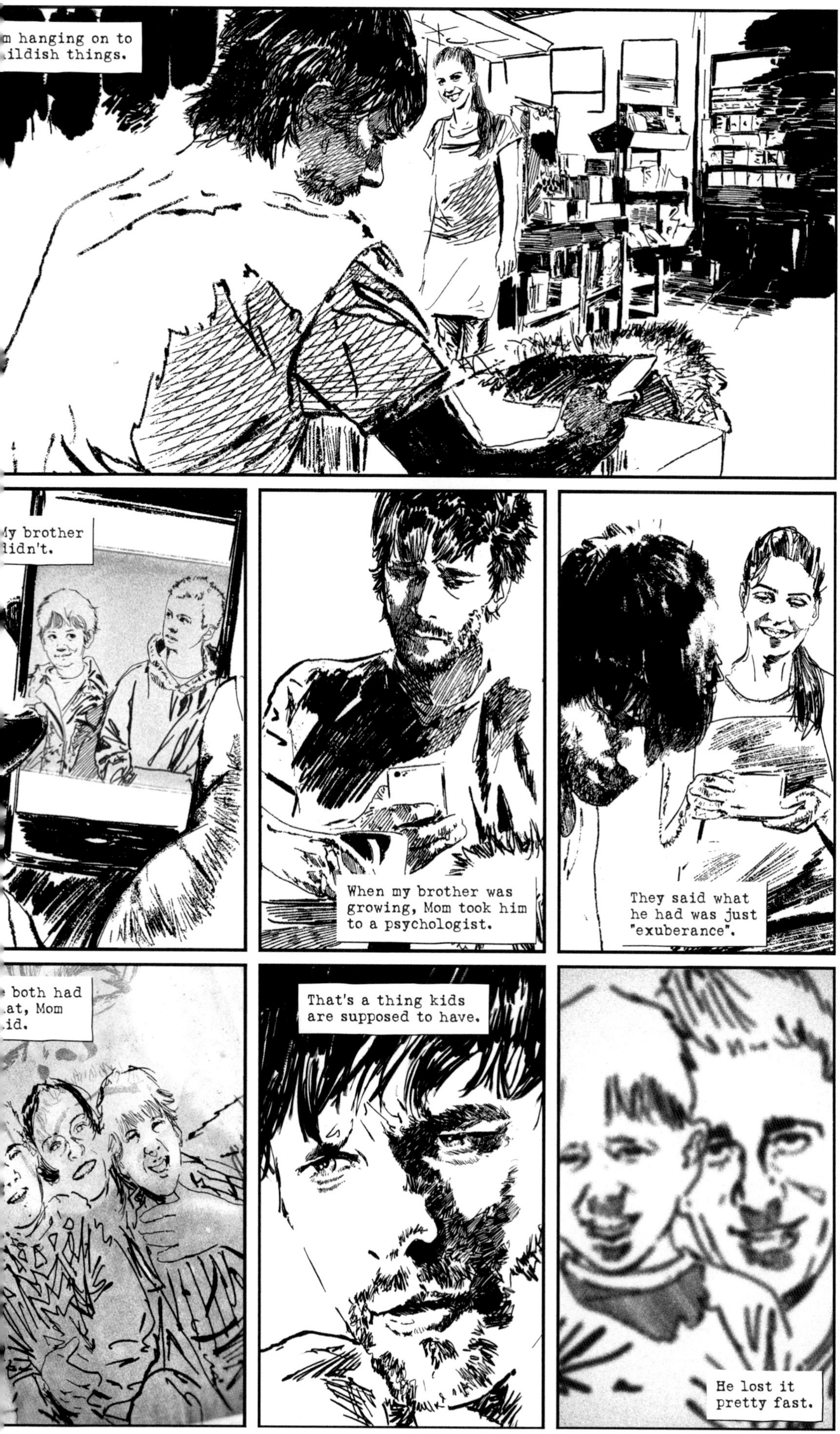
m hanging on to
ildish things.
y brother
idn't.
When my brother was
growing, Mom took him
to a psychologist.
They said what
he had was just
"exuberance".
both had
at, Mom
id.
That's a thing kids
are supposed to have.
He lost it
pretty fast.

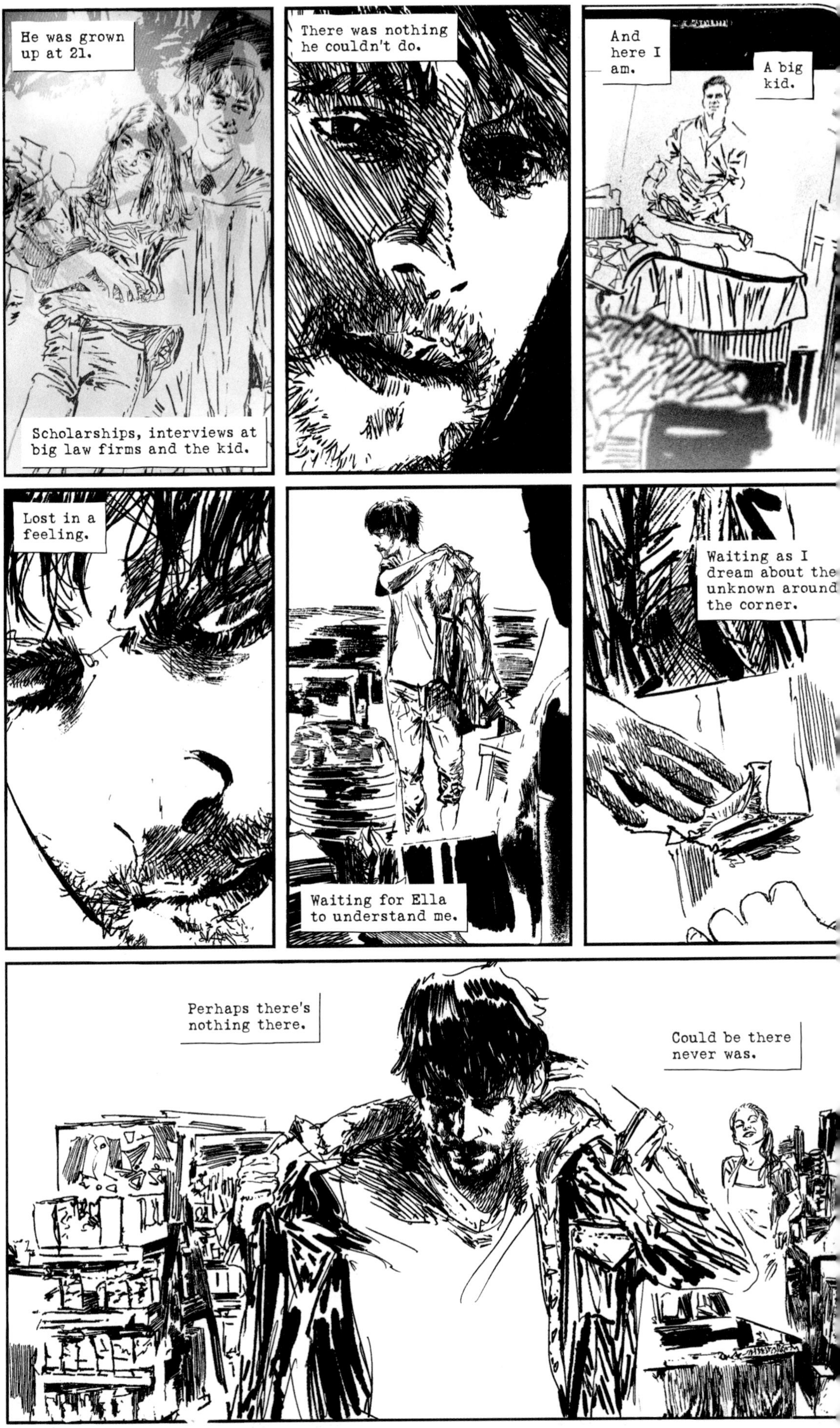
He was grown up at 21.
Scholarships, interviews at big law firms and the kid.
There was nothing he couldn't do.
And here I am.
A big kid.
Lost in a feeling.
Waiting for Ella to understand me.
Waiting as I dream about the unknown around the corner.
Perhaps there's nothing there.
Could be there never was.

There's a Tarkovsky movie where the protagonist says "Weakness is a great thing, and strength is nothing.

"When a man is just born, he is weak and flexible.

"When he dies, he is hard and insensitive."

Yet I realise now that this is also a journey.

One we must all undertake.

It's time to look around the corner.

To see that there is nothing there.

It's time for hardness to have its day.

A seed can grow. And to grow, a seed must start to die.

One must stop being a seed...

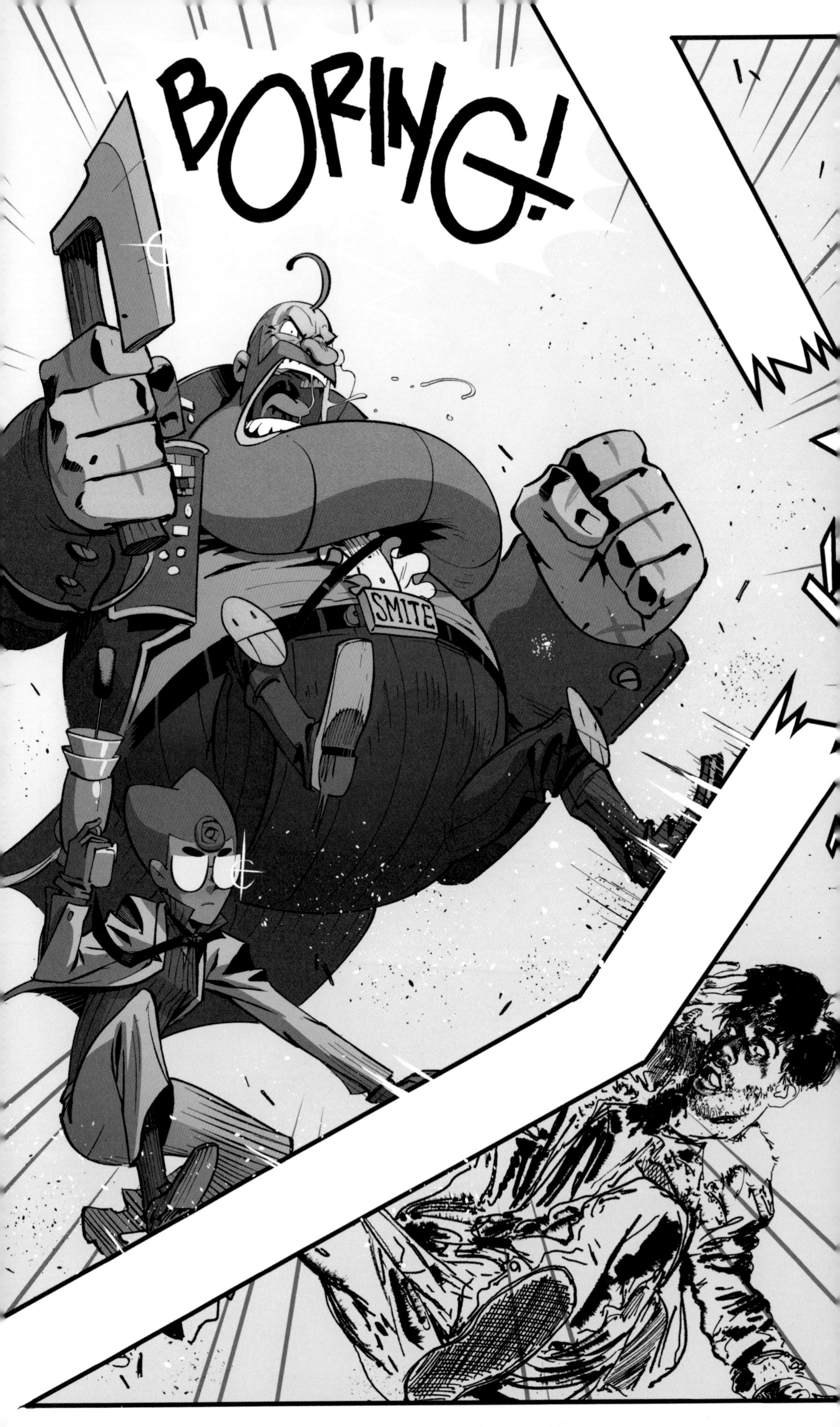
BORING!
SMITE

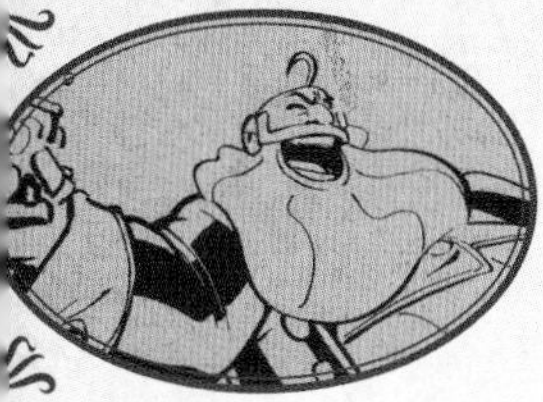

THE Ludocrats

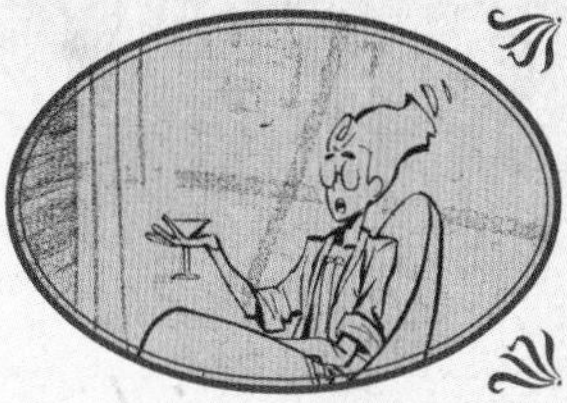

was brought to you by

KIERON GILLEN

LITERARY DISASTER

The wordstorm classified "Kieron" crashed into the literary south coast in the mid-90s as a Class 2 Pretenteosphere and has got worse.

JIM ROSSIGNOL

WORD HERDER

From his base in darkest Avon, Jim sends forth his dogs of yapping to ensure the word-fleece is gathered from the confused, petrified sheep.

JEFF STOKELY

THE MISSING INK

Found by archaeologists in a tar pit, Jeff Stokely's existence revolutionizes understanding of the development of sequential art.

TAMRA BONVILLAIN

LORE OF THE COL

She sits in her fortress, wise and serene, keeper of her secrets. The much-admired Col-lore will bring brightness to this tawdry world.

CLAYTON COWLES

WORD VISUALISATION

Lo! He is the font of all knowledge and is the knowledge of all fonts. His other work includes reality.

FERNANDO ARGÜELLO

JUST LOVELY

Fernando is the sweetest member of team Ludocrats, in that he applies flat colours to the art, with a complete lack of shade.

CHR WIL

CRE

She sigh
job is basica
atin to sea
to corra

SERGIO SERRANO

TACKED RROTS

not mean I
he parrot-
not like
ck birds

MARCO

Ro
han
say
it

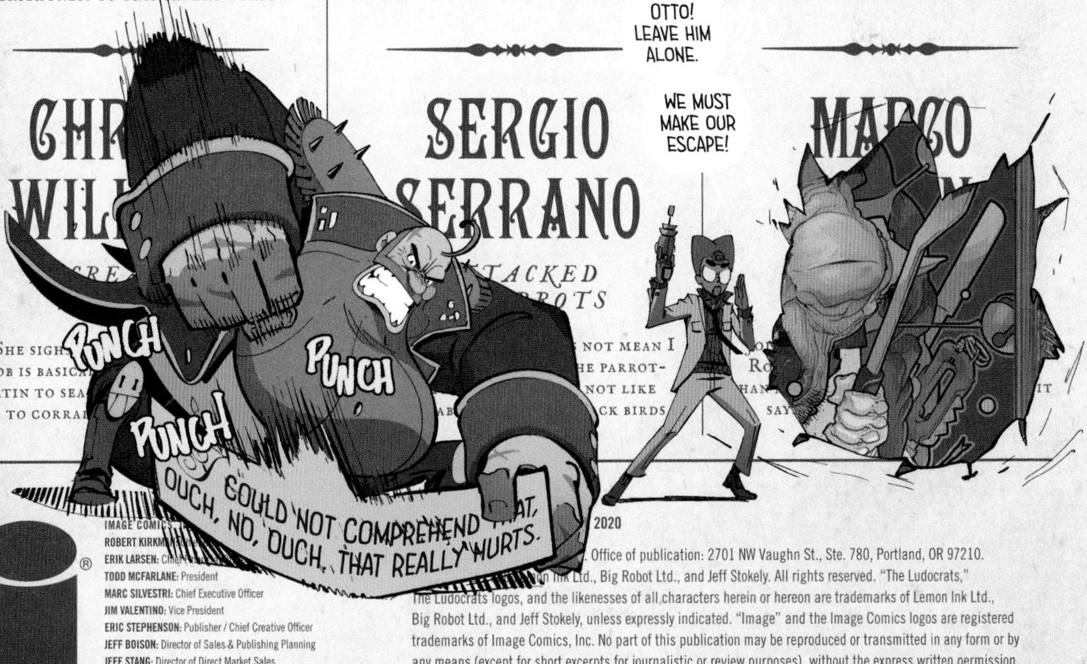

OTTO! LEAVE HIM ALONE.
WE MUST MAKE OUR ESCAPE!
PUNCH
PUNCH
PUNCH
COULD NOT COMPREHEND THAT, OUCH, NO, OUCH, THAT REALLY HURTS.

IMAGE COMICS
ROBERT KIRKM
ERIK LARSEN: Chief
TODD MCFARLANE: President
MARC SILVESTRI: Chief Executive Officer
JIM VALENTINO: Vice President
ERIC STEPHENSON: Publisher / Chief Creative Officer
JEFF BOISON: Director of Sales & Publishing Planning
JEFF STANG: Director of Direct Market Sales
KAT SALAZAR: Director of PR & Marketing
DREW GILL: Cover Editor
HEATHER DOORNINK: Production Director
NICOLE LAPALME: Controller
imagecomics.com

ALTERNATE COVERS

A COLLECTION OF WORKS generated by contemporary artists in response to *The Ludocrats*, specifically being offered money by the creators of *The Ludocrats* to draw something, anything.

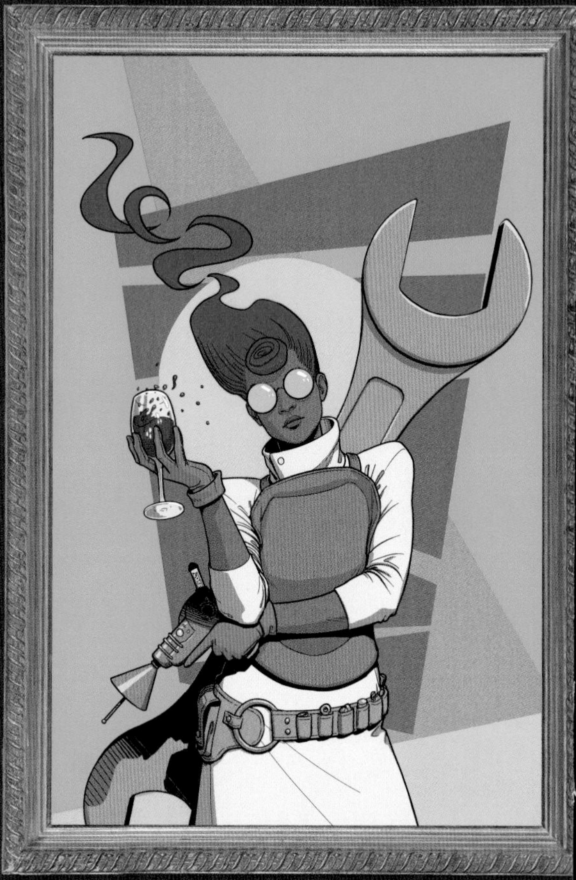

"HADES WITH SPANNER" BY JAMIE MCKELVIE (2020)

Jazzy. Erudite. Cool. Beautiful. Beatific. These are all adjectives. Oh look, there's a Jamie McKelvie drawing. It's nice. It's fine.

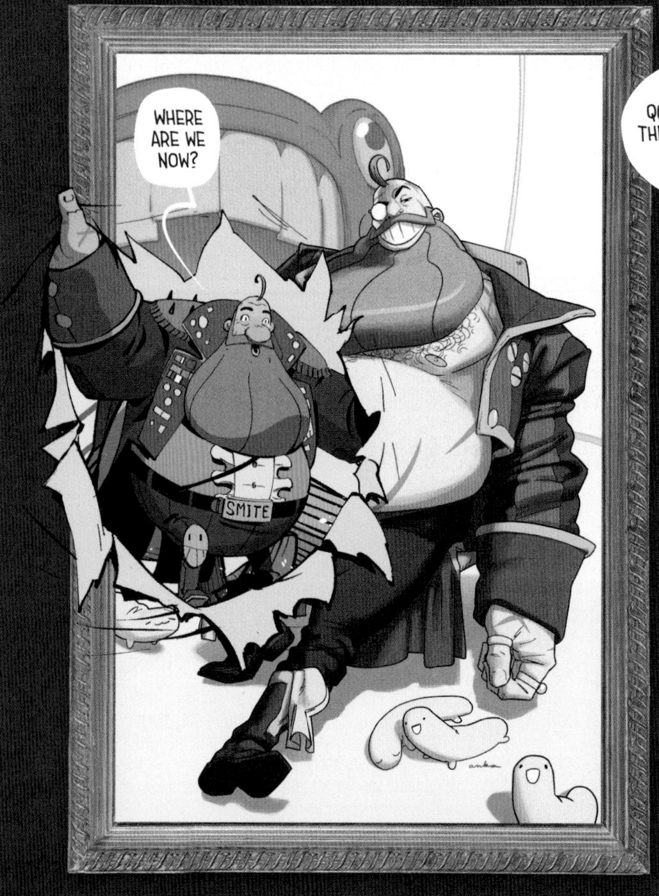
WHERE ARE WE NOW?
SMITE
anka

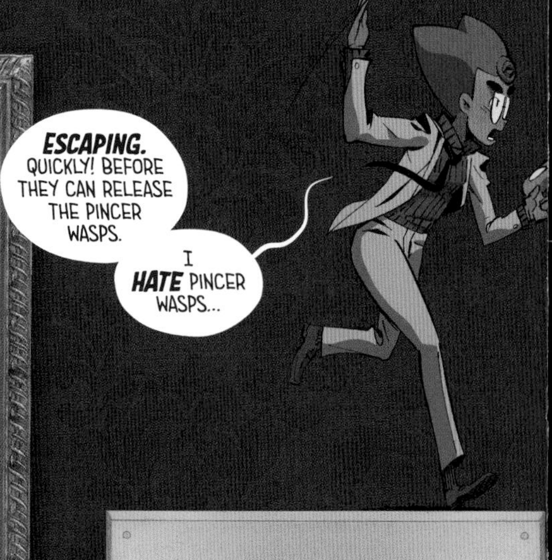
ESCAPING. QUICKLY! BEFORE THEY CAN RELEASE THE PINCER WASPS.
I HATE PINCER WASPS...

"OTTO" BY KRIS ANKA (2020)

This captures the raw, sexual nature of the Ludocrat, as well as their poor posture.

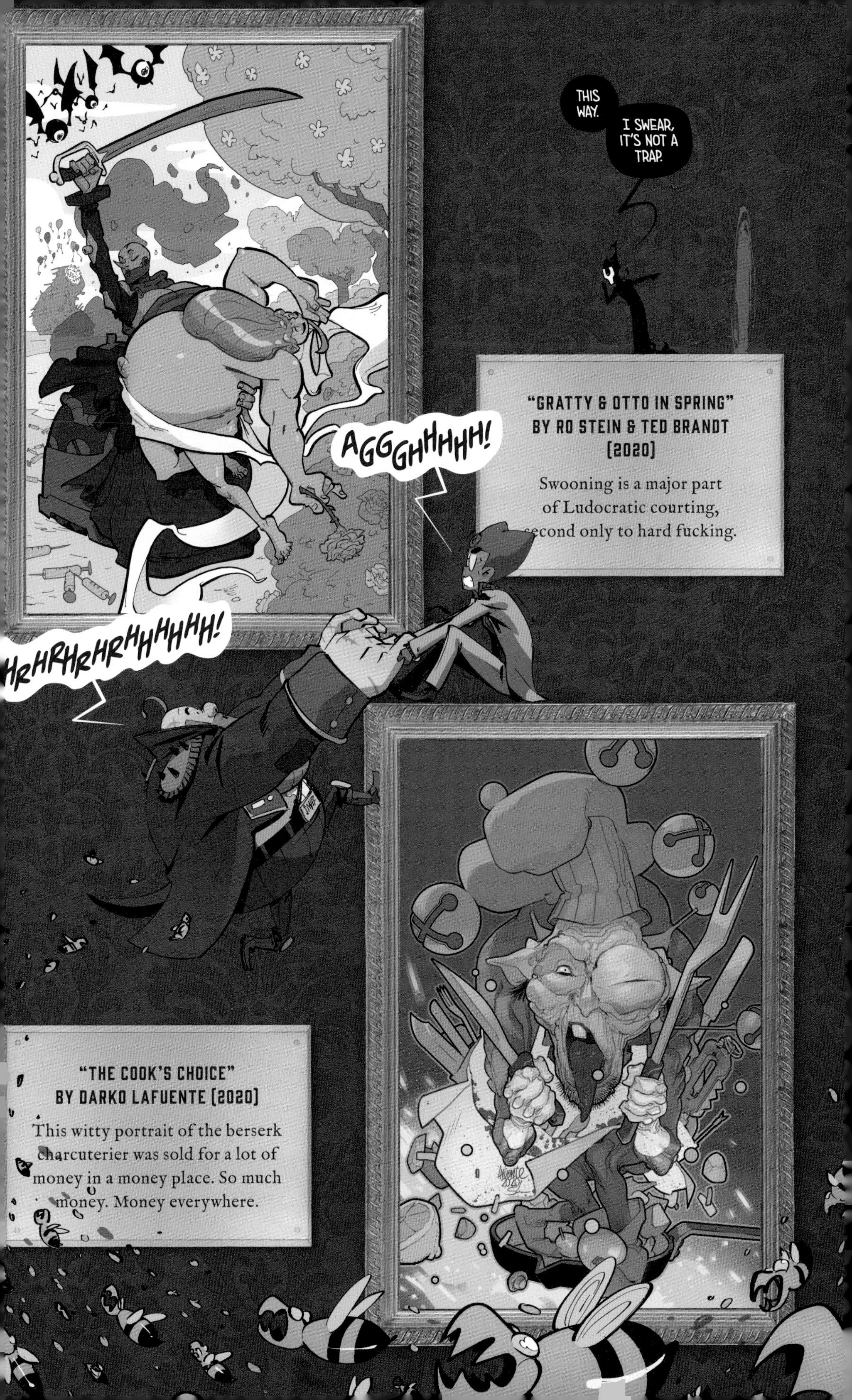
THIS WAY.
I SWEAR, IT'S NOT A TRAP.
"GRATTY & OTTO IN SPRING"
BY RO STEIN & TED BRANDT
[2020]
Swooning is a major part of Ludocratic courting, second only to hard fucking.
AGGGHHHHH!
HRHRHRHRHHHHH!
"THE COOK'S CHOICE"
BY DARKO LAFUENTE [2020]
This witty portrait of the berserk charcuterier was sold for a lot of money in a money place. So much money. Money everywhere.

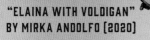

"ELAINA WITH VOLDIGAN"
BY MIRKA ANDOLFO (2020)

A piece best know... ...om Voldian
vs Elaina ("It shou...d ...Voldig...
with Elaina!") which rem...ed i... ...e
minor... ...urts for ...e yea...

"GRATTINA, LEAVING"
BY SKOTTIE YOUNG (2020)

This portrait captures the
Steam-Judge in a moment of
growing bored of an art critic who...
wait. Where are you going? Come—

PREVIOUS WORKS

For those who wish to chart the long underwhelming apprenticeship which somehow coalesced into the staggering work of genius you have just read, one may study the following juvenalia. You'd be better off contemplating *The Ludocrats* again though. Art is over and we won.

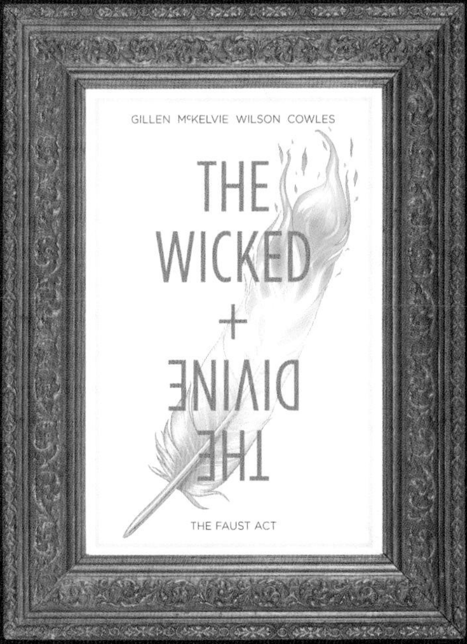

GILLEN McKELVIE WILSON COWLES
THE WICKED + THE DIVINE
THE FAUST ACT

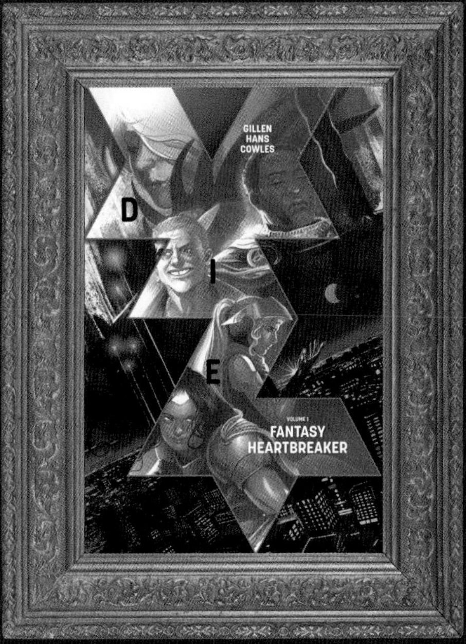

GILLEN
HANS
COWLES
DIE
VOLUME 1
FANTASY HEARTBREAKER

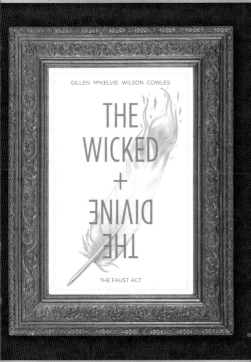

THE WICKED + THE DIVINE (2014–2019)

Nine volumes of gods occasionally being pop stars, but mainly being sad. Sporadic jokes, endemic puns.

DIE (2018–)

An ongoing series about mid-life crisis, the purpose of fantasy and how much of his RPG expenditure Kieron can make tax-deductible.

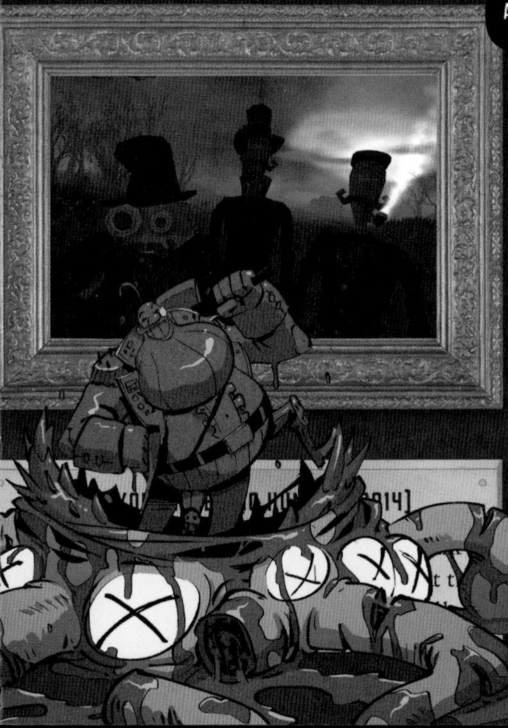

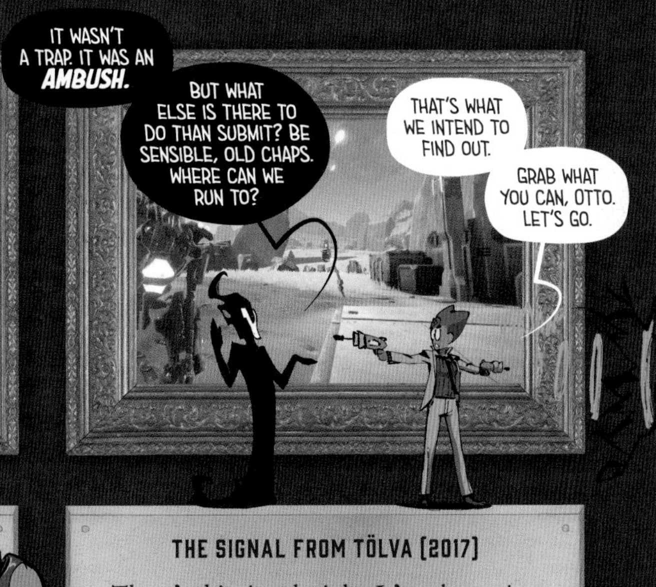

IT WASN'T A TRAP. IT WAS AN AMBUSH.
BUT WHAT ELSE IS THERE TO DO THAN SUBMIT? BE SENSIBLE, OLD CHAPS. WHERE CAN WE RUN TO?
THAT'S WHAT WE INTEND TO FIND OUT.
GRAB WHAT YOU CAN, OTTO. LET'S GO.

THE SIGNAL FROM TÖLVA (2017)

There's this signal, right. It's only coming from bloody Tölva, innit? High graphicosity and playabilitity from Jim & Chums.

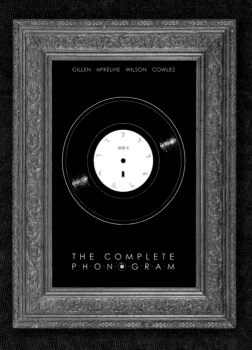

GILLEN McKELVIE WILSON COWLES
SIDE A
THE COMPLETE PHONOGRAM
"The Spire is fantastic! My kind of genre free-for-all." —BRIAN K. VAUGHAN (Saga)
THE SPIRE
SIMON SPURRIER
JEFF STOKELY
ANDRÉ MAY
PHONOGRAM (2006–2014)
Kieron's breakthrough work. He was sleeping on Jim's floor when this was coming out. Jim could have crept in and clubbed him to death and saved us all a lot of bother. Blame Jim.
THE SPIRE (2015–2016)
Jeff brings a whole fantasy world to life with this, and Kieron loves it so much he can't do his usual silly jokes here. You'll like it.
KIERON GILLEN DAN MORA
TAMRA BONVILLAIN
ONCE & FUTURE
VOLUME ONE
JAY ASHER & JESSICA FREEBURG
Piper
JEFF STOKELY
THEY'RE CLOSING IN. IT'S NOW OR NEVER. READY?
YES! MUNDANITY MUST NOT HOLD US!
INTO TH INFINITE, FRIEND!
glorious ratricide.
boys with magical flutes.
Never trust anyone.

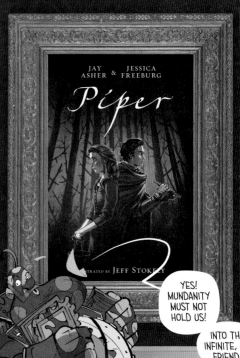

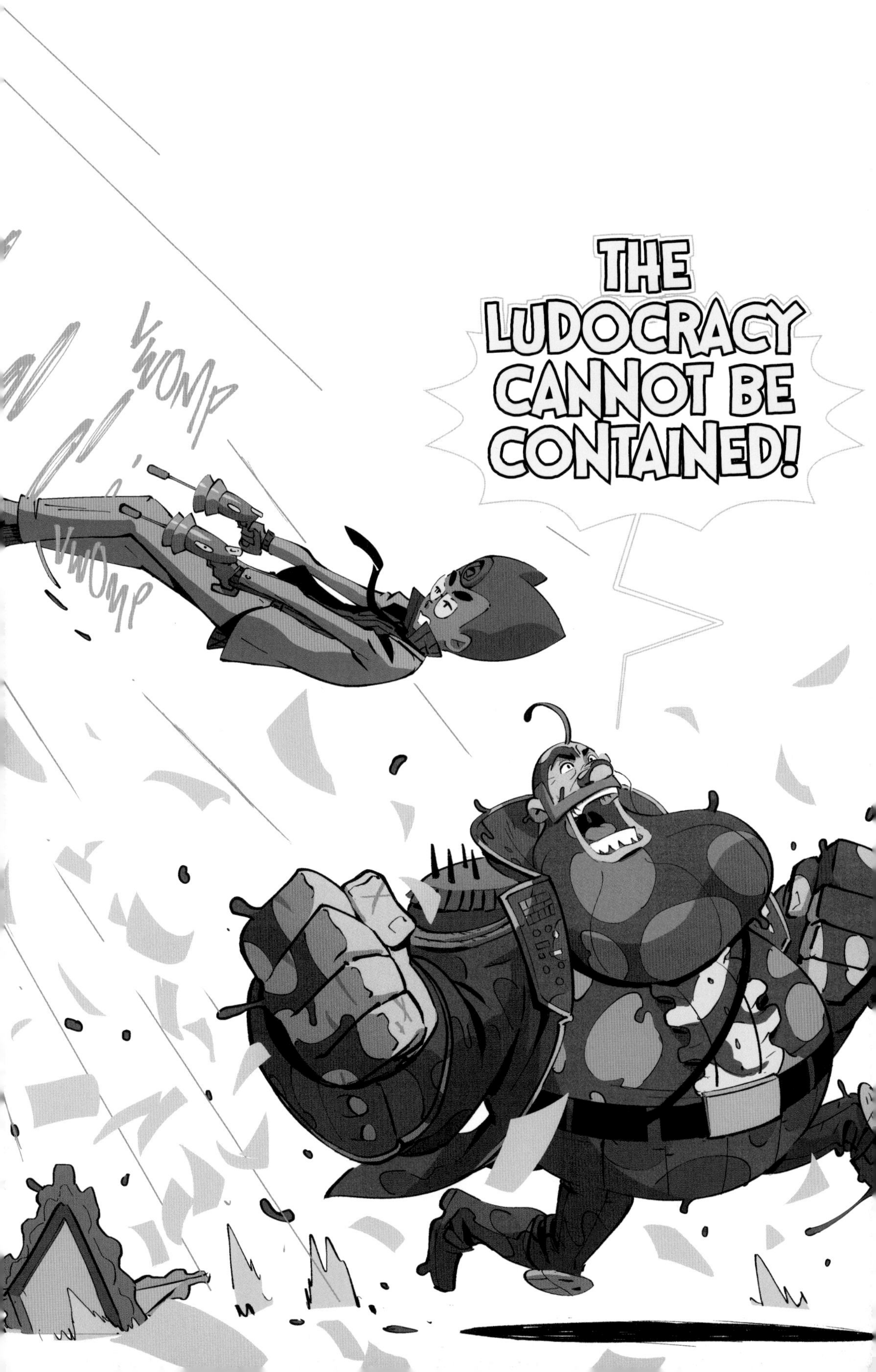
VWOMP
VWOMP
THE LUDOCRACY CANNOT BE CONTAINED!